Marooned

William Clark Russell

Solis Press

ALSO BY WILLIAM CLARK RUSSELL
AND PUBLISHED BY SOLIS PRESS

The Wreck of the "Grosvenor"

List, Ye Landsmen!

A Nightmare of the Doldrums

The Frozen Pirate

*Sailors' Language: A Collection of Sea-terms
and their Definitions*

First published in 1891. This edition completely reset
and published in 2017 by Solis Press

ISBN: 978-1-910146-30-9

Published by Solis Press, PO Box 482,
Tunbridge Wells TN2 9QT, Kent, England

Web: www.solispress.com | *Twitter*: @SolisPress

Contents

VOLUME 3

Volume 1

Chapter I
I Receive a Letter

I RETURNED TO MY LODGINGS in London one night in June in the year eighteen hundred and something, and found a letter lying upon the table. It was from my cousin, Alexander Fraser, and was dated at Rio de Janeiro. This was a man whom I had neither seen nor heard of for some years. We had been sent to sea as boys in the East India Company's service, and together had made three voyages in the same ship to Bombay; which in those ambling days of trade, when a four months' passage to the Bay of Bengal was considered a good run, meant a long and intimate association. Through the death of my dear mother I came into money enough to render me independent, and so I quitted old ocean after three years of seafaring. Fraser made a fourth voyage and I then lost sight of him. When later on I wrote to his sisters in the north of Scotland, I was told he had left his ship at Bombay to accompany a tea-grower, who had been a passenger in the vessel, to his plantations. That was the last I heard of him. As I held his letter in my hand, memory recalled him as a fair, blue-eyed, bronzed young fellow, exceedingly good-looking, a very nimble and alert seaman, fitter for the navy indeed than for the tea-wagon service, full of spirit and resolution and extremely impulsive.

He wrote to the following effect: first of all, he said, he had heard of me and obtained my address from a friend of mine who had sailed a few months before for Lima, but whose ship had been obliged to put into Rio to repair some damage she had sustained in a heavy gale off Cape Agostino. He had a long story to relate about his misfortunes in India, how he had been villainously deceived in the character of his associate and almost ruined by him, and how, as he had no wish to die of starvation, he had shipped as a foremast hand aboard a Yankee vessel, from which he ran on her arrival at Pernambuco—where he fell in with a sugar-grower belonging to Rio, who offered him a good berth on his estate in the neighbourhood of that town. He had not been long settled when he made the acquaintance of a Mr. and Mrs. Grant, with whose only daughter, Aurelia, he immediately fell in love. Mr. Grant was a Scotchman who had married a Spanish lady of noble birth, and their daughter, Fraser went on to say, was the most majestic, stately, and beautiful woman that ever walked the earth. The parents consented to their betrothal, but objected to the marriage until Fraser was in a condition to support a wife in comfort. One night, very suddenly, Mrs. Grant died. Her husband, who adored her, found her dead at his side, and the shock was so great that both his health and his mind gave way. He declared that he could not support life in a town where every object which met his eye reminded him of his loss; and within a month of Mrs. Grant's death he broke up his home and sailed with Aurelia for England. Fraser added that folks at Rio spoke of Mr. Grant as a well-to-do man, and talked of Aurelia as an heiress; but the truth came out when he was gone, and it was then understood that so far from being rich he had just contrived to come to a stand within a few fathoms of the brink of insolvency.

The lovers of course agreed to write by every ship. Fraser was cock-sure of being able to support a wife before another year had run out, and it was settled that he was to send for or fetch her at the expiration of the twelvemonth, as there was not the least likelihood of Mr. Grant returning to Rio.

Eight months after the arrival of the girl in England the father died. She wrote to acquaint Fraser with her loss, and hinted quite enough to intimate that she was not only friendless in London, but in poverty. "And now," continued my cousin, "I want you, who were as a brother to me when we were together at sea, to stand me in a brother's stead again in about as trying and perplexing a passage as ever formed part of a man's life. The business I have charge of is so tender, it needs such cherishing, such persistent personal attention, that I am persuaded were I to let go of it to fetch Aurelia I should return to find myself bankrupt. The population of Rio comprises a great number of rogues, and though the people I employ are not worse than the rest, they are rascals nevertheless, and I make no doubt whatever that if I were to turn my back upon them for three months they would ruin me. Now, my dear Dick, this is what you will do for me: you will call upon Aurelia"—here came in the address—"advance whatever money she may require, engage a cabin for her in the next ship that sails for Rio, furnish her with all such delicacies and comforts as your seafaring experiences, backed by a fastidious appetite, will suggest, and then, all this being done, *accompany her yourself.* You start! But, my dear boy, you will do this! ay, indeed you will; for d'ye see, you *must,* Dick. You will need but glance at her to perceive instantaneously that she cannot be suffered to embark alone. And consider how happy it will make her, thrown as she must needs be into the company, not of *our* polished glittering species—the sparkling dandies of John Company—but of men with faces like walnut-shells, with voices hoarse and raw with hard drinking, whose language is thickened and stiffened with horrid objectionable words—how happy, I say, it will make her to feel that she has the protection of her sweetheart's own cousin, a man of muscle and nerve, who can tell the toughest salt of them all where the flying-jibboom ends and how many gudgeons a liner's rudder hangs on! Consider the ease of mind that I shall enjoy through knowing that you are at her side. Consider again the prodigious delight it will give me to meet you—to thank you—to entertain you—to yarn with you over the past and hearken to the home news you will bring with you. No excuse, as you love me! You *must* come, d'ye see, Dick. Yes, you must absolutely accompany my poor lonely darling girl. You are an idle man, you know; your friend told me you were unmarried when he last saw you, and I have a right to believe, as I certainly hope, that you are single at this minute of reading my letter. The voyage is a pleasant one. Once clear of the Bay, 'tis no more than the pleasant fanning of the north-east trade-wind, with a brief instructive halt on the equator for a glance at John Sharkee and the pretty little flying fishes, and then a delightful run to the noblest bit of scenery the wide world over. Reflect a little upon your health and you are sure to discover that a change of air will do you good. And name me an air sweeter than the ocean breeze! Besides, you were never in South America, and cannot therefore imagine the delights in store for you in the shape of the rivers, the mountains, the shining flowers and exquisite fruits of this grand continent, or at all events of that part of it to which I invite you."

And so the letter went on, terminating in a whole jumble of exhortations to me to come—to squire his sweetheart—to behold from the summit of the regal Corcovado the magnificent harbour, the sparkling city, the green country beyond aflame with coloured growths. ...

It was a letter to set me pacing the room. The voyage was a considerable one; and though I had gone to sea for love of ships when I was a boy, a very few months sufficed to break the spell, and I had long ceased, as I believed, to be sensible of any sort of oceanic influence. I sat down, filled a pipe, and entered into certain calculations. I reckoned that a tolerably true course to Rio from the Thames would come hard upon five thousand nautical miles, and as it was hopeless to expect that any British South American trader would average more than one hundred and fifty knots in the twenty-four hours, I judged that though all conditions should prove favourable, the outward passage alone would run me into five or six weeks. Then of course I should have to return, so that I must look upon the round voyage as promising me three solid months, at least, upon a bosom that had ceased to rock me for some years. The first movement of my mind was one of recoil; but after turning the project over I got to think that, after all, the voyage would prove a complete and healthy change, inexpensive too, and much less troublesome than a trip across the Channel. Possibly the old instincts which had driven me to sea as a lad, and which I had thought dead long ago, lived still, and were now faintly stirring to sudden visions of frothing billows, of the small green moon shearing like a cannon-ball through the flying scud, of the star-touched well rolling in dark folds silently, of the tropic shore that sweetens the warm breath of the languid breeze with the odours of spices and the perfume of a nameless vegetation. London was hot and dull; the seaside tedious and commonplace. My excursions abroad formed no genial memories, for in —— I nearly died of fever at Brussels, and in —— lay ill of a poisonous smell for close upon a month at Florence. Besides, my cousin pleaded to me as a brother and a sailor, and I knew him well enough to feel certain that if he were in my place he would do me this service.

But what sort of a girl was this Miss Aurelia Grant? My cousin expressed her perfections in the impassioned language of love, and he might possibly be very right in all he said; but I remember a man who had passed some years in Spain, and who knew the Spanish character well, telling me that he took particular notice there was a deal of the mule mixed up in the disposition of the women of that country—a quality, as he described it, of bland and even polite obstinacy, that was however very easily excited into a most unpleasant, clamorous, peevish stubbornness. Miss Aurelia was indeed half English; but suppose the other half of her was not to my taste? I do protest on my word that I would rather go to jail for a fortnight than be locked up in a ship for a month with a disagreeable woman. Thus I sat debating; but though I was some distance on the road towards forming a resolution, I cannot say that I had at all made up my mind when I went to bed.

Chapter II
Miss Aurelia Grant

NEXT MORNING I DRESSED myself with more care than I usually took in this way, though twenty-six years old and not without self-complacency in some respects, and about eleven o'clock drove to the address given me by Fraser.

I found the house in a dull and dingy street out of the Edgware Road. Miss Grant was at home. I sent up my name, and was shown into a little front parlour, gloomy with sallow drapery and the bilious atmosphere peculiar to this part of the metropolis. In a few minutes she entered, and I must confess I sprang rather than rose to my feet, so surprised was I by the girl's beauty and deportment. I had indeed conjectured a tall figure in conformity with my cousin's description; but imagination had not gone beyond that, with a pair of dark eyes and an upper lip shaded with down.

Now Miss Aurelia Grant had as fair and delicate a complexion as any that ever I witnessed in the most matchless English-woman's face. Her hair was brown, very plentiful, thick and soft, and it had a kind of light of its own upon it as though dusted with gold. Her eyes were black—profoundly so: Spanish eyes in passion and power and mean-ing, but subdued to an expression of beauty by, as I took it, the English heart in her, that rendered them remarkable beyond my capacity of expression. Her figure was extremely fine, full yet girlish too. She was dressed in mourning, and as she stood looking at me a moment or two in the doorway, I said to myself, This is the handsomest creature I have ever seen!

There was a little blush on her cheeks that brightened the light in her eyes: she smiled and gave me her hand.

"I am indeed glad to see you, Mr. Musgrave. Alexander has talked of you to me again and again. In a letter I received from him yesterday he told me you would call. You are very good to come so soon."

"I shall be truly rejoiced if I can be of service to you," said I, still a tri-fle confused; "my cousin's description of you—eloquent as his devotion would naturally make him"—here I fumbled for the letter,—"would—perhaps, madam" (we madam'd the ladies in those days of high coat-collars, splendid waistcoats and immense breast-pins), "you would like to read it."

She took it eagerly, and her eyes grew so fond as she read, whilst a look so yearning entered her face—such an expression as the memory of her loneliness might put into her when she should meet her sweetheart again after their long separation—that I felt I acted sneakishly in watching her. She smiled happily when she came to the part in which Fraser spoke of her beauty, and when she had made an end she folded the letter carefully as though it were something precious, and pressed it between her hands as if it was her sweetheart's own fingers she held.

It seemed to me as I surveyed her that my cousin exhibited uncommon courage in confiding so much beauty as this to the care and attention of a man whom he knew to be young and single, to say no more, for a spell of shipboard that might last for two or even three months. Our eyes met: her colour deepened somewhat, but her brilliant gaze was as steady as the shining of a star. There was a singularly engaging, most unaffected quality or tone of frankness in her voice.

"Alexander has asked you to do him a great favour. It is really *too* great." I seemed to dissent. "It is positively enough, Mr. Musgrave, that you should hire a cabin for me. To make the voyage also! And yet I know he would be overjoyed to see you. Still it is a tedious journey, and if you are like Alexander you detest the sea."

"No," said I, "I believe I shall enjoy a few weeks on the ocean. The fact is, madam, I want time to realize the thing, so to speak—not to understand it, for of course it is intelligible enough, but to accustom my thoughts to it, you know;" and here I coughed and brought myself up "all standing" as sailors say, for indeed there was something in her shining steadfast gaze that caused me to talk as though I was ill at ease.

"Should you decide to be my companion, Mr. Musgrave," said she, "the voyage will be something to look forward to, greatly as I dislike the sea, or rather existence on board ship." I bowed. "But you will not dream of doing more than securing a cabin for me and helping me in one or two other ways,—if you have the least reluctance. It is quite possible that I may find a pleasant companion among the passengers—if there should be ladies on board. As a rule the captains and mates of the ships that trade to South America are a very rough and rude set of men. Should I be the only passenger, it is natural," she said, with a little droop of the head, "that I should not choose to be alone in such society."

This was like an appeal in its way, and her manner of speaking rendered it irresistible. Besides, there was Fraser's letter calling upon me to protect her, imploring me as one who was as a brother to do him this great service, and these considerations coming on top of my concern for her loneliness and helplessness, my sympathy with her in the grief that was still recent, and above all the perception that she desired my company, and that I should be acting unchivalrously to refuse her, made me whip out, "Miss Grant, it is settled. We sail together. There is nothing to keep me ashore. It will be delightful to meet Fraser again, and I shall find immense satisfaction in feeling that my enjoyment of your society also includes the pleasure of obliging you."

She clapped her hands with a gesture that was like telling you she had something besides English blood in her.

"How good you are! How glad you make me, Mr. Musgrave! I wonder what kind of ship we shall sail in?" she cried, with the vivacity of a mind that has suddenly lost its burden. "She must prove swift! She cannot sail too fast for me!" and here she told me of the vessel in which she and her father had made the voyage home—a clumsy, round-bowed polacca, apparently, that stirred to nothing less than half a gale of wind, and so leaky that the crew were at the pumps for fourteen hours out of the twenty-four; with a bow-legged, beef-faced old swab for captain, whose favourite boast was that he had once swallowed at a draught a bowl of punch containing ten half-pints of rum, whiskey, brandy and water. She described this man and his habits with so much humour as to give me a high opinion of her talent as an observer; and she made me laugh heartily by an account of a quarrel between him and his mate over a pudding—the latter (an Irishman) beginning it by swearing that he had seen dried currants and raisins growing naturally like capers on trees, and the captain ending it by grasping a lump of the hot and steaming stuff and flinging it plump into the mate's face. Maybe something of the merriment of the tale and her delivery of it lay to my mind in the contrast between the rough sea-anecdote and the dignity, refinement, and beauty of the speaker. But I confess I liked her the better for her archness, and for her easy recital of a story which Miss Prim would consider rather vulgar since it referred to such *very* common people.

Our conversation presently went to her father. He died in the house in which she was still lodging, and she declared that when, after the funeral, she sat down to reflect she did not know what in the world she should do. She had not a friend in England, and of her mother's relatives in Spain she knew nothing. The few pounds her father had left were fast giving out, and she frankly told me that the money she still had would not have carried her on another month. "Why did you not call upon me?" I asked her. But it seems that Fraser had omitted to give my address in the last letter but one he sent to her, and it was only a week or two before he wrote that he had learnt it from my friend whose ship had been forced into Rio.

I was with her for two hours, and never did time pass more pleasantly and quickly. We arranged that I should call for her next day and accompany her to the shops she had occasion to visit, and afterwards make inquiries about the next ship and start on all the necessary preparations for the voyage. She cried when she said good-bye to me. Indeed she had suffered grievously, and now that the darkness was passing she could not meet the first of the dawn without tears.

As to myself, I hardly knew whether my resolution made me glad or sorry when I came to turn it over. The girl was exceeding handsome, but then she was not *my* sweetheart. Had her heart been her own a voyage with her must have yielded me a prospect that could not have left me doubting whether I was right in this adventure. But as my cousin's betrothed she was the same to me as if she was his wife. There was no room for sentiment. I was young enough to take this into consideration, and I say, when I reflected upon my determination, I could not satisfy myself that my judgment was as brilliant as my heroism.

On the following morning I called at her lodgings and afterwards passed some hours in watching her whilst she shopped and in paying for her purchases. There was a dignified frankness about her that was very fascinating, and not the less so because it was tinctured with melancholy. Her fine eyes expressed so much spirit, there was so much power in the curve and set of her lips, such suggestion of self-reliance in the peculiar floating pose of her head, I felt persuaded that a very great deal of the heroine went to her composition, that she was a woman whose qualities would best discover themselves in a time of extremity, a person by nature so ardent that no theory about her could touch the limits of the romantic exploits she was equal to in the service of the man she loved. These were my thoughts as I sat watching her whilst she handled the stuffs the shopmen put before her, frequently turning to me to speak, when I would notice that every sudden confrontment of her full beauty surprised me as a fresh revelation.

She managed to buy all she needed in one day, which I thought very clever and very kind also. "How long," said I, "will it take you to prepare for the voyage?"

"Oh," she answered, "if you were to tell me the ship sails to-morrow I should be quite ready."

I told her that I would devote the next day to making inquiries and arrangements, and would do myself the pleasure to call in the evening and let her know what I had done. "At all events," said I, "you would wish me to book ourselves for the next ship?"

"If you please," she answered with anxiety.

"In which case," I observed, "we must not be fastidious. The best procurable cabins will satisfy us, and the skipper's appearance need not count. Yet it will not do to sail away in a vessel whose seams yawn and whose hold has been abandoned by the rats. I have some small knowledge of ships, and if the first that offers is not as she should be we must wait for the next."

"I will leave everything to you," she said, "only," looking around with a slight shudder—we were conversing in her lodgings—"I am so very weary of this gloomy house, this dull street; so longing to see my dear one again, and the bright sun and the flowers of my own home."

"I will do my best," I exclaimed; "there should be and perhaps will be a choice of ships. If we have to wait, you will suffer me to find you pleasanter quarters."

And with that I bade her good-bye and left her.

Chapter III
The Iron Crown

IN THOSE DAYS A large number of vessels bound to all parts of the world loaded in the Pool, a little way below London Bridge. Steam then was young, and not much was made of it. I have lived to see steamers trading to South America big enough to stow away in their holds many of the sailing vessels which were then carrying goods and passengers to all parts of the world. It is difficult in this age to realize the kind of experiences our forefathers suffered when they took ship—it mattered little to what countries—if it were not the ports to which the Indiamen were despatched. I have heard my mother say that in her young days country people who proposed a trip to London would make their wills before entering the coach. I do not know that the coach was much more dangerous than the locomotive, but I am certain that there were no limits to the perils which menace the ocean-borne traveller in the time of the little passenger-ship and smaller passenger-brig; when the sailor was still an exceeding rough son of a gun, charged to the throat with the traditional infirmities of his calling; when no special qualifications were insisted upon as conditions of a man taking charge of a vessel; when ships sailed without side-lights, and when collisions were averted by the easy remedy of whipping the lamp out of the binnacle and flourishing it over the rail; when the cabin provisions were only a little less coarse than the forecastle fare, and when a passage that is now made in a week occupied two or three months.

I had obtained the addresses of a few brokers and owners in the South American trade, hoping thus to find two or three ships proceeding much about the same time, but it turned out that the first vessel on the berth sailed next day and that her cabin accommodation was full. Her name, I remember, was the *Amazon*. The next vessel, a brig named the *Iron Crown*, did not sail until the 23rd, so that even if she satisfied me we should have to wait eight days. The office of the owner of this craft was in Tower Hill, and whilst I was inquiring about her cabin accommodation the person to whom I was speaking, motioning towards a man who had entered a moment before, exclaimed:

"Here is the master himself, sir, Captain Guy Broadwater, and he will tell you that a stouter, swifter, more comfortable ship than the *Iron Crown* never sailed out of an English port. Captain, you will confirm me. What is it now," inclining his head and screwing up one eye as if in thought, "on a bowline with you? A cool thirteen, I believe? Indeed," he cried, chafing his hands and grinning, "we may safely consider the good ship *Iron Crown* the one favourite trader between Rio and the Thames."

"Well," said Captain Broadwater in the hoarse voice of a man who has broken his pipes by rum and years of bawling aloft in gales, "it isn't for me to praise the *Iron Crown*, sir. She can speak for herself. She only needs to know that a man's eye is upon her to talk out. Handsome! Well I knew old Jarge Rowley who laid her keel, and always reckoned him a man without the least flavey of sentiment in his intellectuals until this here *Iron Crown* was launched and lay floating, and then I says to myself, 'Broadwater,' I says, 'swaller your own precious eyes, mate, if Jarge ain't a poet!'"

"You hear what the captain says, sir?" cried the other continuing to chafe his hands.

I took a short survey of Captain Guy Broadwater, and there stood before me a wide-shouldered, exceedingly muscular man of fifty, short, with iron-grey hair and a beard that hung like a bush at his throat, the chin being shaved. He had the smallest eyes I ever saw, and their colour as I now took stock of them seemed red, but I afterwards discovered that this was due to congestion caused by rheumatism, or punch, or both. His nose was of the exact shape of a pear, and being purple at the nostrils and point, looked as if it had been lately stung by a bee. His mouth on the other hand was so small as to correspond, as a deformity, with his eyes. When he was not speaking he seemed from the posture of his lips to be trying, but in vain, to whistle. The skin of his face was much burnt by the weather, and it was adorned with a strange sub-cutaneous filigree-work, or net rather let me term it, of dusky crimson meshes. He was dressed in pilot-cloth, and carried in his hand a bell-shaped beaver, the brim of which was large enough to furnish out a bishop. Yet ugly and queer as he was, there was nothing whatever in his appearance to offend or prejudice me. I put him down at once as a coarse, unlettered, but good-natured sailor of the hearty lively type, whose physical peculiarities were to a certain extent to be attributed to bad victuals in early life, to too much liquor later on, and throughout to the rough usage of the vocation of the sea when followed before the mast. I told him that I was glad to make his acquaintance, and that I had called with the intention of taking a passage in his ship, though I would not decide until I had inspected her.

"Sir," said he, "I am going aboard myself when I have done my business with this gentleman, and if you don't mind lettin' go your anchor here for five minutes I'll carry ye straight to the vessel."

They withdrew to an inner office where I could hear the growling voice of my captain mingling with the sharp-edged tones of his owner as though there was a mastiff and a pug tumbling and larking behind the door.

The skipper presently emerged and put on his broad-brimmed hat, in which he made so strange a figure that I could scarce forbear a laugh. We walked to the river and were rowed to a brig that was moored in midstream.

"Here she is!" cried Captain Broadwater; "look at her, sir! Was there ever beautifuller lines! Observe the lovely swell of the side! It might be the breast of a duck, sir. Mark how clean she comes to the starn-post. In my opinion she's too good to use; she's properer for a show."

There is no reason why he should not have been in earnest, for, as her master, it was conceivable that he should be proud of her. For my part however I could find no hint of the charms which threw him into raptures. The vessel was a stout brig of three hundred tons, an excellent sea-boat, no doubt, with the scantling of a line-of-battle ship, but she was certainly no beauty. She was painted black, with a narrow yellow streak running the length of her sides, and had been newly coppered to the bends; the lustre of the bright metal was under her, and she seemed to float in a little surface of pale sunshine. She was loftily rigged for a craft of her size and carried exceedingly square yards, whence I inferred that with her studding sails abroad she could expand canvas enough in a breeze of wind to start an island from its moorings. We gained the side, climbed up a stout rope-ladder and jumped aboard.

There was a lighter on the starboard bow and a number of intoxicated lumpers were hoisting in cargo. It should have been no new scene to me, yet I found it confusing enough. The sails were unbent, and the running rigging unrove, so there were no ropes' ends to trip over. Nevertheless the decks were encumbered with all sorts of "raffle," as sailors term lumber—casks, hencoops, sacks, planks, and I know not what else besides. There was a full-rigged ship a short distance off getting her anchor, and the fellows at the windlass were roaring out with hurricane lungs one of the many working songs with which the British seaman inspires his heart and nerves, his hands and legs. The melody awoke echoes long ago silent in me. It was at Cape Town that I had heard it last, and the rough salt air brought the picture before me in a vision so clear, sunbright, real—the blue waters of the wide haven, the groups of ivory-white houses upon the low shore, the polished azure back of the huge Atlantic comber poising its arched summit in a ridge of glassy opal light for a breath ere thundering its burthen of snow upon the beach, the great mountains beyond with streaks of lace-like mist crawling along their brows, as though the viewless spirits of the blue atmosphere up there were spinning a white fabric of exquisite delicacy out of their airy looms for the adornment of those giants' heads—that I seemed to waken with a start to Captain Broadwater's invitation to step below and view the cabin.

One hears of the Swiss weeping when some one tunes up their national cow-strain. Mariners are a people who have no tears to spare: what they possess in that way they devote to their private woes; but I do think nothing so stirs a man who has been a sailor as the melody of a forecastle chorus. 'Tis like the wand of a wizard: the curtain rises to it and there before you lies the past—the rolling ocean, the gallant fabric in whose heart you scoured your thousand leagues of sea, your hearty shipmates, the gay Saturday carousal, the girl in the distant home from whose sunny head you snicked the golden wisp, which many a time you have pressed to your lips in some mid-ocean solitude, when there was nobody but the man in the moon and the man at the wheel to see what you were at.

"I have been a sailor myself, captain," said I, as I followed him to the companion-hatch: "and the sound of that stormy chorus out yonder makes me feel a bit swabbish, do you know, for quitting the old life."

"Bin a sailor yourself, hey?" he cried, rounding when at the bottom of the ladder to take a view of me. "Well, an' I dessay it did ye no harm. There's worse people knocking about the world than sailors, though I haven't much respect for that class of 'em which goes by the name of Hands."

"I see. Your sympathies are aft."

"Well, I don't know about that either," he exclaimed rather warmly, as though he objected to my considering that he had any sympathies at all, and methought that his pear-shaped nose as he spoke took a deeper dye; then with a flourish of the arm he said, "This here's the cabin. A noble room, sir. Must board the Indiamen to find the like of it."

The vessel had so much beam that her cabin was larger than I had expected to find it. The furniture was simple enough: a table, lockers for seats, snuff-coloured bulkheads without any sort of ornamentation. At the after end were four cabins, two of a side, whilst forward were other but smaller berths.

"That end's for the passengers," said the captain, pointing aft.

I inspected the accommodation and found it airy and roomy.

"Which are to let?" I asked.

"All," he replied; "how many of you are there, sir?"

"Myself and a lady."

"I reckon there'll be no more then," said he. "Here's four beautiful bedrooms to choose from."

"Where do *you* sleep?"

"Forwards there," said he, pointing with his nose as a negro does with his chin. "Me an' my first mate lodges there. The bo'sun who serves as second mate lies in the fo'k'sle. There's no interference. You'll be as private as a chick in its egg. Case of more coming I'd take the two foremost berths, if I was you. The helm don't feel to kick so much there, and if the chap at the wheel should warm his toes by stamping you won't hear him plain."

I should have been better pleased with a vessel of twice the burthen of this craft; but then to be sure we should start in the height of the summer when the Bay of Biscay is least formidable—though let me remember that the heaviest gale I was ever in was fifty miles south of Ushant in the month of July—and once clear of those waters we had a right to look for quiet weather during the rest of the passage. The short chat I had with Broadwater on returning on deck confirmed my first impression of him: he was indeed no very polished companion for ladies, but he was well enough as sea-captains of his class and in his trade then went. I was not surprised to find that the vessel did not carry a stewardess. You had to look to the height of the Indiamen in those days for luxuries of this kind. I asked him what sort of table he kept.

"An A1 copper-bottom table," he answered. "Salt beef of the primest—roast pork—poultry twice a week—currant dumplings—taking it all round, a list nigh as long as my arm."

"Pretty substantial," I exclaimed.

"Ay," said he, grinning, "there's never no twopenny kickshaws to be found aboard of *me*. No hishee-hashees here, sir, with French names. All's good solid eating,—dishes which makes a man feel that he's dined when he gets up. Give me food that'll coil a chap's appetite down for him. That's why, to my notion, there's ne'er a bit of vittles on this airth to beat a good leg o' roast pork."

I gathered from these observations that Miss Grant and I were not likely to be invariably entertained to our tastes, and that it would therefore be necessary to lay in a stock of wines and stores for our separate use; and having ascertained that I was at liberty to fill one of the hencoops with poultry for ourselves, and that if the other cabins were unlet one of them was at my service as a larder, I took leave of him, and was rowed ashore, and without further ado walked to Tower Hill and engaged two berths in the brig *Iron Crown*, Broadwater master. Also, at this office, to save time, I wrote a letter to my cousin, in which I named the vessel we were to sail in and the date of our departure, and handed it to the owner of the *Iron Crown* to transmit with despatches of his own to Rio by the ship *Amazon* proceeding next day.

Chapter IV
We Embark

A S THE BRIG DID not sail for another week, and as we intended
to join her at Deal, which would give us two or three days ashore
beyond the date of our departure from the Thames, I procured rooms
for Miss Grant in a private hotel near Bond Street, so that I was within
convenient reach and saw much of her. In truth the poverty and melancholy of the street in which she had lodged rendered the very name
of it intolerable to her, and the gloomy influence of the house upon her
spirits was made more oppressive yet by the recollection of her father's
sufferings and death and her own privation in it.

The change from such lodgings to the comforts of a hotel, the sudden removal from her mind of the distracting burthen of poverty and
anxiety, the feeling that I was by her side and that she had a protector
in me, and that in a few weeks she would be with her sweetheart and
married to him, combined to make another woman of her in those
eight or ten days. Her eyes shone with a clearer light, and their dark
luminous depths gathered a softness beyond description from the happiness that was in her. A delicate bloom lay upon her cheeks, her laugh
was sincere, her smiles full of an honest gaiety. As we walked together
I would notice that both men and women stopped to stare after her.
I remember an old dandy with his hat cocked and a tuft on his chin,
coming to a dead stand on seeing her, then following us and passing as
an excuse to turn again to have another look. I will not say that she was
insensible to the admiration she excited—she would have been no true
woman to feign such a thing—but I cannot conceive that any girl could
have shown herself less affected by it.

We took the coach for Deal early on a Friday morning. The journey
was long and tedious. It was after sunset when we sat down to the dinner I had ordered in a quaint hotel that looked directly upon the sea;
but the moon rode high, clear as crystal in the dark blue air, and her
glorious reflection came to the very margin of the beach, upon whose
shingle the rippling summer breakers trembled into snow in a fan-
shaped path of glory that floated as steadily upon the quiet surface as
the orb herself in the breathless sky.

After dinner we walked to the esplanade. The luggers lying high
and dry looked hoary in the clear and icy light: the seaward-gazing
windows sparkled out to the gush of the radiance in silver stars; every

shadow lay like an ebony carving upon a sand-white ground. Far away, past the yellow winking spots of the signal lanterns floating off the Goodwins, was the fitful flashing of violet lightning. The planets hung large and burnt richly, and, clear of the sphere of mist-like radiance that circled the moon, the stars shone in such numbers that I never remember witnessing the heavens so crowded. After the roaring of metropolitan streets, the low washing sound of the surf along the coast was inexpressibly soothing and refreshing, and one's blood coursed to the cool sweetness of the ocean atmosphere as to a draught of rare and generous cordial.

There were many ships in the Downs, wan and spectral in the moon-shine. Their riding-lights resembled a swarm of fire-flies. By bending the ear you caught from the nearer vessels the sounds of laughter, the thin strains of a concertina, the clank of a chain cable dragged along the deck; or from the further distance the faint chorusing of a crew pulling and hauling aboard some hidden craft that had softly sneaked into the Downs on the top of the subtle tide.

"Which amid that ashen muddle of ships out yonder will be ours, I wonder?" said I.

"How ghostly is the atmosphere that is made by moonlight at sea!" exclaimed Miss Grant, sending her glance along the shining wake of the luminary, and then looking into the eastern darkness and talking as if she spoke to herself. "It must be the low-lying stars, I think, which cause the distance to appear so terribly remote. The beauty of such a night as this used to awe me when we were coming to England—it does so now, though I am on dry land. It should be as lovely to me as to oth-ers, but it is not so. The mystery of it is too great—the mystery of the silence and the pale air and the whispering of the sea along the shore."

"It may be that what is mysterious cannot be beautiful," said I, find-ing talk of this sort a little above my art, though not wanting her to think that I did not understand her either. "Yet I don't know. I have seen eyes in my time as secret as the dark sea yonder, and they were wonderfully beautiful, I assure you."

As I said this a rumbling voice close behind me exclaimed, "Bort, sir! beautiful noight for a row, sir! Water smooth as satin, lady."

I turned and observed a Deal boatman.

"No—we shall have enough of the sea presently. Can you tell me if a vessel named the *Iron Crown* has brought up off here?"

"What's she loike?" he asked.

"A brig," I said, "three hundred tons, newly sheathed, painted black with a yellow stripe."

"Is her capt'n a man with werry small eyes an' a nose like a sailor's duff?"

"That's right."

"Then she brought up just afore sundown. Oi was off fishin' with a party at the time, and the chap Oi've described sung out to me to git out of the road;" and he pointed seawards with a shadowy hand, but it was impossible to distinguish any one ship among the congregation there. He hung about me a little as though he would engage me in further conversation, and then said, "Werry thirsty weather, sir." I gave him the value of a glass of ale and he left us.

"At the head of human disenchanters," said I, "stands the British long-shoreman, with his cry of 'Bart, sir.'"

"Hark!" exclaimed my companion lifting her finger.

It was half-past nine, and the bells out upon the water were sounding the hour. There were probably two hundred sail in the Downs; the tinkling ran in ripples as though a wave of air raised scores of metallic echoes of different tones as it swept onwards. Some of the bells sounded simultaneously; some followed one another in chimes; a few were mellow, many shrill, more yet of a silver singing cadence. From the pallid remoteness the tones came in faint and tiny sounds, after which fell the silence, and you heard nothing but the fountain-like seething of foam upon the shingle.

We returned to the hotel, but I lingered, after Miss Grant had retired, for a long hour upon the balcony overlooking the sea, smoking a cigar and musing much on the girl and my cousin Fraser and the voyage on which we should probably start next day. The moon hung over the Downs, and through the steady rain of her silver twinkled the yellow sparks of the ships' lights. There was a lugger heading for Deal and coming fair down the middle of the ice-like path upon the waters. She floated black against the tremulous shining that went up behind her to the sea-line, and as you marked her sweeps or long oars rising and falling you would have imagined her some gigantic marine insect stealthily creeping shorewards. From every lifted blade the water dripped to the moonshine in diamonds, and the *cheep, cheep* of the oars grinding betwixt the thole-pins sent the fancy roaming to the tropic swamp and to the mysterious croakings of the tree-toad.

I was up betimes, but Miss Aurelia was before me. She looked as fresh and as fragrant as Cowper's rose newly washed by a shower.

"The sea," said I, "promises to use you kindly."

"Yes, and I feel well, too, which is better than looking so."

She was robed in black, her dress fitted her excellently, her hair was coiled into the likeness of a crown, her dark eyes were full of fire and life. I did not much like to think of her as being obliged to sit and converse with such a man as Broadwater and with such people as his mates were tolerably certain to prove. But it could not be helped; though when the captain's purple face came into my head I felt that I should have been ungenerous and mean indeed to have suffered her to sail alone. There was a light breeze from the southward. The upward-bound vessels had got under way, and the picture was gay and brilliant with the crowded white canvas of the numerous craft, the sparkling of the sun in the running waters, the fitful flashings of the wet oars of boats, the light blue sky with a stretch of ivory-like crescents of clouds, resembling new moons linked and compacted going down to the sealine, where a leaning sail or two gleamed like little obelisks of Parian marble. Miss Grant came to my side and we stood gazing together. Presently a waiter arrived, asked if my name was Musgrave, and said there was a gentleman inquiring for me. A moment or two afterwards Captain Broadwater entered.

He gave Miss Grant a bow that was a sheer convulsion in its way, and said, "I thought I'd look in here, sir, afore I went aboard. There'll be nothing to keep us when you and the lady are over the side. There's not much weight in this here wind, but the tide serves, and I'm never for waiting when there's a chance to get away."

"You are very right," said I; "but we haven't breakfasted yet, captain. There's time enough for that, I hope?" And thinking he was going to object, I added, "You'll join us? Nothing like shore-going food and cooking down to the last moment."

He answered that he had already breakfasted, but that on reflection he felt himself equal to another meal, and the waiter arriving with the ham and coffee we sat down. I have seen men with immense appetites in my day, but no man who ever came near to Broadwater in this way. It was not only the quantity he devoured; it was the rapidity with which he ate. He took a hot roll, tore the crumb out, buttered and then bolted the whole without winking and in a breath. He picked up an egg-spoon, and after inspecting it an instant, called the waiter and asked him what it was. The waiter explained. "Bring me a proper spoon!" he roared in a voice that caused Miss Grant to start and glance at me with a little air of consternation. The man handed him a dessert-spoon, with which he struck the egg as though it had been a sailor's head, then scooped out the inside and swallowed the whole, afterwards seizing another egg, all so quickly that it was like watching the performance of a conjuror. He never offered to speak a word until he had eaten as much breakfast as would have sufficed me for a week, though he made an end before Miss Grant and I had fairly begun. My companion looked at me as if she would say, "I told you what sort of people the captains are in this trade;" I was more struck however by his manner of roaring to the waiter than by the rest of his behaviour. "If this is not a ship's bully all of the olden time," I thought to myself, "let his appetite be called delicate."

He now began to tell me in a hoarse voice about his passage down the river to the Downs, and how a West Indiaman in bringing up at midnight had fouled his cable and nearly run aboard him. "But," said he, "there's no seamanship to be expected from the men who gets command of them big ships. They're hired for their faces and their tricks of speechifying and caper-cutting and grinning out answers without losing their tempers when the ladies bother 'em with questions. Put them into a situation that requires real nautical knowledge and they can only stand and look on. If you want to be cut down, or your spars brought about your ears, them's the gents to show ye how it's done."

All this was very pig-headed talk; but if he should prove, as I suspected, full of salt prejudices and antique sea-notions, I at all events should not be without one favourite source of diversion during the voyage.

Our baggage was on board the brig. The little we had with us was conveyed to one of the vessel's boats that was lying off the beach waiting for the captain. Miss Grant sprang to the gunwale and thence to a thwart with inimitable grace that was full of a generous disdain of the extended hand of one of the seamen. I followed, and Broadwater bundled in after me. "Shove off!" he bawled as though in a passion. The boat's head was slewed for the brig, and the three men fell to their oars.

There were fifty things to admire as our little keel was swept forwards: the grey bald stare of the Foreland point with the sheen of the chalk trembling off it upon the blue atmosphere beyond; the ships still at anchor growing large to our approach, their glossy sides twinkling to the rippling lustre in the water like the tremble of sunlight amid the shadows of dancing leaves; the sudden flash of a cabin-window to the movement of the hull as though a cannon had been fired from it; the various colours and devices of a dozen different nations' ensigns languidly fluttering their bright folds from mast-head and peak; the line of green and yellow coast sweeping into an airy dimness of pallid cliff as wan in the distance of the brilliant north as the crescent of the moon floating in the noontide heavens; the quaint aspect of the hearty old smuggling town whose foreground of brown shingle gleamed black to the recoil of the washing breaker, whilst it offered the saltest imaginable picture in the shape of fleets of yellow luggers high and dry, and the figures of boatmen lounging, scrubbing, mending nets, and boiling pitch-pots.

There were plenty of things, I say, to look at, yet I do not remember that I took notice of much outside the three men who were rowing us to the brig. They belonged of course to the ship's company. One was a half-blood of a dark olive complexion and eyes like sloes resting on slices of lemon. His hands were as small as a girl's, beautifully shaped, though corned and horny and palm-blackened by the tar and drudgery of shipboard. The others were plain ginger-haired British lobscousers—one with a beard of stubble that projected from his chin like the thatch of a sou'-wester, both knob-nosed and rugged as the shell of a walnut. Their feet were naked, their rough breasts lay bare to the light, their nervous muscular arms were decorated with bracelets, crucifixes, anchors, female figures, pricked in with the pale blue of the sailor's pigment. All three of them wore a sullen look—not the expression of evil-minded men, but of persons rendered sulky and resentful by ill-usage. I saw the half-blood glance at Miss Grant, and a sort of light broke upon his face and swept the dogged air out of it as a smile clears a sour brow; but his eye instantly went from her to Broadwater and fell, a singular look of loathing and hate darkened his countenance, and I witnessed the impulse of a violent emotion in him in the quick, savage swing he gave his oar. It was like a curse!

Here were tokens not to please me who, as a man that had passed some years at sea, had preserved an eye for the interpretation of sailors' meanings. If the crew were dissatisfied at this early stage, then old Broadwater and his mates must have gone to work with an incredible promptitude to make their true characters known to them. Had they a grievance? Their provisions would have been fresh meat and loaves of bread down to this point, and they could not therefore know what the forecastle stores were like. Was the vessel leaky? It was to be hoped she was not. No! it could be nothing less than Broadwater. Well, if the men were growling now, what would be their posture later on? I was sufficiently well acquainted with the character of merchant seamen to know that often the very best sailors amongst them are those who curse the deepest in their gizzards. I was also aware that there was nothing uncommon in a crew finding plenty of time and excuses to mutiny in a run from Blackwall to the Forelands, going ashore with bag and baggage in a body, and obliging the ship to wait off Deal until the crimps could roll a new crew into her forecastle. All this was, as it still is, in the ordinary course of the ocean life. But the looks of the three thinly-clad fellows made you think of something more significant than the familiar causes of the forecastle rebellion.

However they pulled too briskly to give me time to consider them very attentively. The boat buzzed through the water, and the brig ahead rapidly enlarged upon the view.

"Is that the ship?" exclaimed Miss Grant.

I answered, yes.

"Is there anything afloat to beat her?" exclaimed Broadwater in a deep-sea voice.

The half-blood turned his head upon his shoulder as if he would have his mates observe what was in his mind by his look.

"Oars!" bawled the captain. "Out boathook, you dog!" to the man in the bows. "Good thunder!" he growled, "what is there to make the sojers who ship as sailors nowadays skip, if it ain't gunpowder in their shoes and a lighted match 'twixt their toes?"

We swung alongside and gained the deck.

Chapter V
The Voyage Begins

THE MOMENT CAPTAIN BROADWATER'S foot was on shipboard he shouted out, "Man the windlass, Mr. Bothwell! Get this here boat hoisted some of you! Jump, bullies, jump! There's wind enough to blow us away if ye don't stop to curl your hair!" which said, he forthwith fell to bundling about on his rounded shanks, running here and there, looking round and aloft, bawling to the mate who had gone forward, and apparently employing every art of which he was master to render the scene of commotion one of sheer distraction.

There seemed about fourteen of a crew, not counting the captain and mate. A few of them came to the davits to get the boat up, the rest laid hold of the windlass handles and began to heave. You heard the clank, clank, of the pawls and the grinding chink of the cable coming in link by link. "Sing out, my livelies! heave to the girls, lads! heave and sing! Heave and raise the dead! sing out, men! clap a tune to your muscles, my splicers! heave!" cried out the mate (as I supposed the dark young fellow who spoke these words to be); and I was not a little relieved to hear after a minute or two the peculiar long-drawn notes of a seaman breaking into a working song, followed at the proper interval by the whole body of men delivering the chorus with the true old hurricane note. It would have been a bad sign had they not sung. Only a sailor would appreciate the meaning of silence among the crew of a merchantman getting her anchor.

I took Miss Grant below to show her her berth. There was no smiling and curtseying stewardess to receive her; no obliging steward and his mates to fly to my bidding. The very cabin-boy was at the windlass, and there was nothing living under deck if it were not a lurking cockroach or a concealed rat. But then happily we could not miss what we had not been used to, nor complain of the omission of what we had no reason to expect. Put the mail-boat traveller of to-day back fifty years and he would probably be the most forlorn and melancholy sea-borne object under the sky. I had forgotten to ask Captain Broadwater if there were other passengers, but there was no further need to trouble him: the doors of the berths were open, and a single glance sufficed to let me know that Miss Grant and I were alone. All for the best no doubt, thought I; think of some fellow here in these pent-up quarters with a snore like the escape of steam, or of some lean splenetic Spaniard, constantly ill, and full of growlings in smooth water, and of aves and litanies in stormy weather!

"It is not every one who would choose to sail with Captain Broadwater," said Miss Grant, evidently surprised at our being the only passengers.

"You do not like him? I am sorry. I was glad to get an early ship—"

"No, no, Mr. Musgrave, I do not mean that. How could you tell what sort of a person he would prove to be. I think you will find that he treats his crew inhumanly."

I lifted my eyebrows; I had not imagined she would have seen so quickly into such a matter as that.

"Nor," continued she smiling, "do I fancy that we shall find him a very agreeable table-companion. But no matter. Rio is not so very, *very* far off now!"

We exchanged these sentences whilst we stood before our cabin-doors. Our luggage lay in a heap aft against the transom, but it was better there than in the hold. There was no one to help us, and so we shifted for ourselves. Between us we dragged the boxes and portmanteaux into our berths, and I found a new quality to admire in Miss Grant in the form of a sturdy spirit of independence. No complaints, no regrets, no peevish murmurs over our being neglected. I recollect that I thought—were we to be cast away, here is the girl to show the sailors how to manage. Little did I imagine what was before us when that fancy passed through my head!

The necessary furniture for sleeping lay in my bunk, but it was evident I should have to make my own bed. In the spare cabin next mine was our private stock of provisions. I cast my eyes over the hampers and cases, and knowing what they contained, considered that, taking our livestock into account, we should fare on the whole tolerably enough. Calling to Miss Grant that she would find me on deck, I mounted the companion-ladder, and on emerging discovered that the crew had tripped the anchor and were running about making sail. There were many vessels getting under way at this time, and the picture was full of animation and colour. The jib had been hoisted, and the brig's head was slowly paying off; hands aloft were shouting to people below to hoist away and sheet home; the men on deck were hoarsely bawling as they dragged upon the sheets and halliards; purple-faced old Broadwater standing near the wheel was roaring out orders in whole volleys, and the mate in the waist, who had a singularly shrill voice for a man, heightened the general clamour by re-echoing the captain's orders in notes which sounded like screams. As if all this were not distracting enough, the pigs under the long-boat, irritated by neglect, by fasting, or by the hubbub about them, were squealing as though somebody were stirring them up, whilst the concert was still further intensified by the crowing and the crackling of the cocks and hens in the coops. That the sailors should sing out at the ropes was reasonable and desirable; seamen as they haul take time from their songs, otherwise the business of hoisting, bracing up, sheeting-home would be like drawing teeth. But what purpose could Captain Broadwater serve by roaring to his crew as if they were a company of villains whom nothing short of noise and execrations could urge to exertions?

As I stood looking on, my eye was taken by the mate. He was a man apparently of my own age, tall and thin, with nothing of the air of a sailor about him. His complexion was exceedingly sallow, but his features were strikingly handsome—such a nose, mouth, and forehead as you would expect to find only in some marble fancy of a heathen deity. His eyes were large and black and amazingly rapid in their movements, insomuch it seemed incredible that glances could be darted with the swiftness I have witnessed in this man. An extraordinary point was, his hair was that of a negro: as sheer curly black wool as ever adorned the pate of a Mumbo-Jumbo. It was a very puzzling feature, for assuredly there was no more of the African in him than there was in me. He had a small moustache, and only needed a *sombrero* hat, a cutlass, and a girdle full of pistols, to offer the completest imaginable copy of a pirate. His shrill words leapt as rapidly from his lips as his glances from his eyes, but he seemed incapable of delivering even the most commonplace order without temper. His English was that of an educated man, nor could I discover that it was tainted in the least degree by a foreign accent.

Before long all plain sail had been made, and the brig, with her bowsprit pointing to a down-Channel course, was leaning lightly under the pressure of the summer breeze and pushing gently through the trembling blue surface. The men had ceased their songs; there was no further occasion for the captain to bawl, and something like silence was upon the little ship. Well, thought I, here am I fairly started at last! and as I looked at the town of Deal sparkling to the high sun, and at the old chalk ramparts soaring to the brow of the Foreland giant, a queer feeling thickened my sight for an instant, though it vanished with the "Pshaw!" it evoked from me. But this was an old weakness. I believe had I used the ocean for twenty years, and was still going a voyage every twelvemonth, the sight of the cliffs of the old home quietly sliding away on the quarter and melting into the blue atmosphere would affect me as it did in my boyhood.

I turned to join the captain, and was confronted by Miss Grant. The joyousness in her face seemed to rebuke me. She had brought her hands together, and was gazing from the sails to the land with her lips parted, her breath coming and going quickly, her eyes full of gladness.

"There is one gay heart aboard," said I quietly.

"It is like a dream to me, Mr. Musgrave!" she exclaimed, "when I think of my dull lodgings—and the thoughts that terrified me there—the dread of never seeing Alexander again—and now to find myself going to him—only a few weeks between us,—a kind friend by my side—I, who a few days ago had no friend—" She paused and repeated almost in a whisper, "It is like a dream to me."

"It is real enough," I exclaimed; "yonder is stuff much too substantial to serve as a fabric for the manufacture of visions," and I glanced in the direction of Captain Broadwater, who, now that his ship was fairly under way, had started on the regular pendulum walk of the quarter-deck—a true sea-sawing from abreast of the wheel to forward of the main shrouds with a stare aloft, a look to windward, and then a spin of the heels for another turn; and so on as I have seen the thing done right through a four hours' watch.

"Who is that man?" asked Miss Grant, indicating the chief mate, who was standing in the gangway with his eye aloft to witness, if he could, any imperfection in the trim of the yards and the set of the sails. I told her, and added, "He looks fitter for the stage than for shipboard. I hope I do not misjudge him; but if he would not knife a sailor with as little compunction as he would harpoon a dolphin, then the cut of his jib badly libels his soul."

She watched him with fast failing curiosity and presently sent her gaze seawards. The draught of air had slightly freshened; we were slipping past the South Foreland and opening the broad range of the Channel over the starboard bow. There was a small swell here, just enough to give a slight lift and fall to the jib-boom, and to raise a faint seething noise at the cutwater, along with the airy tinkle of foam-bells sliding iridescent as beads of oil into the eddies of the short wake under the counter. There were ships all about us, and upon the far sea-line you saw the snow-like shining of canvas, serenely luminous as any star, and the dim pearly shadow beyond of the coast of France. I walked aft with Miss Grant to survey the brig from the best place in which a ship is to be viewed when you are aboard her, and here we were joined by

Broadwater, who, as he approached us, pulled out and cast his little eyes upon an immense, almost round, silver watch.

"Pretty nigh time to go to dinner," said he. "It's a blessed thing to be born with a good appetite. There's never no harm in a man that eats hearty. I'd rather judge of a fellow-being's conscience by his appetite than by his actions."

"What country does your chief mate belong to?" I inquired.

"That's more than I can tell you, sir," he replied. "He calls himself a Scotchman, but his hair don't look North Country. His name's Bothwell—Neil Bothwell. He's the proper sort of man for sailors. Never was a chap who could work up old iron like him."

"Are sailors animals that they require working up, as you term it?" inquired Miss Grant.

"Well, perhaps they ain't, miss," he replied. "Animal's too soft a term for 'em. The proper word's beast—wild beast, mum; there ye have it!"

I observed that whenever this captain laboured under any sudden excitement his nose reddened to it as though emotion could find no other feature to express itself in; owing to his eyes being much too small to convey his mind, and to the purple meshes which overspread his countenance like a net that prevented any particular expression of intelligence from rising to the surface. Methought there was something malevolent in the air with which he turned his eyes from Miss Grant to cast a glance aloft.

"Nothing off! Nothing off!" he suddenly shouted, whipping round upon the fellow that was steering; "where d'ye think the ship's bound to, you scowbanker? Keep her to her course!" he rolled menacing to the wheel and addressed the man in a low voice, whilst he thrust his face into the binnacle. The fellow put the wheel down by a spoke or two, with a dogged look and a sullen twist of his eye upon the captain. I think he believed the skipper had meant to strike him. A sheath knife lay upon his hip, and the muscles of his arms, which were bare to the elbow, stood up like ridges of iron under the weather-browned flesh. Broadwater after some further muttering returned to us.

"You were speaking of sailors, ma'am," said he; "there's but one way of finding out the sort of people they are. You must take command of a ship. Of course there's nothing good enough for 'em. They come to the vessel imbecile with drink out of the alleys in which they live when ashore, with nothing to wear but the rags they stand up in, and without having tasted food for a week maybe; and they're no sooner aboard than up turns their noses to whatever's offered to them, and the growlin' begins. What's their wittles? Beef, pork, tea, bread, mollasses, winegar—things they'd never have knowed the names of if they hadn't been sailors; for as landsmen they couldn't have earned as much as would have brought their eyes to the sight of 'em. They like the money they take up, but the work don't suit their delicate constitutions. Tell 'ee what it is: there's been a great deal too much said about the British sailor. He's been led into such fancies of his own consequence that he's now ate up with wanity. 'Ne'er another nation, I'm told,' he says, says he, 'can produce the likes of me!' An' he don't know how right he is. Ne'er another nation *do!* For what's the name of the country whose sailors are within hailing distance of him in the art of loafing, growling, mutineering, and giving trouble all round?"

"Your crew are contented, I hope?" said I.

"Me and the mate'll keep 'em satisfied, I warrant ye," he answered.

I must confess I did not like this man's views and talk. But then I reflected that sailors are, on the whole, a long-suffering people; that in every crew there is a proportion of sensible men who keep the others straight by their resolution to out-weather the captain, even if he should prove old Nick himself, sooner than be betrayed by injurious usage into an act that would procure the forfeiture of their wages. I likewise considered that Broadwater had doubtless been master for some years, and that he had experience enough to distinguish the line where surly and dissatisfied obedience ends, and mutiny—defiant, reckless, and often deadly—begins. Meanwhile I held my tongue, for I was in no humour to enter into an argument with him upon the virtues and vices of the British sailor. I observed that Miss Grant watched him furtively, but with attention. Yet his face was but little better than a mask. It was impossible to decipher his mind by looking at him. He had no other faculty of self-interpretation than his speech. Nature had restricted his capacity of expression to that.

Shortly after this the cabin-boy arrived to announce dinner. The time had slipped away swiftly, and it was now one o'clock.

"The lad must mean *lunch?*" said I.

"No fear!" said Broadwater; "dinner sir, dinner!"

"And pray what is the next meal called?" I asked.

"Supper, sir; served at half-past five; much as a man can eat or ought to eat 'long with tea. Should ye feel faint towards bed-time, there's biscuit, cheese an' pickles. No chance of passengers starving aboard *me!*"

"Oh, we shall manage very well, I have no doubt," I exclaimed soothingly.

He trudged below leaving Miss Grant and me to follow.

"A true sea-bear, Mr. Musgrave," she whispered.

"Yet he was fairly well spoken ashore," said I. "But to keep one's temper is the great secret of happiness. And, besides, we need see as little of him as we choose."

He kept us waiting, and when he emerged from his cabin his face shone from what he himself would have called a "wash down." You might have thought he had soaped his hair as well as his face: it lay as a skull-cap on his head and glistened in the light, and I took notice of a polished spike of it projecting beyond either ear as though the old fellow had rounded off his toilet with a couple of notes of admiration. It is not many years since I made a voyage to the West Indies in a mail-steamer that would have carried me on to Rio, had I desired to visit that port; and I well remember that this, our first meal aboard the *Iron Crown*, recurred to me as vividly as though it had been an experience of yesterday when I sat down in the shining saloon of the great steam-palace at a table, white, rich, glittering with damask and glass and silver, and a waiter behind my chair to attend to my selections from a bill of fare which no excellent hotel could go far beyond. The cabin-boy of the *Iron Crown* was a tall, knock-kneed, dejected-looking youth, who was making his first voyage; he was already oppressed with nausea, and his anxiety and fear of the captain were horrible. I think I see him now, breathing hard as he put a tureen of hot pea-soup (at which he was too ill to glance) before old Broadwater, and then staggering back with his eyes half out of his head, as though persuaded he had blundered in some way and that the captain would instantly rise and fall upon him. Our repast—and I will ask you to consider the time of year—consisted of this same soup, a boiled leg of pork, a dish of potatoes smoking in their jackets, and a pudding of the shape and appearance of a small bolster spotted with currants. The captain drank rum and water, and ate like a ship-wrecked man; and that he might not think us fastidious, and so ground and justify to himself a still more objectionable manner than he had as yet discovered, Miss Grant and I partook of the soup and toyed with a slice of the pork, but declined the pudding on the plea that the excellent breakfast we had made had left us without appetite. The skylight lay open, but the atmosphere was nevertheless oppressive, and I was not a little grateful that the brig should be sailing along on a level keel; for though I was never sea-sick in my life I am persuaded that, had the vessel's motion been lively, the hot atmosphere of the cabin coupled with the strong fumes of the repast would have rendered me very uneasy. Broadwater was so well pleased with his dinner that he suffered the cabin-boy to stagger through the task of waiting without giving him one injurious word; but the terrified concern of the lad satisfied me that though the brig had sailed from the Thames but a day or two before, he had in that brief time undergone discipline enough to make him heartily wish himself at home again with his friends.

As I handed Miss Grant up the companion-steps, she exclaimed: "I fear you will have to thank me for some uncomfortable experiences—and yet think of me alone in this vessel!"

"Never trouble yourself about me, Miss Grant," said I, "I shall begin to enjoy myself presently. Here am I face to face with an aspect of life quite worth examining, believe me. One might wish indeed that there were other passengers, for Broadwater has the look of a man in whom decorousness is only to be contrived by a combination of fares. But he shall help to divert us yet!"

I returned to the cabin to get a deck-chair I had purchased, together with a parcel of books, and made her comfortable. But there was nothing in literature to detain her eye or mine just then. The breeze had freshened, yet it blew a little before the beam, and the brig with her port tacks aboard had just heel enough to suggest speed by her posture. We were hauling out from the land that trended away to starboard in streaks of dim green and white and brown, with here and there a brilliant star-like shining upon it from some object that sent back the sunlight. About a quarter of a mile to windward of us, was a large Indiaman, bound as we were, and passing us, but slowly. There were soldiers aboard her, and the line of the forecastle and main-deck was spotted with bright red uniforms; whilst, from under the violet twilight of the awning stretched over the poop-deck, you caught the glance of twinkling lace and metal buttons, and the fluttering coloured drapery of ladies standing or walking. Her large cabin-windows trembled back the shivering lustre that rose to them off the flashing hurry of waters. Her wake followed her like a narrow band of white satin, and as the dark blue curl at the cutwater arched its luminous ridge into snow, the leap of the froth to the afternoon splendour resembled a scattering of gems, or the shattering of a fragment of rainbow. That is the sort of ship to make a voyage in, I thought to myself; but it would not have been kind to say so. Miss Grant's gaze was full of delight and admiration. She let me know that she had a sailor's eye for atmospheric effect when she bade me observe how the white light of the canvas appeared to overflow the boundaries of the gleaming spaces, and dissolve upon the blue beyond like the sheen from a sky-line of snow-clad hills standing fair against the liquid sapphire of the winter heavens. But though the Indiaman was soon ahead of us we were sailing, too, and there was comfort in knowing it. Round as were the bows of the *Iron Crown*

I judged that she had the trick of blowing along whenever the wind found her a chance, and that her run to Rio might prove nimbler than her shape, as she lay in the Pool, had promised me. Thus we slipped onwards, diminishing the land until it fell into blobs of film and hovering streaks of blue; and by sundown we might have been in the heart of one of ocean's deepest solitudes but for three or four orange-tinctured sail, like dashes of light in the far distance, and but for the water our stem was rending being of a hue as different from the deep, dark, beautiful, pure blue of the fathomless surge as were old Broadwater's eyes from those of Miss Aurelia.

Chapter VI
An Incident in the Channel

HAD I EMBARKED ON this voyage despondently, I believe I should have found a reason for the gloom on my mind in a very extraordinary incident that occurred on this the first night of our departure from England.

Supper had been served at half-past five. Broadwater thus spoke of this meal because it was, as it still is, one of the perversities of the forecastle parlance, so to entitle the hook-pot of tea, the pieces of ship's bread, and the remains of the contents of the noontide kid of beef or pork, which form the last of the mariner's three repasts. I had requested the captain to order one of my fowls to be killed and cooked as a provision against the oppressively substantial fare of the cabin; and though to be sure the bird came to the table somewhat tough for the want of keeping, and somewhat prickly with unplucked quills, it at least provided us with a lighter entertainment than we should have found in the cold leg of pork, in the dish of fried slices of pudding, and in the liver and bacon which the cabin-boy placed upon the table. A great teapot was put before Broadwater, who poured out cupfuls of a liquor black as ink; from the depths of which, on stirring it, there arose quite a little plantation of twigs and leaves. He told us that there was milk enough on board to last until to-morrow, after which we must be satisfied to take our tea "neat," as he called it.

"Few vessels of the size of this brig carry cows, I suppose?" said I.

"No," he answered, "nor goats neither. It's astonishing that the art of feeding people on board ship should have rose to what it is, considering how few vittles there are which ain't of a perishable kind. They'll put up effigies to chaps who write books, to play-actors, to folks like politicians who get on for themselves and don't do nobody else any good; but if ever mortal man in this here bloomin' world deserved a statue it was the fellow who first hit on the notion of steeping beef in brine to keep it fit and sweet for sailors' use. Think of being able to get when afloat—mind ye, miss, I says *afloat*—such a dinner as we've had today! The mere sight of such food at sea—not an ounce of salt in the whole biling neither—is enough to make a man think his eyes must have gone wrong!" and he lifted his hands and gazed upwards with the air of a person overwhelmed with astonishment.

At this early stage it was difficult to tell whether he desired us to accept him as a humourist. But it was not long before I discovered that he was neither a wit nor a wag, and that he was only comical when he had not the least intention of being so.

Whilst we were at supper the mate came below and took his seat quietly, saluting Miss Grant and me with a bow. But for his hair I must certainly have thought him one of the handsomest men I had ever seen, now that I could view him closely and observe the delicacy of his lineaments. His woolly crop was however fatal to him. It was a feature that neutralized all others, even when his head was covered; the effect of the exposure of the whole growth fell little short of a shock. I tried to engage him in conversation; but he was very reserved, answering merely in monosyllables with a constant reference in his manner to old Broadwater, whose presence I supposed kept him quiet. Once or twice he glanced at Miss Grant, but so swiftly it was scarcely possible that he should be conscious he looked at her. He despatched his meal quickly, rose, bowed to us again, and went to his berth in the forward part of the cabin.

"Is your mate a smart sailor?" I asked.

"There never was a smarter," answered Broadwater. "See him aloft. He'll spring to the yardarm from the slings, and'll be jockeying of it when the liveliest of the hands isn't up with the futtock shrouds."

"Have you known him long?"

"He was my mate last voyage," he replied, lifting the lid of the locker next to him and pulling out a bottle of rum; and then calling for water he mixed himself as stout a nor'-wester as ever sailor put to his lips, though he had already swallowed three large cups of tea.

"He has not the air of a seamen," said Miss Grant.

"So little," I exclaimed, "that I am surprised, captain, to hear you speak of him as a taut hand."

"Taut? well, that's perhaps the word, sir. I don't know that he's not almost as taut as me, and in saying that I pay him as handsome a compliment as one man could give to another: for let me tell you, Mr. Musgrave, that you might coast the whole of Great Britain and not meet with a shipmaster who could hold a candle to me in the art of managing sailors."

"Glad to hear it," said I, rising, not very well pleased by the languishing glance he cast at the bottle, as though debating whether to take another sup or return the liquor to the locker.

The afternoon had been hot and blinding with sunshine. The evening that now stole down upon us from astern with a single jewel glittering upon its brow, albeit the western sky was still crimson, with lagoons of delicate green amid the amber and rose and scarlet of the light high clouds there, was delicious and tranquillizing, full of dewy softness and the balm of the shadows which trail in the wake of a glaring day. The radiance was so illusive that the sea looked to go bare to its confines, and the sense of solitude you got when you gazed over the rail could not have been more complete had the *Iron Crown* been floating deep in the heart of the Pacific.

Miss Grant and I paced the deck, greatly enjoying the coolness and repose of the night. Our talk was chiefly about her early life, her father and mother, Rio, Fraser, and the like. It seems that on her mother's side she came of a race of grandees, one of whom was an officer under Don Pedro de Valdez when that Admiral surrendered to Drake, and she said it was a tradition in the family that he was the only man aboard the Spaniard who exhibited any kind of reluctance to being made a prisoner by Sir Francis. Her mother took her to old Spain, as she called it, when she was a child, but though she met several relatives she could recollect nothing of them beyond their haughty manners and grandiose airs. Indeed, I gathered that her mother's noble connections accepted her marriage as a blow to the family dignity. "And yet my father," said Miss Grant, "came of as good a stock as any in Scotland. Pray, what Spanish woman of title is too good for a Scotch gentleman of high descent?" I ought to love my mother's native country; but she is poor and has sunk so low that, until she can take her old place in Europe again, the pretensions of her ancient nobility must continue to be almost too ridiculous to laugh at."

Whilst we walked and chatted the time insensibly slipped away. Once Broadwater rolled over to us puffing a pipe. He offered no apology to Miss Grant for smoking in her presence, though those were days when behaviour of this sort was considered a barbarous incivility to a lady.

"There is grog and biscuit to be had below," he exclaimed, "if you or the lady has a mind for a sup before turning in."

"Thank you, we require nothing more."

"The boys lock up at half-past nine," said he. "but the cabin-light's left burning all night. There's never no need for groping aboard of *me*. What I says to my owner is, treat your passengers well and they'll stick to ye. *I'm* not a man to be scared by a ha'porth of ile. Tell 'ee, Mr. Musgrave, how to read a man's character: watch him carve, sir? There's some as'll help ye as though when what they're serving out is gone there'll be nothing more left to eat on this blooming airth. Others'll act as though they understood you was a *man*. That's my kind. Aboard me every-thing's up to the knocker."

He uttered a loud unmeaning laugh that instantly flavoured the atmosphere with the odour of rum.

"We must consider ourselves very fortunate to fall into such good hands," said I. "A man of purple cheer, to use the language of the poet, is a person quite to my liking."

His eyes were so small that it was impossible to judge whether they were unsteady or not. He seemed to look at me as if he suspected a sarcasm in my words, and an objectionable meaning in my employment of the word "purple"; he then with a flourish of the stem of his pipe to his forehead walked over to the binnacle, and after blowing some clouds of smoke with many a long look around and up at the canvas, knocked the ashes out of his bowl, gave some directions to the boatswain, who, acting as second mate, had charge of the deck, and went below.

"He thinks of nothing but eating," said Miss Grant.

"I hope that may be all," I answered: then checking some expression of dislike and mistrust I was about to utter, I changed the subject by calling her attention to the lovely effect of the moonlight upon the sails of the brig. By daylight the vessel was the sheerest bit of commonplace; but now that the magic pencils of the moon were busy with her, every feature was chastened, the homeliest and coarsest detail softened by the rich clear glow into a fairy delicacy of airy outline and silvered substance. She floated clothed with beauty, and swam like a sweet imagination through the shining air. Her decks gleamed out with the whiteness of the peeled almond: the black line of every seam between the planks lay as sharp to the sight as the ebon shadows of the rigging sliding to and fro to the sleepy stirring of the vessel; there was weight enough in the draught of air to hold the canvas motionless, and every hollow was like the image of a sail carved in alabaster. The boatswain stumped the weather-deck, and his shadow at his feet was more keenly black there than his figure against the sky. The fellow at the wheel stood stirless, but for an occasional movement of his arms, and you would have thought it was the stars that ran as they slipped up and down past him, so imperceptible was the curtseying of the brig. The dew along the rail sparkled crisply, as though, since moonrise, some secret fingers had encrusted the line of bulwarks with gems. Forward all was still; save under the yawn of the fore-course I could distinguish the figure of the look-out man stepping athwart the forecastle, sometimes pausing to lean over the side to send his gaze into the pale distance ahead. There was no gleam of light along the range of the starboard seaboard where the coast was.

"If this were to last," exclaimed Miss Grant, "the voyage would be delightful in spite of the disagreeable obligation of having to take our meals with the captain."

"Delightful, yes; but too long I fear," said I. "We want wind, Miss Grant; we need what the shipbrokers term despatch. This moonlight, this quiet sea, this gentle wind, the transformation of this old bucket into a fabric of marble and diamonds and pearl, are enchanting indeed,—but conditions fit only for pleasure-making. You are in a hurry, and I shall not be reluctant to see Rio heave into view either. Give me, instead of the beauty of such a night as this, the thunder of half a gale of wind blowing over our quarter, a high green frothing sea chasing us, that same moon up yonder whisking like a silver round-shot from the edge of one dark cloud to another, and the brig with a reef in her fore-sail and the main-top-gallant sail set over the double-reefed topsail hurling through an acre of foam of her own making, with the white seething and hissing smother boiling into her wake that stretches to the very line of the tumbling horizon!"

"An excellent description, Mr. Musgrave, and it is what we want as you say. You have not forgotten your old calling. You talk easily enough of reefs and sails."

"When," said I, "a man has dipped his hand into the tar-pot the stain of the stuff never quits him. Once a sailor, always a sailor."

At this moment five bells were struck by someone on the main deck.

"What time is that?" she inquired.

"Half-past ten," I answered.

"So late!" she exclaimed; "it is time to go to bed. Good-night, Mr. Musgrave."

"Let me see you to your cabin," said I, and down we went.

The lamp had been dimmed spite of the skipper's indifference to ha'porths of oil, but there was light enough to see by. I was glad to find the little bracket-lamps in our cabins alight. I suppose it was a part of the boy's duty to see to this, but there was really so little to expect in the way of attention in a craft of this kind that I was grateful for the most trifling illustration of our being looked after. I stepped into my cabin for a cheroot, not choosing to turn my back on so fair a night yet a while. Slightly as the brig swayed, the bulkheads and strong fastenings creaked as though a score of rats were worrying one another, and I guessed, unless I should turn in thoroughly sleepy, these bothersome noises promised to keep me awake all night. Cigar in mouth

I walked the deck for some time, finding a constant pleasure in the moonlit scene, and greatly enjoying the delicious hush that rested upon the vessel and the ocean. After all, thought I, this is a voyage to do me a great deal of good. It is a complete change; there is no cold weather to be dreaded, no Cape Horn, no Southern Ocean in June. There should be some fun to be got out of old Broadwater, though I do not like him. And then I fell to thinking of Miss Aurelia. There had been so much moonlight mixed up in our oceanic intercourse so far, that it seemed to me as if I should never be able to cast my eyes upon the planet without thinking of her. Well, no woman could desire a lovelier fancy and habit of association in a man's mind. My humour took a poetic turn; Byron's line—"She walks in beauty like the night," came into my head, along with Shelley's fine thought—"Moonlight and music and feeling are one." Here is plenty of moonlight, thought I, but even if I should call Miss Aurelia the music, where is the feeling? But what wonderful eyes she has! I mused: what spirit, power, life, intelligence! She talks very finely too, by George! Fraser is her dear boy, and deserves to be so, I don't doubt; but the shape of his head must have vastly changed since he was my shipmate at sea, if he is able to understand one half of the fancies which take her.

Presently feeling somewhat lonesome, I crossed the deck to where the boatswain was quietly pacing.

"A fine night," said I.

"It is, sir,—lovely indeed," he replied, coming to a stand and touching his cap very civilly.

"You are the second mate, I believe?"

"Second mate and bo'sun, sir."

"Pray do not stand, I will walk with you."

We started to pace the length of the quarter-deck together. I particularly observed in him a very respectful, quiet manner, the sort of sailorlike civility one wanted to hear of in such a ship as the *Iron Crown*. The moonshine gushed so clearly that my companion's face could not have been more visible had I viewed it by daylight. He was a hearty-looking man of about five-and-forty, clean shaven save in a streak of iron-grey whisker; a real splicer in aspect down to such minutiae as the hang of his arms and the curl of his fingers as he walked.

"Is this your first voyage with Captain Broadwater, Mr.——?"

"Gordon's my name, sir—Zana Gordon. Yes, this is my first voyage with Captain Broadwater."

"I suppose he is reckoned a pretty smart seaman?"

"I don't know I'm sure, sir."

"The crew at least strike me as a lively lot. They tumble about very briskly, a good sign in men newly shipped. But of course most of them will run when the brig arrives at Rio. Jack has his peculiarities as have other folks."

"He has a right to be peculiar, sir. His life's a good deal out of the common; little understood, too, save by them who have to eat and drink and jump aloft with him. And it isn't enough that he's expected to work for twenty-four hours in the day, and that he's got to eat victuals which no man ashore who values his dog would give it, unless it went mad and had to be choked; and that his labour's of a sort ne'er a landsman would undertake, no, not if instead of signing for three pounds a month he agreed for a hundred. That isn't enough, I say. It's what lies behind, sometimes deep, and nearly always out of sight, that's the worst part of all that's bad in the seafaring calling."

"You mean bullying, brutal treatment, injurious language?" He was silent. "I should understand you," said I. "In coming aboard this morning I found a bigger hint than would have sufficed me in the faces of the boat's crew. I was a sailor myself for three years, and one doesn't want to serve longer than that to make plain words of the looks of seamen."

He still held his peace, but he had said enough to let me know his silence was mere wariness. When we got on to other topics he was as talkative as I could desire. I found he had been able seaman aboard the Indiaman I had first gone to sea in, though he had left her before I joined. She had been commanded in his time by the same man who had her when I was a midshipman; so here was a topic that was enough to at once establish a sort of bond between us.

Whilst we were pacing the deck the man on the look-out forward hailed my companion—as he seemed to think. Neither of us caught what he said, and Gordon hallo'd back. The man sang out again, but without making himself heard; on which the boatswain went forward to see what was wanted. He left me standing near the wheel. There yet remained half of my cheroot to smoke out. Six bells—eleven o'clock—had been struck some ten minutes before; but the loveliness of the night still detained me, and I was in no mood yet to exchange the warm sweetness of the ocean night-breeze for the atmosphere of my cabin. On a sudden the man who was steering started violently, let go the wheel, and ran to the vessel's side, where he hung in a strained listening posture, with one hand to his ear. I hastily crossed the deck, wondering what on earth he could have heard to cause him to start so wildly, and above all to desert his post at the helm as though he had gone out of his mind. The moonshine streamed full upon him, and the complexion of that light, combined with his extreme pallor, made the face he slowly turned upon me ghastlier than any dead man's for the very life that worked with a sort of grin in it.

"Did you hear him?" he inquired in the low tremulous voice of a man newly recovered from a faint.

"Hear whom?" I answered, staring my hardest into the distance, misty with the radiance.

"Something away yonder called me!" said he, still speaking in the same voice, weak with terror and astonishment.

"You!" I exclaimed; "called *you!* But there's nothing there, man—nothing in sight, anyway. What should there be then for a human voice to sound from?"

"Hark! There again!" he cried, with another violent start as though he had been electrified. I had heard nothing.

"What is your name?" I asked.

"Jesse Cooper, sir," he responded, trembling pitifully.

I had begun to think that the fellow was ill, or that he had suddenly gone wrong in his head, when he lifted his hand as if to motion silence, and then I certainly did seem to hear a faint sound coming from God knows where, that might have passed for a feeble human cry, though it syllabled nothing that was intelligible to my ears. No doubt it was no more than the sheer imagination in me wrought on by some delicate murmur of wind aloft, or by the stir of one rope lying in the chafe of another, or by the jerk of a sheet to the gentle strain of the sail, or the creak of parrel or truss. But for the moment I was hardly less startled than the man himself.

"Very extraordinary!" I said.

"You heard it, sir?" he cried, looking wildly at me.

"I certainly heard something confoundedly like a human voice hailing," I answered, peering with all my eyes at the sea, as though I must certainly see something there if I stared long enough.

"O my God! O my God!" he groaned. "You heard it too, sir! It's no fancy then. I'm called, and must go. It was father's voice. He was drowned at sea, and three years afterwards called my brother, who fell from aloft and was killed the same night. And now he's called me!"

I saw how it was, and felt very sorry that I should have owned I heard the sound, for I was now persuaded it was pure fancy on my part, that is to say, pure fancy in taking the noise I had heard to be a human voice: though by my owning I had caught the note, be it what it would, I was like to drive the poor superstitious creature clean out of his mind.

"The brig will be aback in another minute," said I. "Catch hold of the wheel, man. There's nothing in all this—nothing but nerves. Dead men can't call out—you ought to know that! If they could there'd be nothing but voices hailing the world day and night."

He grasped the wheel without answering me, and brought the brig to her course. Just then the boatswain came aft.

"Nothing wrong forward, I hope!" said I.

"No, sir. The look-out called to a mate for a chew of tobacco, and thought, when I answered, that I was the man he had sung out to."

"Glad it's no worse," said I. "We've had a bit of a scare aft here,— all happening in a minute—too odd of its kind to require improving by anything of the same sort forward," and then I told him what had happened.

We stood in the shadow cast by the main-rigging as we conversed. He cast a glance in the direction of the wheel, and said, in a voice made up of pity and contempt:

"There's always sailors knocking about with notions of that kind. I've seen a man plump down upon his knees and pray in a loud voice all because he caught sight of a compreesant a-burning at the yard-arm. That there Cooper struck me, on first setting eyes on him, as having a queerish look in his face. If there was more learning in forecastles there'd be a deal less of these here fanciful gallivantins. Fancy a chap supposing that his father, who was drownded t'other side o' Cape Horn, could hail him after all these years out o' the English Channel!"

"Yet wiser men than this same Cooper, Mr. Gordon, hold and stoutly cling to stranger beliefs than the midnight halloing of drowned men!" said I, hammering at a flint for a light for my fragment of cigar. "If any mortal being has a right to believe in ghosts, it should be the sailor. Look aloft, Mr. Gordon!"—he turned up his weather-beaten face— "Mark how spectrally those sails show out to the moonlight. What, to a fanciful eye, should the flitting of the shadows up there to the swaying of the masts signify but the pinions of spirits hovering over those glimmering heights? and what, to the imaginative ear, should the mutterings of the breeze in the shrouds mean but the dark and secret whispered conversation of beings as little like you or me, Mr. Gordon, as the moon is like the sun? Again, look over the side—it is all wide, white silence: mere sea and moonshine to you and me, but to the lonely distempered vision the fittest canvas the wide world over for the magic lantern of the mind to cast its imaginations on."

He tilted the peak of his cap on to his nose as he scratched the back of his head, and said: "Well, if a man's weak enough to believe in ghosts,

I don't doubt he'd get more ideas about them out of such a night as this upon the ocean than maybe he'd collect out of the most crowded of graveyards ashore. But supposing such things as sperrits to be, who's going to make me believe they ha'n't got too much sense to choose the sea to knock about in? A spectre's right enough in an old country house and the likes of them places ashore; for he's not only got a roof over his head and a fire to warm himself at when the weather draws up cold, but the pick of the best room to lay in, and a larder to help himself from—if so be a sperrit ever gets hungry. But what does a ghost do at sea? If he's a land ghost he'll stop ashore; and is it imaginable, d'ye think, sir, that if he's the ghost of a sailor he'd retarn, without being forced, to the life he was bound to hate when he was flesh and blood, and keep company, of his own accord, with such people as skippers and mates, and endure again the cold and wet that 'ud send him from the deck or from aloft streaming like a soaked rag to his thin blanket and leaking bunk?" He shook his head in a way that showed him fully convinced by his own reasoning.

"Isn't that a sail out yonder?" I exclaimed, at that instant catching sight of some tiny object gleaming like a faint dash of light on the sea-line, and doubting for a moment whether it was a star or a ship's canvas or the play of white water.

He looked, and said, "Yes, sir; a yacht, I allow, by the sheen of her sails."

It was as though a paring of pearl reflected the moonlight, so exceedingly dainty and delicate was the lustre of the fabric against the dark obscure of the horizon. I noticed however, whilst I kept my eye fastened upon it, that it moved with a velocity quite meteoric in its way, for when I had first descried it, it showed out a hand's-breadth forward of the foremost mainshroud, whilst before I could have counted ten it had slided midway to the forerigging.

I glanced aft. "Why, Mr. Gordon," I said, "the wheel's deserted; the brig's coming round!"

He sprang to the helm, and ground at the spokes till the tiller-chains rattled again, meanwhile looking right and left.

"Where's Cooper, sir?" he cried; "he hasn't gone forward. I'll swear he never passed us; he wouldn't quit the helm unless he was mad!"

There was a grating abaft the wheel; I sprang on to it and strained my sight at the wake astern. The moon was westering and looking over our foretopsail yard-arm, and her light was very clear and broad. I could see nothing. The wake went away slowly in small black holes and little seething clouds, with here and there a faint flash of green light, as though a strange fish with a green eye floated up to the surface to take a view of us now and again.

"He is overboard—drownded hisself!" cried the boatswain. "Man overboard!" he roared. "Lay aft the watch! lively, or ye'll be too late!" and he fell to grinding at the wheel again to steady it.

The brig came round slowly. His cry was electrical in its effect. I had seen nothing stirring save the man on the look-out, and now in an instant the planks re-echoed the thumping and slapping of the booted or naked feet of the watch tumbling aft as if for their lives. They were busy with the boat, clearing away the falls and casting off the gripes, when up came old Broadwater.

"What's the matter? what's the matter?" he bawled.

"Man overboard , sir!" shouted the boatswain.

"Where is he? where is he? Anybody see him?" roared the skipper, springing with his oval shanks on to the grating alongside me.

"I have been looking, but can make out no signs of him," I answered.

"How long has he been overboard?" he shouted.

"Three or four minutes, I expect," answered the boatswain.

"How did he git there?" he bellowed; "was he knocked overboard?"

"Good God!" I cried, wild to think of the precious time the old fool was losing by these questions, "there's a man overboard, captain, and he must drown if you don't instantly seek him, if indeed he's still afloat."

"Keep all fast with the boat," he vociferated; "if he's only been overboard three or four minutes he ought to be visible if he's on the surface, and since he ain't it's a proof he's under."

"It's murder!" said an angry voice amongst the men standing near the davits.

Just then the mate sprang through the companion.

"Who was it said it's murder?" shouted Broadwater, half suffocated with passion. "Mr. Bothwell, find out the man! find out the man! I must know who it is!"

"Captain Broadwater," I exclaimed, "the poor fellow has only been overboard a few minutes, and you really—"

"Mind your own blasted business, sir," he shouted in such a raging way that I have no pen to portray it with. "Find me the man who said it's murder, Mr. Bothwell! Find me that man, sir!"

Disgusted by the old fellow's insolence and temper, and sickened by his indifference to human life, I walked a little way forward clear of the men, and stood leaning against the rail with my arms folded waiting for what was next to happen. The mate thrust in lithe as steel amongst the sailors, flashing his eyes first into one then into another face, whilst with shrill imperious tones which came back in echoes from the hollows of the canvas he demanded to know who had spoken the words. Broadwater, dismounting from the grating, danced in a very delirium of wrath in and out among the seamen, looking for all the world in the transfiguring light of the moon like a gigantic crab masquerading in man's attire, whilst he whipped out at the top of his pipes with all sorts of menaces, threatening I know not what unless the man who had said it was murder was named or confessed himself. The excitement grew, the hubbub increased. Oaths were so plentiful, I could only earnestly hope that if Miss Grant were not asleep she was out of hearing. I feared it would come to a fight, and expected every moment to witness the gleam of a knife flourished in the air. The men, however, would not tell who it was that had spoken the words. Some blows were exchanged, and presently the sailors came staggering my way, driven and beaten along by Broadwater and his mate.

"Forward with ye! Forward with ye!" roared the old fellow, flourishing his arms like a windmill, whilst the mate shoved and pushed as a drover would thrust a congregation of irresolute or defiant calves. It would have struck a landsman as incredible that the men should have suffered themselves to be thus driven. They were six to two, yet they offered no resistance. But the habit of discipline is strong in the sailor, and the quarter-deck is sacred ground. In no man who has command of his fellow-beings is there vested such despotic powers as in the master of a ship. The spirit of mutiny will skulk long ere it dare show its face. There is no doubt the men would have gone forward quietly enough; but Broadwater's and his mate's blood was up, and the wild and wretched business did not end until the men had been driven forward of the mainmast. Blowing and gasping, though still flourishing his hands, Broadwater came to a stand, his face so crimsoned by his exertions that he looked like a mulatto in the moonlight.

"Now see here," he said, sputtering out the words in wheezy accents, for he was too exhausted to roar, "ontil the name of the man who spoke them words is given to me, you're on bread and water! Mind that! One of you it was, and I must know who; and if bread and water don't serve, I'll stop 'em both, I'll stop 'em both! Hunger'll make a mad beast rational. So now you know what ye've got to expect."

With this he walked aft, followed by his mate. By this time I had had enough of the deck, and was sick, grieved, and deeply worried. Broadwater's insulting expression stuck in my gorge, and I made up my mind to have a short conversation with him next morning on the subject. It was depressing beyond words, too, to think that the unhappy man, who beyond question had dropped silently overboard whilst the boatswain and I conversed forwards, may have perished for the want of a boat nimbly sent to seek him. One of the crew had called it murder, and that would be the universal feeling of the forecastle I was sure. Broadwater was marching to and fro near the wheel, with a lurch in his gait that satisfied me he must have gone to bed pretty well primed. He was talking vehemently to the boatswain, who still held the wheel. The mate overhung the rail, gazing astern. I went below unnoticed by them, and had opened the door of my cabin when I heard my name called. I turned and saw Miss Grant standing in her doorway robed in a pink dressing-gown. Her dark eyes flashed back the light of the lamp in my berth, and with *them* and her pale face and coronal of fair hair and commanding posture she would, attired as she was, have nobly filled the canvas of a painter as the Muse of Tragedy.

"What was the cause of that great commotion on deck just now?" she inquired, without the least exhibition of alarm or nervousness.

"I had hoped that you would have been peacefully sleeping, Miss Grant. A fellow who was at the wheel fell crazy, and quietly slipped himself overboard. He was missed, and the alarm given. Hence the hurried tread overhead which disturbed you."

"Was he saved?"

"No. Broadwater arrived rather the worse for liquor, lost his temper, and prohibited the men from lowering the boat. It is all very sad, and I would rather it had happened on the last instead of the first night of our voyage. But I have told you the worst. And do you know, Miss Grant, that it is past midnight?"

She saw that I did not want to prolong my talk just then. Indeed I was secretly much excited, much perturbed, vexed, and pained, and feared that my speech would betray my anxiety and worry her. She listened a little, and exclaimed, "Everything seems quiet now: is it still a fine night?"

"As lovely as when you left it," I answered.

She inclined her head and closed her door, and without further ado I tumbled into my bunk, though not to sleep for a long while.

Chapter VII
Bothwell, Chief Mate

I WAS AWAKENED EARLY BY the scrubbing-brushes of the men over-head washing down the decks. The movement of the little ship was tolerably lively, insomuch that on quitting my bunk I had some diffi-culty for a few minutes in keeping my legs, nor was it hard to tell, by the dim humming noise that seemed to tremble through the fabric like the vibration in a harp-string after it has been twanged, that it was blow-ing a fresh breeze of wind. I was soon dressed, and on gaining the deck found the brig storming along with her royals furled and her trysail-boom well on the quarter. A high sea chased us, and but for the wind being abaft the beam we must have found no little spite in the weight of the sudden gusts and brisk squalls which distended our canvas until the sheets groaned again to the strain. The heavens were covered with large white clouds, which rolled along very stately and solemnly, with a brownish scud speeding under them like smoke; but there were every-where great breaks of clear blue sky of the true summer tint of the English Channel. The sea was as grand as one could wish it with flying shadow and leaping dazzle—blue ridges with a mile-long head of foam, bits of rainbow in the showering of spray, weltering spaces of violet gloom cast by the clouds and the swift glory that chased them. The brig was buzzing through it as if, to use the sailor's phrase, she had the scent at last. She rose to the head of a sea in a boiling smother, then sank all very solemnly with a leeward heel that seemed to bring the top-gallant rail within arm's-reach of the hissing yeast that went wildly swirling past, and out of which the rush of wind from under the foot of the mainsail would tear up bucketfuls of blobs and flakes, and send them scattering with a scream through the air with something of the pearly glint of the flying-fish in their flight.

My friend, Mr. Zana Gordon, had once again charge of the deck. Bucket in hand, with trousers turned above the knee, he swirled the sparkling green water that was handed to him along the deck, whilst the men scrubbed with their brushes. Recollecting that these were the fellows who were to be disciplined by a diet of bread and water into telling the captain which of them it was who had used the words that had enraged him, I ran my eye from one to another of them with a little attention, but observed nothing particular, unless it were a sort of sullenness in their deliberate manner of handling their scrubbing-brushes, which after all might have been a mere imagination on my part.

It was a lively enough scene in its way, and brought back old memories to me. The smoke of the newly-lighted galley-fire blew swiftly and merrily from the chimney of the caboose into the sea, and you noticed the farm-yard noise about of the crowing of cocks and the grunting of pigs. There was but one vessel in sight, a large topsail schooner heading to cross under our stern for a course to some French port. The sea took her fair abeam, and she rolled so heavily that she looked like a great fan violently swayed by some Titanic hand hidden beneath the surface of the water. Well, it was just the sort of weather I had told Miss Grant yesterday that we needed. A short spell of it would drive us clear of soundings, and I knew it would make one feel as though the voyage was to have an end when one should find the course set fair by the binnacle compass for South America.

The boatswain saluted me with a flourish of a tarry thumb to his forehead, but he was too full of business to talk. After I had been on deck for about a quarter of an hour, by which time the scrubbing was over, and the seamen were smacking the planks with a swab or two, Broadwater came up through the companion-hatch, where he stood a while holding on, and blinking around him as though not yet wide awake. Then going to the wheel he brought his eyes in a squint upon the compass, and after a survey of the fabric aloft, and a slow gaze round the sea, he called out to me, "Good morning, sir. Tow rope's in hand at last, I allow. No hint of kedging in this here movement."

I inclined my head coldly and distantly to him, and then suspecting that any kind of sub-acid or chilly posture would be entirely lost upon such an intelligence as his, I resolved to deal with him in a way that should at least be intelligible.

"I wish to speak a word with you, Captain Broadwater," I called out.

He looked at me a moment as though he feared his dignity and importance would suffer by having to go to me, and then after a half glance at the fellow at the wheel with a slow pulling down of his nose with his fore-finger and thumb, a trick that seemed to help him to arrive at a conclusion, he came to where I stood, but very leisurely, appearing the while to think of nothing but the appearance of the deck and the movements of the men swabbing.

"Well, Mr. Musgrave," he exclaimed, "what is it, sir? Slept pretty comfortable, I hope? Nothing the lady can find to complain about, I trust?"

"Sir," said I, "you were extremely rude and offensive to me last night. You are captain of this ship, and I am a passenger who has paid for certain rights—civility from you amongst the rest—which I intend to claim; and if you do not concede me every tittle of what I have parted with my money to obtain, I will make it so hot for you on my return to England that you shall wish yourself hanged ere you ever set eyes on me. And now, sir," I continued, with the sternest face I could contrive to put on, though my gravity was not a little staggered by the ludicrous expression of bewilderment that overspread his singular countenance, "I insist upon your apologizing to me at once, Captain Guy Broadwater, for the insolent manner in which you addressed me last night."

He cast his little eyes from the deck to the sky and back again, frowned, scratched his head, and by other signs seemed to wish me to suppose that he was in an agony of thought. Then, with an inimitable air of being all abroad, he pointed with his forefinger to his waistcoat, and said, "Me! *me* insult you! You're a-dreaming, Mr. Musgrave."

"No dream at all, sir," said I; "you were confoundedly insolent to me, and ruder even in your manner than in your speech, and I demand an apology."

Again he looked up at the sky and down at the deck, as though the effort to recollect what had passed caused him acute suffering.

"What did I say?" he suddenly asked.

I told him.

"Well, Mr. Musgrave," said he, "you're a gentleman, and I should be sorry for to swear that I never spoke them words, seeing that you tell me I *did*. But I can assure you, sir, on my honour as master of this here *Iron Crown*, that I have no recollection of using the term you mention. If I did, why then I 'pologize, and no man can do more."

On hearing this I bowed coldly and walked aft, congratulating myself upon my resolution, for I believed I had made him understand he would have to be very cautious henceforth in his dealings with me, and I had also got to see that the man, like all other bullies, was very white-livered at bottom. There was indeed danger that a person of this nature would extend something of the treatment he exhibited to his crew to Miss Grant and me; and unless I asserted myself promptly it might end, through a natural aversion on my part from any kind of worry or annoyance, to my insensibly submitting to his rough usage, which of course he would accentuate in proportion as I yielded, until my life on board might become as uneasy as if I had been one of the crew. This is a feature of a voyage absolutely impossible in these days, but in my time it was a condition (in small passenger vessels, of course) as familiar as the coarseness of the food and the gloom and discomforts of the cabin.

I kept my back on the quarter-deck for a little, whilst I stood watching the sparkling race of froth hurling from under the shadow of our counter to the creamy summit of the green surge chasing us, during which I could hear the old fellow calling to the seamen in such a tone as few men would think fit to adopt towards a dog. If it was convenient to him to forget his insulting manner to me, it was plain that whatever else he chose to remember was very present to his mind. For how long a period the men who formed the starboard watch would consent to the discipline of bread and water it was hard to conjecture; though indeed the sailor of that period could scarcely suffer a very severe hardship in the deprivation of lumps of meat out of which, whether raw or cooked, the mariner beguiled the tedium of the voyage by manufacturing snuff-boxes for his grandfather, work-boxes for his sweetheart, and tobacco-boxes for himself.

Miss Grant did not leave her cabin till breakfast was upon the table. Broadwater, who was seated when she arrived, got up and distorted his figure with a bow, whilst he asked her, with much such a pleasant face as he wore when I first made his acquaintance, what sort of a night she had passed, and if the brig's tumblefication troubled her much. This stroke of politeness was meant as much for me as for her. After the exchange of a few common-places about the weather and so forth, Miss Grant said to the captain, "Were they not able to save the poor fellow who fell overboard last night?"

"No, mum," he answered, with a half look from me to a lump of sausage which he held aloft on a fork; "the long and short of it's this. The man was in the water some minutes afore the alarm was given. The surface lay clear under the moon, and had he been showing there was enough of us looking for some one to see him. He meant to drown hisself, and he *did* it."

"But apart from the chance," said I, "of rescuing him as a mere matter of humanity, would not his loss, by weakening your working strength, make you anxious to be sure that he was not to be recovered?"

"There was no signs of him, sir," he answered doggedly. "I don't want to lose no men if I can help it; but if a chap chooses to slip overboard so quietly that no one hears him touch the water, what's to be done?"

"But you didn't know when you first came on deck that he *had* drowned himself," said I.

"No," he answered, "but didn't I act as if I did? which means that I'm one of those men who don't need to know a thing to understand it."

I turned to Miss Grant, and related the strange story of the preceding night, whilst Broadwater worked away at his breakfast with both hands, and masticated with such energy as to apparently hold him deaf.

"Strange," she exclaimed, "that you should have thought you heard the voice that called him. Of course it was fancy, but it is dreadful to think how even a little imagination may overpower the reason."

"There was everything to help the imagination," said I: "the silence upon the vessel and upon the ocean—the wild, straining look in the man's eyes with the sparkle of moonlight in them as he turned them upon me, full, as I can now see, with the anguish of madness—and then the misty silvery distance towards which he bent his ear with his hand to it. I believe had he told me there was a phantom out there, and pointed to it, I should have seen *something*, if not the apparition he himself beheld."

Presently, after a prodigious meal, Broadwater arose and left the cabin.

"Why did not he attempt to save the man?" Miss Grant said.

"I believe the fellow when he first came on deck was still muddled with the fumes of the liquor he had swallowed, and barely understood what had happened or knew what he was about." And then I told her how he had insulted me, and how a little while before I had obliged him to apologize. My mere telling her this thing touched the spirit in her. The look of her as she listened to me made you feel that here was a woman to fill any man who should vex her with the feelings of a dog. Before we quitted the table, the mate arrived to get his breakfast. He bowed to us quietly as before, seated himself without speaking, and fell to his meal with great soberness and civility of demeanour. It seemed hard to reconcile his subdued bearing, which seemed by its air to be habitual to him, with his fierce and passionate treatment of the men, and particularly his desperate and raging behaviour of the previous night. Now that the captain was away I hoped to be able to draw him into conversation, and began by saying that if this breeze lasted we might look for a run of two hundred and fifty knots in the twenty-four hours.

"Quite that, sir," he answered.

"That was a sorry business last night, Mr. Bothwell. If the men forward are superstitious, they will not like it."

"They won't like their company being weakened you mean, sir?" lifting his gaze from his plate and eying me steadily for a moment.

I thought to myself, as I glanced at his woolly head, his handsome features and dark eyes, which when they fell from my face rolled in a hundred nimble glances, fastening upon nothing, and yet seeing everything as you would say, "Lord, what a corsair this rogue would make in the hands of a Byron or a Michael Scott!"

"No," said I; "I mean they won't like Captain Death boarding their craft almost before the anchor they have broken out has dried at the cathead."

His swift glance darted from me to Miss Grant, and then with a smile that exhibited a set of fine, even white teeth, the whiter for his dark moustache, he said, in an almost effeminate way, "Oh, sir, we must not trouble ourselves about what the sailors forward think."

"Why not?" asked Miss Grant quickly. "Are they not men like you and Captain Broadwater? You would be unable to sail this ship without them. A master on land dare not treat his men-servants as captains at sea treat their crews."

He answered softly, "No, madam, because no doubt men-servants would give notice and seek another situation."

"Do you believe it, sir?" she exclaimed, flushing and gazing at him irefully; "indeed you would find they would not rest there——." She checked herself, and added laughingly, and looking at me, "I have not a very high opinion, Mr. Musgrave, of the spirit and courage of lack-eys and footmen, but I truly believe that if they were treated by their masters as sailors are by their commanders there would be a great many mysterious disappearances happening amongst the nobility and gentry."

"I am always glad, madam," said the mate, showing his teeth again, "to hear the ladies championing poor Jack. He has very few friends, very few friends."

He shook his head without any suggestion of sarcasm about him, and the gesture seemed to me to make his eyes shine as if they had been formed of some black liquid with a gleam upon it that danced to the rippling of their movement.

"How long have you been at sea?" I asked bluntly.

"Ten years, sir."

"Humph!" I exclaimed, "a good deal of hard weather and knocking about may be packed into ten years. Apparently you are of Captain Broadwater's mind, that the sailor moves forward the better for being kicked."

He made no answer.

"I have heard," said I, addressing Miss Grant, "of captains whose hatred of the sailors serving under them was really phenomenal. I remember being told of the commander of a ship that he could never bring himself to offer one of his seamen anything with his hand, but that he would put it down upon the deck and *kick* it at him. By the way," I continued, turning upon the mate again, "what'll be the upshot of this trouble with the starboard watch? The men are not likely to peach upon their messmate, and if the man who used the words won't confess himself, what's to follow? The fellows will not surely put up for a whole voyage with nothing to eat and drink but ship's bread—bad enough, I dare say—and a draught from the scuttle-butt?"

Before he could reply, Miss Grant said quickly, "To what do you refer, Mr. Musgrave?"

"Why," I answered, "last night on the captain refusing to send a boat on the chance of picking up the man who had gone overboard, one of the group of fellows who were at the davits exclaimed, 'It's murder!' and the whole of the watch are not to be allowed any other provisions but biscuit until the man who used the words is discovered."

"He is discovered," said the mate almost blandly.

"Oh, indeed!" I exclaimed, "how, pray?"

"He came to me about twenty minutes ago, and said that as he did not choose his messmates should suffer for what he had done, he would own he was the man who cried out, 'It's murder!'"

"He should be pardoned for his honesty," exclaimed Miss Grant. "I hope the captain will let the matter rest. I will ask him to forgive the poor fellow."

The mate softly wiped his moustache, rose, bowed, and went on deck.

"One should say," said I, "that there are the seeds of a startling romance in that chap; but I fear that it is nothing but the vilest sea-going commonplace made a little odd by good looks and Hottentot wool."

"I agree with you," she answered; "he is even more colourless than his captain; yet prosaic as they both are, they are equal to creating a very great deal of trouble; and do you know, Mr. Musgrave," she said, suddenly and even vehemently, "I am extremely sorry that we ever took berths in this ship."

"Oh, but it is a little early to be anxious," said I cheerfully. "I quite know what is in your mind: you fear that the behaviour of Broadwater and his mate may lead to the crew giving trouble. Well, the same misgiving is my reason for speaking out so plainly to both men. If they are made to understand that I am watching them and observing their conduct, they may have sense enough to restrain themselves for the reason that I should be at hand as a witness to testify to their inhumanity, and to justify any act of insubordination that the sailors might be driven to."

She was silent for a little, and then said, "Whereabouts is the ship now, Mr. Musgrave?"

"I suppose we are hardly abreast of the Isle of Wight yet," I answered.

She reflected again, and then clasping her hands and bringing them to her lips, and looking at me with a sort of wistfulness, though she spoke with hesitation, she said, "I almost—I *almost* wish that the captain would put us ashore."

This was a desire to puzzle me considerably I answered, "Of course, Miss Grant, if you are reluctant to proceed I will unhesitatingly ask the captain to put us ashore; but I should not like him to refuse, and unhappily there is no doubt that he will refuse, because of course he would conclude that we should return to London and lodge a complaint against him, and so lose him his berth. Now, if he should decline to put us ashore my position would be an awkward one. He need do nothing but keep the ship heading steadily on her course, and we are helpless."

She interrupted me: "And the passage money would be forfeited. No, I am silly to wish such a thing. I was all eagerness and impatience yesterday. It is just a little passing misgiving." I was about to speak. "No," she exclaimed with energy, "we are here and will remain here."

"Be it so," said I, not a little relieved, for I foresaw a very great deal more of trouble than I had the least disposition to undergo, even to oblige *her*, had she insisted on my asking old Broadwater to haul his brig in to the land, and set us and our baggage once more on *terra firma*.

Chapter VIII
The Half-blood's Punishment

MISS GRANT WENT TO her cabin and I on deck, where I observed Broadwater and the mate marching the length of the quarter-deck and busy in conversation. There was a middling high sea running, which, had it been on the bow instead of on the quarter, would have rendered the motion of the brig extremely uncomfortable. As it was, it swung the vessel with an almost rhythmic steadiness as it under-ran her. It was first a long upward heave to the foaming liquid brow, then a gradual lean over to the full weight of the wind till the lee-channels roared in the smother of spume over the side, and then a steady slide down into the speckled, froth-laced trough, with a recovery of the hull that started us with a level keel for the next buoyant climb. Not above a cannon-shot to windward was a large frigate, close-hauled under double-reefed topsails and reefed foresail. She showed no colours, but to a nautical eye a single glance sufficed to prove her English. She was plunging heavily, and would lift her head out of the boiling white about her bows until eight or ten feet of the keel at her forefoot showed clear, with a dull yellow glancing from the metal sheathing that looked like a mirroring of pale light on the wet, black, gleaming sides of the beautifully moulded hull. As she rolled she gave us a view of a portion of her weather-deck, with a hint of black artillery in certain covered, muzzled shapes, crouching under the defences of her bulwarks crowned with the white line of hammocks. The movement of a spot of red here and there marked the mechanical pacing of a marine. I never remember a nobler sea-show than was offered by this fine frigate, with her broad white line broken by the closed gun-ports, the superb set of her reefed canvas, the airy grace of her rigging ruling the piebald hurrying sky with dark lines of shrouds, thinning as they soared, till they rose delicate as the fibres of a spider's web to the glimmering button of the truck at the royalmast-head, whence streamed the long pennon straight out upon the wind, like a streak of light up there; whilst over the weather-bow there was the sharp and frequent flash of a green sheet of water that broke into smoke as it flew, or a sudden lifting above the bulwark-rail of a column of froth, which the blow of the bow would send arching back till 'twas a sheer huddle of dazzling yeast under the radiant figurehead, that, with some hero's wreath in its hand, plunged to the giddy whiteness only to soar triumphant a moment after.

It was old Broadwater's duty to hoist and dip the ensign to her. This is a civility I should be very punctual in exacting if I were commander of a British man-of-war. The skipper, however, rolling along on his bow-legs by the side of the mate, did not look as if he even knew there was anything in sight. He never threw so much as a glance in her direction, though I could see some men at work on the fore-rigging watching her with an admiration that rendered them, for the time being, insensible to the presence of the skipper and his companion.

There was one of a dozen coils of rope hanging over a belaying-pin swinging to the heave of the hull. I went and sat myself in it, for the shelter of the bulwark there from the gusty blasts which were split-ting upon the rigging full of whistlings and cryings; and there swayed, cradle-like, by the hanging fakes, I leisurely loaded my pipe, and fell to chipping, in the old-world style of that age, at a flint for a light. Whilst thus occupied, my eye was taken by the figure of a man standing at the foot of the foremast. I was thinking of other matters at that moment, and yet I can recollect wondering, as my gaze went from him after a brief glance, that any man belonging to either watch should have the courage to stand idle on deck whilst the rest of the people were at work, when both the captain and the chief mate were pacing within eyeshot of him. Presently glancing his way again, I noticed that he still remained in the same posture, that is to say, with his back against the mast and his face looking a little forward of the fore-rigging, his arms folded upon his breast, and his legs together with the feet turned out, like a soldier in a sentry-box. The mast was painted white, and hence it was, I suppose, that I did not immediately observe that the man was bound to it by turn upon turn of rope, starting from his armpits and terminating a little below his knees. I know not what there was in the sight to startle me, but I believe had a seaman fallen from aloft at my feet, and there lay bleeding and broken, the thing would not have shocked me more than the spectacle of yonder sailor secured to the mast as though he were some dangerous maniac, and rendered motionless by the ligatures, saving that he could use his head and had the freedom of his arms.

I had not been long enough on board to be able to distinguish the crew, but this man I seemed to remember. To make sure, I got out of the coil of rope and went a few paces forward, and recognized in the fellow bound to the mast the half-blood who had been one of the boat's crew that rowed us aboard from Deal. If his face had struck me then you will suppose that it impressed me very strongly now. Whether owing to the strangulation of the rope about him, or to the thoughts in him, his complexion, that I had observed to be of a clear olive, had changed to an indescribably ugly colour, which I can only speak of as an ashen green. It reminded me of the hue I once saw in the face of a dead sailor whose cheeks had been burnt to an almost chocolate tint by exposure in an open boat in the Indian Ocean. He turned his dark eyes upon me with a savage glare in them of mutiny, malice, hatred, and so full of defiance withal, that but for the evil passions his countenance expressed you might have accepted his air as one of bitter and contemptuous pride. It was intolerable that he should think I had inspected him out of mere curiosity, which I saw from his manner he supposed; and since he would be too wild in his mind to interpret the sympathy which I am sure must have been visible in me—for, as I say, the sight of the poor bound fellow inexpressibly shocked and grieved me—I turned my back on him and walked right aft.

Broadwater left the mate and came up to me.

"That's true old North Country style, sir," he exclaimed, "to sit in the bight of the rigging over the pin under the lee of the bulwarks. I've been hove to in the North Sea, and sat for hours along with the rest of my mates, just as you've been a-sitting, waiting for what was to happen next."

"It is hard to find a corner to smoke in," said I, "on board a flush-decked vessel. Where there's a poop or a round-house, a man may discover a nook clear of the gale, and manage to keep the cinders in his bowl till the fire's all gone. Did you ever serve aboard a Dutchman, captain?"

"No, by thunder!" he answered; "what's put such a question as that into your head, sir?"

"Why," I said, "I notice that you have got one of your hands forward there seized to the foremast. The Dutch used to serve their rogues so—sometimes however going a little further than you, for to make sure of the fellow they'd pin him through the hand with a knife."

"You're keeping a bright look-out aboard this vessel, sir," he exclaimed, shooting an odd look at me out of his little eyes.

"My good fellow," I cried, "I should be blind not to see such a sight as that. What has he done? Murdered a shipmate?"

"Almost wish he had," he growled, "for that 'ud bring about the sort of treatment he wants. He's the man who spoke them words last night."

"Ha!" I exclaimed, "and for that you are dosing him with a spell of fresh air that he may go to his dinner with a good appetite?"

He left me under pretence of looking into the compass. I will not say that he was afraid of me, but I am quite sure that if it had not been for my talk with him in the morning, for the manner I then put on,

and which I still wore, he would have dealt with me scarce less roughly and insolently than had I been one of his seamen. I knocked the
ashes out of my pipe, looking away towards the horizon, below which
and out of sight lay the line of the English coast, and felt myself urged
by a very strong impulse to request him to head for the nearest port,
and to put Miss Grant and myself ashore, as his behaviour to his men,
though we were not yet twenty-four hours from Deal, had rendered us
extremely uneasy, insomuch that we were resolved not to pursue the
voyage in his ship. But I was again checked by the considerations which
had occurred to me whilst talking on the subject with Miss Grant. He
might refuse to comply, lose all control over himself in the notion that
my intention was to ruin him, and so affront me that I should be at a
loss how to act. I quite perceived that, unless I could be sure he would
put us ashore, I should be acting unwisely in asking him to do so, for, if
he persisted in sailing away with us, then whilst we remained on board
his ship we should have to submit to any sort of usage he chose to give
us. I stamped my foot on the deck with vexation and worry, and could
have cursed the hour in which I had ever set eyes on the *Iron Crown*.

I had hoped when Miss Grant came on deck that the figure of the
fellow bound to the mast would escape her attention, and was schem-
ing to place her chair close against the wheel on the port side where
the man would be hidden from her; but the instant she came out of the
companion and looked forward she started violently, and exclaimed:

"Why have they bound him? What has he done to deserve such a
punishment as that?"

"He is the man," I answered, "who cried out last night, 'It's murder!'
when the captain ordered the boat to be kept fast."

"And they have tied him to the mast merely for uttering those
words?"

"Ay! It's a bitter burning shame; the indignity of this sort of punishment is the worst part of it."

"I shall ask Captain Broadwater to release him," she exclaimed, with
the indignation in her surging up hot to her face and flashing in her
eyes. "I shall tell him that the sight pains and disgusts me, and that he
has no right to oblige his passengers to witness such painful and miserable spectacles."

Before I could check her she swept up to old Broadwater, and towering over him with such an air as Siddons would have worn in her
tragedy parts, her face flushed, her eyes on fire, her head thrown backwards, she levelled her white forefinger at the half-blood, gazing meanwhile full into the crimson expanse of the skipper's countenance, and

exclaimed, "What has that man done to merit the sufferings of mind and body he must be enduring there?"

The captain was a broad and muscular man, but short; and her erect, swelling, impassioned figure made him look like a boy by her side as he stared up at her. Her sudden dramatic accost took him completely by surprise. His countenance wore a ludicrous expression of bewilderment. He half turned towards the mate, as if to invoke his assistance, and then exclaimed in a hoarse stutter, "Why, mum, that there man— he's about the impudentest son of a swab—the long and short o't is, he as good as called me a murderer last night. Had he been a man-o'-war's man he'd have been spread-eagled to the toon of twelve dozens for saying much less than that!"

I joined Miss Grant and offered her my arm; for though no woman ever stepped a heaving deck more easily and gracefully than she, yet the slope now was sometimes so sharp as even to make Broadwater lurch, and I was afraid of her carrying away, to use the sea term, as she was quite forgetful, as I could see, in the temper and mood that then possessed her, of the tumbling of the platform on which she stood.

"The words," she exclaimed, "were no doubt forced from the man by a sudden Impulse. Why did you hear them? You would not punish a man for *thinking*."

"Yes, I would, if I knew it," answered Broadwater, plucking up a bit, and yet looking uneasy too.

"You must release him, sir," she exclaimed; "it is a sight that makes the whole ship painful and distressing to me."

"You cannot refuse the lady's request, captain," said I.

"But I can; though," he blustered; "why, smother my precious eyes and bile every blooming limb that I own! who's cap'n of this here craft? Release him! Certainly not. If the sight's too painful to view, the lady needn't look. An' what's there painful about it? Why, some men would have chucked him into the forepeak, smothered him up down there in the blackness, with nothen but rats to keep him company, 'stead of benevolently serving him as I do by suffering him to stop up in the fresh air for his shipmates to look at and meditate on. Mr. Musgrave," he suddenly exclaimed, in a bullying, angry voice, "I'll thank you to tell the lady that I'm the commander of this here vessel, and of everything that consarns her and her navigation; and I shall feel obliged, sir, by your recollecting of that fact yourself, sir, for it'll spare ye the trouble of cross-examining my chief-mate here, sir, as if you was a hadmiralty judge. No, by thunder! my name's Broadwater—Guy Broadwater—and I'm master of this vessel, and them there men forrard are my crew, and

I'll thank you and the lady not to meddle with my consarns, but to be satisfied so long as I perform the part expected of me, which is, to carry you and this here cargo to Rio!" and feigning to be in a mighty temper he bowled away to the taffrail, and then came back again breathing hard and looking swiftly up and around him, with a fine air of injury, resentment, and righteous indignation, not ill-managed on his part, though—like the ghost of a squall—it was to be seen through.

There was no affectation in Miss Grant's pity and disgust. She lingered a little while on deck, and then went below to her cabin, declaring that she could not bear to see the man standing helpless and motionless, as if he were dead, suffering grievously as she feared from his posture, which rested the whole weight of him upon his naked feet, and from the many coils of rope which girt him so tautly and plentifully to the spar, that the mere sight of them made one draw one's breadth with difficulty out of sheer sympathy with their suggestion of strangulation. The men at work in the rigging and about the decks did not give him the least heed that I could discover. I noticed one or two of them glance aft when Miss Grant spoke to the captain and pointed forward, but in a sulky, incurious way, as though what was passing had no interest whatever for them. This behaviour might have been due to the presence of the mate, whose rapid glances seemed to dart all over the brig in a breath, and who, as I had already observed, never suffered a man to halt for an instant in any job he was upon. No doubt his almost preternatural quickness in detecting the least hint of laziness or languor was already as well known to the men as if the vessel had been on the high seas a couple of months. Yet Miss Grant's speaking to the captain about the pinioned half-blood was in its way an incident so far removed from all ordinary shipboard occurrences that the sullen inattention of the men to it impressed me greatly. If heavy troubles do not befall this ship ere long, thought I, it will not be because the spirit of mischief is even already wanting amongst her crew; and I sent a gloomy glance seawards in the direction where old England lay, feeling that I would not only gladly forfeit the passage-money I had paid, but ten times that amount over again, to find myself and Miss Grant once more safe and snug in London.

Chapter IX
The Half-blood is Released

HOWEVER, SINCE WE WERE to be locked up with old Broadwater for a spell of weeks that might run into months, our policy was to put the best face we could upon our condition. But Miss Grant was not to be induced to return on deck whilst the man continued lashed to the foremast. I pointed out that he was not suffering as she fancied, that at all events he had not yet been pinioned long enough to be in pain, and I also begged her to remember that a posture and exposure which might strike her as a severe punishment would sit lightly upon a sailor, whose vocation is supposed to harden him into the most extraordinary capacity of endurance. But it would not do. She refused to quit the cabin until the man had been released, and so she remained below the whole day. Indeed I had some trouble to persuade her to dine at the table with the captain, though her good sense helped her in this at last; but throughout the meal she could scarcely bear to glance at him, scarcely endure to listen to him.

On his side he behaved as if he were willing to let bygones be bygones, as if indeed after careful consideration he was on the whole willing to overlook the past. His dinner put him into a good humour. It consisted amongst other things of a large round of corned beef; and when the cabin-boy came staggering with it into the cabin, old Broadwater seemed so much impressed by the beauty of the joint that he lay back upon the locker, with a carving knife and fork sticking up out of his great fists, which he rested upon the table, and in this attitude remained motionless for some moments, as though his transport would not suffer him to move or speak. However, he probably judged by our faces that we were in no temper to listen to his eulogies of the joint. He carved with a countenance of rapture, and with an air of concern, too, as though the cutting up of such a dish as that was a business not to be lightly and irreverently approached.

It was necessary to talk to the man, so I said, "If this breeze holds I suppose we shall soon be swept out of soundings?"

"Yes," he answered, pouring out a caulker of rum, and holding up the glass to the skylight to see how much it held. "We shall be having the Lizard over our starn this time to-morrow, sir, if we keep all on as we are."

"Upon my word," said I, speaking somewhat heedlessly, out of the mere fullness of my thoughts just then, "so much has happened since the anchor was lifted off Deal that it seems as if we had been a week on the road already."

"What's happened?" he asked quickly. "It's all been plain sailing, hasn't it? There's been nothen that you as a passenger have had cause to grumble about?"

"The time seems long, anyhow," I responded curtly.

"It'll have to be longer yet afore it's ended," said he, turning his little eyes upon Miss Grant.

She had hitherto kept silent, scarce glancing at him: now she suddenly exclaimed, with a flash of her dark eyes full into his ruddy face, "When do you intend to release the unfortunate man you have fastened to the mast?"

He took a long pull at his glass of rum and water before answering her, and then said, "Not until I think the weather's had time to purge him."

"Is he to be kept there all day?" she continued.

"Ay, mum, and all night, too. Billy," addressing the cabin-boy, "jump with this here beef, my lad! away with it! if ye drop so much as a toothful of grease, stand by! and mind that the pudden's covered up as ye bring it along, and keep to leeward with it, d'ye hear? for there's a showering of spray to wind'ard now and again, and if you salt the pudden I'll salt *you!* The fact is, mum," he continued, addressing Miss Grant afresh, "there's no use in half-measures with sailors. We've got a crew aboard as wants riding down, and the man as needs it most is the yaller rogue you're a-pitying. Were the fellow an Englishman I don't know that I shouldn't consider a twelve hours' spell at the foot of the fore mast as much as he deserves; but he's a half-and-half, and my experience is, the blacker the blood that runs in a man's veins the longer's the tarm of teaching he stands in need of."

"Is he to be kept without food?" she exclaimed.

"He is, mum," he answered cheerfully.

On this she rose and left the table without another word.

"What makes the lady so terribly sensitive to sailors' feelings?" exclaimed Broadwater, with as much puzzlement on him as his countenance could express. "I see she ain't married. Has she a sweetheart at sea? On less maybe you——?" He shut one eye, and looked at me with the other.

"Never concern yourself about her or me either," said I. "Keep your mind clear, my friend, for you'll be wanting plenty of space presently for the thoughts your crew'll fill you with."

"What do you mean, sir?" he exclaimed coarsely and angrily.

"I mean this," I replied quietly, though my feelings were hot enough, "if you do not shift your course and head on another tack with your forecastle, there'll be a mutiny aboard before we're a week older."

At this his little mouth rounded into a complete circle, the blood came into his face, down dropped the slab of pudding he was in the act of raising to his lips. "Mutiny!" he cried. "Mutiny aboard *me!* Mutiny afore another week's out! Why—why—why," he stammered, "what have ye been hearing of to put such fancies into your head?"

"I judge by my eyes, not by my ears," I replied, still coldly and very quietly, "though I don't doubt that a few minutes of listening at the forescuttle would convince me even more fully than my sight."

Just then the mate arrived, having been relieved by the boatswain that he might get his dinner.

"Mr. Bothwell! Mr. Bothwell!" cried Broadwater, whose face was of a dark crimson, "what d'ye think Mr. Musgrave here's a-threatening? Why—why—why, that there'll be a mutiny aboard *me* afore another week's out."

"Indeed!" answered the mate blandly, but nevertheless exhibiting his teeth in a smile that made his handsome face mighty malevolent while the grin lasted; "I hope not. On what does Mr. Musgrave found his fears, sir?"

"On the captain's and your usage of the men," said I, resenting the sarcastic air of the fellow.

"But what have Captain Broadwater and I done, sir, to justify this terrible apprehension on your part?"

"I want you to understand, Captain Broadwater," said I, not choosing to heed the mate's question, "that you and you alone are responsible for Miss Grant's and my safety. I now warn you that that safety is being seriously imperilled by your treatment of the crew of this brig. Indeed," I continued, suffering my temper to get the better of me, "already the outlook of this voyage fills me with so much uneasiness that since we are still in the English Channel, and—with this wind—within a few hours' run of a port, Miss Grant and I are willing and desirous that you should set us ashore; the conditions being, of course, that we forfeit our passage-money."

Now I had fully believed that on my saying this he would have fallen into a violent passion, raged at and insulted me, defied me to compel him to head the ship for the coast, and so on. Instead, to my very great surprise, the blood faded out of his face; pale indeed he could not become, but the disorder of his mind manifested, itself in a complexion that would answer to pallor in another man's countenance. He pushed his plate from him as though his appetite were gone for ever, and in a wonderfully subdued, changed voice, exclaimed, "Mr. Musgrave, sir, I beg that you'll banish that wish from your mind, sir. To set ye ashore would be my ruination. There's nothing in the world, that I can see, that need make ye oncomfortable. The cabins are roomy, the living up to the hammer, there's ne'er a stouter vessel afloat than the *Iron Crown*; and, though it's me as says so, there's no man living that Capt'n Guy Broadwater'll yield to in the knowledge of navigating and handling a ship under all sarcumstances of wind and weather. There's nothen either in the behaviour of the crew, or in my treatment of 'em, to breed oneasiness. Indeed," he continued, speaking most abjectedly, "if the lady's really so consarned by the sight of that there Ernest Charles at the foremast, why, then, to please her I'll lubberate him in the second dog-watch, 'stead of keeping him there all night, as was my intention."

The mate ate his dinner with a wooden face.

"You can do as you please, Captain Broadwater," said I, rising. "I have not the slightest intention to meddle with your notions of discipline. I simply desire to point out to you that your treatment of the crew is such as to render the prospects of the voyage very gloomy indeed, and if you will head the ship for some adjacent English port, Miss Grant and I will be very glad to leave her."

"I hope not, sir! I'd rather not, Mr. Musgrave!" he exclaimed, speaking and looking so dejectedly that I suspected his manner was to a large degree assumed. "To shift the helm in this here wind would be extremely awkward—extremely awkward; and it'ud ruin my reputation as the master of a passenger-vessel if you was to give out the reasons of your leaving, which are all imagination, sir—the fancies of a gent as has long lost sight of the sailor's character, and forgot that if life was all soup and bully in the fo'k'sle there'd be no work done—no work done whatever!"

I caught one of the mate's swift glances; 'twas as full of malice as could well be packed into such a nimble roll. There was nothing more to be said, and in silence I quitted the cabin, satisfied with my second victory that day over Captain Broadwater; but at the same time also profoundly convinced that a five minutes' conversation with his mate would influence the old fellow into a resolution to keep me and Miss Grant on board at all hazards, trusting maybe to time to soften and extinguish the prejudice and dislike and misgivings we had not scrupled to express in one shape or another.

As Gordon had charge of the deck until four o'clock in the afternoon, I endeavoured to ascertain from him what the men thought of the captain's treatment of the half-blood; but he was very shy and wary, and I believe would not have conversed with me upon the subject at all had it not been for the sort of kindness our chat on the previous night had established between us. His reply was to the effect that the crew were cautious in what they said before him, but that as far as he could gather, the securing of the man to the mast had raised a very strong feeling against the captain and mate; and he said he believed it was only because the culprit was a foreigner that they suffered him to remain in that posture of indignity and pain. "Had he been an Englishman," he added, "my opinion is that they'd have gone on cutting him adrift as fast as the capt'n could seize him up."

The fellow still stood at the mast, bound as I have already described. Thus he had been standing since some time before nine o'clock in the morning. Whether the crew had at any time of the day fed him or put a drink to his lips I could not know; but though it was not three o'clock in the afternoon when I made these observations, the man already—that is to say after seven hours or thereabouts—exhibited such signs of weakness and distress that one would have said he was merely kept upon his feet by the ropes round his body. I never longed in all my life for anything so heartily as for the power to cast the unhappy creature adrift and send him below for a warm meal; but I had spoken out freely and done my best, and more was not to be thought of, though I vowed in my heart, as I saw the unhappy creature wearily pass his hands over his eyes, and drop his chin on to his breast as if his neck could not support the burthen of his head, that if redress was to be obtained for him from such machinery of law as I might find flourishing at Rio I would not spare my purse to procure it.

The wind blew strong throughout the day. Indeed before six o'clock it had freshened into half a gale; the topgallant-sails had been furled, and the brig swept roaring through it under reefed topsails and foresail. The height of the seas which chased us might have made a man think himself in the middle of the Atlantic. Each billow rolled under us with the weight of the ocean surge, and it was hard to realize that we were still in the narrow waters. The sky had settled into that high, hard stratification of greenish-grey cloud, with a dark streak in places, compact and apparently motionless, which nearly always signifies wind, and as a rule plenty of it. The brig steered wildly, and the perspiration poured from the face of the man at the helm as he swung to the wheel, putting it down and up, whilst every floating rush of the fabric off the liquid brows brought the seas boiling about her quarters, till the curl of the yeast there would sometimes be flush with the rail. At sunset the wildness of the glory was more like the rising of the luminary on a stormy December morning, when the heavens open and shut with snow-squalls, than his descent on a summer's night. The heavens flushed to a furnace-glow—an angry, smoking crimson, lightening into pink zenithwards, and thence floating away in rose into the very heart of the east. But the sea kept its dark green colour, and the run of its frothing peaks from one shining line to another made the glow of the firmament as startling as an unreality by the contrast.

Miss Grant remained in the cabin. At the meal called by the captain "supper" I had begged her to come on deck, telling her that Broadwater (and I fixed my eyes on him as I spoke) had promised to free the man during the second dog-watch.

"When he is released I will go on deck, Mr. Musgrave," she said, "but not before. Such a sight is more than I can bear, and indeed it is miserable enough to be down here and feel that the man is still suffering."

"He isn't suffering, mum," said Broadwater; "he'd laugh at you for supposin' it. The calling of the sea turns sailors' skins into hides, and their feelings into horns. If it didn't there'd be no seamen left, for they'd all die off of consumption and other delicate complaints. I've told Mr. Musgrave that to accommodate you the man shall be lubberated in the second dog-watch, and that means eight bells; and obliged he ought to be, for by thunder! mistress, if it hadn't been for the consarn you're under about him I'd have kept him there till eight o'clock in the first watch to-morrow morning!"

Well, by remaining below she missed not only a fine and wondrous scene of sundown, but as gallant and stirring a sea-piece as it was ever my fortune to view. For whilst the sun, hidden as he was, hung, as I might suppose, some four or five degrees above the horizon, a cloud of canvas loomed up almost dead astern. The brig was swarming through it at not less than eight or nine knots, and yet here was a ship growing out of the olive-coloured welter as though in very truth she was the rising moon. She was a large black American clipper, fresh from the Thames, with canvas white as cotton, and she had every cloth abroad, with the exception of her mizzen-royal and her fore and main skysails. The press was prodigious; one looked to see the great, swelling, soft white fabric flashing into a thousand fragments, and melting away upon the roar of the gale like snow-flakes. Her speed was not less than fifteen knots in the hour; I judged it so by comparing her approach with our progress. All forward she was smothered to the spritsail-yard; but at irregular intervals she shot her long black shape clear of the dazzle and fury about her bows, but only to smite the trough with a blow that hurled up a very storm of white waters, until you would have taken her to be a ship sweeping through the first gatherings of a waterspout. She passed us close, flying along as though we were at anchor, and her passage was that of a thunderstorm for the sound of the gale in her canvas, for the rain-like hissing all about her sides, and for the multitudinous shrieking of the wind in her rigging, resonant as fiddle-strings to the enormous strain put upon every shroud, backstay, and brace.

Broadwater gazed at her with an inimitable air of astonishment. I saw him looking up at his own canvas, and then over the stern of the brig at the wake there, as though he could not persuade himself that the great clipper yonder carried the same weight of wind under which the *Iron Crown* was staggering. In a few minutes her elliptical stern was upon us, with swift upward heavings of the gleaming gilt-work upon it, till the letters of her name showed glaring over her rudder, and with flying plunges and slow majestic rollings, the stately fabric swept onwards with the gloom into the west, until presently she was as visionary in the liquid obscurity ahead as the creaming of the seas there.

On eight bells being struck, Broadwater, who was standing near the wheel, bawled out, "Mr. Gordon, cast that there Ernest Charles adrift from the foremast, and tell him to lay aft!"

I wondered what the captain meant to say to the unfortunate wretch, whose long punishment certainly did not need the topping off of a round of abuse; but finding he did not appear, I crossed the deck and observed a group of seamen collected at the foot of the mast. On approaching I saw the figure of the half-blood prone upon his back.

"What ails the man, Mr. Gordon?" said I; "has he fainted?"

"It's exhaustion, I allow," he answered.

"He's been belayed too taut—enough to prize his heart out of its moorings," exclaimed one of the sailors in a gruff voice.

"There's a flask of brandy in my cabin," I exclaimed. "Where's the boy? He'll find it."

At this moment the mate arrived. "What's the trouble now?" he called out in his shrill, fierce voice.

"Charles is in a swound," responded the boatswain.

The mate bent his back, and looked into the face of the prostrate man. The twilight was still abroad, but the gloom of the night, darkened yet by the shadow of vapour that overspread the sky, was fast deepening, and it was already difficult to distinguish objects.

"Up you get!" shouted the mate, suddenly springing erect, with a sharp kick at the recumbent form. "There's no shamming allowed aboard this brig. Up with you! Up with you!"

He kicked him again and yet again, and then, as fiercely as a madman would throw himself upon another, clutched the man about the collar, and ran his back against the foremast sheer on to his feet.

I expected to see him fall, but whether he was actually shamming, as the mate declared, or had been brought to by Mr. Bothwell's kicks and handling, he opened his eyes and kept his feet, though he swayed against the mast, and I do not doubt would have fallen but for the support of it.

"Aft with you!" cried the mate; "the captain wants a word with you before you go below."

"He'd better be helped aft," said the boatswain, "small wonder if he should have lost the use of his legs."

"Aft with you!" persisted the mate.

The inhumanity of the fellow was maddening. "Murder him at once!" I cried; "it would be kinder!"

The mate did not answer, did not even look round at me. One of the sailors muttered something; I did not catch the words, but the growl had a very ugly note in it. The half-blood made a step, reeled, and fell heavily. I walked aft sick at heart, but ere I had made a few paces I heard the mate exclaim, "Take him below, then, take him below!" and passing me he joined the captain, and they fell to pacing the deck together.

The night was damp, and the force of the wind put an edge of cold into it. There was nothing to court Miss Grant on deck nor to detain me there; so I spent the rest of the evening with her in the cabin, though conversation after a time grew somewhat laborious, owing to the dismal creakings and groanings in the heart of the hull as it strained from hollow to summit, and groaned again to the stormy sweep of the blast into the iron-hard canvas aloft. I told my companion that the half-blood had been freed and taken below, but said nothing about the brutality of the mate nor the condition the man appeared in, whether actual or affected, when released from the mast.

And indeed I do not know that I should have entered so closely into these particulars, but for the obligation I am under to exhibit the causes which led to the extraordinary adventures I shall have to relate before I bring this narrative to a conclusion. At the same time, as pictures of the sea-life are so seldom attempted, and as the secret history of the merchant-sailor is so little understood, I cannot but think it proper that all forms of the vocation, whether sunny or sombre, whether elevating or debasing, should, in the interests of the mariner, be described by those who have an acquaintance with the calling, and who are able to plainly write down their recollections and experiences. I am happy to know that many of the old forms of inhumanity on shipboard are extinct, or fast decaying; yet enough survives to render, I am sorry to say, even such a sketch as I have attempted true in many respects of much that happens in the sailing ship of to-day. The coarse, unprincipled skipper still flourishes; mates of the Bothwell pattern still are to be found in plenty; and though the condition of the sailor has been improved and fortified by laws which had no existence in the days of which I am writing, his grievances yet remain sufficiently abundant to render even a recurrence to the usages and practices of half a century ago useful to him at the present moment as much that continues habitual to his hard, toilsome, hazardous and unrepresented vocation. But to proceed.

The wind blew fresh all that night, and did not fail us until we had put twenty leagues between us and the Scilly Islands. It then fell light and drew ahead, and forced us upon a bowline, and for twenty-four hours we were staggering most abominably upon a long swell, with a true Biscayan sweep in the run of it; wrinkled with the wind, but foamless; swollen enough to fetch a harsh voice of small ordnance from the canvas that it swayed into violent slaps against the masts, and into short blasts like explosions with the sudden rounding-out of the cloths. Affairs on board seemed to run during this while pretty smoothly. I saw the half-blood named Charles at work on the day following the night of his release, and I do not know that old Broadwater made further trouble of the matter for which the fellow had been punished. The notion, or perhaps the hope rather, grew in me that he meant to soften somewhat his truculent treatment of the men. I had indeed spoken very plainly, and I took it that he had turned my words over in his mind when he was not too fuddled with liquor to think coherently, and had determined not to put it in my power to create a difficulty for him at Rio or on his return home. The mate, too, seemed disposed to quiet down, as if he had got his cue from the captain. It is true that he could never hail a man aloft, or call him when on deck, without an exasperating note of quite unnecessary temper in the fling of his voice. But it seemed to me as if he was no longer incessantly on the lookout for something to fly in a rage over. I suspected however that both he and Broadwater moderated their behaviour only when Miss Grant and I were on deck. At all events the ship's work seemed to be carried on without much fret and jar; yet, whether it was because the old sailorly instincts in me sharpened my sympathies, or because I feared that the conduct of the captain and his mate had already raised a devil forward, which even the quieter bearing of such men as they was not likely to lay, I confess I could never look at the crew without seeming sensible of an indefinable air amongst them which I can best convey by speaking of it as a sort of morose uneasiness.

Broadwater, I am bound to say, showed no sulkiness towards us for our plain speaking and dealing. You would have thought there had been no trouble whatever between us had you heard him praising the meals at table, bragging of his old experiences, boasting of his brig as though she was the loveliest frigate then afloat, and so forth. As to the mate, we gave him so wide a berth that often a whole day passed without our exchanging a sentence with him. The only companionable creature aboard was Gordon, in whose quarter-deck walk I was always glad to join when the night came round that gave him the first watch as we call it at sea—that is, from eight to twelve. Naturally Miss Grant and I were very much together. This, to be sure, was unavoidable; but I own that I would get a bit troubled in my mind when, after turning in and extinguishing the lamp, I found my imagination haunted by her fine eyes, her noble figure, and above all by a certain sweetness in the tone of her voice that would at all times, long after she was silent, linger upon my ear like a memory of glad and gentle music. I sometimes said to myself, Suppose I fall in love with her? It would be impossible to conceive of a more inconvenient passion. It was idle to argue with myself and pretend that I need not fall in love with her unless I chose. Reason might talk very soberly about such a thing, but my instincts knew better. In short, not being able to make sure of myself in this direction, I arrived at the conclusion that I had acted as a fool in consenting to lock myself up in a small brig with a handsome woman whose heart was another's, and to the fascination of whose person and manners I was expected to oppose as immovable a countenance as old Broadwater's. Had there been other passengers we might have made shift, for considerable intervals at all events, to manage without one another's company; but we were alone—a condition of the voyage I cannot say I had seriously contemplated or even lightly thought of before embarking on this adventure—and the result was we were incessantly together. I had purchased a chess-board and a pack or two of cards, and when the deck bored us, or the weather there was uncomfortable, we would sit down and play a game in the cabin; and I say it was difficult for me to be hour after hour and day after day encountering her spirited, sparkling glances, watching her smiles, listening to her graceful fancies, observing the fifty fascinating elegances of her posture and movements, without thinking a very great deal more about her when I was alone, and perhaps even when I was in her company, than my honour could approve or my judgment understand.

Chapter X
A Midnight Alarm

WE HAD BEEN EIGHT days out when I met with a very unpleasant experience. The brig was still on the Spanish parallels. The night had come down moonless and dark, and the vessel, close-hauled under all plain sail, was quietly rippling over the breathing surface of the sea, with lines of delicate green fire breaking from her cut water to abreast of the gangway, where they trembled out into the deep blackness there. The air was damp with dew, and as Miss Grant was below and there was nobody on the quarter-deck but the mate, I flung my cheroot overboard, and entered the cabin. There I found my companion with a book in her hand, trying to read by the light of the lamp, whose swaying to the movements of the brig bothered the eye with a flitting of shadows. Broadwater was at his usual place at the table, with a bottle of rum and a steaming glass before him. He sat apparently lost in thought, with one eye shut and the other fixed upon the lamp, his little mouth rounded into the familiar whistling shape, his pear-shaped nose as ruddy as the liquor in the bottle, and the expression on his face indescribably absurd with its rubicund cast of tipsy sentiment.

"Have a glass of rum and water, Mr. Musgrave?" he said to me, with a stupid smile, pointing with a drooping finger to the tumbler before him, yet speaking as if the silence had grown oppressive and he was glad to break it.

I declined, and asked Miss Grant what she was reading. Before she could answer, Broadwater said, "Beg pardon, Mr. Musgrave, but can you tell me if you're a married man, sir?"

"I certainly *can* tell you," I replied, bursting into a laugh; "I am not married. Are you?"

"Yes, sir," he answered, "and I wish I wasn't. She's a nice young lady, but," he added gloomily, "I don't like her mother, sir. That there mother of hers is always interfering; and what's worse, she's got no respect for me." His hand wandered somewhat aimlessly towards his glass, which he presently grasped, half emptied, and replaced with a heavy sigh. "Mr. Musgrave," he went on, "you'll excuse me, sir, if you please. You'll be marrying some of these days—bound to it—an' I'd strongly recommend ye to take Capt'n Broadwater's advice—the advice of old Guy Broadwater, who's as well known from Freshwharf down to Blackwall as the Monument is, or the dome of St. Paul's: don't you go and get married to a party that's got a mother. If you do, you'll find you've gone and married 'em both. There's nothing as weighs upon a man's feelings like his wife's mother. You mind, sir. Remember what I says, and you'll recall this voyage as the one sarcumstance of your life that was the making of ye."

He drained his glass, and pulling out his great silver watch, that seemed to pop from his trousers'-band like a cork from a bottle, he cast an uncertain glance at it, and rose with a succession of nods at me, whilst he said, "Recollect Capt'n Broadwater's advice, sir: it'll be the making of ye," fell about a little whilst he replaced the bottle in the locker, and then, saluting Miss Grant with a tipsy smile, lurched towards his cabin, talking to himself as he went, the burthen of his words being, as far as I could collect it, "Take my advice, Mr. Musgrave; it'll be the making of ye."

As he was nightly in the habit of withdrawing to his cabin more or less overtaken with liquor, we had by this time grown used to the practice, had come indeed to view it as part of the navigation of the *Iron Crown*, and had therefore nothing to say about it now. We sat talking for half an hour or so: Miss Grant then went to bed; and after smoking my pipe in the companion-hatchway, from which sheltered point I took notice of the heavy gloom amid which the ship was sailing—a shadow so thickened with the deep dusk of the night, through which here and there a star glanced haggard and sparely, that the fabric of spar and canvas was invisible from half the height of the mainmast—I descended to my berth, and, to use the proper nautical expression, "turned in."

On extinguishing the light and pulling the blankets over me, I found my mind somewhat threateningly active. Maybe I was a bit nervous; why, I knew not, unless I harked back to Broadwater's supper and dinner-table, in whose dishes indeed reasons might be found for an intellectual condition only a little short of lunacy. I fell to thinking of the captain's being in liquor, of the blackness through which the brig was stemming, of our safety being dependent upon the vigilance of the mate, who, for all I knew, might be snoring on his back on the skylight or on a hencoop, whilst the man at the wheel lurched there with eyelids of lead and his chin upon his breast. Now and again came the long-drawn sobbing sounds of water washing along the bends close against where my head lay, with a note of yearning in the small roar of its passage that set me thinking of the cold death in the liquid profound under our keel, and of the slenderness of the structure of plank, treenail, and beam, which was our only barricade against the intrusion of the spectre. Then Miss Grant came into my head, and the thought of

her beauty put a sort of light into my mood, though my fancies continued to hang in a nervous jumble upon my mind. However, after a while
I fell asleep, and lay dreamless for some time, as I believe; and may
have rested so for an hour or more, when I had a hideous nightmare. I
dreamt that the cabin-door was suddenly flung open, and that Captain
Broadwater entered with his eyes on fire and his face blood-red with
drink. He grasped the immense carving-knife he was in the habit of
flourishing at table, and approached me close. Whence came the light
by which I viewed him I know not; but he was horribly distinguishable.
He seemed to say, and I quite understood him, that it was his intention
to murder me because I wished to leave his ship; but that, as his hatred
of me was too intense to suffer him to despatch me quickly, it was his
intention to destroy me by degrees. I lay paralysed, tried to bawl out,
but could utter no sound, endeavoured to stir, but felt as dead as a log
of wood. Agony at length broke the spell; I awoke, sprang into a sitting
posture, with the perspiration pouring from my face, and stared, panting as if I had been wounded to death, into the blackness of the cabin.

As I sat peering and endeavouring to collect my senses, I heard the
sound of what resembled a human groan. It seemed to come from the
floor of my cabin. I was still suffering from the agitation caused by my
nightmare; and my nerves having been unduly wrung, whilst I had
scarcely yet had time to recollect myself, I confess that this strange
and alarming noise filled me with so much consternation that I felt
almost as helpless as when Broadwater stood beside me in the vision.
The extraordinary noise was repeated; I could not doubt my hearing.
It rose from the deck under my bunk, and was so exceedingly like the
groan of a drunken man in pain that I thought to myself, Good God!
there may be more in my dream than I am as yet conscious of!

The sense of the presence of a real danger served to rally me. My
tinder-box—I had no other means of procuring a light—was in the
pocket of my coat that hung near the door, and it was necessary to
get out of bed to obtain it. I threw my legs over the edge of the bunk,
intending to very warily slide round by the bulkhead to where the
coat was, that I might not tread upon whatever the object might be
that groaned upon the deck, when the noise sounded again—a thick,
snoring, choking moan. I whipped my legs into my bunk, much more
alarmed than it pleases me to confess. Great mercy! thought I, is it conceivable that Broadwater in a drunken fit has *really* entered this cabin
with the design of murdering me, and that the liquor he has swallowed
has proved too potent at the last moment to enable him to execute
his horrid project! If he has a knife in his hand, I reflected, starting

as another groan arose, I may stumble over him in groping and fall upon the blade; or if I should roll over him he might not be too drunk to imagine that I was attacking him, when of course he would defend himself and perhaps kill me.

Another groan determined me. This must end, thought I, come what will; and with that I slipped over the edge of my bunk, but instead of touching the deck my feet pressed upon a soft, naked, hairy body. Before I could cry out, the thing started up with a savage squeal and threw me down. It ran over me, but my fright was so great that I had not the least idea whether it was man or beast, until, putting out my hands to protect myself, I grasped a curly tail, to my drag upon which the pig—for a beast of a pig it was!—responded by making his nature known in a series of ear-piercing squealings. I groped for the door, found it open and swinging to the movement of the vessel, and feeling for the hook secured it backwards against the bulkhead. I then sought for and tumbled into my small-clothes; but whilst moving with my arms outstretched to where I thought I should find my coat I fell over the pig again. I was now as angry as I had before been frightened; in truth I was not a little bruised with my falls, and my temper was still further inflamed by the distracting cries of the pig whenever I struck against it. Miss Grant opened her door. She had lighted her lamp, and fearing that the beast would make for her, I cried out: "It's only a pig. I'll have him out of this in a minute. Shut your door quickly, or he'll run in upon you." She instantly did as I told her, but a moment after I could hear her laughing as though she had fallen hysterical.

I stepped cautiously towards the passage, and found the door that shut off the after-accommodation from the state-cabin closed. But for this, I should have had light enough from the reflection of the dimmed lantern that swung in the cabin to have seen by. By sliding my hands about I succeeded in feeling the handle of the door, which I opened; but the moment the light streamed in the pig ran for it, and striking me on the legs as it swept past, threw me again to the deck. The cabin-skylight was opened, and the voice of some one above called to me. I could just distinguish the features of the boatswain, but before I could tell him what was the matter, Broadwater, followed by the mate, came running out from their berths in the fore end.

"What is it? what is it?" shouted the old skipper. "Anybody being murdered?"

But the mate's swiftly rolling eye instantly caught sight of the pig, at which he made a spring. The creature with a prodigious squeal slipped, as though its back had been greased, out of his grip; and with a wild kick-up of its hind-quarters, and a defiant flourish of its tail, made in a gallop in the direction of the captain, through whose bow-legs it bolted, bringing him down as if he had been shot. By this time the boatswain, peering through the skylight and seeing how it was, had ordered some of the men of his watch to jump below and catch the pig, and down they trundled, four of them, filled with anticipations of a fine bout of skylarking—for Jack dearly loves a pig-hunt. The uproar was now prodigious. The pig raced round the cabin and under the table yelling like a steam-horn to every clutch that was made at it; and after it went the sailors, tumbling, swearing, laughing, whilst the mate shouted to them in a shrill voice to bear a hand and catch the brute. Old Broadwater, who appeared somewhat dazed by his fall, sat upon a locker rubbing the back of his head, now and again lifting his clenched fist as the pig galloped past him, and heaping curses upon the thing in a half-smothered tone. The men however enjoyed the sport too keenly to be in a hurry to end it, and a full five minutes of roaring, puffing, laughing, and squeaking passed before the pig was captured. It was then carried away by the fellows, one of whom, it seemed to me, must have tormented it in some secret manner, for the squealing of the beast as it was borne up the ladder and along the deck was so violent and sharp-edged that it might have been heard a league distant.

Scarce had these distracting notes been silenced, and just as I was about to put a question to Captain Broadwater—for talk was not to be dreamt of whilst that noise lasted—I heard the boatswain on deck cry out in a loud and fearful tone, "Hard up! Hard up! Over with it, man, for our lives!" and then an instant after, "Ship ahoy!" he roared, with the same note of violent hurry and sense of danger in his voice, "Port your hellum! Port your hellum, or you'll be into us!"

The mate gained the deck in a couple of leaps: Broadwater followed him as though he had been whipped up by a tackle; and forgetting that I was without shoes or stockings, clad in nothing indeed but a shirt and trousers, I shot up the ladder to see what was the matter. It took my eyes some moments to get used to the gloom, for there was sheen enough in the cabin to turn the night black as a wolf's throat when you rose out of the companion-hatch into it; then close upon our starboard-bow, as it seemed to me, I spied a light oscillating, as though passionately flourished, and I could just distinguish a huge black shadow there like a deeper dye of blackness upon the liquid dusk that overhung the ocean. A minute after, close by the first light up sprang a second—a sea-torch of turpentine, the long sickly flame of which streamed away into smoke, though it had power enough to palely colour a small circumference of atmosphere, out of which there stole glimmering to the illumination the rigging and lower canvas of a big ship. She loomed up so close aboard that the sight was something to hold a man breathless.

In the brief interval of silence that followed the boatswain's cry to her to port her helm, I could distinctly hear the hiss and splash of the curl of water breaking at her stem; the voice of a man rapidly delivering orders as though for life or death; the rattle of tiller-chains to the swift revolution of the wheel; the flap of some light sail aloft buried in the black void, hollowing inwards as the ship, answering her helm, round- ed to the wind. One moment she was off our bow, the next abreast of us, so close that the face of the man holding the streaming flare-tin glimmered out yellow as the rind of a ripe lime; and as he leaned from the bulwark-rail, torch in hand, swinging at arm's length from a back- stay, the figure of him upon the yellow atmosphere of light was for all the world like a human shape wrought in black silk upon a ground of rusty amber. I cowered involuntarily, believing the stranger's jib- booms to be over us, and expecting every minute to hear the rending and crashing of masts and strong fastenings to the sheering sweep of those outstretched spars. She was soon on our quarter, and then it was possible to fetch a breath; though even when there, you *felt* her terrify- ing presence in the oppression of the vast shadow of her black heights upon the dusk. Presently the flare over her side went out—the blotch she made melted into the general shadow—and then she was as utterly gone from the sight, though but a few cables' lengths distant, as though she had foundered.

By this time Broadwater had recovered his faculties, and he now let fly a whole hurricane of questions at the boatswain; demanding to know how it was that the vessel had not been sighted sooner, wheth- er there was a man forward on the look-out, and the like. But neither rage nor rum could blind him to the almost preternatural gloom of the night. Indeed it was like being in a vault. One or two stars showed faint as the dimmest of their own reflections, and it staggered one to see them, so unreal was their wan gleam. What had become of the moon I do not know. The outline of the brig met the blackness without a break, and though I stood within a couple of yards of the boatswain and Broadwater, I should not have known there were people near me but for their voices. Gordon answered the skipper quietly, said that he had been keeping as bright a lookout as was practicable to mortal sight on such a night, but that, had he had as many eyes in his head as a peacock carries in its tail, and each eye a telescope at *that*, it would have been all the same; to which old Broadwater answered with a growling, "Well, boil me, if it ain't so!" and after that cooled down and spoke rationally.

But just before I went below I heard Gordon exclaim, "It was the crying of the pig, sir, that made our presence known. The ship heard it, and showed a light, guessing there was some craft close aboard. If it hadn't been for that squeaking, I allow that we should have been on the road to the bottom before this."

Chapter XI
A Tragedy

YOU WILL BELIEVE, AFTER hearing the boatswain's remark to the captain, that I was no longer disposed to make a trouble of the invasion of my berth by the pig. A trifle light as air will at sea, and often in an instant, become as solemn and as serious a thing as doom. I returned to the cabin cold from the deck, with the chill moreover in me that a sudden danger and swift release will put into a man, and going to my berth I thrust my feet into a pair of warm slippers, wrapped a dressing-gown about me, and re-entered the cabin with a bottle of brandy in my hand for the comfort of a dram. I was waiting for the arrival of Broadwater, desiring to gather, though without temper, how the pig had made its way aft, when I was surprised by Miss Grant peeping through the door that led to our berths, and then advancing.

"I expected you would be up, Mr. Musgrave," she exclaimed, seating herself at my side; "what a noisy time this has been! Far more alarming indeed than the commotion the other night when the poor man committed suicide. I have really felt frightened."

Yet she did not look so. Her eyes were as steady, her lips as composed, her manner as quiet as ever they had been in the tranquillest hour we had passed together since our first meeting. Her hair, roughened by the pillow, made her beauty the more striking for the disorder of it upon her white forehead and whiter neck. It was no moment to take notice of such trifles, but it seemed to me that this woman could never look more fascinating than when newly and hastily arisen from her couch, and hurriedly attired in a pink dressing-gown!

I related my story of the adventure with the pig, at which she laughed continuously, until I came to tell her of our narrow escape, and how, under Heaven, an incident that would seem merry enough to everybody but the person who took part in it, was the cause of our escape from a catastrophe that might have sent every soul of us to the bottom; and then she grew very grave.

"It needs an effort of mind," said I, "to conceive of the genius of luck taking upon itself the aspect of a pig. Henceforward I shall think respectfully of Broadwater's affection for roast and boiled pork."

"I wish this voyage were over, Mr. Musgrave," she exclaimed. "I feel as if we had already passed a couple of months at sea. Do you think if the ship had run into us we should have been drowned?"

"Impossible to say, Miss Grant. She was a lump of a craft, to judge by the huge loom of her shadow; and I fear that, staunch as the *Iron Crown* may be, one thrust from that big chap would have made old staves of the little hooker."

At this moment Broadwater's bow legs appeared in the companion-way. Down he came, pulling off his hat as he arrived. Sleep, and the turmoil of the pig-hunt, and the alarm he was fresh from, had cleared his head, and he was as sober as one could wish.

"Rather late for you to be a-sitting up, miss," said he approaching the table; "there's no longer call to be afraid. It'll be all plain sailing now for the rest of the night."

"What time is it, captain?" she inquired.

He pulled out his watch—"weighed it" would be the correct term, for it was like breaking out an anchor—and said, "Close upon four bells—two o'clock, mum. Is that there bottle yours, Mr. Musgrave?"

I replied that it was, and grasping the hint conveyed by the question, begged him to help himself. He smacked his lips to the draught, for the brandy was of my own buying, choice and old, and said: "A close shave that just now, sir. I don't know that I ever remember a darker night, considering it's fine weather."

"Ay," said I, "dark it is; much too dark for human eyesight, as your second mate truly said. 'Tis fortunate that we are endowed with other faculties than vision only. Had there not been ears aboard the stranger to catch the squeaking of my pig where should we be now?"

"How could the pig have got into the cabin?" exclaimed Miss Grant.

"Why," answered Captain Broadwater, "he must have broken out of his sty under the longboat, and grubbed along quietly in the darkness until he comes to the companion-way, down which he rolls, courted, maybe, by a smell of feedin'. All hands of us aft being asleep, as I allow, there was nobody to hear him. But if that there door was shut," he added, pointing, "I don't see how the pig was to get into your passage; and supposing *your* door to have been shut, how was he to enter your cabin?"

It seems however that the door that conducted to the passage had been left open and unhooked, so that it was likely the pig, in grubbing about, had given it a shove with its snout and slammed it to. But how the creature contrived to enter my cabin, the door of which I remember having shut, I was at a loss to imagine, until, going presently to fetch a cheroot—for I was absolutely sleepless and was in the habit of smoking whenever it pleased me in the cabin, with Miss Grant's good leave, of course—I examined the latch of the door of my berth, and observed that the tongue caught so thinly that it yielded to the slightest pressure.

I think Broadwater would have gone straightway to bed had it not been for my brandy-bottle. Miss Grant protested that she felt too restless to return to her cabin, and said she wished it were daylight.

"The dawn'll soon be coming along, miss," said the captain; "meantime, what's there to be uneasy about now?"

"The lady is not uneasy, captain," said I, "her rest has been broken, and she no longer feels sleepy;" and I wondered that even his little eyes should not have observed her composed and tranquil expression. Indeed it seemed to me that what uneasiness there was lay altogether in *him*. His manner was subdued, he spoke with a note of respect; there was that in his bearing which suggested that the weight of his alarm had not yet lifted, and I would see him sometimes shoot a look at the companion or up at the skylight, and then thoughtfully stroke down his nose, whilst his little eyes met in a squint upon the glass around which his carrot-shaped fingers were curled. He was too much of a seaman not to know that we had all of us come off just now very narrowly indeed with our lives; and though, as I have said, he would no doubt have gone to bed but for the brandy, he could not sit there and reflect upon what had occurred without indications of discomposure, which contrasted strongly with Miss Grant's reposeful expression, steadfast eyes, and calm, sweet utterance.

And yet from the few words she had let fall, I was sure that she had mastered the full significance of the danger we had escaped as completely as if she had witnessed the scene—as completely indeed as if she had been as practical a sailor as the captain himself. Once she lifted her finger to the light moan of a sea running stealthily along the side against which we were leaning, and exclaimed: "How cold the sound is there! I remember once telling Alexander that qualities sensible to the touch may also be so to the hearing. He did not understand me; but surely, Mr. Musgrave, isn't the icy breath of a winter's blast, as it sweeps past the window, as perceptible to the ear as it would be to the face if one should look out of doors?"

"I find nothing hard to understand in that fancy," I replied; meanly willing, I fear, to exhibit my understanding as in some senses superior to her Alexander's. "I once saw a man lying dead in a posture of terror—he had died with a shriek, I learned; but I did not need to be told *that*, for I could *see* his cry in the attitude, though Death's forefinger had been upon his lips for twenty-four hours."

"A queer sort of twisting of the faculties, ain't it, sir?" exclaimed old Broadwater; "to *see* a shriek, and *hear* cold weather! That's a kind of boiling above most men's intellectuals, I should think. With your good leave, Mr. Musgrave, I'll take another drop, sir. Good old Jamaiky, as a standing drink, is to my taste unsurpassable by any sort o' liquor to be found in the first nobleman's cellar in the country; but a drop of brandy after this here pattern is an agreeable change, and I've heard," he continued, helping himself, "that an occasional wariation is recommended by the doctors as serviceable to the liver. Your health, sir; miss, to you."

He nodded with more complacency than I had ever witnessed in him when not in his cups and sighed with satisfaction after drinking.

I thought I would take advantage of his mood to put in a good word for his crew, and said, "Your fellows seem a lively lot—true Jacks when it comes to a bout of skylarking. Did you notice how they relished the pig-hunt? I should say there's nothing to be afraid of in men who possess their capacity of enjoying little things."

I had scarce uttered these words when, through the silence that followed, and through the whole length and breadth of the brig, as it seemed to me, there rang out so wild and shrill a cry of human anguish, that the like of it I could never imagine deliverable by human lips. You would have sworn it was a woman's voice, and had not Miss Grant been by my side I must have thought it was she—as the only one of her sex on board—who had uttered it.

"Great Heavens!" I cried, "what has happened?"

Broadwater had started to his feet at the sound, but he then appeared to be stricken helpless, for he stood staring with a sort of gape in the set of his lips towards the companion-ladder. Miss Grant's face was full of consternation, and she kept her eyes fixed on me with a wild look of consternation in them. I listened, expecting to hear a second cry. There was a sound of swift running overhead; a sharp, angry shout in the voice of the boatswain; a minute after the chief mate came staggering down the ladder with his hand to his side, his dark face dreadful to see with the ghastly colouring upon it. He stood whilst you could have counted ten at the foot of the ladder, swaying, his left hand upon his heart, his right hand extended, his ashen lips inarticulately moving; then dropped without a groan, and lay motionless.

A voice halloa'd on deck. I could not catch the words, but it was easy to recognize Gordon's tone, and it seemed to me that he was bawling for assistance from the wheel, or close to it. The light burnt dully in the cabin lantern; I turned the mesh high that we might see what was the matter with the mate, and then went up to him. He lay on his side, and when I looked at his face I could not question that he was dead. He had run from the cabin in his shirt and trousers on hearing the squealing of the pig, and in that attire had bounded on deck when the boatswain's sudden cry had raised the alarm of collision, and thus was he habited as he lay—a clearly murdered man—at the foot of the cabin steps. His left side was dark in the lamplight with the saturation of blood, and already there was a large dusky patch slowly sifting out, like ink upon blotting-paper, over the sand-coloured planks on which the man rested. His head was uncovered, his eyes half closed, his lips had not yet had time to soften down out of the rigours of their grinning twist of agony and terror; the gleam of his white teeth was as though he snarled, spite of his lying still. God knows, handsome as the lineaments were, it was now a face as villainous for the wrinkled torment and fierce sneer about the mouth, and the sly brutality of the half-closed eyes, and the savage-ness of the woolly hair, that even in life when all was well with him was enough to repel most sorts of sympathy, as imagination could depic-ture. I know that the memory of it, with its base accentuation of stained deck and dyed shirt, haunted me for years, and the thing is before me at this moment, though without the old horror.

This is a passage that takes some time to describe, though the interval between the dropping of the killed man and my bending over him was to have been spanned by twenty or thirty seconds. Broadwater appeared to have been bereft of reason. A professional danger—the thundering down of a squall catching him aback, a big ship under a press close aboard him, white water under the bows—might have found him equal to its confrontment. The vocational instincts would have gone to work, and preserved him from gaping like a fool. But here was something wide of his experience, a sudden violent shock—a frightful menace in its way, too, for it was impossible to say what greater and blacker trag-edy yet lay secret, but sure, behind this first and most bloody one.

I found Miss Grant at my side looking at the body, with a white face, indeed, but with a bearing perfectly collected and self-possessed.

"Mr. Musgrave," she said, in a quick yet firm voice, "what is to be done? Direct me: I am prepared to assist you in any way."

"So far as this man is concerned," I answered, pointing to the body, "there is nothing to be done. Look at his face. There is no virtue for him now in any stanching or dressing. He has been stabbed to the heart!"

She shuddered, and returned to her seat at the table.

"Captain!" I cried suddenly, angered by the posture of helplessness into which this business had struck him, "here is murder—murder, do you hear, sir? If your crew have not mutinied, what else should this signify? There is no leisure at sea, sir, for *goggling*. For God's sake go on deck, man, and find out what's the matter!"

Had I run at him with a pitchfork, the action could not have started him more effectually than my speech.

"Goggling! who's a-goggling?" he roared. "By this and by that," and here he bellowed out a whole volley of curses, "the man who's done this thing shall swing for it! From my own yard-arm he shall swing for it, though there's ne'er a pair of hands on board but mine to run the villain aloft! Murder! Murder aboard of *me!* Why, what do they hope to do? what's their intention?"

He made for the companion-ladder with fury in his looks and gestures; but at that instant down thundered the second mate, with his face as white as its dark tincture of weather would suffer it to be, as wild in his manner as a demented man; so distractedly agitated that his quick, distressful breathing broke up his words as they rolled hoarsely from his lips, and it was with an effort you caught his meaning.

"Captain! captain!" he cried, "there's been a murder done! The mate— ay, there he lies—stabbed, sir, stabbed by the half-blood Charles!"

"Where is he?" bellowed Broadwater, who had come to a stand on seeing the boatswain, but who now gathered himself together afresh for a spring on deck.

"Hold, sir!" cried Gordon, "hold! hear me out. For God Almighty's sake deal with them as though an ill word *now* should tarn 'em all into wild beasts! Mr. Musgrave—sir—you've been to sea. You know that when sailor-men are ripe for mischief the sight and smell of blood will change the most peaceable of them into devils. Tell the captain this, sir! beg him to listen to me, sir, or there'll be not a life of one of us now here collected as'll stand the chance of that flame there if you was to try and blow it out."

"Captain," said I, half wild with the thoughts such talk as this put into my head, as I looked for an instant at Miss Grant to mark what effect the incoherent consternation of the boatswain produced upon her, "you must listen to this man. He has something to tell you. There are three of us; I have weapons of my own, and you will not be without arms. For God's sake, don't let the worst happen without preparation! Sit—be cool. There," I cried, pointing to the body of the mate, "is something to warrant a cold debate!" and with that I grasped him by the arm, with a quick sense of satisfaction coming to me, somehow or other, out of the feel of the mass of muscle my fingers gripped, and shoved him towards a locker. He sat down, with his face as dark as the stain on the cabin deck, without speaking, with a fixed glare of his little eyes at Gordon, and a kind of suffocated heaving of his breast.

"Now, Gordon!" I exclaimed.

The man had already grown somewhat calmer.

"Captain," he said, "this is how it happened. Charles, the half-blood, was at the wheel. When you went below, the mate," here he turned his eyes with a sickly roll upon the body, and a sharp catching of his breath, "came up to me, and talked of the craft that had nearly run us down. He spoke in a passion, gave me hard words—told me I had no eyes, wasn't fit to take charge of the deck, and swore cruelly that he'd reckon his own eyesight to have been blasted if he'd have missed the shadow long afore they showed the binnacle light over the side. We argued, and I fell as hot as he. After a long spell of jawing he went forra'ds, and I heard him talking to some of the men there. His words went with a snap in them—bitter hard words they was, sir!—a sight too fierce for flesh and blood; and the men took courage, I suppose from the blackness, and gave it him back, till forra'ds it grew into a whole growl of curses, and then," he continued with another sickening look at the figure, "he steps aft threatening them with a hundred work-up jobs for to-morrow. He comes up to me, and lets fly again. He talked as if he hadn't his right mind, and I tell ye that I peered for the gleam of a knife in his hand, dark as it was, for he acted as if he were going to run a muck. It was his watch below; there was nothing to keep him on deck; whilst, if I couldn't boast of his education, there was nothing on God's ocean in the seafaring line as he was competent to teach me." He cast another look of dismay and disgust at the dead man, and stopped to take breath.

Broadwater watched him with a fixed gaze. I was afraid he would interrupt the fellow, but he had fallen into his earlier posture of bewilderment and astonishment.

"I could follow him," continued Gordon, "by the white of his shirt a-flitting about the deck, and after a bit he walks to the wheel where Charles was, and spoke to him. There was some muttering; then I heard *him*," pointing with his finger at the body without looking at it, "talking shrill as a fishwife, whilst the half-blood answered sulkily, as a man struggling with his temper; and this went on till of a sudden Mr. Bothwell made the cry ye must have heard, and before I could run aft he had slipped to the companion, where I lost sight of him. I found the wheel deserted. The half-blood had gone forward in the murky blackness along the line of the larboard bulwarks, and though I noticed the slapping of shoes, yet, not seeing him, I supposed he was still at the helm. I halloa'd for some one to lay aft and take the wheel. The moment he came, I says, 'Where's Charles?' 'In the fo'k'sle,' he answers. 'What's he done?' says I, for I couldn't guess at the truth of the matter from the noise of Mr. Bothwell's yell. 'He's knifed the mate,' says he. 'How do you know that?' says I. 'Why,' he says, 'afore dropping down the scuttle he sings out, 'Nat—Dan—Terence—is there e'er a one of you on deck?' '*I* am,' says I, who was standing close. 'By God!' says he, 'the mate'll trouble us no more; my knife has found his heart out! It'll be the skipper's turn next!'"

Broadwater started to his feet.

"For Heaven's sake, hear him out!" I cried; "time may be precious; how on earth shall we know what to do unless we get the truth."

The skipper had lifted his arm with a frenzied gesture, and would have plunged, spite of my entreaty, into one of his now familiar roaring bouts; but happily he was half-suffocated by rage and terror, and scarcely able to articulate. He continued to watch the boatswain, whilst his extended arm fell to his side.

"When I heard this," continued Gordon, throwing a look up the companion-ladder as if he suspected listeners there, "I went forrards, put my head into the scuttle, and called to Charles. He answered without showing himself. I says, 'In God's name, what have you gone and done?' 'I've sent a villain to hell,' he answers, 'let him come back if he can.' Some of the chaps laughed at this. They had trimmed the fo'k'sle lamp afresh, and all hands seemed wide awake, as no doubt they would be after the row of the pig and the danger we scraped clear of; but I tell ye, Captain Broadwater," he continued, with another look up the ladder, "that there was a sound in them men's laughter which gave me to know that a cask of gunpowder, with the head knocked off lying clear for the first spark, wouldn't be a bigger danger in the hold of this vessel than's her fo'k'sle to her as it now stands, sir." He paused, dried his face on a great blue handkerchief, and then went on speaking hurriedly. "I says, 'Charles, you must come out of that! No use skulking below. There's no stabbing men in this here craft and lying snug after it. Up with ye now,—don't give me the trouble to fetch ye.' He bawled out a curse, keeping hidden all the time. I put my leg over, but ere I could lift the other, four or five men sprang under the hatch, and one of them said, 'See here, Mr. Gordon. We don't owe you no grudge. These are your quarters as they are ourn; but the man's not to be touched. Understand that! By the Etarnal! if so be a finger's laid upon him the capt'n'll answer for it with his life; so aft with ye, sir, and give him this piece of news from his fo'k'sle.' I got out of the hatch, and after a look down at the men, came away to tell ye what's happened."

I had made up my mind to offer no suggestions, and so contented myself with watching Broadwater, wondering what measures such a head as his would be able to devise for the remedying of the horrible mess into which he and his mate had plunged us. He seemed to wake up when the boatswain ceased, and fell to pacing the cabin in silence, measuring twenty or thirty strides before he spoke. He then said, "Better return on deck, Mr. Gordon, and look after the brig, sir. Send Billy here." The boatswain ascended the ladder; Broadwater resumed his walk.

One wants a paint-brush instead of a quill for such a picture as this. The dead body of the mate; Miss Grant motionless and composed, though, methought, there was a flash of an almost preternatural vitality in the dark sweep of her eyes whenever they met mine; the short, square, muscular figure of Broadwater pacing the length of the cabin, staring ahead of him with the blind, wooden look of a figure-head; the play of shadows set dancing by the lamp; the midnight silence on deck; the soft, washing sound of water running in some sobbing black fold along the bends; the creak and jar of the fabric as she rolled on the light swell, with many a muffled note like the short laughs or sullen grumblings of a company of giants below, stealing to our ear from the freighted hold beneath our feet—I say there is nothing in ink to give you the colour, the horror, the strangeness of this cabin picture, and the noises breaking into the interval of silence, during which the captain stepped from one end to the other, whilst Miss Grant and I waited for the arrival of the boy, knowing what he was wanted for.

A few moments before he came, Broadwater halted at the side of the dead man, stooped and listened, grasped his wrist and held it, as though feeling for the life there, then shot erect, and cried out, "Never before did such a thing happen aboard of me! never before! And they talk of murdering me too, hey? How many lives must it cost 'em? How many lives must it cost 'em?" He thrust his hand into the bosom of his shirt, and made as if to run to his cabin, but checked himself, wheeled round, and fell to pacing the deck afresh.

The boy arrived. "Here," shouted Broadwater fiercely, "help me to carry that body to his berth."

The unhappy youth stood with his knock-knees trembling one against the other, whilst he stared at the corpse with eyes which threatened to leap from their sockets. If ever human hair stirred upon the head to the agitation of the spirit, his did. But his fear of Broadwater was livelier than his dread of the corpse. Between them they carried the body to its berth in the fore-end, and I had not known how heavily the presence of the thing had hung upon me until it was gone, when I fetched a breath as easy as a sigh.

Broadwater returned, and the boy shambling in his wake went stealthily to the ladder, and then fled up it as though the mate were in pursuit of him. The captain looked through the hatch as if he meant to mount on deck, but hung irresolute, with a short glance round to me that was like a question. I own that the difficulty with which he was confronted was enough to stagger a brighter intellect than his pork-fed and rum-tinctured brains. Yet his hesitation at such a juncture was mighty discomposing too. Observing that he continued to stand in a posture of doubt at the foot of the ladder, I said bluntly, believing that a plain question might help him, "Captain, what do you mean to do?"

He looked at me oddly for some moments, sent a glance into the black arch of atmosphere formed by the cover of the companion-way, and answered in a deep, sea-growling note, "Cursed if I know. What would *you* do?"

"Wait till daylight, anyhow," I replied; "remain cool, and keep my temper. That's what *I* should resolve upon first. For the rest I should be guided by events."

"And who says I ain't cool?" he cried in a quarrelsome way, "and as to losing my temper——" he stopped dead to the sudden choke of rage in his throat, clenched both fists till I noticed the veins stand out black to the tension like whipcord under the flesh, lifted his arms to the deck overhead, and shook them convulsively in a fit of speechless passion; then looking for his cap he pulled it fiercely down to his ears, and went with a heavy tread up the steps.

"We ought to be grateful," said I, "that the fellow's rage is often too great to enable him to speak. His speechlessness was the very petrifaction of his curses!"

"He is not the man," she exclaimed, "for such an emergency as this. Pray God there may be some good sense left amongst the crew. If not, what will happen?"

"I comfort myself with the thought," I replied, "that sailors are slow to mutiny. They know the law. If they refuse their duty, certain and severe punishment awaits them ashore; if they seize the vessel, it is piracy—a criminal act that ends with Jack Ketch. If they murder—but enough of such talk, Miss Grant. Here has been a wild disturbance that may presently settle down into a sulky calm; and let the tranquillity be as sinister as it will, providing we can step ashore at Rio before it ends, we shall have reason to be satisfied."

She glanced at the dark stain on the deck, a slight shiver ran through her, and she folded her arms across her breast as though for the warmth of them.

"What a night this has been!" she cried; "indeed, what a time the whole voyage has been, so far as it has gone! I have heard stories of wild doings in vessels of this kind trading to the West Indies and to South America, but nothing to equal our experiences!"

She shivered again; I caught a tremble in her under-lip, and a swift expression of mingled worry and horror in her eyes, and fearing that she would break down—and surely what she had seen and suffered since she had quitted her berth might well have broken a hardier spirit than ever woman was yet informed with—I poured a little brandy into a glass, and begged her to drink it; but she waved it aside with a sudden proud smile, sweet with kindness too.

"Do not misjudge me, Mr. Musgrave," she said; "if I seem to falter in a time of trouble, it is not, I think, from want of courage. It is the sense of uncertainty that always weakens me most—the not knowing what to do." She suddenly ceased, lifting her hand to motion silence; but the noise was no more than the growling of old Broadwater's voice talking to the boatswain close against the cabin skylight, one frame of which stood open. We strained our ears, but could not catch words enough to enable us to gather the import of their talk. I advised her to return to her berth, and sleep out the rest of the night if she could. She smiled at my speaking of sleep, and said she would go to her berth and dress herself.

"But you will not come on deck, Miss Grant?"

"Why not?"

"Be advised by me, I beg you. It is bleak and black; what can you do on deck? Next, in the present temper of the men, I could wish you to keep out of sight of them. The dawn will soon be at hand, and sunrise may give a new complexion to our affairs."

"I will do whatever you please," she said "I merely need advice. What follows I hope I shall have courage enough to meet," and with another smile—so full of spirit that it was almost enough to make one doubt that she fully grasped the significance of our dangerous situation, in a small brig with murder newly done, and the crew sheltering and making a hero of the assassin—she entered her berth. Ten minutes after, I quitted my own cabin, fully dressed, and went on deck.

Chapter XII
Mutiny

AS I STEPPED OVER the combing of the hatch, I caught sight of the dawn sifting out into dim ash along the seaboard on the port, or, as we then termed it, the larboard side. It was a cold, unearthly light, and against it the sea-line ran in a short clear ruling, black as liquid pitch. The wind was a quiet breeze, as it had been throughout the night; but the swell had veered from abeam to the starboard quarter, and swung the brig onwards in gliding, floating movements, though that her sails were doing their work you knew by the sound of the singing of running waters rising from the obscurity, mingled with a dull noise of moaning, and the flat, echoless plashing of ripple colliding with ripple into short spouts of sea, which leaped without life round about the vessel's quarters.

Even as the dawn broke it was yet so dark that there was nothing to be seen but the filtering light; but this brightened fast into a ragged sort of staring of the radiance over streaks and through tail-ends of clouds, until the whole circumference of the horizon sloped dark to the vague grey of the sky, with a slow writhing, wonderful to behold, of the shadowy substance of the brig's sails, masts, and hull, into determinable forms, out of what was just now mere impalpable blocks of dusk one on top of another.

I can conceive of no spectacle more melancholy and cheerless than the first breaking of day over the wide and troubled ocean. There is a bleakness in the aspect of pallid heaven and yet darkling water, and in the grey complexion of the canvas and rigging of the ship, that enters the atmosphere as a sensible quality of cold; and I have known men who, though they had been on deck for several hours without feeling the edge of the wind, have slapped their breasts with a shudder to the first opening of the desolate faintness in the east. But it was soon broad daylight. The broken, blind sort of stare among the clouds to larboard melted out into the flooding of effulgent pink—the sun lifted a segment of rose-red glory—a sinuous stream of radiance flashed from one blue brow to another down to within a musket-shot of us—and then you saw a piebald sky, mottled into rich marble with dashes of white vapour—a broad-bosomed swell rolling in folds of dark blue and brimming to our channels, freckled with foaming wrinkles.

There were some men talking near the fore-hatch; occasionally they directed their glances aft to the quarter-deck, where the captain and boatswain stood in silent waiting, as it seemed to me, until the spring of the sun from the ocean should fairly settle the dawn into day. I took a long survey of the blue circle, but there was nothing to be seen. Not that there was anything to be hoped from the sight of a ship, unless, indeed, she should prove a man-of-war; for our trouble was not of a kind that a merchantman could meddle with. How could her people serve us? Advice was hardly likely to prove profitable to Broadwater, and more than that he was not going to obtain by backing his topsail to speak to a stranger and asking him to send a boat. And yet even the remotest gleam of a ship would have yielded me a sort of feeling of relief, by qualifying, however worthlessly, the profound sense of loneliness that possessed me on first seeing the vast stretch of liquid waste bathed in the delicate light of the sunrise.

There was an air of surly and defiant stubbornness in the postures and glances of the group forward that was instantly noticeable. I counted seven of them, and supposed therefore that amongst them was one or more of that division of the crew which had the watch below. They appeared to be holding a council; and it was startling, I can tell you, to mark their forms, so to speak, come out from the blackness into the dawn, and to think of them as having been there talking one to another, as they now were when the darkness hid them.

I looked for the man Charles, but he was not on deck. No doubt it was the fancies put into my head by the thought of the dead creature below, which helped my imagination to colour and accentuate the attitudes and expressions of the fellows; but even though the night had passed as tranquilly as the preceding one, I must still, though bending the most incurious eye in the world upon them, have found something in their varied demeanour to render me uneasy. There was doggedness and obstinacy in the plant of the figures swaying upon their legs to the heave of the deck; in the arms squared firmly upon the breast, the rugged wrist of one hand showing out past the dark half-concealed knuckles of the other; in the challenging glances aft; in the well-conveyed indifference to the presence of the master.

The second mate had a very worn and haggard look. He showed like a man worried to the heart; but I think it must have been the shock of Bothwell's murder that paled and lengthened his face, for he had used the sea for too many years, and had lived too closely with sailors, to be scared to the degree that his visage and manner now indicated by mere mutinous mutterings and loafing, insolent attitudes. As to old

Broadwater, it was quite impossible for him to look gaunt; his purple countenance was as much a part of him as his ears or his feet, and he would die with it on him as a negro dies with a black skin. But the incidents of the night had done their work with him nevertheless. The arch over each eye was sharper; in quiet times this would have made him appear as though labouring under astonishment, but there were other features and other expressions to lift this aspect of surprise into a look of savage consternation. Had I viewed him without knowing what was the matter, I should have imagined that he had been on deck day and night for a week, exposed to violent and dangerous weather, during which his mind had been heavily strained by anxiety.

There was a man named Daniel Ladova, another half-blood, as I supposed, standing at the wheel, and I could have laughed outright at the pat fit of the fellow's face to the circumstances of the time; for though I dare say he may have been at bottom as steady, respectable, and sober a creature as one could wish to see in a ship's forecastle, yet he was so confoundedly ugly, with his flat nose, the nostrils whereof were stretched past the line of his eyes, his wide mouth and negro fullness of lips, his coal-black, long, streaky Indian hair, low forehead and complexion of saffron, the whole topped off by the sieve-like pitting of smallpox, that one might have searched every shipping-yard in Great Britain without meeting with a fellow better qualified by his looks to stand at the brig's helm in this particular juncture.

Suddenly Broadwater made some observation to Gordon, and walked aft. The boatswain called out, "Forward there! Send Charles aft, one of you!" but there was a half-heartedness in his way of singing out that made one feel he regarded the captain's command as purposeless and ridiculous.

The fellows lounging about the foremast looked round to the hail, but only quitted their posture to that extent. No one called to Charles, no one even approached the scuttle to do so.

"D'ye hear what I say, men?" repeated Gordon, but in the same half-spirited tone, as though the bother of this time had taken most of the manhood out of him; "one of you tell Charles that the captain wants him aft."

"Charles has got nothen to do with us," cried back one of the fellows huskily; "if the capt'n wants him, he knows where to find him."

Broadwater bawled from the station he occupied near the wheel, "What are they a-saying, Mr. Gordon? What are they a-saying, sir?"

The boatswain replied, "If we want the half-blood, we must call him ourselves."

"Send all hands aft! send all hands aft!" shouted Broadwater furiously, stepping forward by half-a-dozen angry strides, and then halting, with his chest rising and falling to his passionate breathing, that was not all pure wrath either, for I could *feel* the irresolution that lay under all this show of temper, and guessed that but very little likely to prove useful to us could follow on any intentions he might have in his mind.

The boatswain instantly roared out, "Lay aft all hands!" in much such a hurricane note as he would have delivered in a gale of wind, in summoning all hands to reef topsails.

My heart beat fast now, I confess, for the men's refusal to obey this order would signify mutiny; and though from the first hour of my climbing aboard the *Iron Crown* I had been apprehensive of grievous trouble in this way, now that it had come to look as if the thing was about to happen, I was as much agitated as though I had never given it a thought, and it had broken upon us on a sudden. Judge, then, of my relief, when I saw the knot of men gathered about the foremast leisurely make their way aft with a shambling, devil-may-care gait for the most part; one or two with a half grin, which was less suited to my taste than the mulish, sullen countenances the others carried. The captain, leaning forwards and backwards on his curved legs to the swing of the ship, his arms up and down, his hands clenched to the appearance of small rounds of beef, his cap jammed so tightly down upon his head that the upper rounds of his ears forked out with the pressure, stood fixedly regarding the sailors as they approached. Meanwhile the boatswain had gone forward, and picking up a handspike, thumped the deck heavily with it, whilst with his head overhanging the scuttle—by which I would have you understand the little forecastle-hatch through which the men emerged from, or dropped into their quarters—he delivered a second leather-lunged roar of "All hands lay aft!" emphasizing his cry with a further smiting of the deck with his bar, which he then threw down. This done, he came away, and stood a little abaft the main-rigging, the captain having posted himself abreast of the companion-hatch. In a few moments the rest of the men who were in the forecastle tumbled up, hoisting themselves out with their elbows, and vaulting lightly on to the deck, with a sailor's enjoyment of an incident that at least gave them something else to think of than the cheerless, laborious routine of the ship's work.

The sun was now risen, and some degrees above the horizon. It was half-past four in the morning, maybe later; one takes no particular account of time in such passages as these. The warm breeze blew steadily, and the brig buzzed softly over the blue hills of swell, which, as they ran into the south-east quarter, lifted the molten silver of the sun's reflection upon their broad shoulders in regular procession, till the white dazzle there was as blinding as a glance at the luminary himself. I had often read of difficulties of this kind happening at sea, but never been brought face to face with the reality; and I remember thinking, as I stood on the larboard side of the vessel, close against the quarter-boat, and ran my eye over the group that had come to a stand a little abaft the mainmast, that though the perils of the deep be many, some frightful, and all of them formidable, the worst of them, ay, even fire itself, must yield in horror to mutiny—where men arm themselves against their fellows, where the passions of undisciplined minds are let loose, where tyrannic authority and bitter grievance come in conflict, and where the struggle is inflamed and rendered wilder than anything of a like sort could ever become ashore through the forecastle perception that, the bad business once entered upon, there is no mercy to be expected in the event of failure, no hope to be cherished should rebellion prove successful. In disaster men work together for their lives; in mutiny they work together for their own destruction. The sweep of the sparkling sea-line round about us was like the compression of the very spirit of loneliness into our little brig. There was nothing to help the eye, to ease, by a solitary detail of discipline, the perturbation excited by the scene. On board an Indiaman, for instance, there would have been mates and midshipmen in plenty, loyal to the commander; with an array of passengers, maybe, in whose fidelity one could count in the name of self-concern. It would be strange, too, if the whole of a big ship's company should prove disaffected; so that the quarter-deck might reckon at least on the negative services of a portion of the crew. But if yonder crowd, gathered about the mainmast, and staring with mingled derision and hate at the square, round-legged, red-faced man whose lifted brows and whistling mouth put the expression of a gape into his countenance, broke into revolt, what should our case prove? I counted ten of them, and the man who steered would make eleven, and Charles, who skulked below, twelve. Twelve reckless fellows, with the scent of the assassin's knife fresh in their nostrils, with instincts and yearnings perhaps made devilish by the memory of a usage of which I as a passenger must needs have seen but a very little part, though I had witnessed enough to convince me that had I been of their company, and suffered as they had, my resentment would surely not have left me among the hindmost of them in the posture they now exhibited!

The picture was as nautical as the most ardent lover of ocean-pieces could desire. The men were variously attired: in blue dungaree—in patched canvas breeches—in half-boots, and coloured shirts which revealed their brawny breasts bare to the dark moss upon them—here a round hat, there a sou'-wester, and around every sailor's waist was the narrow sea-belt, with a sheath of leather upon the hip, holding, convenient to the grasp, the black haft of a dagger-shaped knife. The shadows of the rigging crawled upon them, as the vessel, with a little humming of water at her bow, floated, with cradling swings, from one sapphire knoll to another; not a feature but had the true oceanic colour: the coils of rigging swinging at the belaying-pins; the big scuttle-butt securely seized under the high bulwark; the little white caboose with its head of black chimney whence blew a vein of blue smoke; the yellow longboat amid ships snugged under the spare booms, with a black snout projecting from the sty under it; and a darting and withdrawal beyond of the heads of cocks and hens glancing like red rags as they showed and vanished through the bars of the coops. Aloft, swelling gently, rose courses and topsails to the little royals, with a breezy stir of shadows in the hollows, and a pearly curve sunwards where the bosom, arching beyond the bolt-rope, caught the full splendour shining out of the east.

Broadwater pulled off his hat, dried his forehead, covered himself afresh, and approached the men by half-a-dozen paces.

"Is the man Charles among ye?" said he; "if so, let him step out, for it's *him* I want, not *you*."

Of course he knew perfectly well that the half-blood did not form one of that little crowd. Perhaps he meant to convey that he had not deigned to glance at the fellows; but this was absurd, for every man as he stepped aft must have observed that the captain watched him as a terrier does an approaching rat. One or two of them glanced over their shoulders, as though believing that the half-blood had come from the forecastle. No answer was returned to Broadwater's inquiry.

"Now, look here, men," he continued, with an air of bluster which I hoped would not increase upon him, "you know, of course, that Charles committed murder this morning by stabbing the mate, who lies a dead body in his bunk below; and you likewise know that for an act of this kind, when he gets ashore, he'll be hung up by the neck, and left to dangle there till his bones blow away. Now, as he's a murderer, it's my duty to put him in irons, and keep him under hatches till I'm able to hand him over to the people employed by the law to sentence and strangle him, and all such folks as he. D'ye see, men?" with a powerful flourish of his arm, and a slight increase of bluster, as though he was gaining in spirit from the air of attention with which the sailors seemed to listen to him. "We don't want no difficulties. Aboard *me* everything has always been plain sailing, and up to the knocker. My mate lies a dead man, and I want the chap as killed him."

He paused, running his eye over them. Two or three of the crew gave their heads a quick shake, but none of them spoke.

"The man," proceeded Broadwater, "is lying snugged away in the fo'k'sle. Now, look ye here, my lads. There need be no trouble about it at all. All that you've got to do is just to remain where you are, whilst me and the second mate fetches him—seeing that he won't come under milder persuasions."

I thought by the manner of the men that they hung in the wind, and would let the captain have his way. He must have fancied this also, for he started to walk to the forecastle with a gesture of his hand to the boatswain; but, ere he could get one leg fair before the other, a tall, powerfully-built seaman flung himself with a stride or two upon the line of deck which the captain was about to measure, and cried out, "Stop, sir! no furder! We don't mean to let you have the man."

If Broadwater had been shot through the heart, the arrest of his movements could not have been more spasmodic and utter. Rage once again rendered him speechless, and the rush of blood to his head darkened his purple countenance into an almost livid complexion. Half-a-dozen sailors thrust up and formed about the man who had spoken. Their looks were so threatening, that I dreaded in Broadwater the least gesture that might be mistaken as combative by the fellows. The boatswain came to the side of the old man, who, gasping for breath, and as voiceless as a person in a fit, fell back step by step till he had put some half-dozen yards between him and the crew, by which time he had recovered his voice; but I protest, had I not looked at him and observed his lips to move, that I should not have known him by his tones. He raised his arm, and shook his clenched fist at the tall sailor.

"Your name's Terence Mole," he said. "If it should cost me every shilling I'm worth so to punish ye for this ere job as to keep ye cursing your mother's memory day and night for ever having bore you, I'll spend it! If, to have ye punished for this, it should oblige me to tear the shirt off my back and pawn it for more law yet to crush you with, I'd do it, and go naked for the rest of my time, and die easy! You scoundrel!"

He fell speechless again, with another mad brandishing of his arms towards the tall sailor. The man watched him with a cold, insolent grin. One of the crew exclaimed, "Soft words, master, soft words. Ye want that there man Charles, and we don't mean to let ye have him."

The boatswain, with a glance at the captain, turned upon the crew. "Lads," he exclaimed, "consider what you're a-doing of! In protecting this here murderer you're making yourselves parties to his crime; and though I don't know much about shore-going law, I can't question that your abetting of the villain may end in stringing most of ye up alongside of him; whilst it should sinnify transportation for life to the rest of ye."

"Mr. Gordon," answered the tall seaman Mole, "we've tarned the matter over, and we've made up our minds not to let the man Charles suffer, leastways aboard this brig, for his act. He's rid us of a devil," he pronounced the word with a sudden snap of the teeth, "and if he hadn't done it some one else would; though it was for him, by rights, to make a beginning, seeing how he was served," he pointed with a dark thumb in the direction of the foremast, "merely for commiserating the fate of a drownded shipmate. If the capt'n's flesh an' blood, so are we. We're willing enough to listen to reason, but so long as we continue to be the crew of this here brig, Charles don't go into irons; nor shall we allow him to be punished in any other way."

With that he folded his arms, rearing his figure erect, and angrily staring at the captain. The boatswain turned to Broadwater as much as to say, "Speak, sir, speak. You hear what the man says." The old fellow swung on his heel and walked aft, and stood with his hands behind him gazing seawards. The men fell to talking among themselves, and there was a laugh or two, but the hilarity had a very false ring, and was instantly checked by a growling "Dowse it, you fool, dowse it!" I observed some of the seamen regarding me, but I pretty well understood that by this time they knew that whatever might be my sympathies they assuredly did not incline towards the cabin end of the ship. Besides, I had a right to listen and look on at all events, and leaning against the rail, with my hands in my pockets, I kept my eyes fixed on them, unmoved by their gaze.

Although Broadwater scarcely remained a minute abaft the wheel, the time seemed so long that I believed that he intended the men should break up and go forward of their own accord, without giving himself the trouble of dismissing them. But I was mistaken. He suddenly wheeled round and came along at a rapid pace, abruptly stopping however at some distance from the crew.

"It's your intention, then," he shouted, "not to allow me to clap this murderer in irons and lock him up?"

"You heard what was said," one of them exclaimed.

"Mr. Gordon!" he suddenly roared, "for-rards with us both! By the thunder of heaven, we'll have a try for the bloody villain, let follow what will!"

I saw him tweak at the band of his trousers with the motion of a man who girds himself for an affray, then make a spring. The men closed in a wall before him. He struck at them, but I could not see that his blows were returned; they did no more than to press upon him and drive him backwards. Gordon threw his arms around the old fellow's waist to drag him away. Sickened and horrified by the scene, I ran to assist the boatswain, dreading lest one of the many blows which the old fellow was raining might lead to a general onslaught on him, and grasped his right arm, and in a few moments we had hauled him clear of the crew, at whom the boatswain continued shouting, as together we pulled the skipper aft, "For God's sake, go forward, men! for God's sake, go forward!"

Chapter XIII
Broadwater Proves Obstinate

WE GOT BROADWATER, WHEEZING, panting, and gasping, to the cabin skylight, upon which we forced him to sit, not a little blown ourselves by our uncommon exertions; by which time the crew had broken up as advised by the boatswain, and were going forward in twos and threes quietly enough. Broadwater sat for some minutes without offering to speak; when he had got his breath again, he flung off the skylight and ran below with the swiftness and gestures of a madman.

"This is a bad business—a bad business, sir," said Gordon, speaking in a voice full of concern.

"The deuce of it is," I exclaimed, "the captain has not the least idea how to act. The men are wildly to blame—no doubt of that; it is monstrous that British seamen should sympathize with a murderer and a foreigner; but I am certain, from signs of a disposition I took notice of in them as they stood together yonder, that were the master of this vessel any other man than Broadwater, the sailors might easily be brought over."

"I know it, sir—I know it," he cried bitterly. "They began well. Had they been properly used they would have gone on and ended well. But though the man's dead I don't mind saying, Mr. Musgrave, that a crueller mate never walked a ship's deck than Mr. Bothwell. 'Twasn't only the words he'd use, 'twas the insulting tone of them—like coating with poison the knife you stab with. The brutal tarms cut to the men's hearts, and lay festering there, sir, with the recollection of the fellow's voice and looks. Ye onderstand me? It rose above the half-blood's restraint. A horrid murder, Mr. Musgrave, but it don't surprise me."

"What will Broadwater do?"

He threw a glance down the skylight and exclaimed, "I'm afraid whatever he does'll be wrong."

"But what would you advise, Mr. Gordon? There is a lady below, remember; I am responsible for her safety; if for her sake only, this trouble should be speedily ended by some decisive course of action."

"Why, sir, seeing how matters stand," he answered—"the mate dead, his murderer screened by the men, the crew in a state of mutiny, the captain ought to head fair for Madeira—'tis the nearest point, where no doubt he'd get help from the shore, if so be there was no English or foreign man-of-war riding there."

"Certainly," I cried; "that should be his plan! There is no man forward, I suppose, capable of guessing the captain's intentions by a change of course?"

"The change would be too small to take their notice," he responded. "But suppose they did guess what he was at, they'd make no difficulty about it—at least whilst their feelings remain as they are now. They hate the vessel, and 'ud be glad of a chance to get away from her, though the road to their liberty lay through a jail."

"Have you suggested this notion to the captain?"

"I told him," he answered, "when him and me were talking before sunrise about the mate's murder, that if the men continued to give trouble, or broke out into regular mutiny, there'd be certainly nothing for it but to head for Madeira."

"What did he say?"

"Cursed and swore, sir. 'Sooner than be driven to Madeira by my crew,' he says, I'd cut away the brig's masts, and let her lie where she is,' he says, 'till she's growed unrecognizable for barnacles!' But," he added, "now that he's seen the sort of attitude the men have put themselves into he may change his ideas and agree with me."

"Was there ever such a bigoted old fool?" I cried. "Did ever one hear of so rum-soddened a dolt placed in such a confoundedly responsible position as that of master of a ship before? I only wish he were as ignorant of navigation as he is of human nature and the art of treating sailors: I'd run him then myself to Madeira, and he shouldn't know where he was bound to until the island was hove up green over the bow. What is the stupid idiot to do if the hands, barring yourself, are against him?" I continued talking hotly, out of the fit of nervous irritability that had seized me. "And what does he mean by saying that he would sooner cut away his masts than haul in for the island and the protection it would afford him? Confound the fellow! Does he suppose that the lady and I parted with our money for the privilege of shipping in a sheer hulk?"

"Well, sir," said Gordon, "I dessay if ye put it to him warmly he'll listen to ye. If not to you, to nobody else for sartain, sir. There's too much feeding mixed up with the brains in his head; and the machinery's got clogged and don't travel properly, spite of his being incessantly greasing of it with liquor. And what's he going to do about the watches, I wonder? Why, it must be drawing on for six o'clock, and here have I been on deck since midnight." He dodged about the skylight in his efforts to command a view of the cabin, to see if the captain were there. "There's ne'er a man more willing to do his bit than me," he said, "but it ain't in flesh and blood to keep all on watching and nothen else."

"If he likes to make you his chief mate, and me his second," said I, "I shall be quite willing to fill the berth, and take watch and watch with you. I shouldn't set myself up as *your* match, Gordon, of course; but if I couldn't trim sail with old Broadwater, or take sights, or note a change of wind, or mark the head of a growing squall with him, he shall tell me I can't distinguish the difference between the sheet of his trysail and the hanks of his standing jib."

"Put it to him, sir; put it to him," cried the boatswain, rubbing his hands with a small emotion of glee in his worried face. "I tell you what, sir, if the capt'n'ud make you hacting second mate—unbecoming as such a post would be for a gentleman like you to occupy—I allow that the appointment 'ud go further to reconcile the men to the brig, and to the voyage, than all the excuses the capt'n could make for himself, and all the wisest sort of kindness he'd be capable of showing 'em. Of course they know that you have been a sailor, sir."

"How?" I asked.

"Why," he replied, "I told them. Next, they're aware that the man Charles was saved from spending the night lashed to the foremast by your and the lady's entreaties and threats to leave the ship. That bit of news was brought forrards by Billy the cabin-boy; likewise by the chap whose trick it was at the wheel when the lady spoke to the capt'n about the half-blood. Depend upon it, sir," he added emphatically, "that if you should be made second mate, or, better still, chief mate, the men 'ud feel so satisfied to know they'd got a gentleman to officer them, that I'm confident they'd give no further trouble this side of Rio. Will you put it to the capt'n, sir?"

"Certainly I will," I replied, struck by the poor fellow's eagerness, though my fancy hung much less in this direction than in a desire to urge Broadwater to make promptly for Madeira.

I left the honest creature and went below, pretty shrewdly guessing that Miss Grant lay all this while sleepless in her cabin, and was in bad need of the encouragement of a chat. I also wished to meet Broadwater, that I might tackle him whilst I was in the mood to pitch my key to any sort of note that he might choose to strike. Billy the cabin-boy, with his lank, yellow hair dangling over his eyes, was on his knees working with a deck-scraper at the dark and ugly stain at the foot of the companion-steps; but blood lies upon wood as upon the human conscience; its sacred magic, its preternatural quality of staining, is no more to be neutralized in timber by the scraper, than in the murderer's mind by the parson. 'Twas a mallet and chisel that the lad needed, and even with them the cleansing of the plank might have ended in a hole in the deck, gaping to the uttermost outline of the horrid blot. I felt a little creeping in my skin as I passed the boy, but then I was desperately bothered, and the eyes of my imagination were out of gear, so that little things put on ugly forms, and through distortion of aspect were cruelly suggestive and abominably significant.

I listened a moment at Miss Grant's cabin door, and very softly knocked, by no means desiring to disturb her should she be asleep. She instantly asked who it was that knocked; I answered and she came out. She was fully dressed, robed in jacket and hat for the deck.

"I am glad you have come to me," she exclaimed; "but you see I have dutifully obeyed your orders. I would not even enter the cabin, though you would imagine how dull, expectant, miserable, I felt alone—listening, waiting, dreading I cannot tell you what—in this gloomy little box."

I took her hand and conducted her to the cabin, and she seemed to lift her head like a drooping lily to the refreshment of water as she entered an atmosphere bright with the sparkling of the sun flowing full upon the skylight, and crawling in sheets of gold upon the bulkheads and deck. She looked with attention at the lad at work under the hatch, as though she wondered what he was doing; then, understanding, she partly turned her back upon him with a manner that was like dismissing the perception of the meaning of the fellow's labour from her memory.

"What have you got to tell me?" she asked, seating herself, and resting her chin in the palms of her hands, whilst she gazed at me from under the shadow of her broad straw hat with such a spirit of resolution in her eyes, that I saw she had prepared herself for the darkest disclosures.

I related exactly all that had happened during the time I had been on deck, and was in the midst of repeating my recent conversation with the boatswain when she slightly coughed, with a significant glance past me. I looked, and saw Broadwater coming from his cabin. He stood near the boy a moment or two watching him, then gave the lad a kick that threw him on to his face.

"Away with ye!" he cried. "Scraping indeed! It's bottle-washing that's in your line, you young scaramouch! Off with ye for a broom, and collect these here shavings, and tell the cook to get the cabin-breakfast ready by six bells."

The boy picked himself up, and mounted the ladder. Broadwater turning to me said, "An all-night job regularly sets me pining for food, long afore I should feel the need of it after a proper allowance of sleep."

I thought to myself, Shall I begin with the fellow at once, or wait till he has broken his fast? A meal might make him more sensible, render him more tractable; but my present mood was an opportunity I ought not to miss; and then time was exceedingly precious. So I began:

"Captain Broadwater, unless you are going on deck to relieve the boatswain, who has had charge since midnight——"

He interrupted me by saying in his roughest manner, "Mr. Musgrave, the discipline of the *Iron Crown*'s my affair. Don't, I beg of you, give yourself any trouble about it, sir."

"Then sit down," said I, warmly and sternly, "for if the discipline of the vessel is *your* affair, this lady's safety is *mine!* So now, sir, give me your attention, for you will find that I am more in earnest than even the most rebellious of your men forward." He did not offer to sit, but contented himself with watching me. "First," I went on, "what do you mean to do?"

"Wait, sir, and you'll see."

"No," I cried, bringing my hand down with a sounding whack upon my thigh; "that answer will not satisfy me, Captain Broadwater. The crew are in a state of mutiny; your mate lies murdered; the only living creature aboard that you can depend on is your bo'sun, and even *he* may fail you—honest to the bottom of his soul as I know him to be—for he is no more than a foremast hand, though he holds a responsible position under you. Now listen, sir. As matters stand, this lady and I are in peril of our lives. Your duty is not only to give us every encouragement, but to make haste to obtain such assistance as shall deliver us, as well as yourself and vessel, from the heavy dangers which threaten us. Therefore I demand to know what you mean to do?"

He eyed me with the same kind of doggedness I had noticed in some of his men when he was addressing them; was silent for a space after I had ceased, and then said, "What was your object in hiring cabins in this brig?"

"The passage to Rio."

"Right! And I'm carrying you to Rio. That's the part you paid my owner for me to perform, and I'll *do* it."

"But," I cried, "how is it possible that you can carry your vessel to Rio with a crew who have already distinctly mutinied by refusing to surrender your mate's murderer to you?"

"The Lord spare me!" he roared out. "If I ain't bound to Rio where else am I a-going?"

"See here," said I, determined to make him understand by my manner that I was in earnest, "you must be perfectly well aware that as matters are you will never succeed in carrying your ship to Rio. A moment, if you please! The crew have rebelled to a man, and have defied you. You know it! The respect you might have obtained you have forfeited, and they laugh at your commands. You know that too! By protecting the half-blood they share in his crime, and every fellow in your forecastle is therefore an assassin at heart. And you mean to tell me that, all this being as I say, you will be able to complete a voyage which may run us into two or three months, but which is as yet but a week old only?"

"Certainly!" he cried; "we're bound to Rio, and I mean to keep all on till we get there."

"If that be so," said I vehemently, "this lady and I decline to proceed with you."

"Decline to proceed!" he shouted, evidently misunderstanding me.

"Yes, sir," I answered, shouting too. "We insist upon your steering the brig for the island of Madeira. The place is within a few days' sail. I don't doubt that the crew would cheerfully help you to navigate the vessel there. They loathe the brig as much as they dislike you, and would exult in their release, even if it came to their going ashore in irons. Therefore, Captain Broadwater, as you are in no condition to continue the voyage to Rio, I must insist, by virtue of my rights as a passenger, and of the claim that this lady has upon my protection, that you shape your course without any further loss of time for Madeira."

He breathed hard, then raised his fist and brought it down with a mighty whack upon the table. His face was dark with passion, his little eyes reeled as they took me in from head to foot. "Sooner than do what you say," he muttered rather than spoke, "I'd scuttle the ship with these hands," lifting them both, "and send every man-jack of us aboard to the devil." He backed away, as though he meant to walk crab-fashion to the companion-ladder, and on a sudden shouted out, "You've been a-talking with the bo'sun, Mr. Musgrave."

"And what of that?" I responded, in a voice that gave him to know I had lungs enough to outshout him even if occasion should render such a contest needful. "Am I to understand that you refuse to head the ship for Madeira, that Miss Grant and I may go ashore there, and escape the barbarous perils which your treatment of the crew is certain to plunge us into if you persist in continuing this voyage?"

"Yes," he roared, "you are to understand it!—you are to understand it a hundred times over! My instructions are to carry this ship to Rio, and sooner than deviate I'll scuttle her!" and flinging his fist at me, so to speak, with a loud snap of his fingers, he went with a heavy lurching tramp up the ladder, growling out fifty curses in an undertone that reminded me of a dog gnawing a bone, watched by another.

I looked at Miss Grant. "Of all pig-headed varlets! Where," cried I, "could have been my eyes, that I was unable to decipher the old lobster's true nature under his complicated purple skin when I first met him?"

"We are confronted with a difficulty, Mr. Musgrave," she said quietly, mechanically twisting a ring upon her finger, with thoughtful eyes fixed upon it, "and we must look at it calmly, and be patient, and consider what is best to be done. First of all," she continued, "I am quite certain, from the man's manner, that you will never induce him to alter his course for Madeira. And then what follows? Perhaps now that the mate is dead the crew will cease to prove troublesome. Mr. Gordon is a quiet man, and the sailors appear to like him. Mr. Musgrave, I believe if this horrid old captain could only be induced by threats or persuasions to use his men kindly, the voyage might be safely continued."

But, unhappily, peace of mind was not to be obtained by contemplation of merely theoretic conditions, though I heartily admired her cool inspection of a difficulty that surely could not have held less terrors for her than for any other woman without her heart to oppose it. If Broadwater was to be terrified into changing his nature, then no doubt we might reckon upon a comfortable and pleasant passage. But the old swaggerer's qualities clung like limpets to his soul. He was not to be cleansed by any process I was master of, at all events. The only hope that I could find lay in Miss Grant's suggestion that, the mate being dead, the sailors' grievances would be diminished to the extent of the bitter usage he had given them. But the scene on deck that morning had been too significant not to fill me with dark and melancholy misgivings, which were accentuated yet by the feeling that, let me talk as hotly as I would, and threaten as clamorously as I chose, I was practically powerless. I had felt this in the Channel, and I felt it more violently now that we were far out upon the surface of the broad Atlantic, at the disposal of a man whose resolutions there were no means of thwarting, so far as I was concerned, unless indeed I sided with the men, encouraged them to deprive him of the command of the brig, and sailed her myself back to England or to the nearest port, leaving the vindication of my behaviour to the story of cruelty and peril it would be in my power to relate—a romantic project indeed, and to be instantly dismissed!

Chapter XIV
The Sailor's Last Toss

I REMAINED WITH MISS GRANT in the cabin until breakfast was served. Our talk referred to nothing but our situation, as you will suppose. Before long I found my worry and anxiety yielding to the influence of her calm yet animated gaze and clear good sense. Indeed there is no kind of human encouragement that equals the feeling a woman can inspire. The moral help a man will get from the posture and language of a brave girl is so invigorating that it will give his heart a new spirit, though there be the pulse of a lion in its beat.

Whilst we conversed I heard Broadwater talking on deck, and it seemed to me as if he were delivering a harangue; but I gave it little heed, being heartily sick of him and the mutinous disturbances raised by his base old tongue. There was a sound of scrubbing-brushes gritting along upon the deck overhead, with a noise of pumping and of water washing about in the scuppers—assurance, at all events, that the crew were doing the ship's work. This I bade Miss Grant take notice of, being now rendered almost hopeful by the fine cordial influence of her intelligent thoughts and by the inspiriting power of her smiles, her sparkling regard, the music of her voice, the resolution of soul that held her beauty as composed as if she slumbered.

Punctually at six bells—seven o'clock—the cabin-boy arrived with the breakfast, and almost immediately afterwards Broadwater made his appearance. I had got my cue from Miss Grant, who had urged me not to question the man, and above all in conversing with him never to lose my temper; so that we had nearly finished the repast before a single word was uttered by any of the three of us. The captain gobbled as heartily as if all had been well with the ship. In truth, his jaws were so incessantly occupied that they gave him no chance to utter a syllable. Then, having somewhat appeased his appetite, he called for another great cup of black tea, which he fell to stirring meditatively, with an occasional lift of his little eyes to mine.

"I hope, Mr. Musgrave," said he, forcing an odd note of rough jocosity into his deep sea-tones, "that you've sent that there Madeiry scheme of yours adrift. Why, ma'am," he continued, turning to Miss Grant, "if so be as I'm given to onderstand that Rio's your home—and Mr. Grant was a gentleman whose name is very well beknown to me, very well beknown to me indeed—if so be, I says, that Rio's your home, surely, ma'am, you must be in a hurry to get there, and wouldn't thank me for carrying out Mr. Musgrave's proposal to delay the voyage by calling at Madeiry."

"Certainly I am impatient to get to Rio, Captain Broadwater," she answered, with a half glance at me, following on the faintest possible blush rising to her cheeks, and quickly vanishing, as though it were the shadow of a rose lifted to her face and dropped again. "But then it is my impatience that wants me to make *sure* of getting there."

He drained his cup and cried, "Never doubt it, mum. Give me wind enough to blow us along, the rest'll be as easy as swallowing whilks."

This new manner of confidence in him made me say, "The behaviour of the crew, I hope, has improved since sunrise?"

"Mr. Musgrave," he exclaimed, rising, "I have to beg and pray of you, sir, that you'll allow the behaviour of the crew to be *my* business. Judging from the observations you let fall this morning, it's middling plain to me that all that you want is to feel sure that you and the lady'll arrive at Rio. Ontil, then, you've got good cause to be alarmed, you've got no right to tell me what my duty is, how I'm to treat my crew, and what port it's my business to head for!" saying which, he picked up his cap, and buttoning his coat around him, with a ludicrous expression of mingled dignity and self-complacency he went on deck.

A couple of minutes later, not a little to my surprise, Gordon came down the companion-steps and stood a moment at the bottom of them, looking shyly at the table, cap in hand. He tweaked an imaginary lock of hair on his forehead at Miss Grant, and exclaimed, with a nervous laugh, "Rather a novelty for me, Mr. Musgrave, sir, to breakfast 'long with ladies and gents in the land o' knives and forks; but it's the capt'n's orders. He's made me chief mate, and I'm to live down here and take Mr. Bothwell's cabin—when he's out of it," with a look at the stain at his feet.

"We are glad to welcome you aft, Gordon, believe me!" I cried. "Take that seat. Here's the teapot—I don't think Broadwater has emptied it."

He sat clown and fell to his breakfast, and I cannot express to you what a new element of cheerfulness came into the atmosphere of that rude old interior out of this sailor's plain, hearty, honest face and bearing. I was extremely anxious to get the news, for the captain had told me nothing, and asked him if anything fresh had happened on deck since I came below. He replied, subduing his voice, with a heave up of his eyes at the skylight, till nothing but the whites of them showed, that the captain had called the men aft and made them a speech, in which he told them that, if they agreed to go on with their work quietly and give him no more trouble, he would not insist upon their surrendering the half-blood, though the fellow would have to come on deck and share in the general work as heretofore. Of course, on his arrival at Rio, he would report the matter, and leave the rest to the law. That was his duty. He further told the men that Gordon would take the place of Mr. Bothwell, and that he—that is to say, the captain—would stand watch and watch with him for the rest of the voyage, unless, amongst the crew, he should later on discover a man fit to take the duties of second mate, when, if the hands consented, he should be willing to bring him aft. Indeed Gordon told me that Broadwater talked so soberly to the sailors that they stared at him and at one another, as though they suspected some ugly scheme behind this sudden queer shift of face. However it ended in their expressing themselves satisfied; and Gordon particularly noticed that when the watch were turned to wash down, they sprang to the work with the liveliness of people from whom a shadow and a burden have been lifted, whilst the watch below, who went forward to get their breakfast, exhibited every symptom of surprise and gratification.

"But it's all along of your doing, sir," continued the boatswain, still speaking in a voice scarcely raised above a whisper; "it was that there demand of yours that he should carry the ship to Madeiry that worked on the captain. He came up to me in a passion, and asked me what I meant by speaking of Madeiry to you; but cooled down astonishingly rapid, and, after taking a few turns by himself, sung out to me to send the men aft, with the consequence as I've related. A leery old gentleman, sir, but what's happened is bound to be well, providing it ends well."

This sudden change in the captain—though, like a shift of wind, it might mean only a short blow from a new quarter, and then a sweep back into a long howling gale out of the same old wild point—was a thing to feel grateful for, when the afternoon came and brought with it an hour's dead calm—a long wash of muddy swell heaving from the south-east, and running a sluggish jumble of folds, round-browed as domes, with never a ridge in twenty miles of them to break the monotony of the hump-backed procession with the sparkling of a glass-clear head—and then a swift rush of breeze that swept the foam out of the water as it broke with a long cry out of the south-east dinginess, and bowed the brig down to her covering-board. Broadwater was ready for it. The topgallant-sails had been furled, the mainsail snugged to its yard, some fore-and-aft canvas (no need to be too particular) hauled down, and the topsails were blowing out from the yards on the caps with the reef-tackles hauled out, and hands dancing aloft to knot the points, when the first of the weather rang between our masts. It was not a moment when one wanted to think there was a mutiny aboard. Broadwater helped the man at the wheel to put the helm hard-a-weather, and to the long wash of the Atlantic swell foaming to the sudden scourging of the wind, with the sail swelling from the foretop-sail-yard, the foresail yearning high as though it would fly into the rush of shadows overhead, hands chorusing upon the main, with Gordon's figure at the weather yard-arm coming out clean as a pencil-drawing against the soft dark race past him, the half-blood Charles swinging upon the Flemish horse at his feet, the other fellows ranged along with many a kick-up abaft of the foot-ropes as they plunged to the reef-points curving out of reach as the line of the band arched to the slings and quarters—the brig, responding to her helm and to the heavy leeward drag of her big thunderous jib, gave her quarter to the tempestuous outfly, and went with long seething rolls through it like a sleigh over falls and risings of snow.

It was blowing so hard presently that they found the reefed forecourse and topsails with a stay-foresail and a fragment of trysail as much as the vessel could carry; and before long there was a plentiful washing of water forward, for she lay now as close to her course as she would come, and the ridged seas foaming on top of the backs of the swell brimmed with a roar to the bow under the larboard cathead, where they rose in a dazzle of white water, then tumbling inboard with the clatter of twenty tons of shingle, and floating coils of the running rigging up amongst the legs of the men, and converting locomotion in the waist into sheer floundering. The men worked briskly and with a will; indeed I accepted this burst of weather as a stroke of Providence, designed to rally the minds of the crew to their strict business of seafaring, and to bring old Broadwater to recognition of the value of willing sailors in the navigation of a ship—considerations which appeared to have fallen asleep in the tender breezes that had fanned us out of the Bay, under clear skies by day and sparkling constellations by night, down to the latitude and longitude our keel was now traversing. Certain it was this half gale—for it came to that—was dead in the road of Madeira; indeed the brig could not have looked up for the island to within six points; and me-thought as I stood near Broadwater, whilst the crew were on the foretopsail-yard, that he turned his eyes from the foaming windward sea-board to me, as if he would say, "You see what chance your Madeiry scheme would have *now*."

This was really the first bit of hard weather we had yet encountered. The brig proved a wetter craft than I should have imagined, though she rose buoyant to each long frothing hill of brine, with a slant of her spars and a shear of her cut-water that made you think she had more of the clipper instincts in her than the mind of her builder had included in his model. But it was dreary, weary work—the air on deck wet with spray and surging down upon you in volumes that often forced you to turn your back upon it to fetch a breath, a melancholy clattering of spare booms forward, the scream and smoke of water hissing inboards through the scupper-holes, and then draining away through the same apertures in long lamentable sobbings, the shrill whistling of the gale splitting upon the curve of the grey ropes, the quick roar of it as it flung as with a sound of cannon from under the foot of the arched canvas to the weather roll of the masts; whilst below it was dismaller yet, bulkheads creaking, cabin-doors ticking like gigantic clocks upon their hooks and hinges to the regular swaying, groanings of strained cargo in the hold, and such a tumblefication of deck, that having once fairly brought up on a locker you loathed the obligation of leaving it.

The storm-shrouded day howled itself steadfastly onwards into the blackness of night, when the scene of commotion took a new character of wildness from the swarmings of sea-fire in the curl of each dark summit, and in the soft sheet-lightning-like flashes of the phosphor flying with the water through our rigging. But though it was a time of discomfort, it was a time of comparative ease, too, for it blew all thoughts of mutiny out of one's head. Recollections of tragedy, anxiety, and distress seemed to have been washed overboard by the first sea the brig shipped; and Miss Grant said to me that she would be glad never to see a sunlit day nor a placid night of moonshine again during the rest of the voyage, providing the *Iron Crown* continued to stem fairly onwards for Rio, and the men remained quiet, and Broadwater too occupied by the weather to bluster and bully as of old.

I confess I had forgotten all about the dead mate, when on returning from a short look round on deck at about half-past ten—Miss Grant having withdrawn to her berth an hour before—I saw Gordon and the cabin-boy staggering out of one of the foremost cabins, bearing between them a long white bundle. I asked the boatswain what it was, and he answered, "The body of the mate, sir." The thing, bolster-shape, was stitched up in sailcloth, and more ghastly, maybe, to the imagination for lacking suggestion of human outline.

"What are you going to do with it?" I asked.

"Heave it overboard, sir," answered Gordon.

I might have suspected as much; yet I could not make sure that Broadwater would have dismissed the remains of his factotum without a benediction.

"The capt'n wouldn't trust the handling of him to any of the people forward," said Gordon, "nor bury him by daylight under their noses. I reckon he's right. This here," said he, with a look at the burden, at one end of which he swayed whilst the cabin-boy staggered at the other, but without the pale consternation in his face that would have shown in it had the captain been his assistant, "is still as a red rag to more than one pair of horns which have sprouted aboard us of late days. Steady, my lad! Slew round now! I'll go back'ards up the steps, and don't you pull!"

The brig rolled so heavily that I expected every moment to see the boatswain plump down with his ghastly burthen and overset the boy. They managed to get it on deck however without mishap, and following, I watched them from over the edge of the companion-hatch swing the white thing with a low growling *one, two,* THREE! from Gordon, and send it with a flash like any one of the sheets of milk-white foam bursting over the weather-rail into the dark waters beyond. The sailor's last toss! I thought, as I re-entered the cabin; and whose child had been that negro-headed, handsome-featured fellow? The wolfish yell of the wind high aloft swept to the black orifice of the hatchway as an answer to the question, and no icy blast could have struck such a shudder through me as the chill that trembled from my hair to my feet to the sudden lighting of my eyes upon the mahogany-like stain upon the cabin-deck. One thing on top of another, 'twas almost enough to make a man feel sorry for the murdered wretch. If ever a creature was charged to the gorge with all qualities which go to the making of a romantic scoundrel, this same Neil Bothwell had been. Maybe he was born a little too late; for the paddle-wheel, if not the propeller, was even now scooping up all idealism out of the sea. If the black flag were not actually hauled down, it was on its way to the locker, there to moulder; the Corsair had buried his Medora, and gone to the Isles of Greece to slink out, oily and filthy, upon the sleepy Turk, or the humming Sicilian. The slaver alone was active. Yet I never can recall Mr. Bothwell's woolly head, his chiselled features, white teeth, and nimble, sparkling eyes, along with the dark brutality of his nature, his piratical voice and venomous language, without feeling persuaded that the knife of the half-blood had cut short a career which, in its continuance, despite the crimson cross and the grinning teeth of the British frigate, must have supplied the naval writer with many fruitful and astonishing themes.

That miserable stain made the atmosphere of the cabin feel as bleak as a vault on a December night; and though we were supposed to be in warm parallels, I could not have snugged me in my blankets with heartier relish of the clinging comfort of them had the gale been splitting upon frozen rigging, and the blackness upon the sea dashed with the iceberg's spectral tinge of faintness.

This dirty weather troubled us for four days. It seemed to have blown the ocean clear of ships and birds, for we sighted nothing, whether winged with canvas or feathers. All day long 'twas the same steadfast rush of the surge, green as bottle-glass, freckled with the foam flying from the champing courser in advance, lifting a head of melting white to the sullen slate of the shadow overlaying the sky; with once—it was on the second evening—a fierce sunset of smoking crimson, red spokes of a dingy brightness cleaving the black scud and the boiling, angry haze of the west, and touching the unmirroring welter into spaces of a rusty blood-like colour, as though—and the fancy was Miss Grant's— each beam of coarse effulgence were a material weapon darted by some mighty hand on high, and making the ocean bleed to the thrust; followed by a sort of melting out of the sun into a brief, shapeless running as of molten ore low upon the sea-line, where the billows leapt black against it; till the gale, like some baffled, sentient thing, stormed up afresh with a long victorious yelling in its western flight, crowding cloud upon cloud there with such rapid smothering of the tarnished hectic, that in a few moments you knew not where to look for the place behind which the luminary had foundered.

Then followed several days of fair weather, and if it had not been for a lurking feeling of uneasiness, a sense of trouble impending, I believe I should have found enjoyment enough in this time to fully compensate me for the worries and anxieties I had suffered. For three successive days a pleasant wind from the north and east blew almost directly over our stern; and the brig, with studding-sails overhanging the water far out on either side of her, and soothingly cradled by a subdued heave of liquid fold, as regular as a pulse, and soft as the rise and fall of a sleeper's breast, floated steadily on her course, irradiating the blue of the surge with silver reflection from her extended canvas, whilst the short wake streamed off white as a looking-glass, as though indeed the lines of dark ripples breaking from the bow shivered spaces of the translucent sheen under the swinging booms into fragments, which veering aft occasioned the lovely metallic shining which you noticed in the furrow under the counter. Already from the slope of the rolling brows of dark blue brine the flying-fish were whisking in short, uncertain flights; the swinish outline of the porpoise rose black and wet to the flash of the sun; afar the snow-white spire of a ship's canvas would break the melancholy continuity of the sea-line. Our shadows shortened at noon, and so fair was the course we headed that the eye had almost the accuracy of the sextant in determining the period of the meridian, by observing the wake of the luminary rising and falling in a fan-shaped stream of gold transversely from the horizon to our larboard cathead.

One scarcely needed the comforts of the pleasure vessel to have found it all as full of such delights as go to a yachting cruise, if the rest had been as well as sea and sky and atmosphere. But, first of all, there was Captain Broadwater again. Now that the dirty sky had been blown away, and the shrill dark gale transformed into a steady gushing of fair blue sunlit breeze, warm as a woman's breath, and filled with the aroma of a thousand leagues of ocean, the reckless old man had warped his mind back to its old moorings, and was once more falling foul of the men, often as I would think without reason, or, when justified, then always with coarse and needless temper. But that was not all. The half-blood Charles was about the deck—for I must tell you, now that we were regularly at sea it was "all hands," as the term goes, from eight bells in the morning down to four o'clock in the afternoon, with an interval of an hour from half-past eleven for dinner; and consequently it was impossible to put your head through the companion-hatch without, after a bit, seeing the half-blood at work, sometimes on the rigging, sometimes with a marline-spike on deck, but most often stitching at sailcloth stretched along the waist. It was not only the knowing that he was a murderer that regularly affected me with a violent stir of emotion every time my eye lighted on him, though I should see him twenty times in a day; it was the shock also, at least to my notion of shipboard discipline, to the marine habits of thought I had carried away with me from my early voyagings, coming from perception of his being at large, when without doubt he should be in irons below, and of the liberty he was now enjoying being the will of the crew. My abhorrence of Broadwater's early usage of him could in nowise temper my loathing of the olive-coloured dastard's act. Of course, the crime of which the fellow had been guilty might well make one suspect a deeper significance in every action, gesture, and speech of his than they in reality possessed; but sometimes, in watching him furtively over the top of a book, or whilst conversing with Miss Grant, when he was not too far off for his features to be inexpressive, I would get it into my head that if ever the swift, askant glance of a human eye indicated treachery and black resolution, matured and waiting only, his did whenever Broadwater's approach courted a glance from under his dusky, drooping lids at the old fellow. I reasoned thus: I said to myself, this man being guilty of murder, albeit he has his freedom in the brig—the liberty of a bird in a cage!—is fully aware that the gallows awaits him on his arrival in port, and that the person who will make it his especial business to procure his prompt despatch is that same red-faced, hectoring, noisy, and tyrannous skipper, at whom, when he imagines himself unperceived, he darts as malignant a glance as ever I witnessed in mortal eyes. What then! Is it reasonable to suppose that yonder half-blood intends to resignedly suffer himself to be carried to Rio, and on the testimony of the depositions of that shipmaster there, whom he abhors, to suffer with his life for his deed? Then I would say to myself, But what is he to do? Certainly he cannot prevent the master from navigating the brig to her South American destination. Does he contemplate suicide as his only chance of escaping the executioner? He is under the protection of the crew; has he any influence with them? Assuming that he has, what use can he make of it? Thus would I sometimes speculate, idly indeed; yet the thoughts that occurred to me were of a kind to rob the smooth ocean of its placidity, and the gay picture of the brig, brilliant with the serene splendour of the heavens, of something of its beauty.

However, I kept my thoughts to myself. I took care that Miss Grant should have no suspicion of what was passing in my mind, nor did I utter a word on the subject to Gordon, mainly because I felt the whole thing was mere foreboding, and that discussion of it could therefore serve no end.

Chapter XV
We Sail Through a Strange Light

I REMEMBER IT WAS ON the third night of this gentle weather that I was quietly walking up and down the deck with Miss Grant's hand lying lightly on my arm. Four bells had not been long struck. The night was dark, but exceedingly beautiful, with a tropical richness of starlight that yet, though to the eye it showed like a wide fine rain of silver light, suffered the sea to heave black to the confines of the hovering firmament—not a break or glance of foam anywhere, not the tiniest sparkle of the sea-glow, albeit with my companion I had overhung the quarter for many minutes to watch for any greenish cloudy rising, any yellow fibrous shooting; for of all oceanic midnight sights nothing delights me so keenly as the movement of phosphoric swarmings in the quiet ebon brine, when the vessel has just way enough to stir the liquid blackness into shining configurations of all sorts along her sides, and to mark her passage by a jewel-like trailing of luminous bells of foam, and the emerald glare of misty puffs of fire. The brig, with studding-sails out on either side, was floating through the shadow of the night at some four or five miles in the hour. Her wide stretch of canvas rose pallid to the gloom, and died upon the eye in mere films and spaces of faintness ere the sight could penetrate to the forms of the little sails which crowned the stone-coloured pyramid. All was silent—every cloth aloft was asleep. Under the black arches of the distended canvas the stars would come and go to the movement of the fabric , like eyes of invisible shapes, peering an instant over the edge of the yards down upon the dim glimmer of the brig's decks. Gordon was in charge. I had killed half-an-hour some time before with him in talk, but when Miss Grant arrived I paired off with her, and left my hearty friend to fill the interval betwixt the wheel and the main-rigging with lonely meditations.

I do not mind owning here, that on such a night as this it was not very easy to check in myself something of those sentimental thoughts concerning my fascinating companion which had bothered me, as I have elsewhere said, at an earlier date, and which no doubt would have continued to worry and vex me down to this hour, but for the murder of the mate and the posture of the crew. The quiet weather, and the apparent peace in the brig during the last three days, had enabled us to be much together on deck again, and to converse on subjects of a kind very different from assassination on shipboard, and the perils of passengers in vessels worked by mutinous sailors. Indeed, the long and short of it is, as we stepped the deck together this night, I felt that if our voyage to Rio should be long delayed, it must infallibly end in my falling in love with Miss Aurelia. It would not do to call the emotion a disloyalty to my cousin. What must happen cannot be helped, and there is nothing in philosophy to balk the issue, though it may teach one how to support it. The utmost I could hope to do was to disguise my feelings, quit Rio as promptly as the shipping there would suffer, and leave the rest to old Time with his brush and whitewash. Still the position was an exceedingly uncomfortable one, and it was likely to endure long enough to render me very unhappy. For in those days I was a young man with the heart and sensibilities of youth; and to fall in love with a woman who was betrothed to another; to find my happiness subtly sneaking away, and making its existence dependent upon conditions which never could be fulfilled; to feel moreover that the emotions, which it was not in my power to suppress, were in a sense unfair to the girl—though I must always maintain that the highest compliment a man can pay a woman is to fall in love with her—whilst they were dishonouring to myself in my existing relations with my cousin, was to place myself, without being able to help it, in a position so immediately distressful as to threaten by and by to become distracting. The worst of it was that, whilst I would wish the voyage over, my conscience was sensible that the desire was nonsense, and that I was in no hurry. To be sure it would be with no common delight that I should part with Captain Broadwater and his odious dinner-table, and take an eternal farewell of a ship's company of whose behaviour it was impossible to make sure from one hour's end to another; but already—already! though Miss Grant and I had been together for a fortnight only—the prospect of turning my back upon her, of saying good-bye to her at Rio, of sailing away and feeling that all I had done was to undergo the miseries of a long voyage merely to hand over the handsomest woman that I had ever met in my life—the only girl moreover I had ever encountered to whom I could have given every bit of my heart—I say, the prospect of this was all so very distasteful to me, that when I came to look into myself I was not at all astonished to find I was secretly willing that this voyage to Rio should continue, at all risks, to a period that might be indeterminable, sooner than sunder my association with the lovely and engaging girl whom my abominably thoughtless cousin had asked me to take charge of.

But these were my thoughts only. It was not to be supposed that she would have the least suspicion of what was passing in my mind. There was nothing of the coquette in her; no capacity of courting admiration for the mere selfish pleasure of enjoying it. As she walked by my side, the warm fragrance of her on the atmosphere, her face white to the star-shine with the sparkles of it in her eyes, I had very little doubt, believe me, that, had she guessed at the thoughts which had my heart in tow, she would have rapidly made shift to conquer the floating movements of the deck without the support of my arm upon which her left hand now rested. Upon my word, the cruellest of all women—not the more forgivable because she is unconsciously cruel—is the girl who, knowing that she is beautiful, acts without perception of the magic and influence of her graces. Fortunately for the peace of men, such women are rare. But Miss Aurelia Grant was one of them; and, though the more intimate our association was the more, in one sense, and in a mean sense I am afraid, I enjoyed it; yet she could never touch my hand, bend her fire-impassioned eyes upon mine, incline her stately figure to me with the gracious, maidenly familiarity of a girl in the society of a man whom she values as a friend, without a sort of wild odd regret in me that Nature, in making her beautiful, had not also dowered her with the capacity of appreciating the significance of beauty's most artless provocation. But then the Spanish blood would account for much in her that was as teasing as it was delightful.

Now, as we quietly moved from one end of the deck to the other, there happened so strange a thing, that the like of it in these parallels, at all events, has, to my knowledge, been witnessed once only. We had been chatting as soberly as though we were uncle and niece: not the lightest of the inspirations of this most glorious night coming out of it to tincture our words or thoughts into any complexion of romance, though never might a scene of starlit gloom furnish a young fellow, already rendered sentimental enough, with a better excuse for frequent poetical flight than this in whose shadow I paced with Miss Aurelia, her ungloved hand (with the gleam, by the way, of an engaged ring meeting my eye each time I looked down) lying white as a flake of sea-foam in the bight of my arm. I was talking about old Broadwater, and expressed my wonder that he should be able to accommodate his love of rum and his taste for "all night in," as they say at sea, with the obligation he had imposed upon himself of taking Bothwell's place.

"Spite of his many shortcomings," she exclaimed, "I should think he is too experienced a sailor, too much a seaman by habit not to be vigilant during his watch."

"Oh," said I, "I don't doubt that he keeps a bright look-out when his turn to take charge comes round. What I mean is, it is odd that he should not have chosen some one from amongst the men forward to act as second mate, Gordon now being first, for then he would be able to go to bed drunk as usual, with plenty of time to sleep off the fumes; but the long and short of it is," I added, "there's no living creature in this forecastle to whom he durst confide his ship."

As I said this, I heard my name called, apparently from the forecastle. We were at that moment close to the wheel, and in the act of returning to measure the length of deck afresh. I was not a little surprised to hear myself hailed from so remote a part of the brig, and as I had not recognized the voice, I sang out, "Who wants me there?"

"Me, sir—the mate," came the answer from the bows; "will you and the lady please step this way?"

I asked Miss Grant if she would accompany me, thinking that she might be a little shy, and very reasonably shy, too, under the circumstances, of that part of the vessel.

"Certainly," she answered promptly. We had to move with caution. The pile of canvas that clothed the brig from truck to waterway deepened the midnight obscurity of the deck, and though it was plain sailing where we had been walking, yet, once abreast of the mainmast, one had to keep a sharp look-out, by groping, for the harness-cask, scuttle-butts, coils of rigging, pump-handles, and other matters which lay between the point where the quarter-deck began and where the brig's forecastle ended. I called out, "On which side are you, Mr. Gordon?" wondering why he wanted us, and what had carried him away from his post aft.

"On the starboard bow, sir," he rejoined; "mind the fluke of the stowed anchor as ye come along! I'm just forrard of it."

I held Miss Grant's hand, walking in front of her. The galley was locked up for the night; there was not the faintest gleam of light anywhere visible, if it were not a sort of ghostly sheen lurking like a churchyard exhalation over the fore-scuttle, from the slush lamp, as I presumed, swinging in the sailors' sea-parlour below. Indeed I was so engrossed by the occupation of picking my way, that I saw nothing until I was fairly alongside of Gordon, who pointed, with a long shadowy arm, the fingers at the end of which showed like a giant's against the stars, over the horizon, and exclaimed, "Mr. Musgrave, sir, saw any man ever the like o' that? What can it be?"

He held his arm levelled, and following its indication I saw, right ahead of the ship, standing apparently upon the ocean at the distance of the horizon, an arch of light, or rather, let me say, a shape of dim white radiance, that arched in perfect outline from one leg to another that appeared to rest upon the black surface of the deep to within three or four degrees of the sea-line, as though its foot had broken away. There is nothing so deceptive as distance at sea. The light, when I first saw it, might have been within gunshot, or it might have been a couple of leagues away from us. The radiance had the tint of moonshine, and was as visibly defined upon the velvet dusk as though painted there by the sweep of a brush dipped in white fire. You saw the stars shining close against the rim of it, all round and under the arch of it, where they sparkled like the riding-lights of ships.

"What is it, Mr. Musgrave?" exclaimed Gordon, in the voice of a man not only awed, but even alarmed.

"I wish I could tell you," said I. "It looks like the fiery trail of a comet that has swept in an arc from behind the sea, and gone to pieces in the blackness before it had perfected the semi-circle."

"We are steering directly for it!" exclaimed Miss Grant.

The watch on deck, disturbed in the naps they were taking in secret corners by Gordon's call to me, had collected near us, and you heard the growling of their voices as they pointed ahead, marvelling, as we did, one to another, at the startling, beautiful, radiant appearance. I heard one say, "Jim, it's a sort of vast compreesant. There's no luck for the vessel as sights them shows."

Another said, "If we are to sail through it, stand by! The likes of them lights, I've heerd, strikes men green if they smites 'em full."

"What in thunder can it be?" repeated Gordon; "'tain't anything burning out there, is it? How fur do it stretch? Can any man tell? Looks to me to be a-widening."

One of the shadowy group beside me exclaimed, "Job is to know how fur off it lies. I allow there's all ten mile between them legs."

"Vast there!" cried another, "ten mile! I'll swap my chest agin your Scotch cap afore eight bells this blooming night if them legs is a mile wide."

"I'll go aft and report it to the captain," said Gordon, in a voice that betrayed the agitation he was labouring under. "Never see'd the like of such a thing in all my time. Beats all my going a-fishing, sir. Why, it's a object that ain't in nature; and if we don't give it a wide berth it'll be a bad look-out for some of us, or I wasn't christened Zana!" And apparently as much subdued as if he had seen a ghost, or heard some spectral voice up in the air bidding him prepare for his end, he slunk away from our side, and vanished in the darkness as he made his way to the cabin.

When he was gone a deep silence fell. The men ceased to speak: Miss Grant and I gazed without exchanging a syllable: nothing was to be heard but the soft shearing of the cutwater beneath us, rending the liquid indigo with the noise as of the tearing of satin. The blackness under the bows was profound—not a sparkle of phosphor to catch the eye, not the sickliest flake of starshine to express the invisible heave of the deep by the wire-like widening of it to the movement. I looked behind me at the towering canvas on the foremast, and found a strange solemnity in the visionary beauty of the silent, swelling, airy concavities mounting in pale vague surfaces into the stooping dusk; but whether near or distant, the mystic arch of light ahead threw not the feeblest gleam upon that soaring surface that spectrally dilated on either hand to the pinions of the studding-sails which faded into a hovering faintness far beyond the sides. The mysterious sheen to our approach seemed to gather a quicker tincture of lustre, as of the diamond, or some clear glittering star. It is impossible to express the startling loveliness of this apparition of luminous arch against the midnight sky, with the stars shining down to its rim, and spangling the hollow to the sea-line within. 'Twas as though God's hand had set up a sign in the sky for us to behold; and the men now were so dumb in the face of it, that you easily guessed how impressed and awed they were. Most of the watch below had come up to have a look, but each newcomer's first murmur of wonder speedily died in the hush that was upon the others.

"What is it, do you think, Mr. Musgrave?" said Miss Grant, in a voice a little above a whisper.

"Were we far north or south," I replied, "one would make it intelligible by reference to the Northern Lights or to the magnificent display of the Aurora Australis, with its sudden pale flashings and spiral coruscations. No doubt yonder beautiful object is something of the kind, electric—phosphoric—call it what you will. But is it not worth seeing? Why, one would sail round the world even with old Broadwater for such possession of memory as that glorious span will yield!"

"It will fill these poor fellows with superstitious fancies," she said, speaking very softly. "Did you hear one of them say that people who sail through such things are struck green?"

I could not help laughing, and said, "Yes; but it is possible to be green without passing through such an arch as that. If these sailors, now, were Roman Catholics after the type of the mariners of Columbus's day, they would be on their knees chanting litanies, and making the air melodious with their *Salve Regina*'s. But is not superstition excusable amongst seamen? Look at that wonderful sight, Miss Grant. Imagine yourself run backwards by the stream of time three hundred years—before the scientific man had broken loose, when the world was bare of problem-solvers, when all interpretation was deliciously romantic and tenderly poetical. What then would you think of such a sight as that! It would be no mere phosphoric or electric arch. No, no; but some paradisiacal bridge of ethereal crystal, such as St. John may have gazed upon without having recorded it; and be sure that your young-eyed imagination, fired by sheer ecstasy of superstition, would readily discern the forms of angelic beings with wings of pearly light, and raiment as lustrous as a moonbeam, flitting along it to the stars upon which its unfinished end to the left there seems to rest."

I merely talked thus to provoke her, delighting in the high moods which even such idle stuff as this would induce in her. But unfortunately it was not only that we were not alone; I had scarcely made an end, when old Broadwater, followed by Gordon, rolled floundering and tumbling on to the forecastle. He came and stood close against me, puffing and blowing in such a manner that my nose was a long way ahead of my ears in detecting that if he was not actually drunk he must have turned in very well primed. He stared for some moments in silence, breathing hard, and then burst out, "Well, boil me alive, if ever I seed the likes of that! 'Tain't fire, neither. What do *you* call it, Mr. Gordon?"

"Got no idea, sir," answered the mate, speaking as before with a note of awe and depression in his voice. "Shall we shift the helm while there's time? It looks close aboard now, and we shall be into it if we don't mind."

"Shift the hellum!" cried Broadwater. "What for? D'ye think it's land, man? Why, what else is it but what they calls a luminous fog? And who's going to diwerge for a thickness you can see through?"

Some man said, "That there's no luminous fog, master. It's a big, strike-me-blind compreesant. Look out! It may foul our mast-heads as we pass under it, and who's to know that we shall ever be heard of arterwards?"

Broadwater, who had been peering hard into my face, seemed on a sudden to distinguish me, and without apparently heeding the man who had spoken, exclaimed, "Hope you're enjoying of it, Mr. Musgrave. 'Tain't often a sight like that's chucked in for naught in a voyage to Rio."

"Am I to shift the helm, sir?" said Gordon.

"Certainly not!" roared the old fellow, "didn't ye hear me say so just now? Cook me alive, Mr. Musgrave, if sailors be men fit even to make soldiers of! Diwerge because there's a lunar rainbow in the road!" He seemed to be struck by his own fancy. "It's a lunar rainbow," he shouted, "one of the finest I ever see."

"Where's the moon to make him?" said a voice.

"Keep all on as ye are, Mr. Gordon; all on as ye are!" said Broadwater, with an ominous growl in his tones, that was like an intimation to the little company of shadows standing near him to hold their peace. "Steady as she goes, sir!" And so saying he staggered away from the rail, and went swinging towards the quarter-deck, singing out to the helmsman as he went, "Steady as she goes, my man! Steady as she goes!"

We had neared the shining appearance so rapidly, that I suspected it must have been very much closer to us when first sighted than we had imagined. It cast no reflection upon the dark waters under it, nor sheen upon the air beyond the line of its own irradiation, as you saw by the shine of the stars close down upon it. As we were under a steady helm, it soon became plain that the sparkling arch was slowly trending to larboard. When it first showed out, our jib-booms seemed to point fair for the centre of it, whereas now the right leg had drawn on to our starboard bow. The obscurity seemed the blacker for that light. I'd look aloft and around, wondering that no illumination came from the mystical burning to touch the sails, or to put a sparkle into the eyes of the staring men. They were grumbling freely, swearing that nothing but ill-luck could attend our passage through the luminous thing, and heaping curses upon the captain for his drunken obstinacy. Gordon had followed Broadwater on to the quarter-deck, but Miss Grant and I held our place against the forecastle-rail. Within half-an-hour of the object heaving into view, we were close upon it. Even when our flying jib-boom end was silvered by contact with the luminosity, the jibs themselves hung black as thunderclouds against the shining. I had just time to note the wondrous sweep of this mighty arch, extending like a vast hueless rainbow into the clear obscure, when the light was all about us. I begged my companion to look aft; the spectacle was incomparable for splendour and shadow, heightened by the elements of mystery and fear. The swelling sails at the fore—studding-sail upon studding-sail to the topgallant yard-arm, and white cloths rounding and rising from forecourse to crowning royal—leapt into spaces of bland, almost milk-white light to the touch of this atmospheric radiance, and floated gleaming whilst the rest of the brig from the fore-rigging lay black and buried; but very swiftly the whole vessel leapt into this midnight effulgent vision, and no searching moonlight could have offered a clearer view of her. Every man's shadow swung at his feet; the atmosphere was a wide white gushing; the very trucks at the lofty mastheads shone out with the dull light of frosty silver buttons. Aft, upon the quarter-deck, you saw the motionless dark figures of Broadwater and the mate, standing as though this mystical illumination possessed some hellish quality that had blasted them into stirlessness. The fellow at the wheel gripped the spokes without a move in his posture that seemed to me full of terror and awe. Many of the crew, whilst our jib-boom was yet penetrating this burning mist, and whilst the forecastle still lay in blackness, had jumped below with sharp cries of alarm, warning one another to beware of the light, that it turned the flesh green, that it was fatal to those it shone on, and the like. But a few men lingered, though when the brig was fair in the radiance I marked them in cowering attitudes, one stooping low at the windlass end, another crouching with his arms against his forehead, a third in a posture of recoil at the heel of the bowsprit, as I have seen people terror-stricken by a sudden dazzling flash of lightning. The heave of the sea was like the swelling of a sheet of silver. But in less than three minutes, as nearly as I could calculate, I marked the jib-boom and jibs turn black, then the forecastle stole into the midnight again, and preternatural beyond expression was the spectacle of the swelling canvas, bright for a breath to us who stood in blackness, then vanishing upon the sight as though the whole fabric had been formed of star-lighted mist that had melted on a sudden. In a few minutes the brig was once more sailing along in darkness, and the glorious arch was over her stern, with what was now its left limb, viewing it from the forecastle, veering away upon our larboard quarter.

Chapter XVI
Broadwater's Proposal

HAD WE BEEN A large ship full of passengers, such an astonishing sight as a silver arch, self-luminous, yet without power to pale the close-lying stars, with overflow of its sheen, spanning a space of the midnight waters and resembling nothing, as I then supposed, ever seen south of the polar verge of the temperate parallels north of the equator, would have given us enough to talk about to serve to the end of the voyage. But wonderment is brief when its sphere of diffusion is slender. Miss Grant and I talked the subject out promptly, and then there was nobody left to say more about it. Broadwater, it is true, at breakfast next morning persisted in declaring that it was a lunar rainbow; though, had he stuck to his first notion that it was a luminous mist, I am not sure that his guess would have been far out.

"How are you going to get a lunar rainbow without the moon?" I said.

"Who says that it *is* to be got?" he answered. "The moon's always somewheres about, I suppose; and why shouldn't she be able to chuck one of them appearances upon the sky when she's out of sight, just as she do when she's within view of the eye? There's no call for her to be overhead for shows of that kind to happen. I once see a beautiful rainbow, right over our mastheads, a full half-hour after the sun had gone down. You may depend upon it that there arch last night was a lunar rainbow."

I liked him too little to argue with him, lover as I am of the absurd ideas of stupid, prejudiced, ignorant old sailors. Besides, the thing was a phenomenon not to be explained by anybody aboard that brig at all events, and to be accepted therefore as one of the many thrilling and beautiful mysteries of old ocean's sombre or sunlit solitudes.

I was not however a little surprised to find that what I had deemed the mere passing depressing influence of the apparition upon the spirits of Gordon continued to weigh upon him. This was made apparent when Broadwater, after favouring us with his views on the subject of lunar rainbows and other atmospheric effects, most of which were no doubt coloured by the bottle of rum through which he had inspected them, went on deck that the mate might get his breakfast.

"Have any of the hands turned green since last night, Mr. Gordon?" said I.

"No, sir," he answered. "Most of 'em jumped below, I hear; t'others dodged the sheen. They reckoned upon some of them showing blighted though when daylight came along; and if the watch had turned out blue, let alone *green*, hang me, Mr. Musgrave!" he exclaimed, hitting the table with the handle of his knife to emphasize his language, "if I for one should have been surprised, for never did a more scaring sight arise before the eyes of a sailor."

His subdued and dejected manner was more striking than his words. I glanced at Miss Grant, whose fine eyes, full of thought, were fastened upon his face.

"The fancy amongst the men," she exclaimed, "must have arisen from the old belief that the shining of the moon full on the face of a sleeper distorts the features, and puts an ugly colour into the complexion. The arch looked like moonshine, and I suppose the sight made the men so nervous that it was enough for one of them to hint at anything alarming to terrify the whole."

"I wish I'd never seen it," he exclaimed; "it's done me no good, miss."

"But surely," cried I, wondering at him, for his had always seemed to me as prosaic a mind as ever I met with in a sailor—nor could I forget his ridicule of the superstitious craze of the man who had drowned himself in the English Channel—"you do not want yourself to believe that there is anything in a mere body of luminous vapour, to call it so, to hurt or influence you, either in body or mind?"

He shook his head very despondently: I observed that he ate little, though he drank a quantity of tea, thirstily and feverishly. "I'm a poor man, sir," he exclaimed, "but, so help me Heaven, Mr. Musgrave, I'd gladly have parted with every shilling of my savings sooner than that the capt'n should have headed the brig slick into that shining. Beg your pardon, miss," he continued, addressing Miss Grant with a sudden eagerness, "but when ye entered that light did it feel cold to ye?"

"No," she answered, without exhibiting surprise at the question.

"You, Mr. Musgrave—did it feel chilly like? not so much upon your skin as here?" and he put his hand to his heart.

"The only sensation I can recollect," I answered, "is one of delight at the glorious picture the brig made, as she slowly floated into the radiance out of the blackness, coating herself with the quicksilver of it from the truck to the end of the swinging boom."

He was silent, then shook his head, and exclaimed: "Well, mere fancy, no doubt. It's all fancy in this here world. Without imagination there'd be nothing to hope for, nothing to be afraid of."

"There might have been a chill in the light, though we enjoyed the picture too much to be conscious of it," said Miss Grant, talking to me though speaking at Gordon.

"The strangest part of it was this, miss," he said, looking at her earnestly, "I felt it was cold afore we entered it. 'Twas that which made me so earnest the capt'n should shift the hellum. I knew so soon as ever I came in contact with that light the bleakness of it would catch me here," again putting his hand to his heart, "and I'd have given all I'm worth— all I'm worth," the poor fellow cried, with a vehemence unusual in him, "to have escaped it. Up to the moment when the light had slided within a foot of me I'd no sensation but the fear of what was a coming; but the moment it touched me I felt the chill. There was death in it, sir, there was death in it! No man'll ever persuade me contrary-wise."

He checked what I was about to say by rising with an apologetic glance at the skylight, to let us know he could linger no longer, and immediately went on deck.

I had so much faith in the steadiness of Gordon's intellect that I could only accept this odd posture in him as due to some trifling functional derangement, which a dose of physic or a few hours' rest would correct. Yet it gave Miss Grant and me something to talk about. I had some knowledge of sailors and their superstitions, and kept her amused for an hour or two with stories of wizards of Finnish origin, who sold favourable gales of wind to credulous mariners; of bald human heads, with little laughing black eyes and capacious grinning mouths, rising to the surface, and terrifying Jack by asking questions in a tongue unknown to any nation under the stars, and then disappearing with a shriek of derisive laughter; of ghostly shapes alighting on the yardarms, and kindling corpse-lights there, by whose dismal illumination the mariner could see phantom faces glimmering out into expressions of sorrow and remorse, as though grieving over the fateful missions on which they had been despatched.

However, though I had no sympathy with the queer notions which had come into Gordon's head, my own misgivings were of a kind which might very well have passed for a sort of superstition too, for they kept me incessantly foreboding disaster, though what form it was to take I never could have imagined; and so, as you will see, the mate's despondency in its way was no more deserving of ridicule than mine. First of all, I was more troubled than I was perhaps conscious of by the recollection of the murder that had been committed. It worried me mostly of nights; again and again in the darkness of my cabin, and in the silence of the long watches, when the brig was sailing smoothly forwards, and

all was still upon the sea, when nothing broke upon the ear but the muffled washing of water outside, and the faint jar and creak of the fabric
within, the vision of the mate as I saw him when he stood at the foot of
the companion-steps with the grin of death in his moving and speechless
lips, his right hand extended, his left hand dabbling in his shirt that was
soaked, where his fingers pressed, with the life-blood draining from his
heart, would rise before me horribly distinct, and keep me rolling and
tumbling in my bunk, till more than once it ended in my jumping up,
lighting the lamp, and clothing myself, and killing a couple of sleepless
hours with pipes of tobacco and a drain or two from the private stock
in the next cabin. Then again, as I have before said, it was a cause of no
small consternation to me, secret as the emotion was, to feel that the man
who had committed this murder moved freely about the ship, enjoying
his liberty and the protection of the crew, and had all necessary leisure
besides to converse with the men, and to influence them to any purpose
he might have in his mind. Indeed I formed a darker opinion of the sailors from their willing association with the ruffian, and the jokes I would
hear them exchanging with him, than from any other sort of conduct I
had as yet witnessed in them. It was un-English—a harsh, bad, jarring
note in the rough and rude harmony of British forecastle-life; and this
feature of our shipboard existence was the uglier to my mind for the man
being a foreigner. Such half-bloods as this Charles, at best, are a people
alongside whom our Jacks do not much care to sling their hammocks
nor eat out of the same kid with; but in addition to this man's deformity
of breed was his proved quality as a "knifer"—a characteristic unpleasantly common to those skins, and half the secret at least of the aversion
they inspire in English crews. Detestable as Bothwell had been as a man,
the crime of his murder was more to be abhorred even than he; and I
say it worked in me like a superstition to see his assassin coming and
going about the decks, fetching his meals from the caboose along with
the others, singing out at the ropes, or hailing from aloft in the voice of
a lively hearty—but always with the same sharp, stabbing gleam in his
eyes whenever he turned them upon Broadwater—and making a part
of the brig's honest routine, when his proper lodging was the forepeak,
his fit equipment the bilboes, and his rightful condition the completest
practicable isolation from his shipmates.

These and twenty more such thoughts were in my mind after Miss
Grant had withdrawn to her berth, and whilst I remained alone watching the shambling figure of the cabin-boy stripping the cabin-table,
with a hungry goggling of his eyes at the remains of the meal as he
staggered up the hatchway with the dishes. I was mechanically rolling

a cigar between my fingers, with the intention of lighting it and going on deck, when Broadwater came below. I supposed he would pass to his cabin, for, now that he divided the look-out with Gordon, he was very punctual in going to bed when it came to his turn to quit the deck. Instead, he halted, took a survey of the cabin as if to make sure that we were alone, and then came and sat down near me.

"Mr. Musgrave," said he, speaking with hesitation and awkwardly, "I knew that you was at sea as a youth, sir; but I wasn't aware, till Mr. Gordon just now told me, that you considered yourself equal to taking charge of the deck and navigating a craft."

I looked at him, wondering what was in his mind.

"I hope," he continued, "you'll find nothing offensive in what I'm about to observe. The fact's this. Now that my mate's overboard, there's no man but me in this here brig, barring yourself, with knowledge enough of the quadrant to know what part to put his eye at, if so be he should need to use it. Now, if I should fall sick, who is there, onless it be you, sir, who'd be able to carry on the navigation of this here brig? Gordon tells me that you yourself said to him a short while ago you'd be willing, if asked, to take a mate's berth aboard of me. Now, Mr. Musgrave, what d'ye say? Gordon's agreeable to fall back into his old *spear*, and if you'll take his place as mate, sir, I should be glad, very glad indeed; though of course I won't say nothing about remooneration, that being a matter you might afterwards settle with the owner."

"I am obliged to you for your offer," said I. "I certainly did say something to Gordon about being willing to lend a hand in the navigation of the brig, should my services in that way ever be required; but as to taking a post of command over your crew——" I shook my head. "I don't like their attitude; I don't like the idea of your mate's murderer being at large; I don't like to think that there's any body of English sailors who can not only protect but remain friends with a half-blood, a foreign miscreant, whose knife, in my humble opinion, is as ready for another man's heart as it was for Mr. Bothwell's."

"Ay," said he hoarsely, leaning towards me with a look at the skylight, and then at the hatch, "that's just it. Ye've hit it true as a hair. It's more because I want to feel that we're stronger than we are aft than because I may fall sick that I'd be glad to see you mate first or second, as you may elect. I don't mind telling you," he continued, in the same hoarse, subdued voice, and with another look up and around, "that the aspect of the present billing don't sit pleasingly upon my eyes, sir. Ye heard what Gordon said that night of the murder, when he came down—how the half-blood 'ud do for *me*, too, if I didn't keep a bright look-out. Well,

I tell you, I've learnt to fear that man. I don't like his looks. I met his eye just now, and it was like the snap of a musket at me. I haven't said much about it, in fact I haven't said anything; and maybe it's weighed the more upon me, 'cause I kept myself shut up on the subject. But it's a long way to Rio yet, sir, and my fear of what that man's capable of is a weight that I must chuck over the side somehow or other. My notion is, then, that if you took the mate's berth the men 'ud like it, you being a gentleman. They'd feel your influence after a bit, and by expressing of your feelings to them in the sort of language that my neglected education as a boy keeps me as a man a-falling short of, they might grow ashamed of their protection of the half-blood, and be willing to let us clap him in irons, when of course I should be able to sleep sound again, and enjoy my meals with the old satisfaction."

He looked at me with a mixture of eagerness and cunning in his little eyes. I did not need to reflect, for whilst he had been speaking I had made up my mind.

"I thank you for your good opinion of me," said I; "I cannot accept any such post as you propose. 'Twas a mere fancy tossed to the bo'sun in the course of a talk, with no wish or resolution in it at all; but, though I decline your offer, you will of course understand that I am quite prepared to support you in any time of trouble; always presuming," I added significantly, "that the authority you exercise, but which may be resisted, is fair, legitimate, and consistent with regular sea-duties."

"Have ye got any weapons of your own?" he asked, with another look up and around.

"Yes," I answered.

"What are they, sir?"

"A brace of pistols," said I.

"Any hammunition?"

"Ay," I replied smiling, "enough to send ten times the number of your crew to their account."

"That's all right," said he; "I'm armed too, armed enough to be able to serve out what's needful to Gordon, and to have enough left for myself and *more*, if we can get others to help us. Would you mind doing this, sir?—get in with the men in a proper sort of condescending way, so as there could be nothing bemeaning in the thing to a gent of your spirit, and find out if there's e'er a man forward who is to be trusted to stand by and look on, should you and me and Gordon arrange to rush the job."

"I don't fully understand," said I.

"Well, I'll tell ye," he exclaimed, with his eyes very full of cunning and eagerness, "the notion that's come into my head's this: if we could count on so many of the men standing aloof, should it come to a mel-hee, then for the safety of all consarned I should propose that you and me and Gordon should arm ourselves, have the handcuffs ready, fall upon and secure the half-blood when no man could suspect our intentions, drag him aft and lock him up down here, and with our pistols keep any of the crew off who should attempt a rescue."

"The scheme is practicable," said I, after a little, "but it requires consideration. At the first sight I don't half like it. I see your difficulty—I clearly perceive that unless this half-blood be secured and removed from all intercourse with the crew, diabolical mischief may follow. I realize this: that at one end of the ship is a murderer, at the other end a man who is only waiting to get him to Rio to hang him." He nodded vehemently. "*He* knows that, and the question is, is he going to give you the chance to hang him?"

"That's the question!" he cried, bringing his fist down heavily upon the table.

"Yes," I exclaimed, "and it has haunted me pretty smartly of late, I can assure you. But, on the other hand, a melhee, as you call it—this project of seizing the half-blood and threatening the sailors with our small-arms—might, indeed it *would*, end in rank, staring, hellish mutiny. What then would you do? There are but three of us against the whole ship's company. The safety of the lady who is on board this vessel under my protection is my first consideration. It would be a poor look-out to set fire to a ship in order to get rid of a rat. It would be an equally poor look-out to excite the men into wild revolt against the three of us, to the imperilling of the life and honour of Miss Grant, for all we dare predict, simply that your mind may be eased by having the half-blood under lock and key."

"Then what's to be done?" he exclaimed coarsely, and in a defiant, quarrelsome way "The safety of the brig depends upon me, and if harm befalls *me*, what's to become of her, and you, and the lady you're so consarned about—and unwisely consarned about in my opinion, for, by not helping me, you'll be chancing to let her go adrift."

"I have told you, Captain Broadwater," said I, greatly disliking this sudden change of manner in him, for I had met his suggestion in a very earnest spirit, "that in a time of extremity, which shall not—understand me—have been brought about by any act of cruelty and brutality on your part, I will support you and Mr. Gordon heart and soul. But I cannot accept the duties you ask me to undertake, nor do I see my way to offering to help you in any wild scheme of seizing the half-blood, under cover of the muzzles of our pistols, with perhaps the obligation of having to shoot down one or more of your crew, to the assured end of raising a murderous spirit amongst the men, and exciting them into God knows what act of terrible mutiny."

As I said this, Miss Grant came from her berth. I made a gesture to him to signify that no more must be said now; on which he rose and went to his cabin. She looked at me earnestly, but was silent. I handed her up the companion-ladder, lighted a cigar, and followed. The morning was deliciously fine. There was a pleasant breeze a little abaft the beam, which enabled the brig to show her lower studding-sail to it, and under broad wings packed to the trucks, the little vessel glided crisply over a sea of blue, the beautiful dark dye of which at the horizon seemed to tincture the line of the sky, bending down past it into an opalescent shimmer through contrast of the sapphire sweep with the azure faintness behind it. The decks were dry and white, with a crystalline sparkling of salt about them. There was a short awning just abaft the skylight, and our deck-chairs were under it; but the sun was not yet high, the wind blew sweet and cool over the rail; life was stirred to her innermost sources by the freshness of the morning, and to sit would have been to forfeit half the delights of this radiant day. On our quarter, steering north, was a brigantine, toy-like in the distance; the sunlight flashed an ivory whiteness on her windward canvas, whilst the violet shadowing on the leeward cloths made them look to be melting on the airy blue beyond. There was a spot of colour in her rigging, and Gordon, from the other side, called out to me that she was a Dane. There was nothing else in sight, and the mighty stretch of water, under the dazzle of the soaring sun, looked the vaster for that fairy-like fabric upon it.

I threw a swift glance along our decks, and noticed that the men worked quietly upon their various jobs. A couple of them were busy on some chafing-gear in the fore-rigging; a spun-yarn winch was rattling on the forecastle; and the half-blood Charles, with his back upon us, dressed in blue dungaree, a red cap on his head, and chocolate-coloured shanks bare to the knees, was balling up the stuff as it was manufactured. The cook was standing in the door of his little galley, smoking a sooty pipe, his naked arms folded upon his breast, watching the cabin-boy close by washing some plates and dishes in a tub. High aloft on the fore-royal-yard stood the figure of a man, who had paused in some work he was upon up there to stand erect with his hand on the truck, and the sharp of his other hand over his eyes, whilst he gazed into the immeasurable distance visible to him from that altitude. The tall, muscular seaman, Terence Mole, was at the helm, his hands carelessly gripping the spokes of the wheel, his attitude full of that indefinable, floating ease that enters as a sort of grace into the posture and movements of the true deep-water sailor. All these were details to fill my eye in a breath; and on the surface the picture was so homely, there seemed so much salt, plain honesty in the complexion, quality, aspect of the full scene, that my instant recurrence to what but a little while before had passed between the captain and myself, affected me as an unreality, as something that I had imagined, as an affront to the truth of this quiet, inboard picture, and to the high, wide, refreshing splendour through which our little craft was softly pushing.

When we emerged from the cabin, Miss Grant made some commonplace remark about the beauty of the morning; but we had scarcely measured half the length of the deck when, looking at me wistfully and searchingly also, she exclaimed, "What has happened to worry you, Mr. Musgrave?"

"I must look worried, I suppose," I answered, smiling, "or you would not ask the question."

"You do, indeed. It is some anxiety that concerns this voyage, of course. There can be nothing else, for there are no postmen here to bring you disagreeable news; at least I *hope* the cause lies in the voyage." "If it does, will you tell me what it is?"

Now my immediate impulse was to answer her evasively; but on meeting her gaze, I observed so much fearlessness in it, so much clear and keen intelligence, along with so direct a challenge to me to be plain with her or not speak at all, and so unmistakable an assurance besides of a guess that had already carried her half-way into the truth, that I said to myself with the swiftness of one who thinks, "Why not be perfectly candid with this woman? The wit and instincts of her sex may help me."

She kept her gaze fastened upon me, and seemed to read my thoughts. She said, with a little smile very full of pride, "Do you know, Mr. Musgrave, if Alexander ever had a doubt, he would come to me to settle it for him. I am fond of problems. If I were a man, I should wish to be a politician above all things. I should love to be in a position where my judgment would be constantly tested, and where I should have to act quickly. What is best in a sailor's character springs from this habit. He is incessantly confronted by surprises, many of them tragical, all of them requiring instant resolution." She preserved her smile, still continuing to look at me. I suspected she talked to give me time to think.

"My anxiety," said I, "concerns our position on board this vessel— *your* position chiefly. What could offer a more peaceful picture than these decks? How softly the shadows sway! The men are working as quietly as if the whole gladness of the morning were in them; and yet, since you wish to know the truth, Miss Grant, I should say that if these planks were growing insufferably hot from fire below—raging, but as yet concealed—our outlook would be more distinctly satisfactory to my mind than it is now, staunch as the brig is, quiet as these fellows seem, calm and glowing as the whole picture all about us shows."

She threw a glance around her, and said quietly, "What has occurred to put these thoughts into you?"

I came to a halt, our faces fronting the forecastle, and indicating the half-blood by a movement of my head, I said, "That fellow there knows that on the arrival of this brig he must be hanged, or in some other manner dispatched for the murder of Mr. Bothwell. He also knows that the man who is resting in the cabin under our feet means to get him killed for his crime." The half-blood turned his head at this moment, and we resumed our walk. "You say you are fond of problems. Here is one for you. That fellow forward has the sympathies of the whole crew. He has more: he has their protection, and they will not allow a finger to be laid upon him. Aft is a captain who stands alone."

"The problem, Mr. Musgrave?"

"How is Captain Broadwater to sail the ship to Rio, and set you and me safely ashore there, with yonder olive-coloured villain closely and intimately associated with the crew—popular amongst them as the hero who freed them from the tyranny of the mate—conscious, maybe, of their willingness to help him save his life, which he knows must be forfeited on the arrival of the brig?"

"What do you fear?"

"That Master Ernest Charles yonder will contrive that this brig shall never reach her port."

"By what means?"

"Ha!" said I, "there it is, Miss Grant."

She threw another swift glance around her and slightly knitted her brows. "Can we not contrive to find out what Captain Broadwater thinks?" she said.

I exactly repeated my conversation with him in the cabin. She listened until I had made an end, and then said quickly, "Mr. Musgrave, if you will be advised by me, you will take no part in any scheme the captain may decide upon as regards the discipline of the vessel. The men know that they have your sympathies, and should trouble come, they will—at least they *may*—remember that you were their friend. But what would be the result of your siding with the captain, helping him to put that wretched creature yonder in irons, perhaps being obliged in self-defence to shoot one of the crew? We have a right to think of our safety. Captain Broadwater has imperilled it by his treatment of the men, and I say we have a right, Mr. Musgrave, to think of ourselves. My advice is, be neutral."

I dare say I was the more impressed by what she said, because of her having given prompt and clear expression to my own secret opinions. The judgment that concurs with our own must be, of course, very shrewd and sagacious. But I could also find a good deal to admire in the quickness with which she had seen into the thing, and the accuracy of her insight. For, after all, it only needed a little thought to enable me to conclude, that as Gordon hardly seemed a man to prove serviceable in a crisis—being just a plain, sober, slow-minded sailor, whose tastes were altogether forward, and who in his heart loved the captain as little as the others—the main burden of Broadwater's project must be borne by him and me; that a conflict between us and the crew must inevitably end in our defeat, and perhaps in our destruction, for the sight of a levelled pistol would serve, as a wand in the hand of a wizard, to raise the foulest of evil spirits among the people of the brig; and that if I were not slaughtered outright in the struggle with the men, they would extend their hatred of the captain to me in an equal measure, so that, in a word, I should be practically helpless as a protector in any form or fashion for Miss Grant. Indeed, this was the essential meaning of her advice to me—her entreaty almost; yet I thought I would sound her womanly judgment a little further.

"You are perfectly right, and I shall be guided by you. But suppose the captain should be set upon by the men—I mean treacherously— without furnishing them with an inch of honest justification, would it not be my duty as well as my policy to stand by him?"

"But is he likely to be set upon unless he provokes them? And judging from what we have seen, if he provokes them, will he not deserve the treatment he may receive at their hands?" she answered, with a flash of indignation in her look which gave me to know that old Broadwater must expect no commiseration from her, happen what might.

"I am heartily sorry," said I, with a smile which instantly brought the light of one into her face, though my own grin was pure admiration without the faintest flavour of mirth; for her beauty showed rich just then to the mood excited in her by our conversation, and admiration will often make a man smile as though he had a joke in his head when, God knows, his heart may be full of mirthless emotion—"I am mightily sorry that I was ever at sea as a sailor. Were I a landsman making my first voyage, I should find little or nothing to worry me in what has happened; particularly now that the roll of the commotion is smoothed out, and everything," I added, with a look along the peaceful decks, "is as placid on the surface as the waters of a canal."

"A little patience, Mr. Musgrave!" she exclaimed. "Rio is closer than it was a fortnight ago." I was not so sure of that, but I said nothing. "At all events," she continued, "we must take care that you return home in a good ship, with a pleasant captain."

"Yes," said I, "we must see to that."

"Alexander will be able to advise you," she said, with a softening of her voice to the utterance of his name. "He is sure to know of a good ship, one that might be quite worth waiting for if she is not at Rio."

"Confound Alexander!" I thought to myself; and her way of speaking of him so teased me, that it would have soothed the momentary irritation to have told her that I heartily wished he stood in my boots on board this brig. But a glance at her made me feel that the expression of such a wish would have been preposterously insincere. No; our situation was uncommonly dark and uncomfortable: no man knowing the truth would have dared venture to predict that to-morrow would find us as we were to-day; and still my enjoyment of her society topped every risk I could contemplate; and how detestable the project of our association coming to an end was to me, I knew by my inward perturbation that followed on her speaking of Alexander and his choosing me a good ship to return in.

An hour passed. Our conversation was chiefly about the crew, and the outlook they threatened, and again and again she advised me not to entertain any scheme old Broadwater might submit, but to view myself wholly as a passenger, without further concern in the voyage than its conclusion. She then, feeling tired, took a chair under the awning and put a book upon her knee, but seemed to have no eyes for anything but the crew, whom she watched curiously, as might an artist who gazes for effects of colour, posture, and expression. All this while Gordon trudged the weather-deck alone. I now crossed over to him.

"Feel more cheerful by this time, I hope, Mr. Gordon?" said I; "a man's spirits must be gloomy indeed that don't brighten out to such a day as this."

He forced a grin, and said, "Worrit, sir, worrit; there's no accounting for a man's feelings. I wish it 'ud come on to blow. This here smiling kind of weather is all very well when ye ain't in a hurry; but when ye've got bows forrard like the head of a puncheon, and beam enough for a score of fandangoes 'twixt the rails, without call to stop even a coil of halliards to the standing rigging to get more room, then what one wants is the relieving tackles hauled taut, and two chaps sweating at the wheel, and the spritsail-yard out of sight in the smother over the bows."

"You're in as great a hurry as Miss Grant," I exclaimed.

"Greater, I dessay," he exclaimed. "To tell ye the truth, Mr. Musgrave, I'm sick of the voyage. None of these here small brigs for me again, sir. Never no more! Nothen less than a thousand ton. A man's nature seems able to stand upright when he's aboard a big ship; in these here small craft it's all stooping for fear of knocking your brains out."

There was a sour expression on his face which strictly corresponded with the sentiment and note of his grumbling. I said to him, "Gordon, an odd thought came into my head just now. Notice the half-blood yonder. He's a clearer menace to our safety than an auger working through the ship's bottom. Now what think you of the scheme of the captain— of you and me arming ourselves with loaded pistols, springing upon him unawares, hand-cuffing him, and dragging him aft under cover of the muzzles of our small arms?"

"What do I think of it, sir?" he exclaimed, without a moment's hesitation.

"Yes," I rejoined.

"This," said he. "If there's any gunpowder aboard, better knock the head off a barrel and snap one of your pistols into it, and blow the whole blooming mess of us to heaven. But you're not serious?"

"No, no," said I; "certainly not. Mere fancy, and nothing more. But not to your liking, evidently."

"Good God!" he exclaimed, "at the first offer to touch Charles, pistol or no pistol, the whole crew 'ud be on ye like one man. *They'd* like the scheme. It's the sort of chance they're waiting for. For Heaven's sake, don't go and suggest your notion to the captain, sir. He's just the sort of man to entertain it, and to come and ask me to help him."

Would you help him?" said I.

"Let him ask me first, Mr. Musgrave," he replied, with an odd look at me out of the corner of his eyes. If this was not news, 'twas what I needed to get from his lips. Even had Miss Grant's advice not already settle my mind, Gordon's askant glance, that was more eloquent than words, would have decided me out of hand, there and then. In truth it could but prove as I had foreseen, should I consent to help the captain; and I remember that I let out my breath in a half-wild sigh of relief over the determination I had formed as I turned from Gordon to take a chair at Miss Grant's side.

END OF VOLUME 1

Volume 2

Chapter I
We Lose the Cabin-boy

Two mornings after this, on going on deck shortly before the breakfast-hour, I found the weather changed. The high sun, the blue skies which had shone over us now for many days together, were gone. The atmosphere was gloomy, with a pale thickness that brought the sea-line to within cannon-shot. Under the lead-coloured gloom over the mastheads one could dimly catch sight here and there of a black curl of scud-like cloud blowing leisurely athwart our track; otherwise there was no break, no shadowed curve or line to tell of a denser or darker vapour yet above the warm and sallow haze through which the wind was sweeping without dispersing it. The sea ran in a slopping sort of way that made a great noise about the brig's sides with notes of hollow plashing, the slap of a leap of water seething to its own recoil, the short, small roar of billows overspringing some backward scend ahead of them, like the groaning of surf tumbling in snow to the hidden drag of the undertow. You would have thought there was a strong windward tide running; yet with all this briskness of surface play, I never saw the ocean wear a sulkier look. The glorious sparkling blue of its brine was gone; 'twas now of a cold, sallowish green, thick and muddy with every heave; as though under its heads of foam, and the short, conflicting runs of its small seas, it had been thickened into sluggishness by upheaval of ooze into its volume.

The atmosphere was like a tepid bath, and the brig was damp with it from her loftiest cloths to the deck from which I surveyed the scene. She was under all plain sail, the yards braced forward, but the studding-sail-booms were still rigged out, which was perhaps as good as saying that old Broadwater found nothing more in the weather that had come down upon us than was visible to the bare eye. She was pushing through it dully, and tumbling uncomfortably, in a most sickening way indeed; insomuch, that for the first time during this voyage I felt absolutely uneasy, though the fresh air speedily relieved me of the disagreeable oppression. There was no weight of surge, and yet she could not have flopped about more drunkenly had a strong sea been running. First she would give a sharp dip forward; but before she could put her round nose well into it a trough would suddenly yawn under her counter, and oblige her to drop her stern sharply, and with a souse that would send a large dark-green, glass-clear curl of water thundering into foam away from her quarter; an instant after she would tumble to windward, as though collecting her energies for a good heel over to t'other side; but whilst you postured yourself for the slope of the deck, she would recover herself with a jerk that made you stagger again. I had never heard so much groaning aloft before. The mandrake is said to shriek when dragged out by the roots; so did every shroud, backstay, and halliard aboard the *Iron Crown*, to the fierce jerking strains put upon them by the giddy, capricious rolling of the spars. Every parrel delivered a groan of its own, every sheave squeaked like a rat in its block; nor though the wind was of some little briskness had it power to keep the courses and even the topsails distended during the leeward plunges, when the heavy cloths would come in to the masts with a blow that sent blasts of noise through the air like boiler explosions or smart claps of thunder.

Broadwater was in charge. I stepped mechanically over to the compass to have a look at the card, though of course it was to be known by the lay of her yards that the brig was steering her true course. The captain was clothed in a long pea-coat and sou'-wester, and his red face, framed in the sea-helmet, showed methought this morning very sourly, with a harsh twist about his mouth that put the look of a sulky sneer into its ordinary, familiar, whistling expression. A large drop of moisture sparkled at the end of his nose. He stood holding on to the weather-vane of the trysail-gaff, apparently as little able as I was to move about the decks. The watch had finished their business of washing down, the ropes were coiled away and everything was ship-shape fore and aft: but the drizzled, weeping aspect of the brig, with shadows of moisture lying in dark curves upon her canvas, and blobs of wet distilling from grey ropes and black shrouds, made her look singularly dejected and forlorn, and I could scarcely forbear a smile, as I glanced from the picture of her to the skipper's face, and witnessed the absurd correspondence between *his* damp sourness and *her* appearance.

He eyed me as if he would like to speak, but I took care that he should find no encouragement in the short "good-morning" that I called to him. The truth is, I had given him as wide a berth as I could possibly contrive since the hour when he had unfolded his scheme to me of capturing the half-blood. I had made up my mind on the matter, and therefore had no desire to hear him again on it. Indeed Miss Grant's advice had so worked in me that my attitude was perhaps more resolved and more sharply accentuated than the occasion demanded. In short, it entered my head that for all I could tell the captain's scheme might finds its way to the forecastle; by what agency of course I could not have indicated, for I was sure that Gordon was not a man to talk. But, nevertheless, I knew that on shipboard there is a species of wizardry at work in the atmosphere, by whose operations the crew do somehow or other manage to obtain a dim intelligence of what passes even in whispers in the cabin; and I was resolved that if the captain's proposal to me should come to be guessed at by the sailors, or reach their knowledge in the indefinable manner in which news creeps through a ship at sea, they should perceive that I had no sympathy with it; which was only to be managed by letting them infer my opinion of Broadwater by my behaviour to him on deck.

It was a gloomy breakfast-table. The morning lay so foggily upon the skylight that I could scarcely distinguish Miss Grant's features without leaning towards her. There were fiddles on the table, but the quick rolls of the brig rendered them useless. A plate of bacon was capsized on to Broadwater's knees, and I narrowly escaped being badly scalded by the sudden fetching away of the skipper's huge tea-pot, which to one sharp heave jumped like a live thing over the divisions, and poured its contents in a boiling stream within a couple of inches of my right leg.

"If we were not clear of the Gulf Stream," said I, "this should make a man believe himself in the heart of it."

"What's the matter with the Gulf Stream, sir," said Broadwater, "supposing this *was* it?"

"You have heard, I suppose," said I, almost amused by the excessive sourness in his face, "of vessels sailing with royals and studding-sails into the belt, and meeting ships coming out of it under close-reefed topsails?"

"Well, I *may* have heard of it, as you remark," he exclaimed; "but I haven't been going to sea all these years to believe all I hear at this time o' day."

There was a note of insolence in the old chap's voice that instantly started me on addressing Miss Grant with the completest air of unconsciousness of his presence that I could command. Once I caught his eye, and the gleam of it was not a little malevolent, minute as the puncture was through which he stared. How unusually quarrelsome and bad-tempered he was this morning was to be noticed in his way of speaking to the cabin-boy. It was inconceivable that the poor lad should be able to cut anything but an intolerable figure on that staggering deck, and it was quite wonderful that he managed to scrape through his business of bringing the dishes along and waiting on us without breaking his neck, not to speak of what he carried. But Broadwater found him unendurable, heaped abuse on him whenever he had sufficiently emptied his mouth to furnish scope to his tongue, and finally exploded in a whole volley of coarse and brutal terms, which caused Miss Grant to half rise from her chair with a look at me to hand her to her cabin. But the old fellow left his seat at that moment and staggered on deck, with a farewell shake of his fist under the hapless boy's nose, whereupon my companion resumed her place.

Gordon arrived, looking grey in the twilight of the cabin, and wretched with the dogged melancholy that hung upon him. He knuckled his forehead with a dismal gesture to Miss Grant, sat down and helped himself to a bit of beef, with the air of a man walking in his sleep. This indeed, to a certain extent, had been his mood ever since the night of the apparition of the luminous bow, but it was so accentuated this morning that the dolefulness of it was absolutely grotesque.

"It seems to me, Gordon," said I, "that a glass of three-finger rum and one-finger water would do you more good than that black fluid you're about to drink. The weather, I admit, is enough for the moment to make life appear as if it were formed of nothing but yellow fog and bilious dots. But, my good fellow, there is really no need for such a mute-like face as yours, as though you had taken a fancy to a hearse's plume to embellish your sou'-wester with, and were rehearsing the proper cast of countenance for it."

He rolled up his eyes to the skylight, and then gazed at me with the languishing expression of a sick man, but did not speak.

"Of all the most miserable voyages," I continued, "recorded or unwritten, I'll venture to declare this tops the list."

"Pray don't say so, Mr. Musgrave," exclaimed Miss Grant. "Think of fire, famine, shipwreck, the uninhabited coast, or worse still, the coast inhabited by savages."

"This voyage ain't over yet," said Gordon, in the voice of a raven.

"I don't say it's *calamitous*," I went on. "Indeed, but for the consideration that your safety and comfort are involved, I should be much too happy to wish the voyage over." She smiled, and inclined her head to this as a mere commonplace of courtesy, and indeed I easily saw that she made nothing of it, and suspected nothing in it, from the serenity and steadfastness of her gaze. "Yet," I continued, "we must call it miserable. As if a fit of superstition ending in the suicide of a seaman shouldn't suffice, there comes the barbarous punishment of lashing a man to the mast. As though *that* were not enough, mutiny must follow, along with a horrid murder. And now here is Broadwater this morning with every instinct of bad temper and brutality in him forking out like the claws of a cat at sight of a dog; whilst on top of all sits my good friend there, bowed down by some sort of speechless woe, for which I am sure that there is no remedy but a good pull at one of my choice old brandy bottles."

I started up, meaning to fetch the liquor, but he arrested me with a solemn wave of the hand.

"No, sir," he exclaimed, "there's nothing in brandy to do me good. It isn't *woe* that's a-worriting me. What it be I'm sure I can't tell. I believe the capt'n's clean off his head this morning. He came up a-cursing of you to me just now as if he'd imagined you and the half-blood was gone into partnership to take his life."

"Do you suppose he thinks this?" I cried, startled.

"No, no, sir," he replied; "I said *as if* he did. There's no telling what passes in such a mind as his."

"I do not see that his fancies, whatever they may be, need trouble us," said Miss Grant quietly.

"No," I exclaimed; "it's not the captain's mind; it's your face, Gordon. Turn to and give yourself a good hearty shaking, my lad, and so get rid of the longshore humour that's come to you with a view of the finest sight that ever mortal eye rested on. Why, man, we look to you for the only gleam of sailorly jollity that's to be witnessed aboard this old hooker. It was but the other day that you were laughing at the notions that dispatched the poor fellow Jesse Cooper over the side. Shake this temper out of you, Gordon."

He passed the back of his hairy hand over his forehead. "Well, sir," he exclaimed, "I will if I can. I hope there's nothing in the queer sensations that have come into me to agitate the lady, I'm sure. I'm but a plain sailor man, and never had no college to go to but the fok's'le, and don't feel that I've got any right to be sitting in the cabin of even such a brig as this, a-talking to a lady and gent like you and miss there. I'm sure I ask both of your pardons if I've at all agitated either of ye by my manner. Sailors are but mortal like other folks; ye know that, Mr. Musgrave. The sperrits of the heartiest of them will fail at times. It'll all come right, I dare say," and with that he left us.

Now all this, along with the darkness of the weather, the drizzle on the skylight, the vile tumbling of the brig, and the harsh groaning of the labouring fabric, was surely enough to render both Miss Grant and myself as gloomy and depressed as poor Gordon himself. I protest it made me feel exceedingly uncomfortable to know that the captain had gone on deck and abused me to the boatswain in terms which it was easy for my imagination to fit to his lips. One felt that everything was wrong aboard the brig, from the eyes of her to the transom, that she was no better than a complicated trap, of which if one piece of mechanism went wrong there was half-a-score more whose action was bound to be sure.

There was nothing to tempt one on deck. It was Broadwater's watch below, but he remained above throughout; why, I could not imagine, unless he was too irritable to rest in his cabin. Thick as the weather was, it was daylight, and one could see a mile at all events, and the risks therefore were as nothing compared with those of that black night on which the pig had broken into my berth, and through which Broadwater would have slept soundly, no doubt, but for the uproar, as he had turned in very nearly drunk. The atmosphere was close below, and the lee skylight-lid lay open, and through it as I sat conversing with Miss Grant, I could hear the captain occasionally bawling in a voice whose harsh, hoarse note struck upon the ear with something of the smart of a blow from a missile on the flesh. Once I heard the men singing out, and gathered from the orders delivered by Gordon that they were trimming sail. The motion of the brig however continued abominable, spasms and throes of motion quite bewildering to the brain at times, accompanied by all sorts of ugly slopping sounds of water, hysteric sobbings and gurglings swelling into a semi-muffled, yearning roar as some windward roll would send a billow howling from the side. Reading was impossible; there was nothing to be made of chess or cards, and we could find no better diversion than sitting and talking.

I think it must have been about noon when I heard the captain's voice suddenly exerted in a number of shouts in which he seemed to be repeating the same orders over and over again, but in the most angry, savage, threatening tones that could be imagined.

"What on earth can the wretched old man be at now?" said I. "I'll take a peep."

I threw a cloak over my shoulders, put on my cap, and went on deck. Broadwater was standing on the weather-side of the quarter-deck, gripping the main-royal backstay, and shouting to somebody on the fore, though I did not immediately look that way. Gordon was near the skylight, his hands buried in his coat-pockets, and his dejected face sulkily staring seawards with an air of petulant, gloomy unconcern upon him, as of a man who had passed through the stages of loathing and disgust into contemptuous indifference. I walked right aft so as to get out of the sphere of the skipper's little eyes; since, whilst I was anxious to see what was going on, I was also disposed to fear that if the old fellow caught me watching he might fall foul of me in his present humour before the sailors. I now noticed that the wind had come a point or two more free since early morning, and that the yards were braced in to that extent.

The foretopmast studding-sail had been set, but something was wrong with the block at the extremity of the boom, and the halliards had been slacked away and the sail hauled in great part down upon the forecastle, where it hung with the watch standing by ready to hoist away afresh when the difficulty aloft, whatever it was, had been remedied.

It is proper I should state here, for the information of those to whom sea-terms are unintelligible, that a studding-sail-boom is a long, smooth spar that reeves through irons fixed upon the yard to which it belongs, and that, when the studding-sail is to be set, is run out far beyond the ship's side for the extension of the foot of the cloths. There is no gear attached to it except the tack at the extremity, so that 'tis for all the world like one of those greasy poles which they project over the head of a moored craft on a regatta day, for marine Jack Puddings to walk out on.

Now as I stood near the wheel, the first object I saw was the figure of the cabin-boy, Billy, as he was called, jockeying the studding-sail-boom at the distance of some three or four feet from the yard-arm. He was supposed to be sliding out to the end of it—astride it as though on horseback—but you saw at the first glance that the poor creature was in a mortal fright; that having been urged by the captain's threats to the point at which he had arrived, he was too terrified to advance, whilst the purple face of the old tyrant on the quarter-deck prohibited him from returning. At any time such a job as this would have been full of danger. Even at anchor on the motionless surface of a river, the task of sliding out to the extremity of a long, naked, and slippery boom, would not have been without its peril. The undertaking was now rendered so prodigiously dangerous by the peculiarly sharp, rapid, jerking, and dislocating heaves, staggers, and rolls of the brig, that the mere sight of the lad up there shocked me as though he were hanging by the neck, or being in any other way done to death by the man who continued to bawl out menaces to him.

"By Heaven!" I cried, with the quick, shuddering sensation of a recoil within myself, so to speak, "he'll be overboard in a minute."

"Yes, by the Everlasting! but if he goes for good, the one that'll follow him ain't fur off," said a low voice close to my side. I turned; it was Charles, the half-blood, who was standing at the wheel. I had not until this moment noticed him. One laughs often at descriptions in novels of the villain of the plot hissing out his threats and imprecations through his clenched teeth; but I protest that though it was impossible this man could have spoken with his teeth clenched, his utterance had the sharp, seething sound which is in the romancer's mind when he endeavours to express it. I started with a sudden uncontrollable shudder of aversion, and went some yards forward.

"Shove along out! shove along out!" roared Broadwater, with an angry sweep of his arm towards the extremity of the boom.

The hue of the sky against which the boy swung was a dull and dingy slate, here and there in it a deepening of shadow where some dark cloud sailed above the haze; and out of the horizon, that seemed to welter within reach of an arrow, the sea came running in short, snappish, colliding leaps, with a quarrelsome, hound-like shouldering of one another, and fretful tossings of their heads of froth into the air, the foam falling back like showers of snow against the dingy background. The sailors stared up at the lad, but though now one and then another of them would make a movement as if he were about to spring into the rigging, no man offered to take the boy's place.

I don't believe however it was so much the peril of the work that held the fellows in a body looking on, as the feeling that the captain had started the wretched boy on this business as a "work-up job," and that he would not permit any other man to take his place. It was the most barbarous piece of cruelty you could conceive—out and away worse than the fastening of the half-blood to the mast. It was not only that the lad had not signed as a sailor, so that the captain had no right to turn him to work of that kind; of all the people aboard the brig the poor creature was the least qualified for so perilous an undertaking as sliding out to the extremity of a long boom that was buckling and jumping like a coach-whip to the tumbling vessel's thrash of spar and shear of yardarm.

"Out with you! Shove along! By thunder! I'll make a *traveller* of you with the end of the tack! I'll have ye *hauled* out and made two blocks of and belayed if you don't bear a hand! There's no ile in that timber—no use you're a-squeezing of it!—so out ye go now!—out ye go!"

The white face of the lad turned towards the captain, full of entreaty and terror. On a sudden his cap blew off. Trifling as the thing was, the mere sight of the headgear dropping with a whirl into the sea and showing black an instant ere smothered by a breaking wave, sent a shock through me.

"I can't get out, sir; I can't indeed, sir," cried the boy in a most miserable, whining voice. I noticed several of the men forward staring my way, as though wondering whether I meant to interfere, perhaps hoping to provoke me to do so with their looks. But remonstrance was too late, even if I had not satisfied myself, by observing the temper old Broadwater was in, that it would be idle. It was quite plain that the lad was incapable of working himself another foot along the boom; and it seemed to me, from the despairful, clinging posture with which he hugged the spar, his trousers ridden up to his knees, and his thin legs and long naked feet swinging in sharp relief against the haze past them, that terror had rendered him incapable of returning. On a sudden the brig pitched sharply, all aslant; then with a stagger recovered herself, instantly following it by another sharp plunge and a heavy seething of water beaten off her weather-bow.

"Mind!" I cried at this moment, "the boy will be overboard."

As I spoke he swung under the boom, still clinging to it with his legs and arms.

"Come in! come in!" roared Gordon, rushing forward; "you can manage it, my lad; take your time. Up aloft some of ye and help him."

Three men sprang into the shrouds, but before they were five ratlines high the lad's legs dropped, and he swayed at the boom with his hands meeting upon it, his figure swinging like the end of a rope. Half-a-dozen throats shouted out as many suggestions. "Hold on, Billy! We'll have a bowline for ye in a moment!" "Work your way in, Billy, hand over hand, lad!" "Don't let go, for Heaven's sake. There are men now running aloft to help ye!"

"In God's name," I cried, making a spring in my excitement towards Broadwater, "put your helm down before he lets go, that the brig's way may be checked when he's in the water!"

He did not answer me, but if ever human eyes flashed a curse at a man his did. There was a life-buoy aft, seized to the rail in the good old English style. Without a knife I could not free it. A steel blade was flourished close to my nose. "Here, sir, cut away with this; it's sharp enough for tougher stuff than laniards." I seized the knife that the half-blood extended to me from the wheel, severed the seizings, and returned the weapon to the fellow, with a horror springing into me even in that wild moment of excitement, to the thought that it was the same knife with which he had murdered the mate! I looked forward; the boy was gone, and the boom reeled naked against the sky. At the same moment, "Man overboard! Down hellum! down hellum!" came sweeping aft in a perfect hurricane roar from the lips of the seamen gathered forward, and the deck re-echoed the clattering of their feet as they came racing in a body to the quarter-boat. I looked over the side, and there on the quarter lay the boy on his back floating with his arms out. I sprang on to the rail to fairly heave the life-buoy, and whilst I stood in that posture for the space of a breath, *I saw the poor creature smile at me.* I vow to God it was a thing almost heart-breaking in its way. It may have unnerved my arm; I know not, I am sure. I did my best, flung the buoy with my full strength and as a sailor would, but it fell far short of him; and though the half-blood ground the wheel down till you would have thought that the passion of the creature had given him strength to twist the head sheer off the rudder it belonged to, yet the lubberly bows of the brig came round so leisurely against the conflicting beat of the snarling and worrying seas, that the floating figure seemed a mile off in less time than it would have taken a man to put up a prayer to God for him.

Chapter II
We Lose Four Men

THEN HAPPENED A SCENE of bitter confusion. Though the men, whilst they stood watching the lad forward, must have guessed as clearly as I what would happen, they had said nothing; but now that the boy was overboard and drowning, they broke into a hundred execrations against the captain whilst they cast the gripes of the lee quarter-boat adrift and cleared away the falls ready for lowering. The uproar was increased by Broadwater's vociferations to them to bear a hand; but each cry of his served but as a challenge to the rage of the men, who roared back every choicest flower of the forecastle dialect which they could summon to their lips. However, they worked nimbly for all that, and in a few minutes the boat, with a couple of men in her and Gordon in the stern-sheets overhanging the stern as he fitted the rudder to the pintles, was swinging at the davits. "Lower away handsomely!" The little craft sank out of sight down the side, and in a few minutes was leaping like an India-rubber ball upon the seas, to the desperate drag of the two fellows at the oars.

The shouts from the captain now brought the sailors to the main-topsail brace, and whilst the men were pulling at the ropes to get the yards aback, hauling in a delirious sort of way, with temper ringing menacingly in the songs with which they accompanied their work, Miss Grant arrived on deck, and spying me before I saw her, instantly approached with a hurried, anxious, "What is it *now*, Mr. Musgrave?"

"Why, another murder, bad as Bothwell's, if there be justice in heaven to decide!" I cried, for I was thinking of the drowning lad's smile at the moment, and the mere having to tell her what had happened made me feel as mutinously savage as, I warrant me, the darkest-minded of the men who were running about.

She brought her hands together in a gesture of terror; there was real fear in the eyes with which she swept the sea. She seized me by the arm, and exclaimed with a shuddering glance towards Broadwater, "Another murder do you say, Mr. Musgrave? Oh, if so—if so—" and then she stopped with a bewildered stare at the jumbled roll of green seas that came with staggers which shook them into snow out of the windward thickness.

I had shocked and startled her from the brave hold she had hitherto kept upon her feelings, and could have cursed myself for my brutal, uncouth candour. "I have put it too strongly," I cried, eager to subdue in her eyes something of that light of horror and fear which gave a kind of madness to their beauty. "It is not murder in the sense you think it. It is but another act of miserable cruelty which I fear must end in the death of our cabin-boy."

"Tell me about it!" she exclaimed, in a breathless way, securing her hold of my arm by clasping the fingers of both hands upon it.

I related the incident as swiftly as I could speak it, and I do not think I shall ever forget the look of tragic loathing and indignation in her face when she turned to glance at Broadwater over her shoulder as he stood on the other side of the deck, huskily bawling instructions to the crew.

"Where is the boat?" she cried impetuously.

I pointed in the direction in which I had last seen it, and walked right aft with her and peered into the windy thickness, but could see no signs of the little fabric; nothing like it saving a darker ridge of green here and there which would melt into foam even as I watched. I abhorred the obligation of having to address the half-blood, but excitement was working in me like a fever, and I could think of little more than that the boat which I had in full view a minute or two before Miss Grant came on deck was now out of sight.

"Do you see anything of her?" I said to him.

"She went out of sight on a sudden," he answered. "She's afloat right enough I reckon; the mist will have swallowed her up." He leaned from the wheel, pointing with a small, beautifully-shaped, but discoloured hand out to sea upon the weather quarter.

The brig's way was stopped, so far at least as forging ahead went; but of her leeward trend dead along the path of the wind the nimbleness might be gathered by looking over the side, where you saw the oil-like smoothness left by her to the distance of a pistol-shot, beyond whose verge the seas were breaking as though they were kept at bay to that point by a coating of oil upon the waters. I thought Broadwater must be stark mad to keep his brig hove-to under a press which every moment was driving her deeper into the obscurity that hid us from the boat as she was hidden from us by it. The vessel was under royals and flying-jib, and to such a surface, helped as the fabric also was by the seas, our drift would be rapid beyond endurance; yet not a sheet was started or a halliard let go. The old man stood on the weather-side, leaning upon the rail, and fixedly gazing seaward under the thatch of his sou'-wester; forward, both watches—the whole of the crew in short, as many of them as were left—overhung the bulwarks pointing and talking, with one man half-way up the fore-shrouds, swinging out from a ratline, and his left hand shading his eyes as he bent his gaze at the brownish drizzle upon the near horizon. Five minutes passed; nothing was done, and nothing said that reached our ears. The captain held his motionless posture, staring as though fascinated. One heard nothing but the wearisome sobbing and plashing of waters, the yeasty seething of brine to the chop of the cutwater forward, the simmering of foam hissing in recoil from the smart shock of the descending counter, with the cheerless clank of wheel-chains and jar of rudder, the melancholy clatter of wet spare booms, the rushing noise of wind aloft to the drunken weather lurches of the brig. Suddenly old Broadwater sprang erect from his squared arms, and came rolling along to where we stood.

"See anything of the boat, sir?" he cried.

"Nothing," I answered, scarcely able to tell him so, for my aversion almost overpowered my faculty of speaking.

"Forward there," he bawled, turning his face towards the forecastle, "any one amongst ye see anything of the boat?"

"Nothing," came back the response, in so sulky a swing through the wind, that it made one think of the sudden dead flap of a sail in the midnight obscurity of an electric storm that has not yet burst. The old man struck his hip violently with the flat of his hand, drove both fists deep into his pockets, then started as if to walk, but changed his mind, and came to the rail again, and stood looking with a creeping consternation in his face, before which one saw the temper in it fading away.

My feelings made me reckless. I said to him roughly and defiantly, "You'll lose your boat if you don't strip your ship. Do you know, man, that you're driving dead to leeward at the rate of three or four miles an hour?"

He sent a glance at the half-blood before answering me, and then in a half-choked voice gasped out with an oath, "If there's a mutiny, you'll be the ringleader! I knows ye; I've been following of ye. *You* teach me my business!" He pulled his fist out of his pocket to shake it in my face. I at first imagined by this gesture that he meant to attack me, and quickly released Miss Grant's hold that I might be ready for him. Muscular as he was, with no lack of weight "of beef" in him, as sailors say, I believe he would have found his match in me at that moment; for his charging me with being the ringleader of a mutiny was an insult to make fire of blood running by luck of disposition in a much gentler stream than mine, I am sorry to say, ever did. But very quietly Miss Grant stepped in front of me, and the old fellow, with a second look at the half-blood, rolled over to the companion, where he stood a few moments staring seawards, and then with an air of sudden hurry vanished below.

He reappeared after a brief absence, grasping an old blunderbuss, the bell-shaped muzzle of which was almost big enough to have received his head. He ran to the bulwarks with it close to where we stood. I confess I was not a little alarmed by the sight of so formidable a weapon in the hands of this enraged old man, and I watched his movements with no small anxiety, as I could not imagine what he intended to do with the piece. On a sudden he lifted the stock to his shoulder, drooped his pear-shaped nose over the trigger, and screwing up one eye as though he were taking aim at a bird in the air, let fly. The explosion could not have been more noisy had he discharged a swivel cannon, and the recoil of the piece was so violent that it came very near to flinging him on to his back. However, I perceived that his object was to signal the brig's whereabouts to the boat, and I should have been glad to help him by discharging another musket, or blunderbuss, if the brig owned a second, but was kept quiet by the memory of his insult, and by the expression of ugly temper upon his face. When he had discharged the gun, he whipped out a great powder-flask and proceeded to reload, but poured in so much powder, whilst he rammed in so large and stubborn a lump of newspaper, that all in silence I took Miss Grant by the hand and led her some distance forward, where on the other side of the deck, should the crazy old weapon explode, we would be out of reach of the flying fragments. Having charged his blunderbuss, he approached the rail again, and taking aim at some imaginary object with as much solicitude of posture, indeed, as if he was shooting grouse or snipe, and screwing up his left eye so tightly, that I burst into a laugh at the sight of that side of his face, showing in a sort of purple blur of wrinkles against the rusty barrel and the dull leaden shadow beyond, he pulled the trigger a second time. The piece exploded with a great blaze of light, and the blast of a little thunder-shock, and down he tumbled to it, quite as I had expected; only instead of measuring his length, he smote the deck heavily with his hams, and preserved a sitting posture, with the blunderbuss across his knees, and his face full of astonishment and anger.

Presently he rose and put the firearm on the skylight, and went to the rail. He stared long and earnestly, then shouted to the men forward to know if they saw anything; afterwards gaped aloft at his canvas, with a slow bringing of his eyes down to where we stood. But for the temper and brutality of the man I should have felt sorry for him.

"Do you think he will be able to recover the boat?" Miss Grant asked.

"I fear not," I answered, "unless the weather should miraculously clear within the next half-hour; and even then the chances should be all against recovery, unless the old fool promptly shortened sail down to his topsails—nay, down to bare poles."

"But surely, Mr. Musgrave, we are not likely to *lose* the boat?"

"At sea things grow horribly serious in a minute," said I.

I crossed with her again to the weather-rail, and telescoping my hands, sent a long, long searching look into the length of the dingy shadow of mist, a little way past the line of which one saw the phantasmal welter of the seas and the scarce determinable flash of foam, vague as an outline instil dark waters, to where they melted into the blindness of the haze. The first clamorous wrath of the men forward had been changed, by waiting and peering, into a sort of angry uneasiness. There were nine of them; they hung in a row along the bulwarks, one repeatedly leaning inboards to look past another aft at the skipper, as though full of sullen, irritable wonder at this waiting and drifting scheme of his. But he made no sign. He went to the binnacle, and lifting the hood laid the sharp of his hand across the card, as though seeking to arrive by memory at the bearings of the boat. I suspected in him some trick of seamanship above my knowledge in his keeping the vessel under all plain sail hove-to; but I could not bring myself to address him. Ten minutes passed—ten minutes of silence along our decks—all of us meanwhile staring our hardest to windward, not a syllable coming from forwards to break the dreary washing noises of water, and the sounds of the restless straining of the yerking, rolling, and plunging brig. On a sudden, Broadwater roared out, "Swing the maintopsail-yard! Sweat everything fore and aft! Get them jib-sheets flattened in!"

The sailors, eager to be doing, sprang to his commands; I quitted Miss Grant to help them, and dragged with the gangs till the yards were pointed to the wind as far as they would go; but there were no songs. Here and there a fellow would raise a low monotonous yowling that the others might take time from his notes; but there was no cheeriness in the sailors' voices, and such few cries as were raised were more like the melancholy groaning of sufferers than the hearty piping of seamen at work. The maintack was boarded in silence, and the jigger clapped on to such sheets and running gear as demanded the extra purchase, as though the brig's company consisted of undertakers' mutes. The wind seemed to come fresher now that the vessel was looking up to it close-hauled, and under the great pressure of her cloths she lay over until her lee-channels were awash amid the smother of spume there, though it was the mere spluttering of her round bows throwing the heads of the seas into cataracts from her that made the tumbling whiteness alongside; for I question if her progress, jammed as she was till the weather-leeches of her royals and topgallant-sails were hollowed aback, was as great as her drift had been when her topsail was to the mast.

It was clear now that the captain's intention was to "ratch" for the boat, as he himself would have termed it—by which I mean that it was his design to beat to windward in short tacks in the direction in which the boat had last been seen; and maybe he had kept full sail on the brig for the convenience of handling her promptly, although I held to my opinion that he had blundered grievously in holding her under cloths that must have given her a drift of hard upon a league since he had first hove her to. It was past two o'clock, and as I saw there was no chance of getting any dinner that day, I procured some refreshments from our private stock, and Miss Grant and I made a hurried, uncomfortable meal in the cabin. Even whilst we sat there Broadwater put the brig about again, and as I felt that it was my duty to help him in such an extremity as this, I hastened on deck and assisted the men in pulling and dragging. The breeze had freshened yet, the seas were running more steadily, but the blank around the horizon had thickened, and there was a deeper shade in the dinginess on high that made it look as if it floated with a stoop towards our masts; but there was no break in it, no faintest flaw for the light behind to steal through, whilst the first weak drizzle of it had thickened into a small, fine rain—so warm that you did not feel the moisture until the wind had chilled it—which blew transversely in horizontal lines over the bow, sometimes clouding up into a gush of white smoking mist like a burst of steam from a boiler, that made a blind stare of the look of the sea till the plunge of the wind with a long cry drove it clear of us.

It was no weather for Miss Grant to show herself on deck in, but she declined to remain below; so I made her as snug as I could with wraps and a waterproof-cloak, and she remained by my side, searching the cold, green, frothing tumble for any black speck that should denote the boat, as all hands of the rest of us did. Whenever Broadwater had his tacks aboard, he sent a couple of hands aloft to the fore and main-topmast cross-trees, with two more in the fore and main rigging just under the tops, and many an earnest glance would I direct at the men in the hope of detecting in the posture of any one of them that his attention had been taken, and that he would be singing out in a minute and pointing. The misery of that time comes back to me strongly. It is not in my pen to express the quality of depressing melancholy that was put into that thick, sombre, damp day, with its cheerless whistling and howling of wind aloft, and the grey sails darkening yet to the beating of the rain, and the chill and stormy washing of water from the bows of the vessel, by thoughts of the lost boat away out in the darkening gloom yonder, and of the anguish of expectation and fear that would fill the minds of the men in her, as, riding to their oars—for they would have long since abandoned the labour of rowing—they leaned over the low gunwale, peering past each green, glimmering curl of sea for any smudge upon the wall of vapour that had closed around them which should indicate the presence of our brig.

They would, of course, be without food or water. Small chance of any such discipline as Broadwater was equal to providing in this way for the hurried dispatch of a vessel's boats!

"Do you think," Miss Grant said to me, "that the poor fellows will be able to live in such a sea as this?"

"Impossible to say," I replied, with a look at the remaining boat that was of the size and shape of the other; "every wave has had a snappish run throughout. Yet the men are sailors, and will know how to manage if management be practicable. I wonder if they picked up the boy."

"I fear the worst," she exclaimed, with a tremble in the parting of her lips to the sweep of the breeze, whilst from the whiteness of her face amid the twilight of her hood that covered her head, her dark eyes shone out bright with a light that was feverish with brilliance.

"Why?" "I asked.

"I believe this to be the fulfilment," she answered, "of Gordon's prophetic melancholy. It was the shadow of this event that lay upon him."

I shook my head. "There was no prophetic depression in the other two; at least one may reasonably suppose so. Of the three, probably Gordon was the most prosaic. Why, since there were four men to perish to-day—supposing that they *do* perish—I include the cabin-boy—why, I ask, to one of them only should the future whisper? No, no; Gordon would have been gloomy whether this wretched business had happened or not."

"I fear the worst for them," she persisted. "Is not the air darkening rapidly, too! Should the night fall without our sighting them—oh, Mr. Musgrave, what a dreadful fate!—what a dreadful fate!"

She swept her hands to her eyes, but dropped them quickly, and running to the rail gazed seawards! and I think had the hour been one of gravest peril to ourselves, instead of to the poor fellows tossing about somewhere out in the windward bleakness, I must have found a moment to admire—and with a stirring of wonder in my admiration too—the character of tragic beauty her face took with the grief, and pity, and eagerness in it, as the flash of the wind swept her hood clear of the soft brown of her disordered hair, and left her lineaments plain against the green hills, and blowing froth, and shadowy steep of the scene of heaven and ocean beyond.

The gathering darkness which she had noticed before I did was to prove a squall. You heard the long moan of it ere it had leapt clear of the near haze, and revealed its approach by the glaring rush of waters at its base. Already Broadwater was carrying on till the covering-board was flush with the water over the side. "Let go royal and t'gallant halliards!" he bawled. "Down flying jib, up mainsail!" and as these last words left his mouth the squall struck the vessel. I had foreseen one consequence, and had provided against it by whipping a rope's-end round Miss Grant's waist, otherwise, to the sudden, fierce inclination of the deck, she must have fallen to leeward as one might slip down the roof of a house. The angle was so extreme that it was almost impossible to stir. The halliards had been let go, but the slope of the masts prevented the yards from travelling. "Over with the helm! over with the helm!" shrieked Broadwater. I sprang to the lee-spokes to assist the fellow who had relieved the half-blood, and who, though he was straining with set teeth, seemed unable to stir the wheel by so much as a spoke. It was now a picture of giddy commotion and bewildering uproar for a long five minutes. The brig was so pressed down, that though we had got the helm jammed hard up, I feared for some moments that she would not pay off. You saw the yeast blowing like cream over the lee-rail, and it was like soapsuds, as high as a man's waist, the whole length of the lee-scuppers. Sheets had been slackened away, or let go, and the rattle of canvas shook the vessel to her heart. The squall was a heavy one, and it blew with a voice of thunder out of the thickness; and what with the roaring sound of the blast on high—an independent noise that dominated all other sounds with the violent ring of gusts or guns echoing through the rushing wind—and what with the slapping of liberated folds of canvas, the hollow blows of seas upon the exposed weather-side of the hull, Broadwater's shouts, the cries of the men, it was a scene that might have made even an old sailor think it about time to go to prayers. Fortunately however the captain's wits were equal to an emergency of this kind. He bellowed lustily indeed, but his orders were right. On the mainsail being hauled up, and the trysail smothered, the brig paid off, and as she recovered something of an even keel, whilst she gradually presented her stern to the wind, the yards descended the masts, instantly relieving the heavy strain up there; and before it we bowled—though towards what quarter of the sea I never thought of looking—with topsail-yards on the caps, the topgallant-sails and royals blowing out like flags from the grip of their clewlines and leech-lines, with the hauled-down jibs making the booms buckle again to the heavy dance of the folds, which the pitch of the vessel would souse and bring up streaming till the air beyond the head was white from the foam ripped away from them by the wind.

However, though full of weight and spite, it was but a squall, and the scream of it had presently fined down into the familiar moaning of the early blast. The brig's company was now a short-handed crew for the work that was to be done, and as every pair of hands was of the utmost consequence, I sang out to Broadwater from the wheel that I should be happy, if he had no objection, to stick to the post, that the man whose trick it was might assist the others. He assented with a wave of his hand. Miss Grant came and stood beside me. The crew worked with a will, thinking perhaps that the lives of the men in the boat away out upon the dirty, shrouded jumble—though God knows where they would be *now*—might depend upon their smartness. But it was three-quarters of an hour before the sailor whom I had relieved came to take the wheel from me again, by which time the brig was once more close-hauled under topsails, maintop-gallant-sail, foresail, and trysail, eating her way into the thickness, that was denser than ever it had been at any other time of the day, and that was already deepening in shade to the gathering shadows of an early night above it. Yet till the close of the second dog-watch Broadwater went on ratching in short boards, the men working without a murmur, without any hint of mutinous reluctance in their movements, for the hope they yet had of surging within sight of the boat. But at eight o'clock it was black night—the blacker for rain and haze—the seas were shouldering blocks of gloom, with wan glares of foam here and there, and a smart rattling of wet flinging to the ear like discharges of musketry from the obscurity along the waist to the forecastle.

I was then below with Miss Grant, both of us as wearied as if we had shared in the toils of the seamen, and as anxious about the lookout as we were depressed by the incidents of the day. But for our private stock of provisions, no food would have crossed our lips, for the cook had been called from his galley to help work the ship; no man had been told off to wait upon us aft, and we must have gone to bed after a fast lasting from breakfast, but for the tins of cooked delicacies, the tongues, biscuits, and wines I had been wise enough to liberally provide ourselves with.

It was two bells in the first watch when Broadwater came below. I had long before trimmed and lighted the cabin-lantern, and was sitting at the table near Miss Grant smoking a cheroot, and endeavouring to extract a little cheerfulness of mind out of a glass of brandy-and-water. This was the first time the captain had left the deck since he had fetched his old blunderbuss. He threw down his sou'-wester that was streaming with wet, pulled off his shaggy pea-coat, which sparkled to the lantern-light with the moisture upon it as though it were crystallized, and all in silence opened a locker, took out a knife and fork, a large cube of corned beef upon a tin plate, a couple of sea-biscuits, a bottle of rum, and a tin pannikin; and then sitting down, squared his elbows and fell to with the avidity of a famished hound, never offering to speak. However, it was ridiculous to suppose that I was to be kept in ignorance of such arrangements as he had made, and such schemes as he had decided upon; and as it was no moment to recall his insult, I waited until he had finished his supper, particularly keeping silent until he had drained his pannikin, and then said bluntly, "I suppose you've given up all hope of finding the boat?"

"All hope," he answered huskily, taking a surly squint at me with his little heartless eyes.

"You are now without a mate," said I, feeling Miss Grant's hand coming to my arm with a sudden pressure of her fingers to the uncontrollable dismay which followed Broadwater's hopeless answer. "You are now in a quandary, and can command me if you like."

"Command ye in what way?" he answered, filling his pannikin afresh.

"I'll take the mate's berth if you choose, but of course only to the extent of helping you in the navigation of the vessel."

"Thank'ee," he answered, in his roughest manner. "I hope to be able to do without you."

"I'm very glad indeed to hear it," said I, and indeed I spoke the truth. "But you surely so not intend to keep a look-out day and night alone?" I added, for it seemed to me unimaginable that he should find a man forward fit to entrust the charge of the brig to whilst he was taking rest.

He appeared to struggle with his temper, as though he could not force his inclination to answer me through his bad and sullen humour.

Miss Grant suddenly said, "Captain Broadwater, we have a *right* to know what measures you have taken for our safety." Her imperious look appeared to affect him as a command.

"You'll not suppose, mum," said he, "that I should be down here a-taking of it easy, with the idea," he continued, dragging his great watch out and looking at it, "of turning in in a few minutes for a snatch of rest, if I hadn't left matters ship-shape up above," with a jerk of his thumb at the deck.

"I am glad you have found somebody you can trust," said I.

"I dessay ye are," said he, "and so am I, I'm sure;" and then rising and returning the remains of his supper and his bottle of rum to the locker whence he had extracted them, he picked up his coat and sou'-wester and went to his berth.

It might have made the stoutest-hearted man feel a bit nervous to learn that this brig was virtually abandoned by her captain to her crew, who were full of mutiny and hatred of him, whilst *he* lay snoring below. Of course, seeing how matters had come about, Broadwater could not help himself; by which I mean that it was impossible for him to remain in sole charge of the deck night and day until Rio was reached; therefore, since he would not let me act as mate—and it was quite conceivable that the old fool may have imagined me as mutinously disposed towards his discipline as he had that afternoon insolently affirmed me to be—it was necessary for him to appoint some forecastle hand to the post; but it was a sort of surrender that filled me with uneasiness. I did not attempt to conceal my fears from Miss Grant; indeed she understood the danger of our situation as well as I.

"Any man," I exclaimed, "would scarcely conceive it possible that an old sea-captain such as Broadwater should coolly go to bed and, supposing he sleeps till midnight, leave his brig absolutely at the mercy of her crew till then—at the mercy of a set of men whose hatred of him all through must have been immeasurably heightened to-day by his barbarous treatment of the poor cabin-boy, and the loss of men that followed. But then, what is the wretched old creature to do? He must get some rest during the twenty-four hours, or else entirely lose the very little sense that he was born with. I'll step on deck and see if I can make out who it is that has charge."

It was a black night. The brig had been brought to her course again, though no doubt some men in Broadwater's situation would have kept their vessel hove-to till dawn, in the hope of picking up the missing boat. The dusk was too thick to enable me to make out what canvas we were under. There was not much weight of wind however, but it was charged with damp, and one found a heaviness in it for that reason perhaps when the weather-roll of the vessel brought it in a gust to the face. I walked right aft to the helm, unable to distinguish anybody on deck, then caught sight of the face of a man named Andrew Wilkins, who stooped his head at the moment into the yellow sheen flowing out of the binnacle to get a better view of the card.

I said to him, "Who has charge?"

"Why, the blooming cook," he answered, with a low laugh.

"The *cook?*" I cried, thinking he joked.

He laughed again, but without merriment, and said, "Yes, sir; it's old Drainings as is boss just now."

"Where is he?" said I, drawing away from the glare of the binnacle-lamp to look into the darkness forward; but it was not to be penetrated.

"Somewheres to wind'ard, sir, if he ain't gone and turned in," he answered.

I was in the act of groping my way to the weather-side, when it flashed upon me that I might be acting rashly in showing uneasiness or exhibiting inquisitiveness; so I just said in a careless voice to the fellow at the wheel, "'Tis strange for a captain to go to the galley for a chief mate. Perhaps the cook may have been a shipmaster, forced by adversity into boiling beef for sailors. I suppose he would know what to do should heavy weather come along?"

"I heard the capt'n tell him what to do," answered the man. "Should anything happen, he's to hammer the deck with a handspike over the capt'n's head. That's about as much as can be expected of a cook."

"Well," said I, "this is a queer sort of voyage anyhow, as the Yankees would say. Goodnight." And with that I made my way to the hatch, looking into the blackness on the weather-deck for the cook's figure, but without seeing him, though I don't say he was not there, for the sky was of a raven hue; the very substance of the quarter-boat melted into it, and the eye sought in vain for a line of shroud, or for any faintest configuration of canvas on high.

"The cook in command!" cried Miss Grant, when I gave her the news; "it is ridiculous! ... It is dreadful, Mr. Musgrave!"

I thought so too, though I could not forbear a laugh at the very fancy of it, spite even of the rebuke my momentary merriment found in the startled expression of her eyes.

"I suppose," said I, "that he is the one man on board who enjoys the captain's confidence. He may be the only creature honestly disposed, for all we know, and let us believe that Broadwater has guessed it. After all, I dare say he is as well able to keep a look-out as any other man in the vessel; and absurd as the notion is, yet on reflection I believe old Broadwater to be right for once, and that our slumbers are more likely to be secure with Master Cookee stumping the quarter-deck with a handspike ready to thunder the skipper into vigilance, than were one of the sailors in charge."

However, though after sitting together another hour I induced her to withdraw to her cabin, it took me a long while to persuade myself to follow her example, and by that time it was hard upon midnight. Once or twice I looked through the hatch, but the blackness as before hung extraordinarily thick; there was nothing to be seen, and the wet in the wind made me glad to return to the shelter of the cabin. The brig rolled uneasily, but the motion was comparatively steady, no longer the half paralysing jumps and souses of the morning and afternoon. There was a heavy gloom upon my spirits. It was not only the memory of the sight of the cabin-boy clinging in terror to the boom, Broadwater's red face full of threats and menacing gestures, and the smile the poor lad gave me as he swept astern; there was the thought of Gordon and the two fellows in the boat; the feelings that would be in them, supposing them still alive, as they tossed in their tiny cockle-shell upon the dark hills of sea, without the leanest phantom of star for them to rest their eyes upon, without a fragment of biscuit to appease their hunger, or a drop of fresh water to moisten their lips. These were fancies to put such a chill into the atmosphere of the cabin even, that one shuddered as to an icy blast to the mere muffled hum of the wind moaning in the rigging. I rose, for sitting below was like keeping a watch without any purpose in it; and besides, if any one of the sailors should peer through the closed skylights, and spy me leaning with folded arms against the bulkhead wide awake, it might enter the minds of the whole of them to believe that I was in league with the captain, practically keeping a look-out for him, though covertly; and I tell you the mere idea of this sent me to my cabin right off.

About ten minutes after I had tumbled into my bunk I heard a dull pounding noise, and instantly sat up in bed, not a little alarmed by the strange unusual sound, until it occurred to me that it might prob-ably be the cook beating with his handspike over the captain's head to arouse him. The lamp in my cabin was alight, though I had dimmed it. To make sure of that strange battering noise, I went softly to my door and looked out. The door that shut off the after-berths stood open, hooked to the bulkhead, and I had a clear view of a great part of the state cabin, including the companion-steps past the table. After an interval of a minute or two the pounding noise was repeated, and now I was certain that it was the cook beating with a handspike. I continued to peer, showing however only as much of my head past the door as enabled me to use my eyes, for I had no mind to be caught keeping such a look-out as this, either by Broadwater or anybody else in the brig. At the same time I was anxious to make sure that the captain responded to the cook's summons, for I felt that it would be possible for me to obtain some rest with the knowledge that the captain had charge of the vessel. A third time the cook pounded, on this occasion very nois-

ily, and with so many hard thumps that one would have thought the
hands were caulking the decks, or, worse still, endeavouring to beat
some planks out. The fellow was evidently growing impatient, and he
used his handspike as though he meant to let the captain know that he
wanted to turn in. Shortly after the third thunderous call, Broadwater
came out growling like an old dog, and giving the cook a number of
hard words, as though indeed the man stood before him. But first he
rolled to his locker, muttering his abuse of the cook without intermis-
sion, until he silenced himself with a full pannikin of rum. He then,
after a slow look round, went on deck, and I returned to my bunk; but
four bells had struck before I fell asleep, so incessantly was I haunted
by the vision of the drowning lad, by thoughts of the missing boat, by
recollection of the strange melancholy that had fallen upon the spirits
of Gordon, by contact as one might say with the mysterious sheen of
the cold bow of light we had sailed through, and above all by considerations of Miss Grant's and my safety aboard this brig, with a drunken
old tyrant for captain, and a cook for chief mate, and as ship's company a short-handed crew charged to the throat with mutiny, with one
malignant and active principle of evil amongst them in the shape of the
half-blood, to whom the *Iron Crown*'s arrival at Rio or any other port
meant death.

Chapter III
I Take Command

I WAS AWAKENED BY A sharp, persistent knocking on my cabin-door. "Who is there?" I called out, scarcely yet awake.

"The crew wants a word with ye, sir," exclaimed a deep-throated voice outside.

"Eh, what's that?" I cried, instantly startled into broad wakefulness.

"The crew 'ud be glad to have a talk with ye, sir," repeated the leather-lunged voice, the tones of which, though I might have had some memory of them had I heard them on deck, sounded most harshly unfamiliar, even malevolent, in the privacy and retirement of these after-cabins.

"All right," I exclaimed; "give me a minute or two to dress. Who are you?"

"Terence Mole, sir."

"Ha!" said I, "and where are the others?"

"All of 'em in the cabin, saving the chap at the wheel, and Charles, who's keeping a look-out."

There was broad daylight on the ocean, as a glance through the scuttle assured me; the flash of sunlight came to the glass of the screwed-up port in a fine-weather tremble off the waters, with a commingling of atmospheric blueness that made one know there was plenty of clear azure overhead. It was natural that I should wonder with all my might what the crew could want with me as I dressed myself, but not hastily; for let what might have happened, I was resolved to oppose an aspect at least of composure to whatever might befall, and the first condition of dignity was a leisurely observance of the wish of the crew to see me. I looked at my watch, punctually timed by every day's meridian, and found the hour ten minutes to five. I dressed myself fully, lingering to wash my face and hands and brush my hair; trifling things to talk about indeed, but useful to recall as an instance at all events of self-control, which to this day I am proud to remember; for let me tell you, knowing the posture of the men as I did, it was enough to throw a heartier mind than mine off its balance, to be suddenly aroused from a deep sleep by the wooden knuckles of a sailor, and to collect with a half-conscious ear from his harsh, gruff accents that the seamen of the brig wanted a word with me.

I stepped into the little passage with a glance at Miss Grant's door, which was closed, though I had no doubt she was wide awake within, and had overheard the sailors' message to me. There were eight men in the cabin, four of them seated at the table; the tall seaman, Terence Mole, leaned against a stanchion with his arms, naked to the elbows, folded upon his breast; the sixth—the cook—squatted at the foot of the companion-steps; two others marched to and fro with their hands buried in their breeches-pockets; but they came to a halt when they saw me. The novelty of the sight of these rough fellows seated or lounging about an interior which I, with a sailor's experiences in me, knew that at ordinary times they would think of, in their own sea-parlour, as a sort of holy ground in which no foremast Jack was ever to be heard of, unless he came to catch a pig or to holystone the deck of it, was, I protest, as much a shock in its way as if one of the men to my approach had saluted me with a levelled pistol. The eastern sunshine streamed upon the skylight, and the place was full of the brilliance of the morning. I noticed a sort of shagged, haggard, worried look in two or three of the hairy, weather-lined faces. Used as I was to their attire of duck-breeches, loose shirts, Scotch and other caps, and half-boots—though some of them were unshod—yet the mere presence of them in the cabin rendered their garb as strange in my sight as if I had never beheld it before, and I seemed to find in the first presentment of them the most genuine imaginable aspect of outlawry, abominably in conformity with every fancy, recollection, or imagination of mutiny that could occur to an observer. The fellows who were seated at the table rose when I entered; Mole quitted his lounging attitude; and the cook, a stout, pale, sandy-haired, man, writhed himself on to his feet off the ladder. I came to a stand a foot or two in advance of the doorway which conducted to the after-berths, that Miss Grant might hear what I said, and gather from my language the import of the speech of the others if their syllables should not be always audible to her.

"What is it, men?" I said.

Mole dropped his folded arms, and passed the back of one great hand in a sort of smearing gesture, awkward yet defiant too, across his forehead, over which his hair lay thick as a mat to his eyebrows.

"We've thought it proper to tell you, sir," he exclaimed, "that the capt'n's a-missing."

"Missing!" I cried; "since when? Do you know?"

The cook came forward, and said in a wheezy voice, striking his chest as though he had taken a chill there, "I was on dooty, 'cording to Capting Broadwater's orders, till midnight; then I thumped him up with a handspike, his instructions being I wasn't to leave the deck on any account till he came. Well, he arrived, and I went forrads and tarned in. At four, Mole here came to say that the capt'n must have gone below, as nothen was to be seen of him. I says, 'That's odd, ain't it?' I says, 'an' he so pertikler!' Jim here had had the wheel since four bells, and I asked him if he'd seen aught of the capt'n, and he says that at six bells the skipper looked into the binnacle, and then went forrads again out of sight, for it had been as black all night as if a man had gone dark hisself, and arter that I saw no more of him."

"All that's right enough," said the sailor, to whom the cook referred.

"Have you looked for him?" said I quietly, for a sense of deep insincerity in all this business was creeping into me, spite of the cook talking like an honest man on his oath.

"Everywhere saving them there cabins," answered Mole, pointing with his muscular arm", blue with devices, to the after-berths.

"There are but two cabins vacant," said I; "come with me and look for yourself."

I threw open the door of the berth in which were our private stock of provisions, then the door confronting it, and motioning Mole to precede me, returned to where I had before been standing.

"Of course you have searched his own berth and those near it?" said I.

"First and foremost of all, naturally," responded Mole.

"What is your notion of the matter?" I asked.

Three of them answered together, "He's overboard." Mole added, "Ne'er a doubt of it. It's all hands' opinion. He wasn't a man to hide himself; why should he?" The half-caste Ladova laughed in his throat. "If he's aboard," continued Mole, "we should have found him. We've so overhauled the old hooker that had he been a rat we must have come across him. Ain't that right, lads?"

"Ay, ay," came the reply in a short growl from them all, and the cook in his wheezy voice added, "If he ben't gone to keep poor Billy company my eyes ain't mates."

The suspicion of the insincerity of all this had now grown into a strong conviction that some black deed had been done since I took my last view of Broadwater as he clambered up the companion-steps. But along with this conviction there came also clear perception that I must not by word or look betray the merest phantom of my thoughts, otherwise I should be held as incriminating as a witness, and dealt with as one, I had no doubt. My secret agitation was already sufficiently great to render the assumption of an air of consternation easy. I looked from one to another and cried, "Though I never liked the captain, men; though I don't mind saying now that he was one of the most tyrannical and ill-mannered shipmasters I ever met or heard of in my life, yet his disappearance is a blow to the lady and myself. The brig is now without a commander, without a mate, without even a bo'sun. How, think you, did Captain Broadwater meet his end? Was it an accident, do you suppose? He could not have *walked* overboard." I shook my head. "My lads," I said solemnly, "I don't doubt but that he committed suicide. He was as a madman all day yesterday—charged me, men, *me*" I cried, striking my breast with a passionate gesture, "with a desire to work up a mutiny aboard! A madman, my lads! a drunken lunatic! Not a shadow of doubt but he destroyed himself in his watch on deck, urged overboard, maybe, by the recollection of Gordon and the poor lad and your two shipmates—of all four of whom he has gone before his God as surely the murderer as if he had slit the throat of every man of them with his own hand."

"Mates," cried Mole, tossing his head to clear the hair out of his eyes, and sending a fiery glance from one to another of the seamen, "Mr. Musgrave's put it as there's ne'er a man of us could have said it. I've been a seafaring man eighteen years, man and boy, in all sorts of craft, from the likes of this snorter"—he spat upon the deck—"away up to the Atlantic clippers; but of all capt'ns"—he raised his arm with a face that darkened to the sudden fierce restraint he put upon himself; "but he's gone," he added, letting his hand fall; "committed suicide, as you say, sir; a thing most sartin—past all doubting in fact; and here we are, Mr. Musgrave, to find out what's to do."

I could see with half an eye that the impression I had sought to produce was made. I thrust my hands in a careless sort of way into my breeches-pockets, and fell to pacing the deck. "One thing," I exclaimed, "has followed so fast on top of another, that though there ought to be something staggering in Captain Broadwater's suicide, I find," I said, with a half-laugh and a shrug of the shoulders, "that it scarcely so much as surprises me. But," I continued, addressing Mole, "you ask what's to be done? Have you and your mates a scheme?"

"Well," he answered, speaking with return to his first awkward, defiant manner, "when these men and me, after giving the brig a thorough overhaul, was agreed that the skipper was *gone*, we tarned to and asked one another what was to be done. It didn't need much debating. It's been onderstood all along forrads that you were a sailor yourself equal to navigating a ship, and so of course we at once settled upon asking you to take charge."

I nodded, taking care to preserve a careless manner to guard against exposure of the worry in me that grew more and more consuming as I listened.

"You will take charge, sir?" said Mole, interrogatively.

"Certainly, if you wish it," said I.

He looked round at the others with a faint inclination of his head, and continued, revolving his cap in his hand with his eyes upon it: "Next consideration was, where to go." He looked up at me without seeming to lift his eyelids.

"Where to go!" I cried, startled out of my feigned posture of indifference by the fellow's words. "We're bound to Rio. Shall we not proceed there?"

Every man of them wagged his head with a sort of groaning "No! no! no!" full of an unmistakable note of emphasis.

"We're all resolved not to sail the brig to Rio," said Mole, in an aggressive way that was like a surly hint to me not to argue the point; "we've been turning the matter over, and as we larnt from Mr. Gordon yesterday that our latitude was a few degrees to the norrads of twenty, we've settled to ask you to navigate the *Iron Crown* to the West Indies."

"The West Indies! You are naming a number of islands which cover a wide area of ocean," I answered coldly; for it had come to me like an inspiration that, if I valued my own and Miss Grant's safety, I must consent to do these men's bidding without so much as even a falter in the speech in which I assented; that practically the brig was *theirs*, and I and my companion absolutely in their power; and that my sole policy was to appear as though I was willing to be of them, though my approach must exhibit a little natural hesitation. "What part of—what island in the West Indies have you in your mind?"

"Neighbourhood of Cuba," answered one of the men.

"Bill, leave it to me if *you* please," exclaimed Mole, turning upon the speaker with a frown. "Our notion is, sir," he continued, addressing me with a touch of respect in his manner that was not a little welcome, "that you should navigate the brig towards the island of Cuba, and give us notice when we're within a day's sail of it. Mr. Musgrave," he continued, flinging down his cap, extending his left hand and resting the fist of the right one in it, "you've been a sailor yourself—you've seen what we've suffered—you onderstand the situation we're in—let it, sir, as between seafaring men, be all plain sailing between you and us. There's been murder done aboard this here craft as you know, sir; and," he proceeded deliberately, almost grinding out the words as he delivered them, "we don't intend that the man as made away with Mr. Bothwell shall be took. We don't want no interference. We don't intend that the *Iron Crown* shall be boarded. We don't mean to be laid hold of, and charged with mutineering, and punished for it. D'ye see *that*, Mr. Musgrave? We've got no idea of coming to any sort of harm that we can provide against. What's done's *done!* Nothen's happened but what's been deserved, sir—by God, deserved, mates," he almost roared out, striking his fist violently into the palm of his hand; then suddenly folding his arms upon his breast, he added, in a changed voice charged with menace, "That's the situation, sir, and we want to know if you'll help us."

"On certain conditions," said I.

"What'll they be?" he exclaimed, quickly and suspiciously.

I surveyed him a moment whilst I thought, then held up one finger and said, "The lady must have the same privileges of privacy which she has enjoyed down to the present moment."

He took a view of the others, and bringing his eyes slowly to mine said, "The lady'll have no call to be afraid of us, sir. She'll find us sailors and *men*." A grunt of assent from the others followed this.

"Thank you for saying so," said I, "if ever a woman deserved the kindness of a crew she does. Her heart has been with you from the beginning in your troubles."

"Yes, by the Virgin that's true!" cried the half-caste Ladova, fetching the table a blow with his fist.

"As consarns the lady, sir," said Mole, "set your mind at ease. What's your other conditions?"

"I must, with her, have the exclusive use of this cabin."

One of them cried, "You're welcome enough to it. The fok'sle's good enough for poor sailor men."

"It's as Thomas there says," exclaimed Mole, "the fok'sle's good enough for us. We don't want no cabin. What's your other conditions?"

"I have named them all," I answered. "You'll provide, I suppose, for our comfort here—tell some one of you off to bring our meals along?"

"You'll see to that, cook," said Mole, turning upon him.

"Ay," exclaimed the other, "that'll be all right, sir. The food'll be cooked as afore, and served as afore, if it comes to my having to wait on ye myself."

"Men," said I, "I can expect no more, and I am satisfied. You have met me fairly and spoken to me honestly; and whilst you continue faithful to the understanding that now exists between us, you'll find me as staunch as if I had been one of you from the beginning, and the most ill-used of you too. There are two men on deck—you answer for it that they will be satisfied with our arrangement?"

"Yes," answered Mole, "specially may Charles be answered for. A man whose soul has turned black inside him, as his has, by the shadder o' the gallows, ain't going to be very exacting in his arrangements to get rid of the cuss. Charles will agree, sir; so will t'other."

"Be it so," said I; "and now I'll step into the captain's cabin for a sight of his charts and the log-book there, that I may shape a course to Cuba. That's it, I think?"

"Right, sir," exclaimed Mole. Then looking at the others he said, "Lads, there's nothing I've forgot to say, is there?"

There was some scratching of heads and shuffling of feet, and then one said, "No, everything's been said, Terry, I think;" and another, "Mr. Musgrave consents to take command, and steer the vessel for Cuba, giving us a day's notice of its heaving into view, and I don't know that there's anything more that we wanted to see him about;" but a third cried, "Ay, but Mr. Musgrave'll want some one to stand watch and watch with him. Who's to do it?"

"You're capt'n now, sir," said Mole, rounding upon me, but speaking very civilly; "it's for you to choose one of us to act as your mate. The crew'll be satisfied with your choice, no matter who you fix upon."

"Then," said I, "Mr. Mole, I choose you."

The calling him "mister" set the whole of the fellows on the broad grin.

"Very well, sir," said Mole. "Lads, ye can get forrads now. I'll keep a look-out, capt'n, until ye come up." Secretly confounded and dismayed as I was by all this business, yet his calling me "captain" made me smile spite of myself, as the others had on my terming him "mister." A general laugh followed, but nothing more was said as the whole body of them went quietly up the ladder and disappeared through the companion-hatch.

I stood a moment or two grasping a stanchion, with a hand to my forehead, oppressed by such a sense of bewilderment that it was as sickening in its way as a bad fit of giddiness. But I rallied swiftly, and observing Miss Grant's door to remain closed, stepped at once to the cabin that had been occupied by Broadwater. I entered it with no small feeling of awe. That he had been foully made away with I did not for an instant doubt, and the shadow of the crime seemed to lie like a material gloom upon the atmosphere of the plain interior.

I was in the mood, indeed, just then to be shocked and startled by little things, and I am not ashamed to own that I recoiled as though the ghost of the skipper stood before me to the sight that first met my eye on opening the door of a pea-jacket and a sou'-wester on top of it hanging together by the same hook, and under the jacket a pair of breeches arched, empty as they were, to the exact posture Broadwater's shanks exhibited in life. I protest, the suit of clothes, with the thatch of the sou'-wester coming down abaft the coat, looked so astonishingly like the old skipper, that for the instant I thought he had hanged himself with his face to the bulkhead. There was a bunk in the corner with the bedclothes tumbled; over it a short hanging shelf holding a few nautical books; in a corner another table on which were a quadrant-case, a chronometer, a few mathematical instruments, and, very conspicuous, Broadwater's huge silver turnip watch. The soles of a pair of sea-boots, one foot lying upon another, glimmered out from the gloom under the bunk, as though the captain lay drunk and silent in the darkness there. I took notice, though now I wonder that I should have had eyes for such trifling details, of a likeness of Broadwater and, as I supposed, of his wife facing each other; two heads cut out in black paper, with streaks of bronze to define the lineaments, mounted on a white ground. There was a canvas bag of charts leaning dropsically against the head of the bunk, and in a roll alongside it was a chart of the North Atlantic, which on opening it I found "pricked" down to noon on the preceding day. The mate's logbook was upon the table. The writing in it was Bothwell's down to the time of his murder; a very neat, clean, almost ladylike hand, that threw into grotesque contrast old Broadwater's sprawling, absurdly ill-spelt entries. Gordon, I suppose, poor fellow, had been without literature enough to qualify him to "keep" the book. Having made the necessary calculations to enable me to shape the course the men desired I quitted the berth, grateful to escape an atmosphere in which I breathed with difficulty, and was passing through my cabin on my way to the deck when I caught sight of Miss Grant looking out through her door. I immediately went to her. There was a resolved, quiet expression in her face, and her voice was without tremor as she said, "I overhead all that passed in the cabin. You do not doubt that the captain has been murdered?"

"I do not," I replied; "but the men must not imagine that we suspect them."

"How will they treat us?"

"Oh, they are well disposed, respectful in their manner to me, and they consented at once to my request that the after part of the vessel should be used only by us. This was more than I had dared hope. You will have heard their demand that I should navigate the vessel to Cuba?"

"Yes," she exclaimed, catching her breath quickly; "it will be a round-about way to Rio, if ever we get there." She smiled faintly and sighed.

"Never fear, we shall get there," said I cheerfully. "Broadwater has to be thanked for this abominable muddle. I foresaw it all. I was certain that the men would never suffer this vessel to proceed to her destination, call it Rio or any other place, under a captain whose evidence would hang the man who had freed them from the mate's tyranny. But let us most anxiously bear in mind, Miss Grant, that our policy is not to know that Broadwater has been made away with."

"Oh, I see that clearly," she answered.

"He has committed suicide. Dwell upon this view, and the thought of it will become a habit, and we shall be the safer to that extent. There is plenty of time before us in which to talk over our position and make plans. I will now go on deck and alter the vessel's course. The men must believe me honestly disposed—indeed I must prove myself so; for let them be called murderers—mutineers—the blood that has been shed is assuredly on the heads of Broadwater and Bothwell."

I raised her hand to my lips and went on deck. The morning was as brilliant as any that had ever shone over us. There was a light wind from the north-east which I might have accepted as the first breathings of the regular trades but for the absence of the familiar clouds which float like signals set in the blue heavens to mark the confines of these gracious and serviceable gales. The whole of the eastern sea stretched in a rippling dazzle as of wrinkled quicksilver, of so fiery an effulgence that the weeping eye went instantly from it to the west for the relief it got from the dark blue water there, and the soothing azure of the sky that sloped down to the soft liquid boundary. I ran a swift glance around the horizon, but there was nothing to be seen. The brig was under the shortened canvas of the preceding night; main-topgallant-sail set, mainsail furled, tack of the trysail hauled up, a jib and the lighter staysails stowed. I found Mole pacing the deck with the conscious looks of a person in authority. Though it was yet early the cook had lighted the fire, and most of the men were gathered about the little caboose, holding pots of hot coffee, some munching at biscuits, others smoking. There was a suggestion of orderliness amongst them that satisfied my eye. It was natural perhaps that, recollecting the ugly stain on the cabin-floor, I should have thrown a hurried glance over the quarter-deck planking for a like hint that *this* time should concern Broadwater; but all glistened sand-white to the sun, with no further dyes than the violet pendulous shadows of spar, sail, and rigging. I stepped aft to the binnacle, where Mole at once joined me.

"The course to Cuba," said I, "running a line to the midship bearings of the island, is west by south. Better get your yards braced in and make sail upon the vessel."

He instantly sung out, "Hands to the braces! Square the yards for Cuba, bullies!"

The men drained their pots and sprang to the ropes. Never from the hour of getting the anchor off Deal had they exhibited such hearty nimbleness. Their songs had the true ring, and their notes swept aloft to the hollows of the canvas, and away into the airy blue over the side with the joyous echo of the homeward-bounder's chorus. I motioned the man at the helm to put the wheel over, and the brig slowly floated round with her stern to the sun, and the wide soft heave of the sea coming along under the light wind to the blue shadow of her starboard quarter on the water. "Steady!" said I; "now hold her at that, my man."

"Cuba'll be under the bow then at this?" said he, with such a puckering of his face to the grin which overspread it, that it made one think of an old walnut-shell.

"Yes," said I, "in heading as you go we'll be running the island down in good time."

He leaned from the wheel to discharge a quantity of tobacco-juice over the stern. "Well," said he, "better a light pocket than a heavy heart. There'll be no paying off this voyage, I suppose. But, thank the Lard, there's been plenty *o' paying out*." He uttered Broadwater's name, calling curses upon it in accents by no means whispered, and out of the fullness of his soul fell a-talking to the brig with his eyes on the compass-card that swung sluggishly to the lubber's point.

I stood alone watching the men making sail upon the brig. Mole worked with the others, pulling hard, raising encouraging shouts, and springing here and there with the zeal of a man who considers it his duty to set an example. Events had come in such a hustling throng that in sober truth I had scarcely yet had time to realize our position. Now as my eye went to the men aloft loosening the sails, and the fellows below bawling out at the sheets and halliards, I could find a moment for reflection. If Broadwater had been murdered, it was hard to imagine, by the hearty, careless behaviour and half-jocose airs of the crew, that they knew of it. Yet if murder had been done it would be sheer idleness to feign that the men could be ignorant of it. There was always the fellow at the wheel to stand looking on as a witness. If Broadwater had made away with himself, the splash of him as he went overboard must have been a distinct sound fit to catch any ear, even above all such surly, weltering noises as were rising out of the blackness last night, from the forecastle head to the binnacle; unless indeed the old man, with the sleek, secret, wary cunning of the sailor who had gone to his account in the English Channel, had slipped in the darkness into the lee main-chains, and then softly dropped into the sea.

But this was to suppose that he had destroyed himself, an idea not to be entertained for the space of a breath in the face of the memory of a nature which proved him to have been so grossly of the earth, that one would as soon think of a hog terminating its existence. No! if he were out of the ship, then he was a murdered man; which being past all doubt, I entered into some swift speculations as to the manner of his death; and there being no hint upon the gleaming platform of the deck of the use of the knife, I concluded that he had been stunned and dropped overboard whilst still insensible. One man could have done this. Heavy as the square form of old Broadwater was, one pair of hands might have sufficed to drag the breathless body to the rail, and with vigorous upheaval swing it into a somersault over the bulwarks. Guilt, like terror, will often put a grip of steel into nerveless fingers.

But it was not to be supposed there were no witnesses to this crime. Broadwater was not the man to let the watch on deck skulk even in the blackest hour; therefore there would have been most of the sailors on the move as observers of all that could happen, from the forecastle to where the quarter-deck began; whilst aft was the helmsman with eyes for the rest of the ship there. Broadwater had been murdered, and all hands knew it! My heart turned sick and cold in me at the bare recollection of what had occurred during our execrable voyage, from the hour of Cooper's suicide to this moment, and I turned with a sense of faintness to the rail, and lay over it a minute or two to recover myself, half-distraught by the conflict of emotions which surged up into my head.

I felt a hand upon my shoulder. I started vehemently to the touch from my bitter mood of apprehension, and confronted Miss Grant.

"There can be no objection to my coming on deck, Mr. Musgrave?" she exclaimed.

"None," I answered; "the men have promised not to trouble either of us. We must trust them—we cannot do otherwise."

She looked at me earnestly. I don't doubt I was worn and haggard enough to account for her concerned, inquiring gaze. She was very pale, but I instantly noticed an expression of decision in her face as of a mind that has formed a resolution from which nothing is to divert it. Her black eyes looked at me with a full, steadfast shining. It was manifest that the true spirit of this girl, which had been bowed a little as I had last night remarked, had recovered its old natural, erect, heroic posture.

"Let us walk," she said. "It cannot matter that the men should see us together conversing. They must know we do so below when out of sight of them."

"A moment," I exclaimed. "Mr. Mole!" I sung out, "get topmast and topgallant-stunsails aloft. Crowd on all canvas. You want heels, as we do."

"Ay, ay, sir!" He re-echoed my orders promptly. Had he been mate throughout he could not have fitted the post more intelligently, nor exhibited shrewder perception of the dignity of the berth he filled in his manner of calling to the men, that was as good as saying to them, "I'm still your shipmate, lads; but don't forget that I'm *mister* also!"

Miss Grant and I fell to pacing the weather-deck, speaking low, and taking care to slew round for our forward pace whilst the fellow at the helm was still a little way off. We spoke of the disappearance of Broadwater. She did not doubt with me that he had been murdered, and that the whole of the crew were acquainted with the deed. I said to her, "But glance at them, Miss Grant; see how nimbly they run about; hear the cheeriness in their voices, and the occasional laugh! It is hard to believe they can be conscious that a second dreadful crime was committed in this ship in the dark hours of the morning."

"You will find it was the deed of one man," she answered; "the others feel themselves guiltless, and are happy because they are free. But who is the criminal? Is it Charles, do you think?"

"I *dare* not think," I exclaimed. "As it is, he must regard us as witnesses to his murder of the mate. His dread of Broadwater may be extended to us for the same reason. I am infinitely bothered—infinitely bothered," I exclaimed, with an involuntary clenching of my fist to a fit of exasperation that came to me with the thought of the horrible muddle we were in, and my helplessness and my inability to perceive the least gleam of light upon the heavy surrounding gloom.

She looked at me with a light smile, and said with a sort of peremptoriness, fascinating for its spirit and kindness, "If *I* can be cool, you must be so. Mr. Musgrave, I really do not feel the least bit afraid; certainly I have no fear for our lives. The hearts in those men are not black; they are not *pirates*; at least they are not pirates yet! They are wretched human creatures, who have been driven to this by ill-treatment, and now that the captain is gone they will stay their hands. Indeed, I have no fear. The future, to be sure, is a gloomy problem, but have not we courage enough between us to wait until it is solved?" She continued to look at me, preserving her light smile.

"We should change places," said I, feeling a trifle of colour in my cheeks; "you have twenty-fold my heart. Yet I should feel less worried, I believe, if I were alone here. It is my duty to see you safely to Rio—I embarked for no other purpose."

"But supposing *I* were alone!" said she.

"Ha!" I exclaimed; "and yet I don't know. I believe your nature would top the whole difficulty as a sea-bird a surge big enough to founder a line-of-battle ship. Indeed the mere circumstance of your being alone might win you more consideration from the sailors than they would show you with a male companion to look after you."

"Well, Mr. Musgrave," said she, and her voice still maintained its character of peremptoriness that rendered it, to my ear at all events, not a little engaging by the quality of half-conscious coquetry that I found in it, "bemoaning our position will not help it. I am certain you will yet discharge the obligation you generously, most generously, undertook; and how Alexander will thank you when he hears of our adventures, and of your heavy anxieties, my heart tells me."

She laid her hand upon her breast as she spoke; the Spanish blood in her indeed was confessed in many of her gestures. And though her accent was entirely English, yet perhaps in her choice of words you missed the ease and simplicity you would expect in a girl whose blood and lifelong surroundings were purely British. "A plague on Alexander!" thought I. It had come, somehow or other, to my never being able to hear her mention his name without a feeling in me that she was a bit maladroit in referring to it. "A plague on him!" I repeated to myself, spite of the glowing glance she shot at me through the fringes of her white lids, as if to an instant's curiosity as to what was passing in my mind.

"Under Heaven, Miss Grant," I answered, "I hope indeed to be able to discharge my obligation, though 'tis a word that I don't like—indeed, it is quite the other way. But," said I, with a touch of impatience, "this is no time for ceremonies of speech. We are talking of Rio and Alexander; and here, confound it! are we heading away on a crow's course for Cuba."

"Why do the men want to go to Cuba?" she asked.

"I may find out," I answered; "at present I have not the least idea. The West Indies, to be sure, suggest piracy; but *that* dream is gone. If the cross-bones and skull be not hauled down and stowed away, they are scarce now flying half-mast high. No! yonder live lies will not put this ship to any felonious use! I am to give them notice when we are within a day's sail of the island. That sounds queer—they don't name a port."

"It will all come right, Mr. Musgrave," she exclaimed.

I viewed her with an admiration I could not disguise. It was not only the challenge of her pale, flashful, resolved beauty just then; it was the high courage, giving her faith in the future, that won my eyes to her with an expression in them that must have conveyed more than the message I intended; for her own gaze drooped to it on a sudden, and went away seawards with the merest flutter of a smile upon her lips.

Chapter IV
We Are Spoken

PRESENTLY THE MEN HAD packed studdingsails to the royal yards upon the brig. The increased pressure raised a little yeasty hum at the forefoot. The warm blue gushing of the wind had weight enough in it to steady the canvas. The lower studding-sail overhanging the side by many feet rounded yearningly forwards cloud-like to the pressure; the foot of the mainsail, the weather-clew of which was hauled up, lifted, with scarce a swing-in, to the light heave of the fabric; aloft 'twas all luminous stirlessness, one sail looking to float upwards to another, till on high the little royals blended with the dainty tropical blue till the azure seemed to flow through the whiteness of them, as the pearly chip of new moon in the midday heavens will seem to be tinctured with the sapphire along which it slides. But I took notice that the crew did not intend to wash the decks down; and that I might satisfy myself on a head or two concerning the ship's discipline, and what was expected of me, I called to Mole, having Miss Grant still at my side. There was little of the cut-throat in the appearance of the seaman as he approached and stood before us, civil, but with a determined manner running through his respectfulness. He was indeed as fine a specimen of an English sailor as one could wish to see; tall, muscular, well-shaped, and with the grace begotten by years of rolling decks in every posture and movement; eyes full of sensibility, a cheek burnt by many months of high suns, and handsome features which seemed the manlier for the shaggy cast his thick, plentiful hair gave them.

"Mr. Mole," said I, "I am captain by the wish and consent of the crew, but have no ambition to venture a step further than they require me to walk. I therefore propose to give no orders until I have ascertained their views. They will work the ship, of course, brace the yards about to the wind, and make and shorten sail, and the like. And what more?"

"Nothing more, sir," he answered promptly. So I might have guessed "There'll be no money to take up, Mr. Musgrave," he continued, "and he's a good dog that'll work for a bare bone."

"There'd be money enough to earn though," said I, "should you feel disposed to turn to and make a salvage job of this business. Here's a brig without a commander, with her hold full of mixed commodities——"

He raised his hand with a glance forward. "No, sir. All hands is agreed. If we could stick the blooming hooker up for Lunnon town in a twenty-four hours' ratch, we'd sooner see her chivvying her hell-born skipper and mate that way," pointing down with a wild romantic gesture, "than handle a brace for her salvation." He took a steadier grip of the deck with his feet, so to speak, and looked at me as much as to say, "Hold to your first kind of questions."

"Then," said I, "I am expected to do nothing but navigate the brig?"

"To Cuba! Yes, sir, *that*, if you please, along with looking after her in dirty weather, for we know from Mr. Gordon that you're sailor enough for most things that can happen at sea."

It would have been idle to dispute this high opinion; the result no doubt of poor Gordon's hope that I might take the mate's place, and of his wish to confirm, by his ardent representations of me as a seaman, such satisfaction as the men might feel had I consented to Broadwater's appointment of me. "The crew will find me as dutiful to their desires, Mr. Mole," said I, "as they are faithful to the promises they made me."

"Mr. Musgrave," he exclaimed, "I'll be plain with ye. There'll be no call for you to take any notice of what goes on. The ship's stores aren't over good, and there's no reason why the cook should not tarn to and serve up a forecastle mess from time to time out of the cabin provisions. That there livestock," he continued, pointing to a hencoop, "belongs to you and the lady, I believe, sir?" "I said "yes." "Well, it won't be touched; but all the rest we shall take the liberty of claiming for ourselves."

"Of course," I said, "you will do as you please. But what about the liquor?"

"Ye needn't feel consarned about that," he exclaimed, understanding me; "every man's allowance'll be increased, and why not? But there'll be no drinking. If ever you should observe one of the men half so slewed as Broadwater used to be day arter day and night arter night, the crew'll give ye full consent to have him seized up, and their own hands'll do the rest. No, no, there'll be no drinking. The look-out ain't cheerful enough for the likes o' *that* sort of jollification. There's one thing, perhaps," he continued, changing his tone from the high, almost angry, energy in which he had been addressing me, "that is proper I should tell'ee, sir. The crew don't want to have nothen to say to any ships that may chance to pass. They desire to keep themselves to themselves."

A thought coming into my head on his saying this, I looked from Miss Grant to him and said, "If a chance offered for this lady and me to trans-ship ourselves, you would not object?"

He answered quickly and sternly, "Mr. Musgrave, there must be no meddling with other vessels. Please to understand *that*, sir."

I gave a little involuntary stamp of impatience, but said nothing. Miss Grant's hand stole to my arm with a gentle rebuking pressure of the fingers. The man added, softening his manner, "If you left us, who's to navigate the brig?"

"The ship that received us would lend you a mate."

"Oh, but you *don't* understand," he exclaimed, with a sour lowering of his face. "Well, sir, 'tis settled, of course—there is to be no conversing with anything that may heave in sight."

"I have told you I will do what you ask."

Just then the cook came up to us, to ask if we were ready for breakfast; and simple as the thing was, yet on the top of the shining morning and the quietude of the men, the touch of homeliness in the question put a sort of ease into my mind that was as useful to me just then as a small stroke of good fortune. It half rose to my lips to gratify Mole by inviting him to use the cabin for his meals, and had I been alone in the brig I should have done so; but the thought of him as society for Miss Grant checked my intention, though I protest he would have furnished her with out and away better company than ever Broadwater was, whilst it was not to be questioned that he had much more to talk about, having served in many different kinds of ships and visited many lands; whereas I believe Broadwater had passed most of his early life in the coasting trade, and never weathered either Cape in all the years he had used the sea.

The cook arrived with our breakfast in due course, and made some show of setting the dishes upon the table, as if he had taken more trouble than usual in the cooking of the meal, and was desirous we should value him for it. We were in the cabin waiting for him when he made his appearance, and after preparing the table he asked me if he should attend upon us. I thanked him for his civility, and added that we should be able to do without him, and told him very plainly that any attention he showed us now would not be forgotten by me hereafter. I shall always remember this man for the peculiar dingy pallor of his face, so much like the complexion of the "duff" he cooked for the sailors that no painter could have copied it more inimitably; also for his large, moist eyeballs, whose protrusion gave him a stupid, staring look, whilst at the same time the sky-blue pupils were so bleared with damp and the cloudiness of congestion as to make his wide-open gaze a sort of blind hunt in the direction of what he looked at. Though I had told him we could do without him, he still lingered, as though the novelty of being in the cabin pleased him. I thought I would ask him a question or two.

"Didn't it strike you as odd, cook, that Captain Broadwater should have chosen you to stand watch and watch with him?"

"Why, yes," said he, in his slow, wheezy voice. "I don't know what there was to make him partial to me in that way. He was no more belov-ed by me than he was by the others. He had such a choice of foul words as never I heard in a man's mouth afore. 'Sides a trick of hazing just proper to break the heart of a carthorse. Perhaps his feelings made his way towards me through his stomach. He was much in love with that end of him, sir, and yet coarse as a Finn in his eatin' too. He was born in the latitood o' roast pork. Had he been given birth to higher north he'd ha' asked in his prayers for nothen better than slush."

"He must have destroyed himself very cunningly last night, or rather this morning," said I. "No doubt he sneaked overboard into the black-ness of the lee-channels, and thence dropped." I glanced at him care-lessly as I said this.

"Can't tell ye how it happened, I'm sure," he answered. "I was tarned in at the time, as you know. Hope that there bacon's broiled to your liking, miss?"

Miss Grant thanked him with a smile and a bow.

"Were you ever at Cuba, cook?" said I, in an offhand way.

"No, sir," he answered, making a step towards the companion-ladder, as though he considered it time to be gone, and then stopping to answer me.

"Havana's the chief port," I continued. "There should be no difficul-ty, I suppose, in meeting with a ship bound straight on for Rio. We're both," said I, smiling and preserving my careless manner, "in a bit of a hurry, and I heartily wish that the crew had selected waters nearer the South American seaboard than the Caribbean Sea."

"We're bound to Cuba, anyhow," said he, with another stride towards the steps.

"Do you know what part of Cuba the men design to touch at?" I asked; but as I said this I felt Miss Grant's hand upon my knee. I looked at her, and marked a lightning-like lifting of her long lashes to the sky-light, where, partly through the glass and partly through the raised sash, I caught a sight of the figure of Mole standing in an unmistakably listening posture, though you would have said his attention was fixed by something that was happening forward. "No further need to detain you, cook," I exclaimed, loudly and cheerfully; "if you can persuade the crew—for your influence, you know, as 'doctor' ought to be consider-able—to let me navigate the brig to any point nearer to Rio than Cuba, you will be doing not me but this lady a prodigious service."

The figure at the skylight moved away. He probably guessed by the change of my voice that I knew he was listening. The cook exclaimed,

"The destination of this here wessel is a matter as consarns all hands. It's not for any one man more 'n another to interfere. Cuba's been settled upon, and I allow that the arrangement had best be left alone." With that he went on deck.

"I think you are a little indiscreet," said Miss Grant softly.

"Perhaps so," I replied, "but the fellow with his pale face and projecting eyes had, I thought, an honest look, and I seemed to find a suggestion of garrulity lying behind his loitering here. But I am mistaken. I must be cautious, as you say; still it is distracting not to be able to make even a *guess* at the intentions of the fellows."

"You must expect to be watched," she continued. "We shall have to be exceedingly cautious in conversing, and, Mr. Musgrave, it will not do for you to question any of the men. You must be as reserved as they are, attend to the navigation of the ship according to their requirements, satisfy them with your honesty as a navigator by such proofs as their ignorance will suffer them to understand, and leave the rest to time and to chance. It *must* be so!" she cried, still softly, yet with impetuosity in the drawing of her breath. "It is for time and chance to decide all things. Let one's condition be that of a princess, or as dark and as full of care as ours now, it is the same."

"You shall control me as you desire," said I, gently; "you have more wit than I, more patience, more courage, and will preserve me from doing anything that I may repent for your sake. I feel myself to a certain extent responsible for the dreadful position in which we are placed." She motioned dissent with her hand.

"Well," I continued, "first of all, I ought to have know human nature too well to have been duped by a man like Broadwater."

"Oh, Mr. Musgrave, we do not know human nature even when we are white-haired," she cried, "and you are so young yet!"

"That is so," said I, stealing a look at her to see if there was any correspondence between her eyes and her words. "But I am not so young as not to have known better than to suffer ourselves to proceed on this voyage, when perhaps, by insisting upon it, I could have got Broadwater to set us ashore in the English Channel. One hope I have, however," with a further lowering of my voice; "it may not have occurred to the men. We have ships of war in the West Indian waters, and it is impossible to conjecture what might come of some smart sloop heaving us into view, and desiring a closer acquaintance from symptoms which the astute naval eye can often discern in what to another is mere timber, canvas, and an ugly head or two peeping over the rail."

But the idea of a cruiser overhauling us was a vague hope at best. I might think to lighten Miss Grant's anxiety, and steal a little ease for myself too, out of the fancies that came into my head by talking of such things. But as the nations were then at peace, as piracy was pretty nearly extinct, and as there was nothing to suggest the slaver in the aspect of the *Iron Crown*, what excuse should a naval officer find in the mere cut of canvas, and trim of yards, and run of rail, whether ornamented or not with an ugly head or two, to send a boat aboard for a look at the brig's papers? The island of Cuba bore about two thousand miles distant from us. How many days' sailing that might signify no man would have cared to conjecture. We might indeed look for the trades anon, and blow along briskly to the quartering gale, without need for days at a stretch perhaps to check a brace or stand by a halliard. But the sun eats out the heart of a steady blowing as the Antilles are approached, and the sweeping wind that has been whitening the curl of the dark blue chasing billows, and putting a windy sparkle into the glitter of the foaming huddle of gem-crested waters flashing from under the counter in a long race towards the leaping sealine, dies out into parched catspaws, brief bursts of fiery squall, and long intervals of glassy, rotting calm, with nothing to tarnish the surface of the blinding mirror but the jump of the skipjack, or the thin blue line that denotes the wake of the wet black fin of the shark.

But at sea what happens for the day must suffice for it, and the breeze had now settled into so fixed and pleasant a humming, that I was scarce surprised when returning on deck after breakfast to find a hint in the blue shadowiness in the north-east, with here and there a head of cloud listing out of it, of the presence or the approach of the regular tradewind. All hands were on deck forward saving Mole, who was aft, and Charles at the wheel. They were lying sprawling, sitting about, smoking to a man, yarning, with often a loud laugh breaking from one or another of them. Indeed, it was more like a dog-watch scene on a fine summer's night than such a picture as one would look for in the workup, hard-going hours of the forenoon watch. Over the side the seas ran short, and broke friskily. Again and again, from either bow, a score of flying-fish would dart from the arch of wave there as though some young sea-god leaning against the shearing forefoot was showering barbs of mother-of-pearl up through the blue translucency into the sunny air.

It was my watch on deck, and Mole on my arrival was going forward, when I stopped him.

"Is there a man aboard this vessel," said I, "who has any knowledge of navigation?"

"Not going to such lengths," he answered, "as taking the height of the sun and discovering our situation by celestial observations. But I don't doubt, if I was put to it, that I should be able to find my way about with the log-line, supposing my departure's correct."

"Then," said I, "I may judge, even from what you say, that you are able to follow my navigation, and to form an opinion of its correctness by looking at the course I mark down on the chart."

"Yes, sir, I should be able to do that."

"I am glad to hear it. I desire that my goodwill should be appreciated. The men would not doubt my sincerity or my capacity with you at hand to tell them that you have checked my reckonings, and that I am heading true to their wishes."

"We're all quite satisfied, sir," he responded, with a falcon glance at me under the careless droop of his lids. "We have no fear of your deceiving of us;" and with a half-flourish of his hand to his head he went towards the forecastle, leaving me under the impression that I had said too much, and that it would be as well for me in suture to rehearse whatever I might wish to say to the men with Miss Grant before expressing myself.

As I walked the deck alone, I would catch now and again an odd, inquiring sort of look from Charles, who grasped the wheel. It was almost wistful in its way, and with the idea of giving him a chance to interpret it, I came presently to a stand at the quarter, sending a light glance astern, and then made a stride to the binnacle from which I peered to the canvas aloft, as though to remark with what steadiness the craft swung through it under the dead weather drag of the great studding-sail. My aversion from the fellow was not without a weak element of pity too for him. I seemed to remember now, oddly enough, as I held him within the sphere of my sight without regarding him, the kind of light that had come into his face like a smile when, as he tugged at his oar in the boat that carried us aboard in the Downs, he had let his eyes rest on Miss Grant, before sending them on to old Broadwater who sat abaft her.

"Sir," he suddenly exclaimed. I turned with an air of surprise at being accosted by him. "It's known to you and the lady, sir, that I killed the mate. He drove me wild in the dark, as I stood here, with more outrageous language than the captain himself could use. He rose the devil in me, and I drew my knife—though the moment after I could have stabbed myself for doing of it." He dragged over a spoke with a mechanical twist; his olive-coloured complexion had perished into a sickly, sallow green which his dark eyes, gleaming with the contending passions in him, so accentuated that the memory of his visage was for long one of the ugliest phantoms that troubled my slumbers. I drew a pace away when he spoke of killing the mate; he continued talking hurriedly, as though he feared I should leave him before he had had his say. "You and the lady, sir, thinks of me as a bloody murderer, and so I am—so I am! But it began and ended in what you know and saw. So help me all the good angels I was taught to pray to when I was a child, and so help me the blessed Virgin herself"—he let go the wheel with one of his little hands to make the sign of the cross upon his breast—"whatsoever may have been the cause of the capt'n's disappearance, I am innocent of it. Do you believe me, sir?"

I looked at him a moment and said, "I do. But do you mean to suggest that he met his end by foul play?"

He made a passionate gesture and cried, "I know nothing about it, sir. I want you to believe *that*, and I want the lady to believe it more'n you. She had pity for me when I—when I—" He paused with a gasp and a swift pointing towards the foremast with a trembling hand.

She came on deck at that moment.

"I am glad to learn what you have told me," said I, and I added coldly, for aversion was strong in me again, and besides, his very words were as good as owning that the captain had been murdered, though not by him, "No doubt the unhappy man fell crazy with drink and temper, and through the loss of the boat, along with his conscience over the drowning of the cabin-boy, and quietly sneaked overboard;" and so saying I walked over to Miss Grant,

I called to some men to spread the little scrap of awning the brig carried, and three or four of them came instantly tumbling aft as willingly as one could wish. I then placed a chair for Miss Grant to windward, where I could sometimes halt in my walk to have a chat with her, for now that I had charge of the deck, her accompanying me in my pacings would scarcely look ship-shape in the eyes of the seamen. But I made no reference to my conversation with the half-blood, beyond merely telling her in a half-whisper that the fellow had, in an odd way, protested himself as innocent of whatever the cause might have been of Broadwater's disappearance; whence I thought it was certainly to be gathered that the old man had been made away with. However, it was not a little comforting, I can tell you, to feel that this Charles, whom I held in secret dread, was equal to feeling grateful to Miss Grant for the concern and indignation his punishment at the foremast had excited in her. It was gratifying to me, moreover, to know that he had conscience enough left in him to shrink from suspicion of another dark deed. Indeed my talk with the fellow, followed on by the lively willingness of the men who responded to my order to lay aft and spread the awning, would have put, I believe, something of lightness into my tread of the quarter-deck, specially with the radiant scene of heaven and ocean to turn from to Miss Aurelia's dark eyes, which often followed me as I walked, but for the dull, oppressive wonder as to what project the crew had in mind in making me head for Cuba, a thing that gnawed in the secret recesses of my mind like some sulky throbbing ache of a nerve.

Before my watch was out however there happened an incident which gave me to know very plainly that the sailors' resolution was fixed in one direction, at all events. The breeze had freshened—it was a little before ten o'clock in the morning—clouds rounded and of silken texture, like growing puffs of powder-smoke from great ordnance fired below the horizon, were sailing up into the blue hollow which the sunshine so filled that it was all azure dazzle over our mastheads; the brig was sliding along at some five knots, cradling her form from one dark blue brow to another, with the whipped waters merrily sparkling into billows and melting into cream all along her as she ran. Suddenly a man, who was standing on the forecastle head, bawled out, "Sail ho!" to which cry I noticed that the others, who lounged or lay sprawling about the deck near the galley, immediately started to their feet and ran to the rail to look.

"Where away?" I sang out.

"Broad on the weather-bow," came back the answer.

I looked, and at once descried a sail leaning like a white shaft in the quarter the man had indicated, and, as I might judge by the heel of her, by which one saw that she must be hugging the wind, heading directly for us. I went to the companion for the glass, and bringing the tubes to bear, made the stranger out to be a small brigantine. The hands forward over the rail watched her steadfastly. I waited and had another look at her, and found her growing rapidly. Indeed, that was to be expected, for our united pace would probably be closing us at the rate of some ten or twelve knots in the hour. I hailed the forecastle, and desired that Mr. Mole should be roused up and sent aft to me. He sprang through the hatch within a minute after he had been called, blinking with sleep and the darkness in his eyes against the splendour on deck, but laying aft nevertheless as briskly as if he had the scent of danger in his nostrils.

"What's the matter now, sir?" he cried out, as he approached.

"I simply want to be advised," said I; and pointing to the little brig-antine that was coming along with her wash-streak down in the smoth-er, and the weather-leeches of her topsail and top-gallant-sail and royal shivering like the fly of a flag in a breeze to the grip of the helmsman's luff, I said, "You see that fellow out there?"

He shaded his eyes and answered, "Plain enough, sir."

"Take that glass," I exclaimed, "and look at her, and tell me what you observe."

He worked away with the telescope, and then suddenly exclaimed, "'Tain't English colours, is it? No, it's Norwegian—Jack down—flying half-masted."

"Exactly," said I; "it is a distress-signal, and she wants to speak us. Now, I don't mean to accept any responsibility in a business of this kind. There may be people yonder perishing from some want which it is in our power to supply——"

"Can't help it if there are, sir," he cried vehemently. "We're bound to shove on; there's nothen that must stop us!" and a dark look came into his face, as though he supposed I was going to argue, and was angry by anticipation.

"Be it so," I exclaimed. "We'll keep straight on, as you say." He sent a look full of significance at the man who had relieved Charles at the wheel, and then went forward and leant upon the rail alongside the others, staring his hardest, as they were, at the approaching vessel.

What they had suspected in her appearance I don't know, but I gath-ered he had told them of the distress-signal and of the nationality of it—scarce yet visible to the naked eye—by the lapsing of most of them from their intent, strained, eager posture into a half-lounging, careless attitude. I waited a little, and then viewing her again through the glass, I was not a little surprised to remark that she appeared to be full of people. I examined her carefully, and was sure I could not be mistaken. If the swarm of glimmering dots along the whole length of her rail were not human faces, it would puzzle a man to guess what else they could be. Presently the men noticed this too, for I saw some of them give their breeches an uneasy hitch as they brought their eyes away from her to our own canvas with sharp starings aft, as though they feared I might play them some ugly trick if I were not closely watched. The size of the brigantine scarcely exceeded a hundred and fifty tons, and I never remember seeing a prettier model. She had a true piratical sheer forwards, a run of bow into a knife-like cutwater, sheathing green with usage, that flickered with a sort of emerald sheen to the light of the snow that boiled about her forefoot as she rose to the fine-weather surge. The swells of her well-cut canvas leaned to us sunwards with milk-white softness in the shine of them; nothing afloat could look more saucy, taut, and seaworthy, and one almost suspected some sinister device in the dumb appeal of the speck of crimson bunting with its blue cross, white margined, and inverted Jack, only that the crowd of heads, now distinctly visible, made such a puzzlement of the sight as effectually checked speculation. I watched her intently through the glass, and noticed much motioning of arms, and brandishing of caps and other headgear amongst her people. It needed no specially clear eye for human distress to interpret those gesticulations into an earnest entreaty to us to boom-end our studding-sails and bring the brig to the wind. I stood at the rail watching her, and Miss Grant came to my side.

"There are women aboard, and children too," I cried; "at least a hundred people, I should say. They will think us demons for not attending to their signal."

"What do you imagine they need?" she inquired.

"They may have run short of provisions, or worse still, of water," I answered, steadfastly examining the length of her black sides for any bright spout from the scuppers that might tell me her pumps were going.

The men along the line of bulwarks watched her with faces as hard as figure-heads, with here and there a jaw moving upon the quid that stood high in the cheek-bone, whilst at intervals a fellow would drop from his akimbo arms upon the rail to light his pipe at the galley fire, returning promptly however and resuming his place, where he would stand quietly with a wooden-headed look, but nevertheless with sooty pipe in mouth, blowing out clouds that told of some inward perturbation. On a sudden the brigantine put her helm up, slackened away her sheets fore and aft along with the lee-braces, and headed direct for us. Her manoeuvre startled me, for I thought she meant to run us aboard. The clipper hull of her, now that she was making a free wind of it, swept like the shadow of a cloud over the water. She piled the foam to her hawse-pipes, and a yeasty hillock went along with her on either quarter, with the flash past it of her wake, whose giddy dazzle would have made a near eye reel again. Mole sprang aft to the quarter-deck in a few bounds.

"What's she up to, Mr. Musgrave?" he shouted. "Does she mean to board us, think ye?"

"No, no; to speak us, man—to speak us," I answered, for already her intention was made manifest to me by a subtle shifting of her helm, that would enable her presently to range within speaking distance of us, heading as we were. In another ten minutes she was within a biscuit toss, almost directly abreast to windward, but they had to let go their royal and top-gallant-halliards and *scandalize* their mainsail, as it is termed, to keep their position; for though the brig was under every stitch of canvas that would draw, with studding-sails swelling cloud-like one on top of another far beyond her weather-side, the clipper to windward with all her canvas abroad would have forged ahead like a steamer, and been out of hail in five minutes. There were twenty or thirty women amongst the crowd, some of them with babies in their arms, and forty or fifty men, and at least a score of children. The vessel, being small and somewhat deep in the water, showed her decks to us with every floating slide to leeward. The picture, for strangeness, wildness, and I may add for beauty, was in its way incomparable. The flash of the low black hull through the milk-white boiling along her bends, the ivory gleam of her canvas melting into soft shadowing beyond the central curves of the cloths, the crowd upon her decks so variously and oddly apparelled that nothing short of the paint-brush would put the scene before you—red and green handkerchiefs round the head, caps like inverted flower-pots falling with a tassel to the shoulders, coats of frieze with great metal buttons, yellow half-boots, red petticoats, the gleam of gold or silver earrings—such a huddle of bright colours defies the pen; one thought of an opera troupe, with its choruses and orchestra to boot, as having taken ship for a pleasure cruise, and fallen into some dreadful condition of incommunicable distress. The Norwegian flag, as I have said, flew Jack down half-masted from the main-topmast head; but though she might have been a Norwegian ship, with a Norwegian crew in her, I cannot persuade myself that the women, the children, and most of the men were of that nation. Yet it was impossible to understand a word of what they said. Perhaps they would have been as unintelligible had they yelled in English, for every throat in the craft was strained at the same moment, and the wind brought the hubbub along to fall in a blind dead way upon the ear like a fog upon the eye.

A man, presumably the skipper, an old patriarchal-looking fellow, with a long white goat-like beard, and a white fur cap as it seemed coming close down to his shaggy eyebrows, got into the main-rigging, with a speaking-trumpet in one hand, through which he roared a sentence that was as Hebrew, afterwards pointing with his trumpet to his flag. I said to Mole, "Shall we hail them?"

He answered with a stamp of his foot, "No, by——, not if they was on fire. What do the dogs mean by sticking their craft alongside of us?"

Besides continuously shouting, the queer kaleidoscopic crowd convulsed themselves with every imaginable kind of gesture. Some pointed into their wide-open mouths: others clasped their hands upon their stomachs, with grimaces inimitably expressive of suffering; many motioned as if in the act of drinking; one man held a bottle aloft upside down, tapping it with his finger, and shaking his head most dolefully. There was indeed no need for them to tell in words what was the matter with them.

I cried, "Mr. Mole, you see how it is; those people want water—*water!*" I repeated, emphasizing the words, for if there's a human need that thrills to the heart of the sailor on the high seas, it is *that*. "It is in our power to relieve them to a small extent at least. Look at those children! No possible harm can come, man, from our allowing them to send a boat to us."

He turned upon me savagely. "Mr. Musgrave," he exclaimed, in a voice like a snarl, so hard did his passion make it for him to speak," "if ye have an atom of consarn in *your* safety—in the lady's safety—you'll hold your *jaw*."

I took Miss Grant's hand, and walked with her right aft, and seated myself by her side on the grating.

"You must let them have their way," she exclaimed; "they are devils, not men."

I was too sick at heart, too enraged by the man's insolence, too shocked by the picture of the gaping crowd to windward, to be able to answer her.

Presently there fell a silence upon the little brigantine, and you heard nothing but the seething of the water past her as her sharp stem sheared through it with a hissing as of red-hot iron. The hush was broken by the old white-bearded man bellowing again to us through his speaking-trumpet. Mole, with folded arms, stood looking on without a stir in the scowl of his face. Not a voice disturbed the stillness forward, where the men hanging over the rail were gazing with an air of mere idle curiosity. Twice the old man hailed us; he then got out of the rigging, and on reaching the deck flung his trumpet down with a furious gesture, sank upon his knees, and lifting up his hands to God, seemed to invoke a curse upon us, varying his dreadful tragic posture of denunciation by pointing at our brig with his eyes upturned. At the sight of this the rest of the people fell to menacing us with brandished fists, shouting and yelling at us till their voices blended into one long howl of execration. Yet had our crew been statues they could not have surveyed the dreadful scene more impassively. Presently the old man rose from his knees, and motioned to the fellow at the wheel to put it over; the topgallant and royal yards were hoisted afresh, the peak-halliards manned, and in a few moments the swift and beautiful little vessel was hauling away from us, buzzing round to the brilliant breeze with a wake following her white as the shining of the sun on the polished surface of a scythe.

I thought by her ranging to starboard that she meant to round into the wind, and so get her port-tacks aboard for the ratch that she was upon when first sighted. Instead, when she had stood away far enough to come round to the wind under her starboard helm without chance of striking us, over went her wheel; she spun on her heel like some saucy, frisky woman in a waltz, and flattening in and bracing up fore and aft, sweep! she came for us again, passing close under our quarter, from no other motive that I could see than to furnish her people with another opportunity of uniting their voices in a long, raging and shrieking curse upon us. Then like an arrow she was away astern crossing our wake; but whilst it was possible for the naked eye to hold her, one saw, as it were, the throbbing of the crowd along her as they shook their maledictions at us with flourished arms and fists.

When she had fairly settled away into toy-like dimensions, Mole, who had been watching her from his position near the main-rigging, came up to me, and said with the civil air of his former behaviour, "Sorry to have lost my temper, sir; but you know that all hands is resolved not to speak anything, from a scow to a line-of-battle ship. That's our resolution, and it 'ud make things easier if you was to be so good as to keep as clear an eye upon it as you're fixing upon the course to Cuba."

Miss Grant said quickly, as though fearing an indiscretion of temper in me, she wished to interfere between myself and the man, "Hunger and thirst are dreadful things, Mr. Mole. Those people made their necessities very plain to us. It was the sight of the women and children that moved Mr. Musgrave."

"That's right enough, miss," he answered; "but who's to know what ailed them? Supposing it to have been thirst, what amount of fresh water calculated to be of any use to such a army of folks have we got to spare out of our stock? There's all the way to Cuba before us, with the sun pretty nigh overhead every day, and we've got a right to think of ourselves first, I allow. 'Sides," he continued, putting the sharp of his hand to his forehead to gaze at the now distant sail, and frowning to the brassy glare that came in folds from the running waters off each head of sea, "who's going to 'leviate people there's no onderstanding? Human they was, I dessay; but the likes of such a lump on a little vessel's deck, swearing, motioning, patting their guts, making pretend to drink, and then apparently falling down and cussing of us, ain't altogether the sort of stroke you'd look for in natural things, 'specially when the whole biling is rigged up as if a body of organ-grinders had turned pirates—stole some blooming Dutchman's vessel, and then missed their road."

He talked as if he wished me to find something humorous in his fancies. Bitterly indignant and resentful as I secretly felt, I was not such a fool as to despise an attitude of conciliation in the one man in whom I had now had time to observe the others had confidence, who indeed headed, and no doubt influenced, the crew; so I returned him a few civil, commonplace words, after which he went forward, where he stood talking a while.

Chapter V
A Festive Dog-watch

A T SEA SO MUCH which is strange happens, that no man who has any knowledge of the life will trouble himself to hunt about for solutions. I remember a sailor once telling me, that his ship being blown to the westwards off the Chilean coast, deep in the heart of the Pacific waters, they fell in with a Chinese junk, with three men and a couple of women on board. The wonder of this junk lay not in her sides grey with barnacles and green with weeds, nor in the queer, weather-befouled aspect of her faded Asiatic sails, nor in the ragged look of the blue-gowned, betailed, mustard-coloured creatures that were on deck; but in her being where she was. How came she in the South Pacific? It was like the fly in the amber. The Chinamen made passionate efforts to represent their condition, but to no purpose. Not a motion of a hand of theirs was interpretable, and the captain of the ship growing wearied, filled on his vessel and proceeded on his course.

There are confrontments, I say, in the sea-life, which, being unintelligible on the face of them, no man who has his reason will attempt to explain. It was as likely as not that the brigantine was a Norwegian that had fallen in with an emigrant vessel in distress, had taken off all or most of the people, and then run short of provisions and water. But there was so much to keep me thoughtful in other ways, that, though tragically strange as it was, it was not an incident to constrain my attention to it as though all had been well with us, and the thing no more than a brief break in the monotony of a sunny voyage. The reflection that grew out of it was—what sort of treatment were Miss Grant and I to expect from men in whom selfish fear could so work as to render them insensible to the most piteous of all the demands which the stern usage of the sea can force from human distress? It was the same selfish fear that kept them quiet. One might guess there would be no mad broaching of rum-puncheons with them. They were too much alarmed with their situation to risk anything for the want of unclouded brains. Indeed, their sobriety was as good as a hint of their distrust of me. They very well knew that my one consuming desire must be to escape with Miss Grant from the brig; also that I was sailor enough to perceive there was no chance for me in that way outside the speaking of a ship that would be willing to take us off. They treated me with a sort of negative civility indeed; that is to say, they kept away from our end of the brig, and jumped to my orders; but then my knowledge of navigation rendered me so important to them that they could not do without me; though what haunted my mind as I stood with Miss Grant, watching the dim flicker of the brigantine's canvas on the edge of the wide blue sweep of sea, was, that a day must presently come when the high land of Cuba would be heaving into view, and what then would happen? There was something, too, inexpressibly malignant to my fancy in the request of the men that I should let them know when we were within a day's sail of the island; and the mere inability to gauge the meaning of this desire was enough to keep every instinct in me writhing in a torment of uncertainty.

It was noon however, and I went below for Broadwater's quadrant. It was a primitive appliance, and likely as not to be inaccurate. However, I made eight bells with it, watched closely by the men as I screwed away at the sun, and then returned to the cabin to work out the sights. I used Broadwater's room, as the conveniences I required were in it, and whilst I sat at the little table Miss Grant arrived and stood behind me, looking over my shoulder as I jotted down the figures. She was anxious to know where we were. I unrolled the chart, and pointed to our position.

"It is still a long way to Cuba," she exclaimed, bending her stately figure over the chart. Her mouth was as firm, her face as composed, her gaze as steadfast, soft, and serene as though she were viewing some picture in a book.

"Yes," I groaned, "a weary long way."

She seated herself on a little locker at the foot of old Broadwater's bunk. Her beauty was like a light upon the atmosphere of the quaint, somewhat darksome interior. You would have needed to peep in at the door to appreciate the curiosity of contrast wrought by her warm and glowing presence, the glimmer of amber light in threads of her hair, as though the brown of it were self-luminous, the unconscious graceful dignity of her attitude, and by the odd, rough furniture of the cabin; the suit of clothes with the tarpaulin hat on top, swinging like the figure of Broadwater himself at the bulkhead; the soles of the jack-boots sprawling in the shadow under the bunk, with *her* little feet a yard away from them; the rough time-bronzed pilot-coat, hanging behind her as a canvas, so to speak, for the perfections of her clear skin and the flash of her dark eyes to show on.

She leaned towards me, folding her hands over her knee, and said, "Will it be possible to escape from this brig?"

I started and exclaimed, "I have been full of that fancy since the brigantine hauled off. No; I do not think it is possible. We must take such luck as we may find here."

"I want you to understand, Mr. Musgrave," said she, "that if any scheme of escape should occur to you, you will find me equal to it. I shall not mind what I do, indeed. I will dress up as a man—I will row an oar—yes! I can row. I am not afraid of firing pistols. Alexander will tell you I am a good shot."

She looked down into her lap with a faint smile, then her eyes met mine again—a full gaze, brilliant with inquiry.

"Well," said I, "I had not been in your company ten minutes before I guessed that you would be the proper sort of girl for a pinch. I was right, and so you see, spite of my being so *young*, I am capable of taking a correct view sometimes of human nature."

She laughed softly, and with a foreign gesture of her hand said, "You are too impetuous, too emotional. One would hardly think you an Englishman, you abandon yourself so readily to impressions."

"It may be as you say," said I, feeling somehow almost as much confused by her manner and by her beauty as on the day when she had first stood before me in the parlour of the London lodging-house; "but this anxiety is new in you. What makes you talk of escaping from the brig?"

"Simply—as I have said, Mr. Musgrave—that if you have any scheme I am willing to bear as good a part in it as if I were a man." She drew herself erect, as though she would suggest physical as well as intellectual strength.

"I have no scheme," said I; "would to God I could see my way to one!"

"Might we not lower the boat that hangs at the vessel's side?"

I shook my head quickly. "No," said I, "there is always the fellow at the wheel. How should we be able to lower a boat, even on the blackest night, unperceived by him?"

"But could you not gag him?" said she. "I could help you to pinion him, and then stand over him pistol in hand," smiling, yet with a world of resolution in her gaze, "whilst you let the boat sink to the water."

I went to the door and peeped out to make sure that nobody was listening.

"Supposing," said I, approaching her close that she might hear my voice, which was scarce more than a whisper, "we should succeed in getting away in the boat, what would be our fate in a little open ark in the middle of the great Atlantic, exposed all day to the broiling sun, and all night to the heavy dews, to say nothing of squalls, thunderstorms, gales, putrefying calms, and the rest of the conditions of the glorious ocean life? No, no! dismiss *that* from your mind—for your own sake, Miss Grant—my cousin would shoot me for subjecting you to such risks and privations. But," I continued anxiously, for I thought

I might find a hint in her woman's cleverness, "this thought is new in you. Why do you wish to escape from the brig? A bitter strong wish it must be when, to gratify it, you are willing to face the hazard of an open boat."

"Oh, Mr. Musgrave, I am shocked by the inhumanity of the crew. I had believed them plain sailors forced into evil by bad treatment, but whose better natures would appear again when the tyranny they suffered from had ceased. I think so no longer. I fear their intentions towards us may be—may be—I am frightened by the vagueness of their directions to you. They speak of Cuba, but they name no part of it."

"Hush!" I cried, hearing a footstep. Mole put his head in at the door, knocking with his great knuckles on the bulkhead as he did so.

"Beg pardon," said he; "I thought I'd just come along and see how the land lies with us to-day."

There was insolence in this intrusion, but then I had to consider it was my own bringing about. He stood in the doorway, peering in, in a posture civil enough, cap in hand, filling the frame of the door with his great figure.

"Here," said I, putting my finger upon the chart, "is the brig's position today at noon."

He came to the table and peered close.

"The vessel's heading west by south," said he, after a pause; "this here map don't show the West Indies."

"No," said I, "it is the North Atlantic only; but there should be a track-chart in that bag to give you all the bearings you want."

There were nearly a dozen charts rolled up in the bag. I pulled out four, and on opening the fifth found it to be what I needed—a track-chart of the world. This I spread before Mole, and left him to find out for himself whither a west by south course would carry us from the point of latitude and longitude I penciled upon the chart. It is an old saying, and a terribly trite one too, that a man must go afloat to see the wonders of the Lord; and 'tis equally true, that a man who is a lover of strange, odd, surprising pictures, will find them nowhere in greater perfection than at sea. When I recall that little cabin, with the dim blue light sifting through the glass of the closed scuttle—the muscular, swaying figure of the sun-darkened seaman stooping over the chart, his great hairy paws flat upon the table, his hair hanging from his brow like a fall of rain from the edge of a cloud—Miss Grant sitting silent and watchful, her white fingers clasped upon her knee, with the flash of a gem there that seemed to be reflected in every slight movement of her dark eyes—myself subduing the worry and anger within me to the best careless demeanour that I could contrive by leaning my cheek upon my hand, softly whistling some light sea-tune, to which I kept time by an easy striking of the table with the pencil I held—Broadwater's clothes swinging with the swaying of the ship from pegs in the bulkhead, with other rude, homely details of ocean furniture, already described, to fill, as it were, the spaces between the human interests of that interior with novel colour and touches remote from all shore-going experience;—I say, when I recall this picture, I ask myself, Where's the like of such a scene to be encountered save on that liquid surface, whose cradling respirations deepened yet the strangeness of the whole by communicating those vitalizing elements of sound and motion incommunicable by the pen?

Mole stood erect presently, and looked for his cap.

"Well, I hope the course I am shaping satisfies you?" said I.

"It'll work out as true as a hair, it seems to me," he answered.

"To what part of Cuba are we sailing, Mr. Mole?" inquired Miss Grant, in her most natural manner, without any attempt at an artless voice or a face of innocent wonderment.

"We ain't decided yet," he answered promptly, picking up his cap and going to the door. "We mean to keep Charles clear of the gallows if we can. Cuba's a good bit off yet, and when Mr. Musgrave lets us know that it's within a day's sail, we may have to tarn to and discuss what's to be done, onless we've come to an agreement before hand."

He gave a nod towards the state-cabin, and turning upon us again, said, "The cook's asked me to say your dinner's ready, sir." He then went on deck.

We found a very tolerable meal prepared for us. The cook, having put the dishes upon the table, left us to ourselves; and as we sat close together we were able to talk freely without fear of our subdued voices penetrating to any attentive ear that might be lurking at the sky-light. I told Miss Grant it would need very little consideration to assure us both that, if we valued our lives, we must make no effort to escape by the hazard of such a deed of violence as that of gagging and pinioning the man at the wheel. Failure, I said, must lead to my being murdered out of hand, and then she was to think of herself as alone with a lawless body of people, who, on the strength of our attempt, would hold themselves discharged from the obligation they now recognized to keep their distance and treat us civilly.

She shuddered at this. "It is the dread," she exclaimed, pressing her hand to her forehead, "of anything happening that might separate us, that might end in leaving me alone with these men—it is *this* dread,

Mr. Musgrave, which makes me talk of attempting to escape whilst we are together, and whilst I feel my spirit equal to any call that you can make upon it. The prospect of an open boat is dreadful, I admit, but it would be paradise in comparison to my finding myself alone in this brig."

"It is because we must remain together, come what may," said I, speaking with a degree of emphasis and passion, as I can now recall, to which I have little doubt in another mood her eyes would have sunk with such a little trembling play of smile on her lips as I had once before noticed, "that I dare not risk our being separated by so much as the movement of a finger, without feeling sure of the result. Besides," I continued, sinking my voice again, "even if we should agree to attempt to escape by the boat, it would be better to wait until we had closed the Cuba coast than commit ourselves to the heart of the great solitude we are now in." I said, gently and soothingly, "You have been shocked by the cruelty of the men in refusing help to the people of the brigantine. Their behaviour has excited a new dread of them in you. You have suffered a little shadow to darken your glorious courage. But again and again you have told me to believe that all will be well. All *will* be well!' I exclaimed, taking her hand in both mine; "you have too much of the heroine in you to render the issue of this horrible voyage uncertain. Your courage will shine out afresh. A little patience and the gloom will have passed. I need every bit of encouragement you can give me, and shall be the pluckier and the stronger for your own strength and bravery."

She kept her face averted, and a tear fell from her cheek. I believe I never acted more wisely in my life than by leaving her without another word and withdrawing to my cabin, and remaining there until I felt calm enough to be able to talk to her with clear perception of the meaning of my presence on board, and of the object of our journey.

When the dog-watch between six and eight came round, the evening was so gentle and lovely that I cannot remember the like of it. All day long we had kept the brig under the same canvas which had been set in the morning, and she still floated forwards to the tender propulsion of the white cloths, rising in soft spaces to the sun-gilt trucks, whilst the sheen flowing off the studding-sails, which overhung the sides, trembled in the blue surface under the swinging-boom as though the water were touched with a beam of moonshine there. But the breeze had weakened into a quiet wind that scarcely gave us a speed of three miles in the hour. The sea was tremulous under the warm breathing of the wind, but every ripple ran foamlessly, and the swell was so faint you had to watch the mastheads to make sure that the airy life you felt in the deck was not fanciful. I had charge of the brig, and often stopped in my walk to exchange a few sentences with Miss Grant, who was seated near the skylight. The ugly half-caste Ladova was at the wheel. A few seamen were sitting on the forecastle-head smoking, but presently I noticed the cook come out of his little caboose with a small kid or tub in his hand, the steam of which seemed grateful to him, for as he walked on to the forecastle he kept his head overhanging it as though inhaling it. He set the kid down very carefully near the scuttle. The loungers in the head gathered round, and seemed to sniff up the incense with great satisfaction, as might be gathered from their several postures and the expressions on their faces, though I was at too great a distance to hear what they said. The cook returned to the caboose, and shortly afterwards emerged with an armful of pannikins, which he placed close alongside the steaming kid. I eyed these proceedings uneasily. It was not hard to guess that the steam yonder rose from something stronger than water. One of the fellows put his head into the scuttle and called out, and in a few moments the rest of the crew came on deck. Amongst them was Mole, who sprang through the hatch with a fiddle in his hand. His first act was to step up to the kid, dip a pannikin into it, and take a sip. The brew was evidently to his taste, for he gave the cook a nod, drained the pannikin; and screwing the fiddle to his shoulder, fell to tuning it.

"They mean to be merry," said I to Miss Grant.

"Will there not be enough drink in that wooden tub," she said, "to make them intoxicated?"

"Depends on the strength of the mixture," said I. "Mole gave me his word that there should be no drunkenness aboard us. I fancy the fellows are too distrustful of me to swallow more than will hearten them to a couple of hours of jollity. Strange there should have been a fiddle aboard all this time, and it should never have been played until now. 'Tis to be Jack's *requiem* over Broadwater. God help us! what a muddle that creature has brought us into."

Just then Mole held up his hand to attract my attention. "Jest a bit of sailors' pleasuring, Mr. Musgrave," he sang out; "no more'n'll help us to tune up our pipes, and put a bit of spring into our flat feet."

I responded quickly, with an answering flourish of my hand. "You're quite right, my lads. Never was there a crew more fairly entitled to a spell of merry-making."

"Boys!" shouted Mole, who seemed somewhat excited, "to the lady, bullies! Dip to her and to his honour atop, my livelies. Time from me, my noble fellows!"

"Hold!" I cried, entering into the spirit of the thing, "let Ladova be of you."

I went to the wheel. "Jump," said I, "and drink our healths!"

He ran forward. Mole then dipped for a second draught, and stood with his pannikin poised, waiting for the others to fill. It was a sea-picture just then to haunt a man to his grave, so charged was the colour, the beauty, the freshness of it, with the horrible significance of the condition of things aboard. The manly, handsome figure of Mole, in white duck trousers, blue shirt leaving his mossy breast bare, round hat perched on the back of his head, arms of a giant naked to above the elbow, holding his pannikin high in marine festive posture—the group behind, with their pannikins upheld in imitation of him, here and there a bright eye gleaming out of a shaggy face past some brawny shoulder, the olive features of the half-blood contrasting with the dingy white of the cook—the smoking crimson background of the west, against whose effulgent reaches, rising from scarlet at the sea-line to a sweep of delicate golden haze over the mastheads, each figure stood out clear cut—the loveliness of the great circle curving from the glory over one cathead into the dark blue of the east, and back again to the effulgent sky and sea over the bow;—it was indeed a scene not to be lightly forgotten, charged as it was with the spirit of the beauty of the evening, and with the memory of murder and of bitter wrongdoing, and with our present fears.

"Time from me, my livelies!" cried Mole, with a look over either shoulder; then holding his pannikin high and gazing aft, "One—Two—Three!" At the last word, and in utter silence, flash went every man's pannikin to his mouth, and in token that our healths had been effectually drunk, every fellow held his pannikin inverted. The thing was done with a military precision that must have won a laugh from me at any other time; but before merriment was practicable, one wanted to know how much liquor the kid held, and how much spirit had gone to the manufacture of the contents of the little tub.

Miss Grant rose and courtesied towards the forecastle with inimitable grace, whilst I raised my hat to the dumb salute of the inverted pannikins. Then Ladova returned, and I fell to pacing the deck again, saying to Miss Grant, as I lingered abreast of her a moment with a careless glance aloft, that this was a sign of goodwill on the part of the men that ought to help the courage of us both.

Mole seized his fiddle afresh, and vaulting on to the forecastle-capstan played a brisk polka. Next to jigging, Jack loves polking; the hornpipe heads the list, but the polka stands next. The sailors formed

themselves into couples, and in a few moments were twisting and sliding round the musician. There was fun to be got out of even the mere
sight of the capers their legs cut, and the enjoyment on their faces grinning over one another's shoulders as they revolved. The cook, wanting
a partner, danced alone, a detail of this little passage of jollity that rendered the whole scene inexpressibly childish. I said to Miss Grant, "Is
there in all human nature a simpler-hearted creature than the sailor?
What landsman could find diversion in dancing as those fellows are?
In fact," said I, "Jack has all the simplicity of the savage, with a touch of
the savage's unpleasant qualities. There is nothing in memory to hinder
him. Observe how heartily Mole saws, as if all had been and still was
as well with this ship as at the day she lay in the Pool. Only a few hours
ago one or maybe more yonder struck Broadwater down and tossed
him overboard. Yet the punch is not the less sweet to their palates. They
shake as lively a foot as any sinless soul could."

"See the half-blood! He dances all over. Every bit of him to his very
eyes is on the move. He hops about with pure Spanish enjoyment. That
rude deck there might be a ball-room for him, and the rough company
of the sailors a polished fandango," said Miss Grant.

"Ay," said I, "and I dare say he would not quiver about the less briskly
for the thought that the shadow of the gallows which awaits him lies
dark to the light of the setting sun, somewhere behind the slope of that
sea-line."

And yet somehow, spite of the gloomy thoughts which came to me
out of these merry-making Jacks, there was something in the sound of
the fiddle, and in their skimming and twisting figures, to give a deeper
oceanic meaning to the whole picture of the brig, slowly pushing her
way towards the crimson west, with the ripple from her stem curling
into a flash of golden fire as it arched round to the sun, than it got
from the mere sapphire and scarlet and hectic of the heavens, and the
lovely blue of the sea floating ahead of us, and melting into the brightness under our jib-boom. I thought to myself, What ship sailing within
earshot of us would guess that this peaceful brig had been the theatre
of tragedies as dreadful in their way as anything of a like kind that has
ever happened upon the high seas? But every vessel afloat has an inner
and secret life of her own. A procession of ships is like a concourse of
human beings; no man can imagine what is passing in the hearts of
them—what wild, what glad, what frightful, what pathetic memories
may linger in their dark and sealed depths. Viewed from a distance on
this evening, the *Iron Crown* would have presented a spectacle full of
beauty, of softness, of gentleness, into which there would have entered

a seeming element of happiness, of peace, and of innocence, from the cheerful notes of the fiddle over which yonder manly-looking sailor's head drooped, and from the brisk and hearty figures which slided round about the capstan, with a sailor's true delight in every heave of the leg and in every revolution of the body.

When the polka came to an end, Mole dismounted and handed the fiddle to the half-blood, who, grinning with an almost negro-like countenance of enjoyment, took the other's place, and struck up the well-known hornpipe air, "Jack Robinson." Mole took the deck alone; the others, every man holding a pannikin newly dipped, drew off hot and merry to look on, some sitting, some lounging. Carefully screwing his hat on his head, Mole took the preliminary walk round, and then broke into the ocean-dance, with the perched figure of the half-blood behind him fiddling most ably. I never in all my life saw the hornpipe better danced. There was so much expertness indeed as almost to make one forget one's dislike of the fellow. The admiration of the spectators sobered their grins, and they gazed with sedate appreciation. Sometimes one or another rapped out, "Hurrah, bully! You're the lad for the girls!" "Swing to it, my lively!" "Bully for you, Terry, bully for you!" and the like, accompanied by a frequent lifting of the pannikins. With his hat "on nine hairs," as sailors say, his arms sometimes folded upon his breast, sometimes one hand upon his hip, the other lifted, his loose white trousers fluttering against the scarlet background, his rough hair tossing upon his brow, with the spirit of the thing shining in his eyes, Mole slapped the deck with his feet till it rattled like castanets in the hands of a Spanish dancer, jigging it so inimitably well indeed that Miss Grant could not remove her eyes from him, whilst I gazed positively fascinated by the gilded sea-picture. Indeed, it stirred old memories in me as nothing else had done since we first weighed anchor. It took me back to the forecastle of the grand old Indiaman when the sultry dog watch was growing cool to the dewy eastern shadow. I clapped my hands loudly when Mole, half-breathless with exertion and purple with heat, brought his dance to an end with a smart blow of his foot and a bow to us aft, as finely managed as any courtier could have contrived it. Then after an interval he took the fiddle again, and the others fell a-dancing, and when they were tired they sang songs.

By this time the evening had drawn over us. There were long lines of hectic in the west and rusty streaks of expiring scarlet, but the stars were shining brilliantly, and the gloom of the night was already darkening out the forecastle upon the eye into an airy dusk, amid which the shapes of the seamen were scarcely visible. But I had already noticed with satisfaction that the tub, which had been tilted that the last drop might be dipped out of it, was left unreplenished. One fellow sang with a fine voice—who it was I knew not; it was a clear rich baritone, and went floating up amongst the sails, whose wan hollows gave the notes back in dim echoes. I leaned with Miss Grant over the rail listening. An occasional delicate sob of water rose from the clear profound, clouded with misty bursts of sea fire, which, mingling with the fellow's voice, gave a quality of softness and even of pathos to it. Nearly all the songs sung were of a sentimental cast, and were accompanied by either Mole or Charles with the fiddle; and though broad daylight would no doubt have found the sounds for the most part commonplace enough, yet the airs, even when delivered by some hoarser pipe than usual, took a note of romance and a quality of unreality from the overshadowing presence of the liquid night, the melancholy spaciousness of the dark sea extending on all sides, the dimness of the extended wings of canvas on high, the stillness upon the deep that was scarce disturbed by the breathing of the warm, dew-laden night-wind into the sails, and the almost oppressive hush you found when amid the intervals of the songs you sent your gaze into the dark blue dome brilliant with stars which jewelled every point of spar, every shadowy end of boom, every phantasmal length of yard of the faint, pale fabric, looming large above the delicate glimmer of the decks.

All was hushed and in darkness forward; one figure alone could be made out crossing the stars in a regular pendulum tread on the forecastle, when Mole came aft to relieve me. The excitement of the drink and the dance had gone out of him. He said, "Ye see the men are well in hand, Mr. Musgrave; there's nothen to be feared from their *liquorizing,* as I told you."

"I was glad to notice that," I answered; "your jollifications, indeed your doings of any kind, are no concern of mine outside the lady's safety and my own. I heartily wish that you understood navigation, and that you could take charge of the brig, for in that case you would have no objection to putting Miss Grant and me aboard the first craft that would be willing to take us. The deuce of it is, Mr. Mole," continued I—for I hoped he might have come to me with a disposition rendered a trifle generous by the dog-watch festivity, and would be willing therefore to talk a little more freely than at another time—"the lady is bound to Rio under my charge, to be married to a cousin of mine who lives at that place, and the road there by way of Cuba threatens so long a delay, that besides the secret grieving of the lady over her prolonged separation from her sweetheart—and you, Mr. Mole, as an English sailor, will understand her feelings—there is the worry of my cousin to be considered. He will think the ship lost; he may fancy me false to my trust perhaps."

He waited a little before answering, and then said very civilly, "I can quite onderstand yours and the lady's feelings. We're all sorry for ye both, I assure you; but we don't mean to let Charles swing; we don't intend to put ourselves in the way of the law, and so, as you've been already given plain to onderstand, Mr. Musgrave, there mustn't be, and there won't be, no speaking of ships. 'Sides," he continued, with a sudden rounding upon me, so to speak, in his manner, "supposing the hands consented to your trans-shipping yourselves, ain't it a million to one that the vessel *wouldn't* be bound to Rio, or anywheres near it? In that case," he added with a laugh, which he instantly checked, "you're as well off here; for Cuba's nearer to Rio than the Cape o' Good Hope or the Indies 'ud be, and for all you know, the ship you enter might be bound to them parts, or further off still—to Chiney or New Zealand."

Spite of his civil manner, I judged there was little more to come from a chat with him than ill-temper on his side and increased mortification and anxiety on mine, so telling him that the course to be steered throughout the night was the course we had been heading all day, I went below to join Miss Grant. I told her what Mole had said, and we sat talking till about nine o'clock; and then observing her to look very weary, for she had slept but little during the previous night, I begged her to withdraw, saying that I myself needed rest, as I should have to turn out again at twelve o'clock. Nevertheless, though professing myself tired, I was in no humour to go to bed. It was impossible to sit alone in that cabin without thinking of old Broadwater, a fancy that sent the eye instinctively to the smudge that still lurked darkly in the stain of the wood at the foot of the cabin-steps. A stouter heart than mine might have owned to a sense of timidity without a feeling of shame. The voyage indeed had been more like a nightmare than the grim reality it was, with its teeming life of brutality and ugly deeds. It seemed but yesterday that the brig had floated past the bald terrace of the South Foreland, and yet in the brief interval of the few weeks seven men of our slender company had vanished one after another, and every man to such an accompaniment of tragic and scaring conditions as to cause the memory of his death or of his going to lie upon the mind with the significance of yonder stain upon the planks. Then again I was haunted by the recollection of the gaping and supplicating figures which had that morning piteously motioned to us for help, and of the white bearded old man whose uplifted eyes and trembling, pointing hand had made his curse upon us as articulate as though the ear had received every syllable of the malediction.

But this sitting alone, with nothing to break in upon one's thoughts but the thin, weak groans of the fabric stealthily swayed, was but melancholy work. I went to my cabin, and was about to undress myself, when it occurred to me, that since the brig was now in possession of the crew, whose condition might not be quite so sober as that of Mole, it would be as well for me to look to my pistols. I charged and primed them both, and then remembering that Miss Grant had talked as though she could handle a firearm with thorough knowledge of its use, I resolved to give her one of the brace to lodge under her pillow, or to place ready to hand. I did not doubt that a spirit such as hers would find something tonical and supporting in the mere notion of a loaded weapon lying close to her grasp. In sober truth, I feared more for her than for myself. My life was too serviceable to the men just now to render me uneasy on my own account; but it was otherwise with Miss Grant. Who could tell but that amongst that lawless band there were some—even one—with instincts to be easily rendered devilish with liquor? I see myself now, standing in that little cabin, grasping a pistol in either hand, my imagination forward in the forecastle, picturing the dim light of the slush-lamp there, flinging its faint, wavering illumination over the seamen sitting in their bunks, or with hairy faces overhanging the edges of their hammocks, dangerously gay-hearted with the drink they had drained, and with the dance and songs, which, coming into their hard lives, were a sort of intoxication in themselves, talking of their jinks ashore, of their carousals, of their Polls and Susans, till one of them perhaps would speak of Miss Grant——

I opened my door, crossed the narrow passage, and gently knocked upon the bulkhead of my companion's cabin. She instantly asked who it was that knocked. I answered. In a few moments she opened the door. The light from my own cabin-lamp was upon her, for the berths were exactly abreast. Her hair hung upon her shoulders, one hand grasped the neck of her dressing-gown against her white throat, giving her an aspect of sudden alarm, which the peculiar brilliance of her steadfast eyes could not have defeated but for the composure of her lips.

"What is it, Mr. Musgrave?" she asked.

I now regretted my action. Here was I grasping a brace of pistols, and it seemed a stupid and nervous bit of behaviour in me to disturb this girl, and thus confront her.

"You have told me you are not afraid of firearms," I exclaimed. "It has occurred to me that one of these—"

She looked at the weapon I extended with a smile, then without a word entered her cabin and returned.

"There," she exclaimed, "you will see that I am as fully prepared as you. Indeed I think I am better off, for yours, I fancy, are a little old-fashioned, whilst mine I am sure would prove the deadlier weapon."

She stepped aside that the light might shine upon the pistol she held. It was a very handsome piece, with a long glittering barrel, mounted in silver. "See," she exclaimed, raising it. Her nostrils trembled, she drew herself erect with a slight backward leaning of her head, and levelled the pistol past me with a smile that was made almost scornful by the proud, sparkling determination of the gaze she fixed upon me. Oh, for a painter's brush to give you the queenly figure and pose of her as she thus stood! Her arms sank to her side, and she said quietly, "Have no fear for me, Mr. Musgrave. Should I be called upon to defend myself, I shall know how to do it."

I again wished her good-night, and returned to my cabin, feeling somehow, as Jonathan says, a bit mean, though for what reason I do not know, unless it was that such a combination of beauty, coolness, and courage made one fancy that the best sort of manhood in comparison with it could not but be somewhat insignificant. Indeed it did me good to think of the tear she had let fall that day, and to remember that now and again a natural timidity and fear had broken out. After all, thought I, as I looked round for a convenient hiding-place for my pistols, it is always the woman that forms the most admirable part of the heroine.

Chapter VI
Marooned

HOWEVER, AS IT TURNED out, the fears which had led me to the handling of my firearms and to my disturbing Miss Grant, proved groundless. The night passed quietly. Mole roused me at eight bells by beating over my head, and when I went on deck I found him as vigilant as need be, the ship sailing quietly along, the watch below turning out, everything as orderly, in short, as though Broadwater still had charge, with Mr. Bothwell at hand as an instrument to drive discipline home with.

So it was next day, and so it was next night, and for many days and many nights afterwards. For a whole week together we sailed along without handling a brace or lifting the clews of a royal. To be sure, it was weather to be expected in those parallels. The trade-wind hummed over our quarter, sometimes merrily enough to put an edge of froth to the curl of dark blue ripple, sometimes so softly that I would think we had lost it, when I noticed the light, long, azure swathes winding as unwrinkled as a surface of polished steel to the blue distance with the shadowing of the tender draught between. The men were very orderly; they kept to their quarters, and never one of them, with the exception of Mole or the cook, who punctually waited upon us, so much as put a foot upon the companion steps. They did no work; the decks remained unwashed; what trifling decoration of brass there was about the vessel grew green; the paintwork became grimy and blotched with heat and neglect; the sailors lounged about the deck all day, smoking and yarning, and then when the cool of the second dog-watch came, they would fill their little tub with punch, dance, sing songs, and fall to the sort of merry-making I have described. The pigs belonging to the brig they killed by degrees, and also made free with the cabin provisions and the livestock; but our own private stores they never offered to touch. Every day, after working out my observations, I would show Mole our position on the chart, but I was careful not to question him. In fact his own and the resolved attitude of the others satisfied me that they had made up their minds, that they had agreed upon a scheme from which nothing was to divert them, and of which it was their intention to keep me in ignorance; and I saw there was no remedy for Miss Grant and myself but patience.

Well, the time passed in this way, one day being the counterpart of another, and the hours seemed as minutes when one looked back, so monotonous it all was, though our consuming expectation and anxiety made the end seem so remote that I would feel sometimes as if I must fall mad from the mere waiting for it. Now and again, but at long intervals, we sighted a sail; but it was always at a distance, and I would bring my eye with a sort of loathing in me from the gleam of it, so ironical would be its accentuation of our condition, so idle and distracting the yearnings it awoke in me. But one day there came a change of weather. A shift of wind had happened in the morning watch when I was below, and when I went on deck I found the atmosphere thick, the breeze off the port-bow, and the brig under all plain sail, with the yards braced fore and aft. I made nothing of this at first, for I never doubted that it would brighten out into tropical fairness again in an hour; but finding that it continued, I grew uneasy. For, as I could catch no sight of the sun, there was nothing for it but to depend upon dead reckoning; and as throughout I had no very profound faith in myself as a navigator, and less faith still in the accuracy of old Broadwater's rusty appliances of aged quadrant and infirm chronometer, I feared that my earlier calculations, supplemented by such guesswork as dead reckoning implies, would find me all adrift when the time came, as I should suppose, to report that Cuba might be looked for in twelve or twenty-four hours. I say I was afraid, for reassuring as might be the behaviour of the men *now*, it was impossible to foresee what posture they would take if they should find me wrong in my navigation. Indeed my very life might depend upon my accuracy. They would suspect I had wilfully deceived them, and God alone knows what usage I should receive from them if they worked themselves into a passion over this fancy.

The nights were as thick as the days. I never turned out in the dark without an eager look aloft; but the gloom came down to our mastheads; not the leanest phantom of a star was ever visible, and the dawn was again and again the same feeble filtering of granite-coloured light through a sullen greyness of heaven that yet left the sea-line bare to its confines; and the breeze blowing warm and moist as a woman's breath over the olive-tinctured deep, never once parted this melancholy shadow into a break wide enough to give us the dimmest view of the azure behind it. I told Mole that as the brig was off her course, with a certain amount of leeway to be accounted for, and as I had nothing to depend upon but the log-line, it would be impossible for me to guarantee that we should hit the Cuba coast. I said this to him at noon on the second day of the thick weather, whilst with quadrant in hand I stood hoping for an apparition of the sun.

He looked at me suspiciously under the mat of hair that drooped upon his brow, and said, "But we ain't outside five days' sail of it, are we?"

"About that," I answered.

"Then how can we fail hitting the island?' he exclaimed. "It's long enough; there's range of coast to keep it in sight if it was as high in the air as the moon is. The brig's head's west by north, half-north, two and a half points off. Our position being known, we shall be able to tell when it is time to go about."

"Ay," said I, "but put her about, and where will she be heading to? South-south-east won't serve our turn, Mr. Mole. Besides, I'm not sure of the currents hereabouts. Captain Broadwater's instruments are not of the best, you must know, and his charts are as old as his quadrant. He had made the run to Rio so often that he could smell his way along; but here am I, no experienced navigator, mind you, heading right away off Broadwater's course, and thrusting into a smother that leaves me nothing but the log-line to work my way by."

I saw he did not like this at all. He eyed me very uneasily, with a shadow of temper rising to his face.

"Should be mere crow-flying work, it seems to me," he exclaimed; "'tain't as if it was a rock you was heading for. Look at the length of the Cuba coast, sir, on the chart. West by south's the course; that's ondoubted, if the compass don't lie. Werry well; you're within five days of a range pretty nigh as long as one side of Europe. How can ye be a-missing of it with the log a-going every two hours, and the course showing clear in yonder binnacle?"

"As you are so cock-sure," said I, defiantly, "I heartily wish you would relieve me of the responsibility of navigating the vessel. Since you know all about it, take charge of her! I've done my best, and will resign my trust gladly."

"No, no, by——," he cried, with an oath; "we've kept to our side of the agreement, you keep to yourn. You ondertook, under conditions which the crew's complied with, to navigate this brig to within a day's sail of Cuba, and then tell us when we was arrived at it. We must hold ye to that, sir," he added, with a dark look.

"What I've done, I've done honestly," said I; "I have been as loyal on my side as I admit the crew have been conscientious on theirs. Use me as you will—I am in your power and cannot help myself, and you know it!—I have performed *my* share of the cursed compact!" with which I turned on my heel, leaving him standing and following me with his eyes.

Well, for five days and five nights the thick weather lasted. The end then came, very fortunately for me, for had this spell of bitter anxiety been protracted another week, I believe my mind would have become unhinged. The distrust of the men had grown so keen that they watched me as if I were a rattle-snake. Their very ignorance of navigation rendered them the more suspicious. Every day Mole took the chart forward and showed them where we were, by dead reckoning, and you would see them shouldering one another as they looked, flinging a note of growling upon the air with their combined utterances, pointing to the chart with their thumbs, and then gazing around the sea as if there should be something *there* to furnish them with a hint of the true situation of the brig.

At four o'clock on the morning of the sixth day, when Mole arrived on the quarter-deck to relieve me, the ocean lay as darkly shrouded as it had been at any time since the first of this gloom had gathered around us. The wind had shifted at noon on the previous day, and the course I then shaped was west-south-west, but at midnight it had headed us again, and the brig had broken off to west by north. Yet the breeze had been steady throughout; we had shown royals to it the whole time, and it had made life as easy-going aboard as ever the steady wafting of the trade-wind had; that is to say, it demanded no pulling and hauling from the men, no furling or setting again. Under a close luff the *Iron Crown* broke the short grey seas with her larboard bow with a handsome trend to leeward, as was to be noticed by the run of the short streak of oily wake veering away on the quarter.

Mole was grim and surly as an unshaven sailor newly awakened when he arrived. I was not less sullen than he, sick at heart with the four hours' straining of my eyes in search of a star, and weary besides with the fatigue that comes to a man out of anxiety, idle conjecture, and a sense of uncertainty, that in my case was heightened by waiting into a sort of anguish. I briefly and sulkily gave him the news of the four hours, which amounted to nothing, and with a yawn and a shiver went below, and to bed.

I was awakened from a deep sleep by a thumping of heavy knuckles on the bulkhead outside. I started up, conceiving I had overslept myself; that it was past the hour, in short, when I should have relieved Mole; but on looking at my watch, which hung at hand, I observed it was but seven o'clock. The knocking was repeated.

"Who's there?" I sang out.

The gruff voice of a seaman named Williamson answered, "Mr. Mole wants ye on deck, sir."

"Right," I answered, jumping out of my bunk, whilst I wondered if some fresh tragedy had happened, for my being called in this way brought the morning of Broadwater's disappearance to my mind, and that was a memory to crowd my imagination with a score of black fears and anticipations. Meanwhile I took notice that the weather had cleared, and that it was a fine bright morning. The shining of the sunlight upon the scuttle puzzled me. It came full to the glass in a brimming of white splendour off the sea, whereas if we were holding our course the luminary should be nearly astern, with a slanting of his radiance along our sides, out of which no beam could twist to lie as the light now lay in a circular tremble of pale gold upon the door facing the scuttle. Nor could I immediately fail to observe that the brig floated steady. My ear was too practised not to rightly interpret the slopping sounds of water against the run. She rolled slightly with much internal creaking, as was natural to her; but I did not need to go on deck to gather that either her topsail was to the mast or that her anchor was down.

What had happened? I lingered a minute or two outside my cabin-door, with my ear against the bulkhead of Miss Grant's berth. All was still within. I knocked, then called out gently, "Is it well with you, Miss Grant?"

"Yes; what is it now, Mr. Musgrave?" she replied.

I answered, "I cannot tell. I am now going on deck."

"I will join you shortly," she said

It was comforting to hear her voice. In such a vessel as the *Iron Crown* it was impossible to know what might happen from hour to hour, and I protest, when I listened and heard no sound in my companion's cabin, such a chill of dismay for an instant fell upon my heart, that the sensation was as bad in its way as the realization of a fear. But all was well with her, and without further lingering I stepped on deck.

It takes a man a little time to collect the details of a picture. For a moment perhaps I stood in the companion-way, looking aloft and upon the decks, and then round upon the sea. The brig, as I had expected to find her, was hove-to. Her mainsail was hauled up, the topsail aback, the royals clewed down. It was a very clear, brilliant morning. Every vestige of the leaden, oppressive atmosphere that had environed us throughout the week had disappeared. The sea-line ran with a crystalline sheen like the edge of a lens out of the west; carrying the airy, delicate gleam with it in its curvature to the east, where it broke into white flame under the hot and mounting sun.

Directly on our starboard-beam, at the distance of a mile or less, stood an island. The blue went past it on both hands and the atmos-

pheric hue of the sky beyond was assurance positive to the nautical eye
that the ocean was on *that* side as well as on this. It showed a seaboard
of a couple of miles; the foreshore of it apparently coral sand, which
to the sunshine dazzled out almost blindingly against the dark green
background of bush, tree, and small savannah. Here and there that lustrous beach curved into a little creak with an overhanging of palm-
trees on either side of it, like human beings bowing to one another.
The breeze was light, there was scarce an undulation of swell, and the
thin line of surf crawling out of the blue surface on to the sand came
to the eye in a radiant tremble; the shivering of it seemed to put a sort
of pulsing into the whole of the foreshore, as though the steamy heat
of the atmosphere caused the land to writhe upon the sight. It was a
low island, a Cay, as I might gather, of the true Bahaman type, with a
green hummock or two amidships of it; here and there a volcanic-like
protuberance of land, with verdant slopes refreshing to the eye to rest
upon, and a kind of swarming of trees in places, their tops above the
sky-line of the shore, and their branches defining a fibrine conforma-
tion as delicate as coral against the liquid azure past them.

The sailors leaned over the side of the brig looking at this island.
Mole stood gazing at it close to the companion, with his arms folded,
manifestly waiting for me to appear. I was a minute however in the
hatch before he was sensible of my presence.

"That's not Cuba, sir," he exclaimed, instantly levelling his finger at
the island.

At the sound of his voice the fellows who were hanging over the rail
looked round, and two or three of them dismounted and drew near;
but merely, as I believed, the better to hear what I had to say, for there
was nothing threatening in their manner or faces.

"No," said I, stepping out of the hatch to command a clearer view of
the horizon, "that island is assuredly not Cuba, as you say, Mr. Mole.
'Tis a Cay, with a name of its own, I don't doubt. Our drift must have
been to the north of west, with a set of current that has thrown me all
abroad in my reckonings. I'll step below for the chart."

"Never mind about the chart," he exclaimed, with a note in his voice
that brought me to a dead stand in a second; "that island's beknown to
us."

The half-blood Charles came from the rail with his hands in his
breeches-pockets. "*I* know it," he exclaimed, with a peculiar expression
in the roll of his sloe-like eyes upon me; "it'll do as well as Cuba—
maybe better," he added, speaking the words through his nose with a
Yankee drawl.

"What is the island?" I asked.

"It'll be in the West Indie boiling, anyhow," answered the half-blood; "it's all right. No civilization on it; no blasted lawyers to choke a man for doing his messmates a good turn." He whistled softly, with a half-smile at Mole, then swung on his heel and returned to the rail.

Mole eyed me steadfastly, like a man considering; the others methought with something of pity mingled with rough curiosity in the air with which they surveyed me. A miserable feeling of uneasiness possessed my mind. Mole's manner was authoritative, and even insolent, a behaviour he had no need to open his mouth to utter. But the others showed a sort of indifference; the men at the rail just looked at me, then resumed their posture of surveying the island; the two or three who had drawn near eyed me, but, as I have said, with curiosity only, for I could witness no malevolence in their regard. I confess I would have been less scared had the whole of them closed around me on my arrival in a hubbub of savage cries and threats, charging me with having deceived them, and the like. This at least would have been consistent with the apprehensions which had almost worn me out during the past week; but the careless, half-composed demeanour they now opposed to me was absolutely terrifying, and I vow 'twas almost a relief to turn from those inquisitive faces, as of those of a crowd in a street staring at some one injured, or in a fit, to the more defined expression on Mole's face, showing sullenly some dark resolution at heart.

I put my hand to my brow and swept the sea-line. It ran without a break to the resplendent shaft of sunlight in its bosom.

"Is this the only island in sight?" I asked.

"Yes," said Mole curtly.

"Ay, but I mean," I exclaimed, "is there no more land visible from the masthead?"

"There's a film away to the west'ards in sight from the cross-trees, that's all," he answered grimly, no longer softening his words with the "sirs" he was used to give me. "We should have been ashore had it held thick. The course ye gave me was dead on end for it."

I glanced at the topsail hollowing backwards to the mast, then at the island, then at him, and said suddenly, "What do you mean to do?"

He fetched a deep breath, and said, "After you and the lady have breakfasted, we'll put ye ashore."

On hearing this, the men who were standing near us at the bulwarks approached, and looked on and listened; yet they exhibited little more than curiosity in their manner.

"Do I understand," said I, controlling my voice, "that it is your intention to put the lady and me ashore upon that little island, and *leave us there?*"

"Yes," he answered, trying to look me full in the face; but his eyes fell to my stare of horror and astonishment.

"Men," I cried, rounding upon the others, "this is hard usage to give a man who has served you as I have. Even though *I* should have deserved this treatment, what has the lady done to merit it? Her sympathies were with you all from the very hour——"

"For God Almighty's sake, don't *argue*, Mr. Musgrave," cried Mole, stamping heavily with his foot, and accompanying the gesture by a nervous sweep of his arm. "Our minds are made up. Had yonder island been Cuba, it would have been the same; we'd have set ye both ashore. You and the lady are witnesses we're bound to leave behind us, no matter where. It *must* be done!"

He stamped again. I looked at the half-blood, and was about to address him, but he immediately returned to the rail, and there hung whistling, keeping time by drumming with his fingers.

"Mr. Mole," said I, "it is in your power to give us a better chance for our lives than yonder island will provide. Why do you fear us as witnesses? I am willing to take any oath you and the others may require to keep the events of this voyage secret. Miss Grant will do the same. Put us in the way of reaching some inhabited coast—send us adrift, if you will, within a day's reach of a town, I do not care where it may be—but to land and leave us *there!*" I pointed to the island.

He turned his back upon me, and walked without reply a few steps forward, then turning suddenly and extending his arm, with his great hand clenched, cried out, "Mr. Musgrave, I have begged ye not to argue. It'll do no good. When a man's in hell he's got damnation enough." He swept his hair off his brow and continued, "Your breakfast'll be served afore long, and we shall then want you to be ready. She'll carry ye," nodding towards the quarter-boat; "the water's smooth, and you can take what you will that belongs to you. Best bear a hand to get your traps together, for we've got no notion ourselves of hanging hove-to here." He turned his back again upon me, thrust in among four or five men who were at the bulwarks, and stood with them looking at the island.

"Do they mean to set us ashore, Mr. Musgrave?"

Miss Grant was at my side, glancing from the island to around her, with a face in which one saw the first flushing of consternation yielding to a cooler mood even as one watched it.

"Yes," I answered.

"What island is that?" she exclaimed.

"I do not know," I replied.

"Can you not find out?"

"It is doubtless one of the Bahama group, but which it is impossible to say, seeing how wildly wrong I have proved in my reckonings. It is seemingly known to the half-blood, but there is nothing to be got from him or from the others, the merciless villains!"

"Is it inhabited?" she inquired.

"No. If it were I should welcome the act of cruelty as a deliverance from an intolerable situation."

She took me by the arm, and led me a little distance aft out of earshot of the men. Mole peered at us past the rounded back of another fellow, with irritable impatience in his posture of doing so. She viewed the island for a little while without speaking, apparently lost in thought. Her breath came and went tranquilly. The fear that had for a moment or two shone in her eyes being gone, I could not discern the least symptom of alarm in her. I stood silent, marvelling at her composure, wondering indeed whether it did not owe much to her inability to compass what the men's intentions signified to us. Presently she said quietly, "Will not the chart in the cabin tell us what this island is?"

"I will look when I go below," I replied; but added bitterly, "How should the name of it concern us——?"

She interrupted me: "No; but if we can discover its situation, the chart would show us which is the nearest inhabited land, so that we shall know in which direction to steer when we leave that place." I was about to speak. "Oh, Mr. Musgrave," she exclaimed softly, with the faintest tremor in her voice, though her face flushed to the spirit of resolution in her, "I would rather things should be as they are—I would indeed! Our life in this vessel has grown unendurable. My nights are miserable. I can scarcely rest for thought of the plans those fellows there may be hatching. We shall be together on that island; the nightmare of fancy that haunts me of being left alone on this brig—of our being separated through some deed of violence—will be ended. The worst has come, so far as *they* are concerned," she continued, with a shuddering half-turn of her face towards the seamen, "and there at least," directing her glance at the island, " I shall be spared the hundred daily and nightly dreads which terrify me here. It is hard, it is hard!" she muttered in an almost musing way, "but it is less than I feared. They never meant that you should be able to bear witness against the half-blood, against themselves. Some kind of end must have come, Mr. Musgrave. It is miserable as it is; but time after time my terror has foreboded something infinitely worse."

It was afterwards that I recognized the truth of her words; but just then I was so wild and crazed by this blow, by the cold, calculating inhumanity of the men, in whose demeanour I had never witnessed the least hint of such barbarous usage as they were now about to give us, which throughout had been their intention towards us, and which doubtless was the reason of their demand that I should let them know when we were within a day's sail of the Cuba coast—I say that at that time the conflict of emotions was so violent in me, I could get nothing out of the composure and thoughtful words of the sweet and noble woman at my side but a sort of dull wonder at her tranquillity.

"Your breakfast's gone below, Mr. Musgrave," shouted Mole; "me and my mates'll be obliged by you and the lady bearing a hand. Another half-hour's as much as we can allow ye."

"Let us go to the cabin," said Miss Grant; your heart will come to you again soon. I declare I thank God for this thing as a deliverance."

She led the way, and I followed. The cook was lingering at the table, as though adjusting it to his taste, but on our showing ourselves he ran hastily up the steps, fearful perhaps that we should address him. It was not a time to think of eating. For my part, I believe a crumb of biscuit would have sufficed to choke me. In truth, the long hours of bitter anxiety I had suffered had unnerved me; but to what extent I should not have known but for this sudden testing of my courage. I saw Miss Grant look as though she meant to force herself to partake of the meal, to embolden me by a further illustration of her coolness, but she turned away after a minute, and said, "What is next to be done?"

"We must pack up our traps," said I; "we are at liberty to carry our luggage ashore. Ashore! Good God!"

I could scarcely utter the words. You talk of going ashore when newly arrived off a town; or if off a coast, you go ashore to return again to the ship; but to think of going ashore to this little island, to stop there with nothing in sight but a blue streak of haze, visible only from the elevation of the cross-trees——

"Shall we take all we have?" asked Miss Grant, as collectedly, I protest, as if this Atlantic Ocean were the English Channel, and there was a boat alongside ready to carry us to Plymouth or Dover.

"Yes," I answered, almost mechanically, for this was a detail indeed I found it hard to bend my mind down to; "throw what you have into your boxes and portmanteaux. I will wait for you here."

In five minutes I had stowed my possessions away, and then going to Broadwater's berth, drew a chart of the West India Islands from the bag, and returned with it to the cabin. I overhung it eagerly, but to little purpose. Here was a stretch of islands starting from high abreast of the Florida coast and trending away down to Dominica, and which of them that green and gleaming spot of land out to starboard was, it was hopeless to conjecture. At a later date I might have put my finger upon it without much trouble, but Broadwater's charts were exceedingly old, and this one of the West Indies was complicated and disfigured with ink-marks and dim tracings like a school-boy's lesson-book. However, there could be no doubt that this island fringed the thicker zone, that it was some eastward sentinel Cay, such as Rum, Cat, or Watling Island, and that civilization therefore bore from it as the sun set; so that our course, should we make shift to get away, must lie to the west and south.

Whilst I pored upon the chart, the companion was darkened by the figure of a man, and the imperious voice of Mole rang down, "Are ye ready, Mr. Musgrave?"

"I am waiting for the lady," I replied.

I took the chart, and went to the foot of the companion-steps with it. "Mr Mole," I said, "I have served you as honestly as it was possible to me in the navigation of this brig. It is surely not too much to ask you the name of the island over the side, that I may fix its position here," pointing to the chart, "so as to be able to tell in what quarter of this bare sea the inhabited lands lie?"

"The name's of no consequence, nor its bearings either," he responded gruffly; "ten to one if it's wrote down on a chart that's brought us up with around turn leagues and leagues clear of the coast we aimed at. Bear a hand, if you please, sir; the men are growing impatient."

I flung the chart down on the deck. It was a merciful thing I had not armed myself, for I was so mad just then it was as likely as not that I should have drawn upon the ruffian, and paid the penalty by being tossed over the side with a lump of holystone seized to my feet. Miss Grant came out of the cabin.

"I am ready," she exclaimed; "are we expected to carry our luggage on deck?"

I called to Mole, who still stood at the head of the companion-ladder, "You can send a couple of men for the boxes," and so saying, I conducted Miss Grant through the hatch.

They had lowered the boat and brought her alongside under the gangway, that was unshipped with steps over it. A few of the men eyed us askant as though ashamed, yet too curious not to steal a glance.

The half-blood was one of these. I thought to myself—"You beauty! Old Broadwater after all had the true gauging of your nature. If ever the gallows were put to a profitable use, it will be when *you* dangle from it, bleaching to the wind!" I stood with folded arms, my eyes rooted to the deck, Miss Grant by my side, neither of us speaking. Somehow the sense of bitter humiliation induced by the thought of the sort of men they were who were using us thus, weakened the deep emotion of dismay with which I contemplated our abandonment upon that island. In a few minutes a couple of fellows arrived, bearing our luggage. There were four or five boxes and portmanteaux, along with a carpet-bag or two, some bundles of rugs, a hat-box, and the like; and I cannot express the horrible accentuation these prosaic things gave to our condition when one looked from them to over the rail at the line of white surf melting into the sparkling sand, with the greenery beyond, without a hint even of savage human structure to relieve the spirit of wildness which was swept into the heart of the lonely place out of the infinite ocean distance by the blue line of the horizon going past it on either hand. The two men who had brought the luggage dropped over the side into the boat; the boxes and portmanteaux were handed over.

"Now, sir," said Mole.

I was about to speak. Miss Grant clasped my hand. "Hush!" she whispered, "come!"

Without a word I got over the side and helped her to descend. Suddenly some one cried out, "They're going ashore without anything to eat or drink."

"'Vast with that boat, Jim!" shouted Mole.

There was a pause of a few minutes, then what was left of our private stores was passed over, along with a couple of beakers of fresh water and a jar of spirits belonging to the brig. "Shove off!" sung out Mole, "and bear a hand back, lads."

The two fellows threw their oars over, and the little boat, deep with the weight of the provisions, the luggage, and the four people in her, glided shorewards over the blue rippling surface. It happened strangely enough that the two men were of the three (the half-blood being the third) who had pulled us aboard the *Iron Crown* from Deal. They were both Englishmen, with a ginger-coloured fork of beard, a wrinkled skin, dingy with weather, and covered with knobs like the foot of a sea-boot. They never offered to speak to us, and strenuously avoided meeting our eyes, watching indeed the sheering of their blades through the clear under the sapphire edge, as though indeed they were a couple of draper's assistants out for an hour's row. I held Miss Grant's hand, scarce conscious of what I was doing, though I afterwards remembered that she cherished my hold of it, as though, with a woman's sympathy, she believed I drew courage from the pressure of her fingers, and for that reason let me have my way. Had we been going ashore to some bright town full of life and conveniences, whence in a day or two we should be able to start for Rio, she could not have shown herself more perfectly tranquil and easy. Once she looked behind her at the receding form of the brig, and breathed deep a moment, but the respiration was not a sigh. For my part I never turned my head; my eyes were fixed upon the island we were approaching, but with a feeling of numbness in my mind which rendered curiosity so languid that I gazed as if it were some passing scene in which I had no other concern than that of a spectator.

The men made for the nearest of the creeks, where the tender lift of the summer sea ran seamless to the shadows cast by the leaning trees on either side; the boat's forefoot struck the almost snow-white sand, which went winding up like a silver trail through the herbage, as you notice it on the Mozambique or Natal seaboard, and the sailor in the bows jumped out. The spit of shore that formed the right-hand shoulder of this creek, looking seawards, shelved so flatly to the wash of the surf, that you saw the ocean spreading beyond it to the open sky, with the brig, her topsail still aback, barely leaning from the wind, her canvas and hull dark against the flashing water and the airy splendour beyond her. I threw a look at her *now*, and thought I could distinguish the tall figure of Mole, watching us through a glass which he steadied against a backstay. The seamen who remained in the boat handed out our luggage and provisions, parcel by parcel, to the other, who dragged or carried them a few yards clear of the water's edge. On this freight being discharged, I went into the bow and stepped ashore, Miss Grant springing easily from the gunwale with her hand upon my outstretched arm. My inward rage and despair raised so great an aversion in me to the two sailors, that the mere being addressed by them would have been intolerable, and I was brisk in quitting the boat and in assisting Miss Grant, that they might have no excuse to *order* us ashore. But I had no sooner felt the ground under my feet than the conviction seized me that we were to be left without a boat! I had not thought of this. My consternation, ever since Mole had apprised me of the intentions of the crew, had been so great that such considerations as had entered my mind were, as I may say, instinctive only; by which I mean, that when a thought occurred to me it was accompanied by a sort of dull notion of its being true. I had—I know not why—reckoned in this mechanical, instinctive way upon our being furnished with a boat; had looked at the chart with that fancy in my mind, and concluded that when we left the island we must steer to the west and to the south; the unconsidered idea in me being that we should be provided with a boat. But now I understood that these men, to return to the brig, must go away with the boat, and that the girl and I were to be marooned to the very height of the meaning of the wild old buccaneering word!

One fellow sat ready to back water; the other, standing in the bows, was in the act of poling the little craft off to get her head seawards. I sprang in a bound to the very lip of the shaling water.

"My God, men!" I cried, articulating with difficulty, so tremulously was my heart beating, so choking was the sense of constriction in my throat, "you do not mean to leave us here without any means of escaping? Lads, as sailors and Englishmen, show some pity. We are without a refuge!" I cried almost hysterically, pointing inland; "without tools, without skill to contrive a fabric to escape from this horrible solitude. Men, as you are English sailors——"

"Shove her off, Bill," growled the fellow in the stern. "Away with us! There's no use *talking*, and nothen can come of listening."

The boat's head sped round to the thrust of the oar; the two blades dipped—sparkled—dipped again; in a few moments she was clear of the creek, with the two rowers bending to their toil as though they were pulling for a wager.

I walked slowly to where Miss Grant was standing. I think for a little while I must have been off my head, as the common saying goes, for I recollect shaking my fist at the boat and the brig beyond, and heaping fifty curses upon the crew; until exhaustion, combined with the sweltering heat of the sun striking off the white dusty dazzle upon which we stood, came to my rescue, and most mercifully silenced me. Miss Grant never spoke, never offered to interrupt or check me. She allowed me to talk myself out, and then taking hold of the sleeve of my coat, quietly drew me to one of the trunks that stood under the shadow of a tree, upon which by a gentle movement of her hand she induced me to sit, and then extracting a little silver-mounted bottle of refreshing scent from her pocket, she damped her handkerchief with it, and held it to my forehead.

I believe, had there been a tear in my composition my eyes would have distilled it at that moment.

I broke from my spell of womanly weakness with a very passion of resolution.

"I will not ask you to forgive this failure in me," I cried, "heartily ashamed of myself as I am. A little patience, and I shall hope to prove myself worthy of so noble, so courageous a companion as you. I should not have suspected so much weakness in me. I cannot believe it a part of my nature. I have been unduly, most heavily tried. But so have you!" I exclaimed, finding more strength coming to me out of the clear serene beauty of her eyes than any cordial could have inspired. "Oh, we will make it well for both of us yet."

I sprang to my feet with a shake of my body that was like flinging away the whole miserable girlishness in me to the winds.

"Nay," she exclaimed, "keep your seat. I will sit by your side. We are not separated yet, Mr. Musgrave. I swear," she cried, lifting her eyes to heaven, "I would rather that this should have happened than that we should have had to endure another week of the horrible life we were leading in that cruel ship. We are not separated; but who knows that another week might not have found us so—might not have found me alone?" She shuddered almost convulsively, then instantly rallying with an effort of will that was a miracle in its way for the energy of it, she added, in a changed, softened voice full of sympathetic sweetness and the melody of her tones, "How refreshing is the shadow of these trees! how soothing this stillness! We shall be able presently to think what is next and best to be done. Let us meanwhile wait and see what they intend to do," pointing to the brig.

Chapter VII
We View the Island

THE BOAT, CREEPING ALONG the water with a spark of light to the rise of the oars on either hand of her flashing out as regularly as a revolving lantern, regained the brig, and in a few moments the little fabric mounted jerkingly to the davits; then round swung the topsail-yard, the royals mounted slowly to a taut leech, stay-sails were run aloft, and as the brig gathered way she fell off a point or two with her head to the east of south, the sea opening beyond her to the clear horizon, that just past the vessel's stern ran with a sort of *seething* of its blue into the hot and tingling glory that came in a blinding shiver from the edge of the ocean there to the very feathering of the surf upon the southward-facing beach of the island.

We watched the vessel receding from us in silence; fathom by fathom she crept seawards, with her canvas trembling amid the swimming sultrinesss of the atmosphere, and a short polished tape as of shot satin dragging in tow of her rudder.

"Distance makes her beautiful," exclaimed Miss Grant, "but she has proved a most ugly ship to us."

"What do they mean to do with her, I wonder?" said I, watching the flickering of her high sails as she drew along a slope of the shore whose shoulder would in a moment or two conceal her.

"What do you suppose?" she asked.

"As they have two good boats," said I, "they will probably scuttle the vessel when within convenient reach of some habitable place. It is clear that they know their whereabouts; and as Mole can use the log-line, the chart will give him the rest of the information he needs. They'll arrive ashore, or be picked up as ship-wrecked mariners, earn a deal of pity, pocket some dollars in addition to what they may plunder from Broadwater's and the mate's cabins, then scatter and never more be heard of. There! She has vanished!" I cried, rising.

I turned to survey the island. It was partly coarse, thick guinea grass, and partly soft, glittering, dusty sand where we were, with a group of trees winding to the place to which the sailor had dragged our luggage out of a line of palms marshalled for the space of a couple of hundred steps along the shore of the creek, with others opposite, both bending their ostrich-like plumes to a combining of their boughs that formed a little cool green tunnel under which the bright shoaling water ran darkling, though it sparkled out green as emerald in the opening beyond, with a rounding at the extremity like the end of a thumb, where the white sand came down to it. The land went in a slight rise to a grove of trees that was almost a little forest in its way, with a twilight amid the greenery, spiked by hazy beams of sunshine striking down any opening the light could shoot through. Here and there a great red toadstool showed like a small scarlet shield in the herbage. There was a clump of coconut trees standing isolated to the left of the grove. The white and flowing-like streams of quicksilver wound in paths through the grass in all directions, and made one wonder that the tropical vegetation one saw could take root and find nurture in such soil. The air, blowing softly from the south-west, was tremulous with the humming of many kinds of insects, and sweet with indefinable perfumes as of convolvuli and the passion-flower—a commingling of nameless aromas. I watched a frigate-bird come out from the mere black spot he made seawards, and glance like an arrow without stir of its wide and graceful pinions to some haunt of its own past the little inland forest. In places close beside us the long grass stirred, as though there were human fingers beneath, to the movement of a lizard perhaps green as a bottle, with eyes like rubies, and a flickering fork of tongue as if it was breathing fire; or maybe some dingy thing that might have been a land-crab could be made out creeping for a space through the fibres of the grass, and then falling motionless as though, mole-like, it had sunk deep out of sight.

"I hope there is nothing poisonous in the way of snakes hereabouts," said I, pulling out a stout stick from one of the bundles that lay strapped near a portmanteau, and very warily I strode into the thick of the herbage, beating right and left, keeping a bright look-out, and listening intently. I started nothing but a lizard or two, and one of those half-lobsters called *soldiers*, and a vast spider with a body as big as a crown-piece, magnificently marked like the leopard, with the hues so brilliant and shining that it was as good as beholding some marvellously-wrought mechanism glorious with jewels to watch the scamper of the thing with its long legs over the heads of the spears of grass that bent to its weight. I returned, and opening my portmanteau, pulled out the pistols which lay there loaded, and thrust them into my pockets.

"I'll go and take a view of the scene," said I; "there may be land in sight away west from the tallest of those hummocks. This island must form one of the Bahama group certainly, and if so, others cannot be very remote, though hidden from this elevation. Will you remain here until I return?"

"No, I will accompany you," she answered; "there's nothing to be afraid of, yet I do not like the idea of being alone." She sent a swift glance round her with a faint smile that was like asking forgiveness for this little show of weakness.

The length of her dress made me feel a trifle uneasy. It was impossible to know what small murderous fangs lay hidden among the long coarse grass that showed yellow and bald in places to the roasting eye of the sun. The folds of her gown formed such a flowing drapery that the skirts of it trailed a foot or two in her wake—a regular net for the ensnaring of anything venomous or distracting. Let her courage be what it would, methought if she should hook up such a spider as the chap I had just put to flight, it might go hard with us both. It was no time for ceremony. It is simply impossible for a man to be marooned with a girl without the vessel that makes castaways of them carrying off a mass of the superfluous decorums which on shipboard kept them at arm's length.

"Miss Grant," said I, "excuse me—your dress is too long."

She gathered the folds of it in her hand, and said simply, "Yes, much too long;" then going to one of her trunks she produced after some fumbling—a pincushion!—(to think, now, of a pincushion on an uninhabited island!)—and handing it to me, bade me help to pin her dress up for her. It was a task in its way to reconcile one almost to being marooned—for the moment, at least. I don't think I had known how perilously emotional this woman had made me at heart in all thoughts that had reference to her, until I put my hand to the sweet and careless intimacy of this pinning job. It was a sort of haunting of her closest presence whilst it lasted, like bending the face to a flower that one has long been able to admire with the eye only. She watched me with a half-smile as I stooped round her, whilst I trimmed her canvas suitably to the best of my judgment for our adventure; with an air of unaffected indifference touched but very subtly with the most delicate imaginable spirit of coquetry. It was more like a flirting passage, indeed, in some merry picnicking jaunt—as though we two had strolled from the rest of the people, and I was clumsily trying to make good the dilapidations following an airy frolic—than a detail of one of the grimmest of all ocean incidents. She again explored the box she had recently rummaged, and took from it the silver-mounted pistol which she had shown to me on board the brig, and after deliberating a minute or two thrust the barrel into the bosom of her dress.

"I will carry it for you," said I, with a small recoil from the reckless-ness with which she had slided the loaded weapon aslant her beautiful figure. "Should you stumble—let me hold it for you."

She withdrew it, saying, "I must be armed as well as you. I shall know how to carry it." With that she opened another trunk, and after a brief hunt drew forth a dainty leathern belt of South American make and fashion, into which, after clasping it loosely round her, she stuck the pistol, where it lay safe enough, and ready to her hand besides; and then equipping ourselves with a cotton umbrella apiece, we started for the green hummock that rose at about half a mile inland, taking a bit of a circuit to the left so as to go clear of the trees, into whose cathedral-like dimness it was difficult to peer without uncomfortable fancies of savage things—imaginations of bright hungry eyes glisten-ing between some mighty spikes of aloes; the small head of a serpent half-way up a tree, with fold swelling upon fold of spotted, bloated skin, rising corkscrew-fashion to the green intricacies atop—all helped, as such notions would be, by the novel tropical smell of flower and gum in the wind, and the innumerable murmur of flies and insects shirr-ing across the sight on wings of translucent pearl, and the melancholy, unmusical pipings of birds, one wailing to another and waiting for the answer, as it seemed.

We stepped along very cautiously, Miss Grant looking down for the most part, and I round about. The greenery soothed the eye, but there was a savageness put into everything you saw by the loneliness of the place that weighed perilously upon the spirits. For my part, I felt as though the sand we trod had never before received the impress of a human foot, and there were moments during that walk when the helplessness and hope-lessness of our condition affected me so violently that I could scarce draw a breath, and I had to call a halt, feigning, with my hand to my brow, that I had paused only to obtain a better view of the island.

From the summit of the hummock we could see all around us. The sea went in a brilliant blue slope to the sky, the great dome of which, brassy with the glory of the sun that was but a little past the meridian, set you thinking of some mighty, brightly-burnished copper-bell charged with fiery splendour shutting down over you, with this green spot of earth parching in the midst of it to the roasting metallic glare. A little leaning shaft of white, with an ice-like gleam upon it, broke the continuity of the southern seaboard. It was the canvas of the brig. From *her* right round to back again to her the clear horizon ran without a flaw. If land were visible from the cross-trees of the *Iron Crown*, it was concealed from us here. The little forest betwixt us and the creek hid the foreshore of the island past it; but one knew how it would be there by how it was wherever else the eye turned. The surf rimmed the white sands with three or four lines of flashing snow, which seemed to melt into the coral beach like liquid light, and the seething of it fell as delicately upon the ear as the hissing of champagne in a glass poised to the lips.

"It is all clear sea, apparently," said I; "the blue seems to me to spread everywhere the same. There is some chance for us in that, for in such soundings there can be no danger to navigation, and a vessel may heave close enough into view to perceive our signals at any hour."

"We should have some signals ready," said Miss Grant.

"Nothing to catch the eye like smoke," said I; "I will build a big bonfire up here this afternoon, ready to make a blaze when the time comes."

"The island is certainly uninhabited," she said, exploring it with her dark eyes. "It is hard to imagine that it has ever been *discovered*; but it is best as it is, Mr. Musgrave. Surely the very worst shipwrecks are those in which sailors and passengers have been thrown amongst savages."

"It is blisteringly hot up here," said I; "let us return to the cool of the trees. A moment though! You have a keen sight. Can you distinguish anywhere upon this island the least gleam of water?"

She searched slowly and narrowly, as did I for the matter of that. Again and again I was deceived by some thin sinuous streak of sand that had the very sheen of a limpid stream in the dazzle of it, as it seemed to creep like some little brook amid the herbage of the denser growths; but my eye could regularly follow it to broader tracks which were unmistakably sand to the sight; and I was about to give up, when Miss Grant, who had been looking steadfastly in one direction for some minutes, said, "*That* must be a little waterfall yonder, Mr. Musgrave; look past the curve there, over the head of that clump of bushes."

She pointed to the foot of the slope of another hummock, lower and smaller than the one on whose brow we stood, and in a breath I caught the sparkle of a waterfall shivering like splinters of bright steel against the green edge of the rise, and amidst the interlacery of the bush whose density a little lower down hid it. If it were fresh water it was of the first consequence in the world to us, and without another word we started for it. It proved as thirsty, bubbling, and murmuring a brook as ever lipped glass-like to an English river. Its source was some distance away; it flowed freshly in a channel of its own, fretting to the spot at which we had arrived, when it sulked again in a wide pool, passing on afresh in a mimic torrent, narrowing for a space till its volume made a foam of it, then running clear under the sky for twenty fathoms, after which it pierced the herbage and vanished amidst the trees. I scooped up some with my hand and tasted it. New milk was never sweeter. I had a brandy-flask in my pocket, and with the help of the silver cup attached to it we drank our fill of this delicious water. No wine was ever so well tasted; it was ice-cold too, and of so diamond-like a clearness, that but for the whispers of it as it ran, and the hue of the blue sky in it, it would have been as invisible as water in a crystal vase. Short of the appearance of a ship promising deliverance to us, nothing, I am persuaded, could have so helped my spirits as the discovery of this fresh water. There was thirst in the dry and blinding sparkling of the sand; there was thirst in the aspect of the tracks of rusty yellow herbage which dashed the vegetation with their sickly tint like gangrenes spreading even to the gaze of the eye; there was thirst in the hot air that everywhere trembled like the atmosphere over a flame, until in places the horizon waved as though a high swell were running out there, and the slender trunks of the coconut trees wound upon the sight with the movement of an Archimedean screw slowly revolving. Here then were inspirations to make the discovery of this brook of running waters a positive rapture in its way. Suppose it had no existence, I thought; what should we have done? The beakers the men had dispatched us with held but a few gallons. Rainwater might have been found perhaps by digging in the sand, but I had my doubts of that when I came to look at the dust of the milk-white foreshore. The mere fancy of our condition without this brook— the central roasting Eye sending an atmosphere of brass flowing to the furthest confines—the thirsty, *salt* noise of the surf—(you could *hear* the saltness of it in the seethe of each little recoiling breaker)—was almost enough to make one keep one's hot lips steeped in the crystal coolness and sweetness of the prattling stream.

But my heart fell again as we walked slowly towards the spot where our luggage was. Indeed, the mere sight of these details of civilization— portmanteaux, trunks of the latest fashion, rugs, camp-stools, walking-sticks, the twenty odds and ends which had gone to our equipment— made such a contrast of the inhospitable desolation of the spot of land on which we were imprisoned, that the stoutest spirit must have yielded, I think, to a feeling of hopelessness. How were we to obtain a shelter for the night? When our slender store of provisions gave out, where were we to look for a further stock? Again, unless we were taken off by some passing ship, what was our chance of escape? There was no lack of wood on the island, and with tools I might have contrived to put together some sort of log-fabric on which, under Heaven, we might have made shift to blow away to within reach of succour, whether of land or of ship; but without chopper or saw yonder grove was of no more use to us than a handful of the white sand by the creek there. However, it was a little soon for lamentation, though on such an occasion as this a man's groans would be deepest when his experiences were freshest.

"It is about time we broke our fast," said I; "perhaps we should feel faint had we nothing to think about but our appetites. The men were merciful to send our luggage ashore with us. Those camp-stools of yours are worth a million."

I opened one of the cases containing our provisions, and prepared a meal of preserved meat and biscuit, along with the remainder of a bottle of Madeira. The camp-stools made us seats, and our table was the lid of a trunk. Of all the passages of this particular nautical experience of my life, our first meal on this little nameless island recurs to me the most vividly. I think I hear now the hum of the sultry sea-breeze amid the boughs overhead, rendered refreshing to the ear by the metallic-like rustling of leaves, yet always blowing vibratory with the innumerable buzzings of flies and insects. I see again the green lizard, scarcely distinguishable from the foliage amongst which he lurked, viewing us with brilliant eyes from some limb on high. Occasionally there would come a harsh, short scream from a parakeet, and a flash of lustrous plumage from one verdant shadow to another, like a fragment of rainbow borne along by the wind, accompanied by the sharp rushing *skirr* of beating pinions. The sunshine was alive with the glancing forms of coloured things—now a great dragon-fly, a golden shaft propelled by wings of gossamer—now a butterfly of glorious hue—now some tiny red-breasted bird, a sort of woodpecker, maybe, for I noticed that a drumming as of bills would spring up out of the quarter in which the streak of radiant feathers had vanished. Had all been well with us, good beds to look forward to at night, with even such necessaries to support us as a backwood settlement might supply, why, this little island, with my beautiful and courageous companion to talk to and have by my side would have been something—say even for a fortnight—to have entered into the realities of life as a sort of paradisiacal dream, a fancy for whose brief fulfilment under happy conditions I would barter a dozen years of the delights of the gayest and most showy cities of Europe. But 'twas sheer nightmare and nothing more, spite of the waving verdure of the savannah, of the glitter of the tropic bird, of flowers lovely as the constellations of the midnight of the Antilles, of the rain-like pattering of the leaves of the palm-tree, of odours as of the lime and the citron, when one sent one's gaze seawards, and *felt* the whole solitude of the mighty deep melting through and through into one in a kind of swoon, as it seemed, of the very soul.

However, we ate and drank, and were the better for it. I lighted a cheroot, and fell a-thinking with my eyes on Miss Grant. She was equally thoughtful, with a far-away expression in her face.

"There are nervous folks," said I, "who would not accept the gift of looking ahead even for a fortnight if they could make their fortunes through it. Throw me back a couple of months ago into Piccadilly, with leave to peer far enough to divine old Broadwater's nature, and to guess at the issues it must shape, and we should not be here."

"It is all my fault," said she.

"Mine!" I exclaimed. "I should have insisted on being put ashore with you in the English Channel."

"I mean it is my fault that you ever made the voyage," said she.

"You would not wish to be alone though?" said I, smiling.

She shook her head with an unaffected shudder.

"What conclusions will Alexander arrive at," said I, "when day after day goes by, and no *Iron Crown* arrives at Rio?"

"I don't like to think of it," she answered; "but he will have to be patient. He must wait as *I* must wait."

"Pity it is not the other way about," said I. "*He* ought to be here, and you safe at Rio."

She looked at me quickly, with a half-formed fancy, as it seemed, hovering on her lips, parted as if to speak, faintly coloured, and plucking a blade of the coarse grass at her side, appeared to study the texture of it.

"Alexander will conclude that the brig has gone down with all hands," I continued. "The men are sure to scuttle her, and as they know if rescued they will have to account for us and the two men they have made away with—Broadwater and Bothwell I mean—it is odds if they don't invent the name of the ship they profess to have belonged to, so that the truth will never reach my cousin until we carry the news ourselves to him."

"Poor boy! his anxiety will be cruel. But perhaps we shall be with him sooner than we expect."

"I hope so, indeed, for your sake," said I, with a lift of my brows to the tormenting puzzlement of how it was to be done. "But sufficient unto the day, Miss Grant. Here are we *marooned*, and what's next to do? that's the question. No chance of our being taken off this afternoon, nor of our escaping in any other way. The night then is before us, and we must provide for it. I have no means of erecting any sort of shelter, and the island offers nothing. For my part, one of those rugs and a stretch of that dry sand will make me as good a couch as I need, spite of the land-crab and whatever else crawls hereabouts at night. But the notion of *your* lying on the cold ground is intolerable to me," said I, turning my eyes about in vain search of any hint for a high and dry bed for her in tree or slope.

"I have a net-hammock in one of those boxes," she exclaimed, "unhappily only one. If you——"

"*I!* Lord love you, Miss Grant! Why, if it were not for the lizards aloft, I'd seize myself to a bough, make a bed of one of those leafy forks up there, as Robinson Crusoe did. But there may be monkeys in this island for aught I know, and on the whole I fancy a sand-mattress promises me a quieter couch than a tree. If you can find the hammock, we will turn to and rig it up in as snug a place as we can light on."

She immediately explored one of her boxes, and presently found the hammock. It was formed of net, but very strong, though so portable that one could have stowed it away in one's hat, with ship-shape clews and eyes and lengths of lanyard ready spliced for lashings. This, it seems, like her pistol, her belt, and divers other matters, had been one of her Rio possessions. It was an odd thing to carry home from South America to the English climate; but it was an old home relic, she told me, in which she had passed many a long slumbrous hour under the scented and myriad-voiced shade of the cotton-trees, of the gleaming leaves of the star-apple, and the slender branches bending to the weight of the golden shaddock. Besides, she knew little of Great Britain, and might have believed that the sun was as constant to the garden plains and smoking cities of the greatest maritime nation on the face of the earth, as it was to the country in which she had been bred. But a spell of the Edgware Road would suffice to correct even odder fancies than *that*.

I swung the hammock between two trees which exactly fitted the length of it. They stood somewhat forward from the group where our boxes were, with a tract of white sand hard by, which I had resolved should furnish me with a bed that night; so that she would swing close over me, and be as free likewise as one could possibly contrive it, from all risks of visits during the dark hours from the lizards and tree-toads in which I reckoned this island abounded. I formed a mattress and pillow for her of shawls and rugs, and learning that she had some mosquito-curtains in her boxes, I borrowed a roll of white tape from her, wanting a better kind of line, and made a ridge-rope of it along her hammock, with a couple of pieces of wood cut from the bough of a tree to serve as stanchions, that the ends of the curtain might float fair past the clews, and so protect her at both ends.

"Perhaps there are no mosquitoes," said she, watching me as I worked.

"I hope not," said I doubtfully; "anyhow I shall borrow one of your curtains, and roll myself up in it when the time comes. Unless my system has undergone a change since I was at Bombay, a mosquito-bite with me signifies a lump rather larger than a crow's egg, and as red as Broadwater's nose."

"We have plenty of them at Rio," said she, "but they never tease me. Though the species may be different here," she added, with a glance at the contrivance I had rigged up, which made me fancy that, bad as our melancholy and dreadful situation was, there would be nothing in it to hinder her from objecting to the defacement of her fair face by the singing pests of these rich and sparkling parallels.

I now found that occupation of any kind was helpful to my spirits, and thereupon pulling off my coat and waistcoat, and baring my arms, I went to work with a tolerably stout knife I happened to have in my pocket—one of those useful combinations of corkscrew, gimlet, finger-long saw, and the like—to cut as much dried stuff as I could make shift to deal with; of which I manufactured faggots by securing them with ligatures of grass strong enough to knot. Miss Grant insisted on helping me. She had replaced the somewhat small-brimmed hat she had come ashore in with a great yellow sombrero-fashioned head-covering that sheltered her like an umbrella, and I see her now bending her graceful figure to the faggot at her feet, her white hands, with a flashing ring or two upon them, nimbly and swiftly knotting the grass bindings, lifting her face occasionally to address me, with her dark eyes the brighter, her teeth the whiter, her complexion the fairer, for the softness of the shadow which lay upon her beauty. We manufactured a great number of these faggots, and conveyed the whole of them between us in several journeys to the summit of the hummock, where we built them up in a goodly pile, taking care to fence them about, that they should not be blown away by a sudden squall or rising of wind, and further protecting the whole by a thick cover of live branches, densely leaved, which would also thicken the smoke whenever the time came for us to set fire to the heap. The great heat made this labour very arduous, but though its completion left us both wearied, it was a thing to be done, and we felt the easier in our minds when it was finished. It was impossible to know but that at any hour we might happen to look seawards and spy a vessel slipping fleetly past, too far off to witness any waving signal of shawl or handkerchief, but well within view of such a volume of smoke as our body of faggots would make.

We paused a moment on the brow of the little elevation, before returning from our last excursion to the hummock, to take a long look round. The sun was sinking in the cloudless western heavens; he was a great shield of fast reddening fire, and the placid purple ocean beneath him seemed to rise with a rounding of its polished bosom to the huge luminary, as though he were some mighty magnet up there drawing it. One could not look a moment, without a weeping of the sight, into the blinding ardency of the western atmosphere, so charged was it with the ceaseless gushing of the crimson glory; it seemed to palpitate and contract and dilate like a lake of liquid glowing iron newly poured from the heart of a blast-furnace. But the sea went from there into a tender deepening of turquoise against the orange reflection in which the eastern sky was bathed; the rippling of it was so exceedingly delicate, that it looked more like the shimmering of light upon it than the fine wrinklings of the wind; the thin edge of surf broke with a tincture of lemon upon the sands, that now shone golden to the evening radiance. The air blew very gentle and warm. The tropic picture was deepened to every sense by the strange uncommon sounds rising from the island— queer chirpings and snorings; sharp, short cries from the greenery, like women's voices calling hoarsely; brief melancholy pipings making answer to like notes, sad, low, and more distant. The sound of the surf seethed through this curious concert, but nothing moved, look where one would, if it were not the flash of a bird of gorgeous plumage, a stir of some near tall spears of grass, or the curled head of a palm slightly swayed by the wind into a beckoning posture or an airy salutation. There was a quality in the light of the waning day that put a melancholy into the spirit of the solitude of this place far beyond the reach of moonlight or the starry darkness of the night. Fresh as we were from days and days of the loneliness and immensity of the deep, yet there was something in the boundless aspect of the ocean, as we surveyed it from the height of that hummock, which, speaking for myself, shocked and scared one's instincts as though one gazed at some preternatural revelation of sea. I saw Miss Grant droop in her posture, so to speak, to the sight of it; her clasped fingers holding her hands before her relaxed, her arms fell to her side, her head sank as she slowly brought her eyes from the flawless ocean to my face. She breathed slow and deep, as one in whom perception has grown to the weight of a burthen upon the heart.

"Come," said I, taking her gently by the hand, "there is a morrow, and yet a morrow, before us. The good God is over all besides."

We walked quietly, but in silence, back to the spot where we meant to pass the night.

Chapter VIII
The Midnight Bell

THE CLEAR, FINE, SPANGLED dusk speedily followed the setting of the sun. The night lay dark upon the sea before we had finished the meal to which we had sat down when the hot crimson of the luminary was still flushing the heavens to the zenith with a blood-red atmosphere, against which the trees behind us on the west side of the island showed out black and lovely with the effect of the rich light between the boughs and the leaves, as though some hand had studded every interstice with a red-hot ember. The discordant cry of the parrot ceased, the multitudinous buzzing that had been going on all day came to an end, the melancholy wailing whistlings that had been answering one another down to sunset were hushed as if by magic as the last of the brief twilight glimmered off the sky. It was now the cricket's opportunity, and from every part of the island there rose up a very storm of bell-like chirruping, mingled with the sultry horns of the sailing beetles, odd whistlings and strange groanings coming from heaven knows where, along with the confused croaking of reptiles and the wild *snoring* call of the tree-toad. Here and there upon the darkness, in small hovering constellations, appeared a swarm of fire-flies. In places, these little galaxies of yellow-greenish points of light seemed to combine with the dust of the stars beyond them, and the eye catching them on a sudden would be startled for the moment by the fancy of some astral dance up there in the dark blue obscure, as though a fragment of the milky way had parted from the main body and was making a night on't!

The sea-breeze blew languidly, cool with dew, and fragrant with borrowings from the moist vegetation it breathed over as it floated down to our part of the island from the south and east. The wash of the light and lipping surf right around was as soft as the voice of a child; the sea spread out black as ink from the ivory of the beach, touched at wide intervals with the gleam of phosphorus or the silver wire-like wake, tremulously riding the ripples, dropped by some particular bright star. The moon would be rising anon, and we waited for her coming; for the dusk, clear as it was, rendered movement uninviting and even menacing. In fact it was impossible to tell what creeping thing might squirm to the tread in the darkness that blackened nearly everything but the sand. We had not, it is true, observed the least hint of snakes about throughout the day, but if any there were, the night might tempt them forth to walk. The puff-adder loves to stalk in gloom, and the rattle-snake's delight is the forest shadow. That we might not give anything poisonous a chance, we planted our camp-stools in the centre of the broad tract of sand that flowed fan-shaped to the creek betwixt the herbage, where even to the starlight it glanced out clear as a ship's deck, so that anything that stirred upon it we should instantly perceive.

Happily for me I had a good store of cheroots in my portmanteau. The fragrance of the tobacco seemed to civilize the island.

"Even with a companion by one's side," said Miss Grant, speaking softly, "the loneliness, now that the dark has come, of such an ocean spot as this terribly oppresses the spirit. But to be alone—without hope of escape, without the means perhaps of prolonging life beyond a little while—oh, Mr. Musgrave, there are some forms of human suffering of which the world can never know anything!"

"I should go mad if I were left alone in a place like this, after a bit," said I; "imagination would prove too much for me. Even when all's well I find myself ill-trimmed in that way. But to be alone here, without a chance, as you say, of escaping—I protest I would not give myself long to witness shapes as wild as ever the sailors of Columbus dreamt of, stalking out of the blackness of that grove yonder; to behold grotesque forms sliding out of the gloom of the sea into the gleam of the surf to have a look at me; to hear airy voices syllabling my name—well, fancy does make horrid fools of us certainly!"

It might have been the chill of the dew in the dark sea-breeze that blew with a little moan past us just then that sent a chill through me, but I must own to being possessed by a wild fit of dejection at that moment also. It did not linger; it was like one of those giddinesses which come and go, but which whilst on you make you grip anything for support with your eyes shut. Doubtless it came to me out of the boundless surface of liquid blackness broadening out to the low stars. I could not see how we were to get away from this island, and the briefest mental look ahead shrunk up the very soul in one to the prospect of days passing into weeks, weeks into months, with God knows *what* in the far end for some newly-arrived people *then* to stumble upon as a memorial of nameless human suffering.

Presently the moon arose, throwing up a delicate rosy haze first, then mounting into it red as a rose, which changed into greenish silver after a brief climb, with an icy sparkling upon the sea-line just under her, as though the edge of the ocean there were a long single breaker arching over into foam.

"What is that?" suddenly exclaimed Miss Grant, pointing to the sandy spit that formed a shoulder of the creek.

In the gathering light of the moon it might have passed for a circular mahogany dining-table that had been stranded by the tide, and that having felt its legs had started on an excursion inland. I was exceedingly puzzled, and as I could now see to walk, I approached the black object full of curiosity and wonder; but it was not till I was within ten yards of it that I made it out a vast turtle, weighing, I dare say, four or five hundred pounds. I knew very little of the habits of these animals, but I had somewhere read that the creatures are easily frightened, and so returning to Miss Grant I told her quietly what the thing was. "It will have come to lay its eggs, I dare say," said I; "I have often handled a turtle's egg, but never tasted one. I believe they are very good eating. Let the thing by all means contribute to our stock of provisions. Since there is one there will be others, and if I can manage to turn one of them over, I will; though how to get steaks and soups out of her I'm sure I don't know, unless we can rig up some sort of an oven; but even then what are we to boil the meat in?"

"We shall be very poor creatures indeed, Mr. Musgrave," said she, "if we cannot overcome difficulties of that kind. The one problem is how to get away from the island. We *cannot* stay here, you know."

The black figure of the turtle crawling steadfastly along the sand, like some gigantic spider from which a mischievous boy has cut off all but a little bit of its legs, slided behind the tall grass and disappeared, but I marked which way she went, for I meant to have her eggs if she laid any. The moonshine on the water was now glorious, and came rippling in pure silver to the very wash of the surf; the trees rose pale, and the foliage trembled to the breeze with the sheeny glitter of the South African silver-leaf. Our shadows lay black as sketches in India ink upon the coral sand. Oh! there was wonder, there was beauty, but there was terror too in the marvellous gush of haze which swept smoke-like from the bland planet eclipsing the stars in her vicinity. Distance grew horribly infinite to it, and the sense of isolation a physical torment.

"If the ruffians had but spared us a boat!" I cried. "We could have provisioned and watered her for days and days, and sailed in her too without risk on yonder equinoctial surface. There is nothing for it but to wait, Miss Grant. This is a great sea, steep to our foreshore, or I am much mistaken. The island is bound to be in some kind of highway, and to-morrow, pray God, may give us the sight of a ship."

With this kind of talk we killed some time. The light of the mounting moon was so brilliantly clear that I could witness every varying expression in my companion's face as plainly as if a shining dawn had broken; only that the moonlight gave a spirituality to her beauty which her charms were perhaps the richer for not discovering by sunlight. When the time arrived for me to press her to seek rest, I found her reluctant. And small wonder! It was not that the hammock was uninviting. Indeed, nothing fitter could have been devised for the languid, dewy warmth of such a tropical night of pale gold-like splendour as this, than the airy couch that spanned the black pillars of the two silent trees. One thought of what was up *above!*—some scaly betailed thing, creeping down the dry bark with a clawing of its armoured feet like the pattering of a land-crab upon an uncarpeted floor, to awaken one by a cold pressure of its belly upon one's brow—pah! The tropics are a glorious region to read about, to be sure; but give me an English summer evening dying out—with the lowing of a cow or two, the chime of a distant church-bell, a drowsy chirp stealing from the shadow of some sweet-blossomed orchard—into the delicious repose of night, unbroken by a note louder than the dim *cheep* of the grasshopper, or the faint midnight crow of an uneasy cock. Why here, now, as we sat, if we paused in our speech for a moment, the ear carried even engrossing thought away to the rickety chorusing of the million crickets; winged things as prickly as a cork stuck over with needle-points would sail into one's cheek with a *hum* that was like a little trumpet-blast in its way, so near and sudden was the sound of it; the snore of the tree-toad too awakened an echo as of an innumerable croaking of frogs; and if ever this sultry and unwholesome concert sank a little, it was only, as it seemed to me, to give one a chance of catching more distinctly the thin, red-hot-wire-like singing of a mosquito hard by the ear. The fireflies were wonderfully plentiful. A little cloud of them hovered for nearly ten minutes in front of us, within arm's reach almost; and bright as the moonlit air was, they glittered so sharp and clear, that I believe had the night been dark they would have shed illumination enough to enable us to have seen each other's face by.

Finding Miss Grant reluctant to go to her hammock, I proposed a little stroll along the glittering beach, and for over an hour, I think, did we measure to and fro some quarter of a mile of the sparkling shore, pausing often to watch the curl of the little breaker, arching black against the moon an instant ere seething into foam, or to direct a searching eye seawards for any inky spot upon the tremulous stream of brilliance, or any pallid shadow in the deep blue obscure on either hand of the showering moonlight, or to listen to some few brief, flute-like notes breaking from the inshore forest, or to mark a meteor of magnificence hurling westwards comet-like, and leaving a white, steam-coloured scar upon the sky long after it had burst into spangles and vanished.

At last she consented to "turn in." I dragged a trunk to the hammock to enable her to step to her swinging bed, and when her head was pillowed I made her snug with a shawl, and then enveloped her in the floating gauze of the mosquito-net, through which I could see her dark eyes watching me. The spreading branches of the trees screened her from the moon, but here and there a ray fell through, and one white beam rested upon the hammock. I doubt if any dream that ever sweetened man's rest was more enchanting than the vision of this girl's face under the moonlit, gauze-like transparency. Though no vision, indeed, yet it affected me as with the unreality of one. I could see a smile in her eyes as I raised my hat with a little bow, and wished her goodnight. One must go to sea for such experiences as this. Name me such a conjuncture ashore as could produce it. When I stole a peep at her again, the moonbeam had slipped off her, and the hammock was in gloom.

"I hope nothing will tease you on the sand," I heard her say.

"I hope not," I answered, looking at the branches overhead to make sure that the coast was clear up there.

I had now to make my own bed. The boxes were of unequal height, or I should have stowed them together into a couch. I stretched out a rug to lie upon, brought a small carpet-bag to the head of it to serve as a pillow, drew a mosquito-curtain over me, and lay down, pistols in pocket within ready grasp, and covered myself with such another rug as I rested on. The dry sand yielded with a sort of spring in it, and I found it a very tolerable mattress. But I lay extremely uneasy in my mind however for some time, constantly imagining that something was stirring on one side or the other of me. But I was more wearied than I was sensible of, and presently felt a pleasing sense of drowsiness stealing over me. There was something now almost soothing to the ear in the myriad chirpings of the crickets, and in the subdued soft creaming of the surf. Just over my face hovered a swarm of fire-flies, and I watched them sleepily. The night wind sighing through the trees filled the air with a fountain-like murmuring of rustling leaves.

I was nearly asleep when I started, instantly broad awake, to a peculiar, melodious, but most melancholy whistling of a bird amid the branches of the tree to whose trunk the head of Miss Grant's hammock was attached. What sort of bird it was I cannot say. Maybe it was one of the species which induced Columbus to believe that there were nightingales in these islands, when he sat hearkening at sunset to the gush of melodies which came floating out of the foliage to mingle with the *Salves* and *Aves* and the litanies of his crew. The few rich flute-like notes were plaintive beyond expression. Aroused as I was from my first noddings, it took a little thinking to collect the quarter whence the piping flowed, and what it was that made it. Indeed, to open one's eyes at all upon the bright moonlight, the white sand, the froth of surf, the ocean washing out black from the steel-like sparkling under the luminary, was surprise enough after long weeks of waking up to nothing but my coffee-coloured cabin in the *Iron Crown*, specially when the whole was blended into a sort of mist-like dimness by the fold of mosquito-curtain through which I peered. Indeed, if the sad musical pipings from the boughs overhead had come instead from some creamy-bosomed sea-nymph glimmering out white as ivory waist high past the foam that was shaling upon the sand, the sight must have occupied some little time in filling me with astonishment, so magic and unreal did the bird's awakening of me make me find the scene; so likely a theatre did the island seem for the wizardry of the deep, and so qualified was my mind at the instant for the contemplation, without wonder, of astonishments.

But the song was brief, and after a little my mind came round to its old bearings, and being now wide awake, after a glance at the hammock, which I observed to hang stirless in the gloom, I fell to some practical, anxious considerations of our condition; and the current of thought being set a-flowing ran into twenty different channels. I recalled my first meeting with Miss Grant, my instinctive hesitation in undertaking to escort her, the bewilderment her beauty had raised in me, and how, as I believed, nothing but the tender unconscious pleading of it could have triumphed over my reluctance to embark on this adventure. Then I mused upon the tragic and distracting incidents of the voyage, and my lonely quarter-deck walks with my lovely companion. I dared not deny to my own heart that I was already perilously fond of her. Indeed, had my reason been half imbecile it must have guessed at a growth of passion in me by a trick of meditating and endeavouring to interpret the meaning of her behaviour and looks as I could recollect them after passages of conversation and prolonged association. 'Twas a time for such a reverie as this, believe me, with her fair and stately figure airily resting within hail of a whisper from me, and the sweep of the silent sea round about closing as if to combine us. By Heaven! I thought to myself, though I know my duty, yet should a time ever come when I must hand her over to my cousin, it will be a bitter parting for me. Fool that I was to mix my heart up in a business in which I had no concern! If the forfeiture of her companionship is to be the condition of our escape, will my growing emotion presently leave me with disposition enough to lift so much as a finger to procure our deliverance?

"Tut!" thought I, with a waft of the mosquito-net at a little dance of fire-flies hovering over my knees, "it is about time I went to sleep!"

I had scarcely got my head down on the carpet-bag afresh when I was indescribably astonished by hearing *the chimes of a bell* rung swiftly. I listened breathlessly for an instant, believing the notes to be an illusion of my senses, but it was impossible to mistake. No village church belfry on a Sunday morning ever echoed a clearer summons to the faithful. The ringing suggested the sort of agitation you notice in the quick, eager pealing of a steamer's bell rung as a final warning to passengers to step ashore. It continued without cessation. I sat up, then clearing myself of the mosquito-net, leapt to my feet. I saw Miss Grant sitting erect in her hammock.

"Oh, Mr. Musgrave, what is that?" she cried.

"It will be some vessel," I exclaimed, "close aboard the island; perhaps ashore."

"No; it comes from those trees yonder," pointing to the little forest.

She threw the net like a veil off her head, sprang from the hammock to the box, and thence to the ground. "Oh!" she exclaimed, seizing my arm, "what *can* it be?"

The bell was no longer ringing rapidly; a sexton might now be tolling it. The slow, punctually-recurring chimes came along like a knell; they then ceased, and all was still. I paused a little to make sure if possible of the direction whence the sounds proceeded. On a sudden the ringing started off afresh—such a reckless, rushing, clattering of noise that my conviction was there was a madman at large upon the island, and that this was his way of killing the midnight hours! The whole place seemed distracted by the clamour. Queer grunts rose out of the grass, hard snoring noises out of the trees, with a universal groaning of frogs far and near, the hoarse inquiring cries of parrots, whilst you caught a shriller edge in the shrill minstrelsy of the crickets. The violent ringing of a bell in the dark hours of the night, even when one is as secure as a safe lodging and all the contrivances of civilization can make one, is, to say the least, an alarming disturbance. But to hear such a sound in this lonesome island, apparently amongst the trees yonder where they rose blackest to their topmost foliage against the moon, when it seemed as sure as sure could be that there was no living human being within God knows what distance of us, was such a trial to the nerves that I own to having hung in the wind for a space, amazed almost to a condition of semi-stupefaction.

The tumultuous harum-scarum ringing came to an end, and was succeeded by a melancholy tolling, as though there were a funeral somewhere under way. Bidding Miss Grant stop where she was a minute, I ran swiftly—I was a very nimble runner—to the head of the creek, whence in a few moments I had gained the beach on the north side of the island, a part that would have been hidden to us on the hummock by the forest. The pale golden light of the moon flooded heaven and ocean, and objects could not have been more visible had the effulgence been of the noontide. There was no sign of a ship hereabouts. The deep ranged with a bare breast steeping and soaking to the indigo of the sky; nothing stirred along the platform of sand that went twisting out of sight in a pearl-like haziness round the bend of the island, veering westwards. All this time the bell was tolling, and now I could not doubt that it was being rung in some part of the island, for as at the creek, so here, the chimes appeared to float directly from the black shadow of the central grove. I returned to Miss Grant, by which time the sound of the bell had ceased.

"It is no ship," said I, "be it what else it may."

"It is a real bell, though," she exclaimed.

"Ay, real indeed," said I, "too real for superstition to find a footing on it, though it is a chilly sort of thing to happen at this hour, amid this wild loneliness too. It needed to have been but a little less real to have thickened the blood with fancies of an enchanted island."

We waited, expecting to hear it again, but the ringer had apparently exhausted his merry-making fit for the time being, and all remained silent, saving the chirp of the crickets and the wash of the surf, with here and there a sulky croak.

Had I seen some figure stalking towards us out of the wood, I don't think, armed as I was, and free from all superstitious stirrings, that I should have been wanting in courage; but I confess I hesitated when it came into my head to penetrate the deep ebon shadow of the forest, and search for the ringer and his bell. In the wide glittering open, with the moon riding high overhead, a man rendered desperate by such a condition as mine might find heart enough for any sort of search or encounter; but the wood was as black as the bottom of a well. Here and there one could just catch sight of a faint oozing of moonshine into the dark blot which the trees made upon the land and against the sky; but it was easy to guess that one's entrance into that heavy obscurity must signify a groping rather than a peering bout. Who or what might be there, who could say?

"No," said I; "I'll not venture it."

"Venture what?" asked Miss Grant.

"Why," said I, "I had a mind just now to explore for that bell."

"You would be mad to do such a thing," she exclaimed with energy; "indeed I should not permit it," and she grasped my arm. "There must be a man in that wood," she continued, lowering her voice. "There must be human agency to set that bell going. Perhaps after all the island *is* inhabited, and there may be a nest of savages in that forest, who hid themselves on seeing us, and now dream of scaring us away by ringing a bell. Oh, I wish we *could* be scared away!" she continued, as with a shiver she glanced over her shoulder seawards.

I shook my head. "No," said I, "I'll swear there are no Indians here-abouts. Had they existence, we were bound to have met with some signs of them; a canoe—a wigwam, or whatever else their dwelling-place may be called—remains of fires—relics of feasting. I should like to have a good look round from the hummock. Will you stay here? I sha'n't be gone long."

"Certainly not. I would not be alone for—" she broke off, whilst she stepped to where her hat lay and put it on, and I saw the glint of her pistol-barrel in her hand. "It is wicked to feel nervous," she exclaimed, "but what could be so unnatural as the sound of a bell here?—and then not to be able to imagine what dreadful creatures may be hidden amongst those trees."

We walked to the hummock, thinking much more of the sound of the bell and of the hidden being that had swung it than of the noi-some or venomous objects we might by chance tread upon, and having gained the elevation, sent many a look round the sea and into the heart of the little island; but all this side of the ocean was as bare as the north-ern quarter, whilst not the faintest movement of dark substance or of black shadow could we see, scrutinizingly as we gazed, on any part of the land. The night breeze had died away; there was scarce movement enough of air to breathe cool upon the moistened finger. South and east the ocean stretched, motionless as a surface of polished black wood, and the languid seething of the near surf was so delicate that it stole into the air like the moan of breakers leagues distant. We lingered ten minutes, then returned.

It took me some time to persuade Miss Grant to enter her hammock afresh. I told her that I would keep watch; that there was really no more reason to be afraid now than there had been before we heard the bell; that if the bell had been rung with the idea of scaring us, it was plain that, whatever might be *our* alarm, we also were held in fear; that if there were Indians in hiding, treacherously disposed, they were not very likely to arouse us from the sleep in which they could have stolen upon and murdered or otherwise dealt with us as it pleased them.

"It is a puzzle," said I, "that we must wait for the daylight to resolve. Meanwhile rest is necessary to you, and you must please lie down. Trust to my vigilance, and sleep without misgiving."

Eventually she complied. I made her comfortable as before, carefully enveloped her hammock with the mosquito-net, then with a look at my pistols to see that all was right with them, I lighted a cheroot, swigged off a dram of brandy, and fell to pacing the stretch of sand, sentinel-fashion, close to the hammock, and keeping a bright look-out on the trees beyond, believe me.

Chapter IX
A Piratical Lair

THE TIME SLIPPED WEARILY and heavily away. The march of the moon was so slow that it was enough to make one think sometimes she had come to a stand. I paced the breadth of white sand till I was weary, then sat down, nodded, perhaps dozed, sprang to my feet again with a keen look towards the density of trees, which, as the moon floated westwards, stole out black and yet blacker, till the whole block of it was like a great staining of ink upon the liquid silver atmosphere behind, and resumed my pacing. Now and again Miss Grant lifted her head, bride-like with the drapery of the mosquito-curtain; but a time came when she lay still, and on stepping close very softly and peering, I found her sleeping peacefully, breathing gently and regularly, and looking the very phantom of a lovely woman under the filmy texture of the curtain, with a sort of lunar twilight sifting through the umbrageous shadow to her out of the soft, golden-tinctured air where the open was.

It was as if the night were bewitched, so hushed it was; I never witnessed a movement anywhere save the black shapes of turtle crawling up the sand by the creek side, or on to the beach facing the east. How puzzled I was by the ringing of the bell, by its ceasing for the rest of the night, by nothing whatever having encountered my eye as a hint of inhabitants, by the dead repose in the little forest, with never a shadowy flicker anywhere about to define the flitting of a human form, I cannot express. At last, having seated myself to rest after a considerable spell of walking, I fell asleep, and so lay till I was awakened by the rising of the sun, and opened my eyes upon his blinding stream pouring aslant from three or four degrees above the horizon.

I stepped to the hammock; Miss Grant still slept, but so sweet and fair did she look that I could not break away from watching her. My fixed gaze aroused her; she opened her eyes suddenly, and I backed a step, confused, and perhaps feeling a little mean at being detected. However, she awoke with too much wondering at her own situation and the strangeness of her surroundings to imagine my inquisitiveness, or to note the admiration which I doubt not would have been perceptible in me by her clearer vision. She threw the mosquito-curtain off her, and sat erect, and exclaimed, "Thank God, it is daylight!" looking in a restless way around her, with her hands clasped, her cheek with the hectic of slumber still on it, her beauty rich with the disorder of her hair, and the light in her eyes of transient bewildered thought that fired them like contending passions.

However, she had slept for three or four hours, and was the stronger and fresher for it. For my part, I felt so jaded and stale that every instinct in me clamoured for a plunge, so I trudged away past the head of the creek to the north shore, and spent ten delicious minutes amid the surf there, venturing however no further than waist-high; for whilst undressing I had spied seawards, within musket-shot, a motionless black object, with a lean of it that made me fancy at first it was an empty bottle, but which, when it flashed out on a sudden with a wet gleam, I very promptly accepted as the dorsal fin of a shark.

I returned to Miss Grant feeling years younger, and found her dressing her hair before an ivory hand-glass, which she had hung against the trunk of a tree. Well, thought I, marooning brings about strange intimacies! Perhaps it might be married people only that a scrupulous mutineering crew would think proper to set ashore. But it was no time for fastidious feelings, quite the wrong sort of occasion for prudery of any sort, for any kind of modesty and decorum outside the dictation of plain good sense, realizing accurately the conditions of the situation, and admitting no other government than wholesome honest instinct. In fact you must be cast away with a girl to find out how artificial life is, and how much fairer the virtues show for being purified by stress of obligation into artlessness. I was for turning away, with the idea of searching for the eggs the turtles might have laid in the night, but she continued placidly brushing the long lengths of her glowing hair, with a smile on her face as she looked at me out of the mirror; so I walked straight on, and set about overhauling our provisions with the idea of preparing a little breakfast for ourselves. I had taken a view of the sea from the north side, and now I searched the horizon on this, but no sail broke the shining line. At a rough guess I reckoned that the remainder of our private stores, which had been set ashore with us by the men, might with great care be made to carry us through another fortnight, helped by such food as we should find on the island. Indeed, this question of provisions did not very greatly worry me, for there was not only promise of a bountiful supply in one direction in the shape of turtle; there were coconuts, also oranges in plenty, green or ripe, on the north-west side of the little forest, as I had perceived whilst I sat drying myself after coming out of the sea. We could count too on a good store of craw-fish, which fortunately I knew how to catch. There were iguanas besides, delicate to the palate as spring chicken if properly dressed, though loathsome in their lizard form to the eye. No! the fear of starving did not visit me, but mainly I believe because the mind resolutely shrank from the contemplation of the possibility of our imprisonment lasting long enough to render famine imaginable. The consuming thought was, How if no ship should approach the place were we to escape? This consideration engrossed me even whilst my mind seemed busy in reckoning up the stock of provisions, and again and again I would find myself pausing in that work, with a dull sense of hopelessness that was a sort of distraction in its way, whilst I looked round the island wondering if it was in human ingenuity to manufacture out of it any sort of floating fabric to which we might commit ourselves without the certainty of perishing by drowning.

Miss Grant was full of the subject of the bell. She could talk of nothing else, and whilst we sat at our little repast of preserved meat and sweet biscuit, she was incessantly directing her looks towards the wood.

"There may be people there," she said, "watching us all the time. I thought I saw something move when you had left me just now. We *must* find out to-day if this island is inhabited. The approach of the night will be intolerable if we are to expect that bell to ring again without knowing where it is, or what produces the sound."

"I shall explore those trees shortly," said I; "let me have your pistol. With mine it will give me three shots without obliging me to reload."

She drew it from her belt where it had lain all night with her. I thought I would try its quality, and taking aim at a leaf that stood in clear green outline against the sky, I pulled the trigger, and the leaf fluttered slowly to the ground. The sharp *ping* of the pistol was followed by many hoarse cries of parakeets, and a large bird broke like a shape of burnished gold out of a dense cover of leaves in the heart of the tree at which I had fired, and sailed away towards the forest, waking many hideous echoes with its discordant notes.

"An excellent little weapon indeed," said I, going to my portmanteau for a powder-flask, and reloading the pistol. "Pity it is not old Broadwater's blunderbuss though. The blast of that bell-mouthed engine would be the sort of hint one would like to give if there be ears yonder to receive such messages."

"I will accompany you," said she; "it is inaction and expectation that keep me frightened."

"Lord preserve you," said I, "look at that growth of grass! You would need to be dressed as I am to penetrate it."

Indeed it was only too plain that nothing in the shape of petticoats and skirts could be forced, short of one's wake after a plunge or two becoming a raffle of shreds and tatters, through the dense, coarse, bush-like herbage which stood to the height of a man's waist among the trees. Indeed, the better to equip myself for this adventure, I laced on a pair of stout leather leggings, whilst I buttoned myself up in a short pea-jacket so as to oppose the trimmest figure I could contrive to the stubborn dusky confrontment of bush and guinea-grass. Leaving her standing and watching, I walked briskly towards the trees, with the butt-end of a pistol projecting from either side-pocket, and Miss Grant's weapon in my hand. Piercing as the sunlight was, the foliage was so dense, the intermingling of boughs so thickly complicated, whilst the trees, moreover, stood so close together, that within half-a-dozen paces of the eastward opening of this little forest the green gloom lay beyond belief heavy. The obscurity brought me to a stand at least a minute, until the blinding glare of the open had gone out of my eyes, and I could see plainly. Climbers and creepers of all kinds, training and coiling like serpents, added yet to the dusk by filling the spaces between the trunks with a vague showering of crimson, star-shaped blossoms. After the heat outside, the atmosphere here struck almost chill; there was a sickly smell of rotting vegetation too, and nearly every tread of mine was upon something pulpy that yielded to the pressure with an ugly, juicy sensation as if 'twas soddened through with centuries of black miry damp; though maybe it was no more than a toadstool, or a frog, or a bunch of decaying fruit. Through a little cleft at wide intervals you'd catch a glimpse of the sea spreading brimful of soft blue light to the sky, with a wild buzzing of insects coming in through the opening on a gush of hot air.

I moved with a vigilant eye, crushing warily through the quickset understuff, gazing at every tree-trunk as though another step should open a figure behind it watching me. I need not deny that I felt very timid. The mere cathedral-gloom made by this dense interweaving of greenery was almost preternatural in its way, when one thought of the dazzle that was just outside. Then again, even if there should be no human beings here to suddenly let fly at me with a spear, or arrow, or fusil, how was I to know what savage beast lurked in this wild tangle of shadows? Some of the snaking branches wore the very aspect of giant serpents writhing in folds off one tree to another. Here and there fell a smoky, golden haze of sunbeam, but it only deepened the obscurity of the leafy aisles; though had I had an eye for such matters at that time, I must have found something lovely beyond imagination in these dashes of soft radiance, bringing out some bunch of huge leaves, some cluster of green fruit never maybe to ripen, some scarred and ragged elbow of bough, forking black through a drapery of runners and white-hearted flowers which looked to be falling like a cataract of green waters flecked with foam from the confused darkling roof of branch and foliage on high. Whether the sight of my moving figure alarmed the scores of birds amongst the trees, I know not; but the cries, pipings, hoarse parrot-like bawlings which broke from them, fell tormentingly upon my nervous ear, that longed for peace that it might hearken for any signal of danger.

I had been pushing my way forwards for seven or eight minutes without catching sight of anything more than the flickering plumage of some strange bird here and there, with the glint on it as of a self-luminous object, or as if it still carried the brightness of the sunshine it had been steeped in, when on my left, just past a couple of trees whose trunks rose to their branches with a twist in them which made one think of a pair of petrified boa-constrictors, I caught sight of a bell hanging from under a cover like the lid of a box, supported by two stout stanchions, the whole as green as the wooden piles of a pier washed by salt water. "*That's it!*" thought I. "Come! here is discovery number one. It is a real bell anyhow!" and somewhat marvelling at the sight of such a thing, I made for it. The frame that supported it might have been a hundred years old, and the bell itself twice as ancient as that. The metal was green and bronzed with time and weather. I made out some faint lingerings of what had been an inscription upon it, but the characters were indecipherable. I opened my knife and put the blade of it into the wood of the frame, and it was like sticking a cheese, so damp and tinderous too was the timber, like soaked matchwood. A piece of grass line was attached to the clapper, and hung a foot below the mouth of the bell. It looked rotten, though I gave it a tug without parting it. To make sure that this was the same bell we had heard in the night, I struck it two or three times. The tone satisfied me. I also knew that Miss Grant, by hearing the notes, would conclude that I had discovered the bell. But who on earth could have rung it? I sent as penetrating a gaze as the twilight of the forest would permit in all directions, but nothing approaching human shape or signs of human life was to be seen.

It was clear enough that this bell was seated in the very heart of the little forest, and as I was resolved that my over-hauling of the place should be thorough, I pushed on to the western extremity of the trees, till I could see the sea opening like a great blue eye over the slope of down to the ivory of the sand; and then worked my way with a fight for every foot I advanced, so dense, spike-like, and briery was the tangle. Again and again I paused, always with Miss Grant's pistol ready cocked in my hand, and gazed earnestly right and left and behind me, till I presently came to where the trees thinning gave me a view of the smaller of the two hummocks, with the herbage and trails of sand rounding north-east to the spot where we had passed the night. The daylight here lay broad, and after walking a little I came to sheer sand, with patches of grass sprouting out of it, a clump of cocoas flourishing beyond, which made me wonder again, for I could see no sign of soil.

I halted a little while to recover my breath, and cleanse my face of the sweat that poured down it. I could no longer doubt that the wood was as untenanted as the rest of the island. What hand then had rung the bell? There had been no draught of air to stir the weight of metal in the night. The alighting of some heavy bird upon it might indeed have caused it to sway, but there was nothing living with wings the wide world over to account for the several sorts of peals which had rung forth—the dirge-like tolling, the quicker beat, then the mad helter-skelter clattering, and then the solemn *requiem* chimes again. It was enough to put the wildest thoughts into the most prosaic brains that ever mortal head carried, and I must confess to looking backwards into the dim twilight from which I had emerged with a sort of shrinking feeling in me, and with a bit of wonder too that I should have found heart enough to carry me through the exploration with the stoutness I had exhibited.

I started to walk afresh to join Miss Grant, when, having made three or four steps, forgetful perhaps of preserving the shambling gait I had used in the high grass, the point of my boot struck something in the sand, and down I went, measuring the whole length of me, the pistol I grasped exploding as I fell. I jumped up not a little flurried by this unexpected capsizal, and on looking to see what it was that I had kicked against, I observed a large iron ring lying black upon the sand. I thought to pick it up, but on grasping it I discovered that it was fixed to an eye screwed or bolted into either wood or masonry hidden by the sand. I was busy in scraping away the sand lying around about the ring with the sharp of my foot when Miss Grant arrived.

"What have you seen, Mr. Musgrave?" she cried. "At whom or what have you fired?"

"Oh," said I, "I tripped over this ring just now, and the pistol went off as I fell."

She barely glanced at the ring; her thoughts were elsewhere.

"I heard the bell; did you ring it?"

"Yes," I replied.

"What else did you see amongst the trees?" she inquired.

"Nothing else. It is some old ship's bell," I replied, "hanging at a kind of scaffold that might be a hundred years old, perhaps more."

"No man?" she asked.

"Nothing in the faintest degree approaching one, black, white, or yellow," I replied.

"But, Mr. Musgrave, *who* could have rung the bell then?"

"We may yet find out. At present I have not the faintest notion. But see here, Miss Grant; what is the meaning of this ring? It is a fixture. There will be some sort of trap down here, or I am much mistaken. If I had but a spade now!"

She looked again at the ring, and her interest came to it. She stooped and pulled at it, and then finding it fixed, recoiled a step or two and said, "We had better not meddle with it. The bell is wretched enough as a puzzle. Don't let us seek fresh adventures, Mr. Musgrave."

I mused a bit. "At all events," said I, "no harm can attend our seeing to what sort of arrangement the ring is secured."

There were shells of many kinds strewn about the beach, some of them as big as dishes, sharp-edged enough to cut a man's head off. I picked up three or four, and brought them to where the ring was, and fell to scratching and digging with them, Miss Grant helping me. The shells spooned up the sand plentifully, and after working a little we laid bare what had unquestionably been some small ship's hatch-cover, about four feet square. On scooping yet a little at the lap of the edges, I found that this cover rested upon a timber frame, which in its turn was doubtless steadied by piles driven into the earth under the surface of sand. I tugged with all my might at the ring, but could not lift the hatch. Miss Grant, whose curiosity was now aroused, and who seemed willing that we should look a little further into this business, put her hands to the ring too, but our united efforts could do nothing with the cover. I had no mind, however, to be balked, and after considering a while what I should do, I pulled out my knife, and opening the saw-blade, swarmed up a tree to a stout, straight, marline-spike-looking bough that had caught my eye, and putting my knife to it, worked away patiently till I had cut three-quarters through it, after which I sprang on to the bough and came down with it in a fall to the ground. It was as good as a handspike. I reeved it through the ring, using it as a lever, and pressing it upwards with my shoulder, I so jarred and shook the hatch-cover that it was presently loose enough to lift.

On removing it, I found that it had concealed a tunnel which vanished after a gradual slope of a few feet into utter blackness. Three or four rude steps fell in a flight to where the slope began, so that on descending a man needed but stoop his head to move clear of the roof of this strange cellar. I kneeled down to peer sideways into the obscurity, but saw nothing for the blackness there. An old faint, damp sort of smell arose.

"We had better put the cover on and go away," said Miss Grant; "there may be something horrible hidden in that grave."

"Nothing living, at all events," said I; "it is some old freebooter's lair, some ancient piratical hiding-place, or I am very much mistaken. That secreted bell yonder is a part of the equipment—set up to serve as an alarm, and to signal with, and perhaps to tell the hours too. I must probe that hole; there may be a discovery under our feet worth making."

"Mr. Musgrave, you will not be so rash! *What* can you hope to discover—that can be, I mean, of the least use to us?"

The sense of our helplessness seemed on a sudden to smite her as a shock; she drew a quick breath, and sent a yearning glance along the ocean line, almost unconsciously, as one looks up to heaven in a prayer. I thought to rally her with a stroke or two of idle fancy, and said, "Time was when many of these Bahaman Cays were the haunts of the picaroons; swift and tidy little schooners, loaded to their ways with the treasure of plundered galleons, came ratching to these secret verdant islands; the treasure was brought ashore by the beauties who had stolen it, and buried. Occasionally a black man was murdered, that his ghost might haunt the sepulchre in which the booty lay, and sentinel it against other marauders. Maybe it was the ghost of a murdered black man who rang that bell last night. Miss Grant, I give you my word I am speaking the truth. The Goodwin Sands themselves have scarce gorged more wealth in their time than the pirates and buccaneers have buried in the islands and *costa firme* of these waters, though I don't say *there*," said I pointing into the square hole that looked like the mouth of a well. "Yet when we have made our escape from this place, and are safe and snug in civilized quarters, should I on recalling this secret vault, endure to think that I had wanted spirit enough to explore it? Conceive of our coming across several chests down there crammed to the lids with golden doubloons, crucifixes of the precious metal sparkling with gems, chalices which might make a Jew kneel to the Sacrament for love of the beautiful workmanship." She smiled; I burst into a laugh. "No," said I, "my expectations are not so high-pitched. Nevertheless, I must take a view of that interior."

"Mr. Musgrave," she exclaimed, with a little pout and some warmth of feeling in the look she shot at me, with a droop of the lids instantly afterwards—the most womanly touch that could be imagined, with its flash of reproach and the pleading of the averted eye that followed, "pray do not forget that if anything should happen to you, *I am alone.*"

I hung in the wind, for it grieved me to give her a moment's anxiety. But unless a ship took us off it was certain that we must regard ourselves as prisoners for life, if we failed to devise some fabric for making our escape in. It was impossible to know but that we might discover something in this cave which should prove of inestimable value to us, even as a step towards our deliverance, and on my dwelling upon this and assuring her that I could not imagine there should be any risk in my taking a view of the interior, her face cleared, and she seemed to agree with me; but I could read in her that though she had the heart of a lioness, it fell short of prompting her to offer to accompany me. I doubt if there was ever yet a woman who would have found courage to have entered the black hole, even though her refusal should have cost her her lover. For my part, I felt no reluctance whatever, and yet Miss Grant was so much more heroical than I, in the truest sense of word, that recollection of the disparity tempts me almost into egotism in illustrations of my own humble doings.

I had a parcel of sperm candles in my portmanteau—useful articles to carry to sea in those, as perhaps in these, days. I fetched and lighted one of these, and slinging it by a length of tape, lowered it into the square to test the atmosphere below. It burned brightly. Indeed my nose had given me sufficient assurance of there being nothing wrong in that way. Then bidding Miss Grant to remain where she was, and not to feel uneasy, I descended the steps, and holding the candle up, took a look ahead. I found myself on a shelving floor of hard sand and mould, walled on either side with stanchions and pieces of timber, running athwart into a slender passage, which, however, opened rapidly into an apartment, the roof of which was about a head higher than my full stature. This room might be about nine feet square. Beyond it, led to by a doorway that had in its time been screened by a curtain, as I gathered from the sight of a small metal pole bracketed athwart it, was a second room, black as any tomb, as you will suppose. The flame of the candle burnt bright, yet it was but a feeble light for the illumination of such an interior as this, and I found it difficult to distinguish objects. On the left-hand side of this first room in which I stood was a low structure of bricks, which, on approaching it, I found had served in its time as a furnace for cooking. Over against it, suspended by nails driven into one of the beams which formed the transverse supporters of the wall, were several quaint, extremely old-fashioned cooking utensils, such as saucepans, frying-pans, a kettle, and the like. Two or three articles of a similar description lay under them upon the ground, whence they had dropped through rottenness of the spikes or timber, like over-ripe fruit. On the right stood a queer rustic-looking table very rudely made, the legs branching out like open compasses. I had seen such tables with villagers drinking at them outside old rural public-houses in England. On either hand were a couple of high-backed chairs. I approached the opening conducting to the inner apartment somewhat timorously. I was never a superstitious man, but there was something in the aspect of this dim, mouldy underground haunt that, affected as the imagination might also be at such a moment by recurrence to the mystery of the midnight bell-ringing, might well have set the hair of a stouter-spirited man than mine creeping and lifting upon his head. I listened attentively; the stillness was unutterably deep, something to make one think of the silence that a man interred alive might *hear* in his coffin. However, I had talked somewhat big to Miss Grant, and perhaps was in no temper to be dismayed by my own fancies; so breaking from my posture of hearkening, with a look round at the shadows flitting to the movement of the candle in my hand, I advanced to the threshold of the second chamber and peered in, holding the light in advance of me.

There was some furniture here, and consequently objects sufficient to excite a passing emotion of consternation by the dark flickering, so to speak, of several kinds of outlines. I stood staring, and presently made the chamber out to have been a bedroom. A four-post bedstead, the uprights of which however had been cut short to admit of their erection in this low-ceiled apartment, stood opposite the entrance. The candle-light seemed to find a dull reflection in the legs of it, and on drawing near I saw that they had been gilt. It had been a very magnificent bedstead in olden times, no doubt. The feet were richly-carved figures of mermaids, the posts of ebony, with signs lingering of a once gaudy inlaying. There was a mattress upon the bed and a great bolster, along with a huge, coarse, dark rug. Slung by straps to the wall were several firelocks of the pattern the buccaneers of the seventeenth century were wont to level, and the like number of pistols, all nearly of the dimensions of a fowling-piece of our time. There was also a small array of broadswords and hangers, some fallen, having rotted from the straps by which they had hung. I spied a small chest in one corner, of black oak, and walked to it, having by this time got rid of my timidity. I opened it—let me admit, with a pulse accelerated by expectation—and holding the candle close, looked in; but alas! instead of massive treasure the chest contained nothing more than a quantity of fish-hooks of various sizes, a ball or two of rotted cotton-thread, and three or four parchment-like rolls, which proved to be charts, of which the tracings were rendered indistinguishable by dirt and mildew. The side of this cavernous chamber where the chest stood was papered, as it were, with a sort of loose hangings. I had not noticed this but for their swaying to the little current of air wafted by my moving the lid of the box. This drapery was of yellow silk, covered with strange devices wrought in black, but time or damp had obliterated so much of the figuration, whilst my candle gave forth so uncertain a light, that it was impossible to make a guess at the nature of the designs. Here too were a couple of black wood stools, the legs showing traces of gilding, and a circular steel mirror cut in facets, so tarnished that I viewed it for some time without knowing what it was. Whilst I was gazing around me lost in wonder, but with a tolerably clear conception of the character of this subterranean dwelling-place, my eye was taken by a faint reflection directly amidships of the roof, and on elevating the candle I observed that a large frame of glass had been let into the ceiling, every pane lozenge-shaped. It was indeed like a skylight on a ship's deck. I passed into the first room, and observed the same contrivance there. The sight of these windows gave me an idea, and I at once stepped into the shelving corridor and mounted the steps, blinking like an owl at the brilliant morning blaze.

"Oh, Mr. Musgrave," cried Miss Grant, "I was afraid you would never return! I have been expecting every instant to hear the report of your pistol. What have you seen? Oh, something, I *do* hope, that will explain that bell-ringing last night."

"What I have seen you shall presently see," said I. "It is as snug a two-roomed dwelling-house as one could wish, a bit mouldy perhaps, but a tidier lodging than a tree anyhow. There will be two windows under the sand here. How will they bear now?"

"Two windows!" she exclaimed; and there was little to wonder at in her surprise either, for the sand trended smooth to the dense thickets of herbage, where the trees went huddling into the forest as though it were formed of the quicksilver which the metal dazzle of it—like the fiery points of new tin flashing back the sun—made it resemble; and it needed something more than imagination to enable one to conceive of such a thing as a *window* having anything to do with this surface of coral, almost powdery, softness.

After pondering a minute, I walked to the spot, shells in hand, where I reckoned the window of the kitchen underneath to be situated, and fell a-scraping; and when I had made a hole about a foot and a half deep, the edge of the shell scratched crisply over something polished.

This proved to be a frame of glass. Miss Grant stood beside me, looking on, scarcely understanding what I was at, whilst I shovelled away with a couple of big shells, tossing the sand aside as a child digs for sport on the seashore, until I had laid bare a good space of the skylight. It was easy work, for the admixture of soil was too trifling to give much density and weight to the sand; yet it took me near an hour to lay bare the first skylight. I found it formed, as I had previously conjectured, of the frames of some vessel's skylight, but of a vessel that had been afloat in an age when, as I supposed, shipwrights were here and there to be found willing to embellish the fabrics they launched with lozenge-shaped windows in the deck fittings. The frames lay flat, like the cover of a hatch, solidly overlapping the edge of a timber casement. With the help of the handspike I had manufactured, I prized one of the frames out of its fixings, which had been tautened by wet running sand into a kind of cement, then with my hands tore it bodily up. The high sun struck full through the opening; Miss Grant peered down.

"It is a room!" she cried.

"Yes," said I, "and it will furnish us with the sort of asylum we stand in need of until the moment of our deliverance arrives."

"You do not intend that we should *sleep* down there?" she exclaimed, flushing to the startling thought, whilst her eyes brightened with the dread in her.

"You shall judge for yourself presently," said I, laughing.

"Sleep in such a hole as that!" she cried, with her white forefinger dramatically pointing downwards, and a fine imperiousness in the pose of her figure springing as it were out of a sort of passing indignation at my suggestion. "Why, Mr. Musgrave, supposing the man that rung the bell last night should discover that we were underground; he might put the covers on these holes, and then—and *then*—"

"We should be buried alive," said I; "only there is no man here, so I am not afraid."

"Who rung the bell then?" she asked.

"No *man*, I'll swear," I answered, "unless he be endowed with some mystic power of converting himself into a bush or tree at sight. Indeed I hope we may not be able to find out who *did* ring the bell," I continued, sending a look at the ocean, "for I should like to be taken off at once, at this very minute indeed. But if we are forced to tarry we shall solve the mystery, depend upon it. There's another window somewhere to be cleaned, Miss Grant," I continued, speaking cheerfully, "and when that's done I'll show you so quaint and surprising a curiosity in the shape of a piratical lair, that if I had it within reach of the millions of

Great Britain I should make a fortune in a month by exhibiting it at a shilling a head. But how goes the hour?" I looked at my watch; it was after eleven. "It is time," said I, "to take a peep at the sea from the hummock. Pray God some gleam of canvas may be showing."

She refused to remain until I returned, and so we went together. I must own to finding her most fascinating when she was most timorous. In her fearless moods she seemed to be withdrawn to a distance from me, so to speak; but her manner grew tenderly clinging when she was nervous. She passed her hand through my arm as we walked away, giving a glance over her shoulder at the dark square hatch upon the sand, with an unconscious pressure of her fingers upon my sleeve. It was strange that she who had sat calm in the presence of the body of the murdered mate, who had confronted with wonderful composure the most threatening and malignant experiences of the voyage, should tremble at a black hole in the sand, and at my proposal to tenant a lodging which would protect us at least from the dews of heaven, from the sting of the mosquito, and from the jaws of the land-crab. But may not one read of a field-marshal fainting at sight of a mouse? It might not have needed more than a spider on her petticoat to wring a wilder screech from Joan of Arc than ever the stake extorted. One is sorry to say it—but it is true, nevertheless—that it is in the weaknesses of human nature that one finds its lovableness.

There was nothing in sight. I searched with a shipwrecked eye, but the brim of the ocean ran in an unbroken sweep of blue to the mirroring of the sun. The heavens were cloudless, not the faintest feather of vapour in the whole spacious dome from its azure at the horizon to its brassy central glare. The heat would have been unendurable but for the shelter of the wide umbrella under which we both stood. The faintest draught of air was stirring, sometimes expiring, to let the fiery buzzing of the island swing tingling to the ear, then floating afresh, hot as a fold of atmosphere from a furnace, driving the sound of the feverish concert back. The atmosphere trembled to the drawing of the sun; branch and tree and every spear of grass, the slim length of the coconut to its tufted head, the plumed arch of the palm, the great drooping leaf of the wild cotton-tree, faintly writhed upon the sight, till you thought you could *see* the mass of tropic vegetation growing—with many a crackling noise as of growths rent by the roasting glare cleaving the shrill, fierce humming with a strange and startling edge of sound.

Miss Grant brought her eyes away from the sea, and looked at me as we stood close together under the shade of the umbrella. "What is to become of us?" she exclaimed thoughtfully, without expression of alarm or dejection.

"We must trust to God and to our own energy," I replied, "and above all keep our hearts up. Some means of escape, if nothing comes from outside, will suggest itself. Meanwhile we have abundance of fresh sweet water, there is no fear of our lacking food, we have found as decent a lodging as marooned people have a right to expect." She sighed and tried to smile, but you saw she could get no comfort out of the thought of the lodging. "Our health is good, and one wish at least of yours is gratified—we are not separated."

I know not in what sort of tone I may have uttered this last, but I noticed that her eyes fell at the close of my speech, her white teeth shone over her under-lip to the just breathless biting of it, and then she said in her purely natural manner, "And we must not be separated, Mr. Musgrave, until—until—I mean you ought not to undertake anything rash—such as exploring tombs, for instance."

I smiled and said, "A mouthful of something to eat will not hurt us, and I am pining for a long draught of yonder cold bubbling brook. Afterwards we will have another look at the tomb, as you call it. Only think of a kitchen ready-made to our hands! We shall be having turtle-soup to-morrow, and delicate fricassee of iguana. There are some plantains t'other side there, past that hump of green, along with an orange-tree or two, and with patience, Miss Grant, we may even yet see our way to a fruit-pie."

"Oh, dear, Mr. Musgrave," she cried, with an almost hysteric laugh, and an eloquent impassioned toss of her hands that could only have come to her with her mother's blood, "if we could but have foreseen all this in London when we were talking over the voyage!"

I fancy she read the thought that was in my mind at that moment, and to rescue myself, I said, but perhaps too sedately, "It will make a thrilling story for you to entertain Alexander with."

"Ah, poor dear old boy!" she exclaimed, taking my arm as before, and we walked to the spot where the luggage lay.

Chapter X
An Underground Lodging

BY TWO O'CLOCK THAT afternoon I had entirely cleared the second window of the sand that rested nearly two feet thick upon it. I prized open a casement that the apartment beneath might obtain purification from the air as well as from the sunshine, and I then asked Miss Grant to step below with me and view the rooms. She had seen enough by peering through the skylights to excite her curiosity, and moreover to reassure her mind; and so she now let me hand her down that black hole from which she had shrunk with her eyes ashine with dismay in the morning.

The coolness of the atmosphere in this cavern was nigh as refreshing as a bath after the roasting glow up above, and the softened light of it fell soothingly upon the eye, fresh from the blinding whiteness of the sand and the blue brilliance off the ocean, where the atmosphere was sheer effulgence, though the afternoon sun had carried his wake around south, away from the quarters we had confronted. Miss Grant looked quickly about the place, advancing to the doorway of the inner room with a hurried survey of the chamber, and then her manner lost its restlessness.

"Do you know, Mr. Musgrave," she said, "I expected to find that you had missed some secret way of getting out of this place. I felt almost certain that this was the haunt of the person who rung the bell last night."

"You are satisfied, I hope?"

"I see two rooms, and only one entrance. Yes, I am satisfied," she said, continuing to look round her penetratingly. "Have you lifted that faded silk hanging?" referring to the yellow drapery against the wall in the inner apartment.

"No," I answered, "but I'll do better than lift it," and so saying, I went and pulled it down. It was like dragging at a cobweb. No stagnant flag rotting in the gloom of an abbey's roof over an aged stall would have parted more easily to a pull. The wall the stuff had concealed was like the others, soil and sand, solidified and shored up by a great number of stanchions and transverse beams. Miss Grant now behaved as if she were in a museum. Her face was lighted up by curiosity, and she peered at everything with the liveliest interest. The daylight lay bright in each room, and the damp and mouldy smell was fast yielding to the aromatic air gushing warmly in, laden with the island's multitudinous voice, through the open casements. I overhauled the contents of the old black chest afresh, in the hope of meeting with some hint of the story of this queer dwelling place, but found nothing to suggest an idea even. The charts, so far as I could make them out, were buccaneering maps of the Antilles and the Panama main, with here and there a rude, ill-digested, most deceptive outline stealing out of the grimy thickness of dirt and mildew. I stretched the silk to the light, but the figurations were as vague as they had shown by candlelight. The firearms were crumbling, rusty old pieces, great curiosities no doubt in their way, as were the pistols and the hangers, and indeed every piece of furniture in the place.

"And you think," said Miss Grant, coming to a stand after the narrowest imaginable inspection of everything in true womanly style, and gazing around her with wonder unmixed any longer with apprehension, "that this was many years ago the home of a pirate?"

"Ay, no doubt of it," I responded. "A hundred and fifty years ago I dare say this was a very glittering and sumptuous interior. Look at the legs of that bedstead. Saw any one the like of such carving, I mean on so prosaic a piece of furniture? It was the princely decoration of some rich galleon's state-cabin, I dare say, and one need not shut one's eyes to realize the idea of a head like Cervantes—who, by the way, was an exceedingly ugly man—snoring on a pillow there, the figure concealed to the throat by some exquisitely-worked counterpane of silk. Here is enough to set the imagination off into a brisk trot. The high-sterned polacre, striking the glory of the westering sun from her windows into the dark blue beneath, is riding within musket-shot of the beach; her captain, mate, and boon companions of the crew are here carousing. See them in their great flapping hats, their yellow belts, their big jack-boots, their spiked beards, and moustaches curled to their piratical eyes, roaring out some song of old Spain, with goblets before them filled with a vintage of which we, a debased posterity, can never know the generous, the magical qualities. The old villains! they drank all the fine liquor, and left us the gout!"

"Your picture wants a heroine," said Miss Grant, laughing.

"Oh," said I, "I have not forgotten *her*. She must be yellow-haired; some Saxon sweetheart, captured out of an English ship, bound shall we say to Rio, Miss Grant? She has exhausted the language of entreaty, wept her glorious eyes dim, and grief as she sits yonder is eating away her trembling little heart as she listens with a loathing ear to the deep-throated chorusings of the black-browed roysters, as they sit clinking their silver flagons *at that very table there*, perhaps! The Lord preserve us! what a brush has fancy—to one's own intellectual eyesight, I mean—when her pigments are such realities as yonder bedstead, those high-backed chairs, those queer-looking frying-pans, in which many a hearty turtle-steak has hissed, many a Friday's absolving fare of fish has spluttered! But to be serious, Miss Grant, will not these rooms yield us the accommodation we require?"

She shook her head a little dubiously. "If we could remove that gloomy old bedstead—" she said.

"Oh, certainly," I interrupted. "A little hammering of it with one of those muskets should render it portable. Your hammock will take its place excellently. Then, with the skylight casement a bit open for the fresh air it would let through, and a shawl swung from that metal rod over the doorway, the room would provide you with as snug a retreat as any hotel could offer; whilst I should make my bed here"—we were conversing in the room which I must call the kitchen—"ready at a moment's notice to interpose, pistol in hand, betwixt that entrance which your presence beyond will render sacred, and the villainous bell-ringer, whoever he may be."

"You do not think of sleeping here to-night, at all events," she said.

"No, since I see how reluctant you still are. But your health is precious, and mine too is precious for your sake. A few nights of exposure to the damp of these moonlit heavens would, I fear, tell upon us both, breed a fever, afflict us with the ague, disable us by some sort of sickness, and leave us in a very bad case indeed. We have to get away from this island, you know; and if we design to achieve our deliverance we must keep well."

Her good sense came to her rescue; she perceived the truth of my words, and said she would do as I wished, only—not to-night. When that terrible bedstead had been removed the place would look more wholesome.

"Whatever I propose," said I, "is with thoughts of your comfort, your health, your security chiefly—indeed nineteen times out of twenty *wholly*. 'Tis a bitter, hard experience for you, and would to God I knew how to soften it, better still how to end it. But the thing looks us in the face, and we must meet it as bravely as we can. My part is that of a protector. If I know myself I shall play it dutifully."

She glanced at me a moment as if she would speak, then hung her head to hide the tears which filled her eyes, whilst she extended her hand, saying, "I thank you—I thank you, Mr. Musgrave," just above her breath.

I never recall this strange wild time without asking myself whether I acted as a true, upright, high-minded gentleman should towards this lady, situated as she was, forced by stress of ocean into intimate association with me, at the mercy of my feelings and instincts as a man. I did my best. I know that my one whole-hearted desire was, she should never suffer an instant's pain, be sensible of a moment's grief, of the lightest stir of uneasiness, through this obligation of bare unconventional companionship with me. I could summon no better government of thought for my behaviour than this resolution. But then her own frank, fearless, beautiful nature helped me. Her very purity was like a meeting of my efforts half-way. A little too much of modesty in her would have constrained me with a constant sense of embarrassment by which I might have been led into blunders. Indeed I have to thank her own heroic, honest nature for the successful accomplishment of my desire, that our association on this island should be as painless to her modesty as a woman as though the formidable conditions of our isolation, which forced us close and bound us, so to speak, together, had been as stringent as they were indeed relaxing.

I devoted the rest of the afternoon to dismantling the underground rooms; again and again however intermitting the work to repair to the summit of the hummock for a view of the sea, but without beholding the least sign of a vessel, though never could despair have rendered human gaze more strenuously eager and searching than mine. The task I had set myself distracted my thoughts; yet it was extremely depressing too. It was as though we felt there was no help or hope for us, and that there was nothing for it but to reconcile ourselves to our miserable lot, and effect the best settlement upon the island that could be contrived by persons who were almost wholly without resources. I caught Miss Grant eyeing the aged saucepans and frying-pans with an air of mingled doubt and thoughtfulness, and then she presently made a little collection of them, and was going up the steps. I asked her what she intended to do with the things. She answered that she meant to clean them; they were not fit to use as they were. I looked at her delicate white hands with a movement of remonstrance in me, but then I reflected that occupation of any sort was good for people situated as we were, and that the soiling or coarsening of her hands would be but a very small matter indeed side by side with the desperate needs which might presently grow upon us. But it was with something almost of a laugh of bitterness that I turned from her handsome form as she mounted the steps to the open, and resumed my work. "A pretty leveller is the sea!" thought I. "To think of this stately and lovely lady, who ought to be drawing close to her sweetheart, and to the comforts and refinements of a sunny and pleasant home, scouring old pots and pans upon a desert island; with myself, a gentleman at ease, forsooth! a Piccadilly dawdler, knocking an old bedstead to pieces, as though he had bound himself apprentice to some old rag-and-bone merchant, and furbishing up a residence which even a mole might eye with distrust!"

Nevertheless, denuded of my coat and waistcoat, and my shirt-sleeves rolled above my elbows, I continued to toil manfully, making very little account of the gloomy thoughts that weighed on me. With the stock of one of the muskets I speedily demolished the bedstead, carrying it piecemeal above, where I found Miss Grant seated, shaded by an umbrella, polishing the saucepans and other contrivances with a wet rag and sand. One showed bright to her scrubbing, and she watched me with a well-pleased face as I inspected it. The fact was, there had come to my mind the story of a party of shipwrecked people who had been poisoned by eating food cooked in utensils which they had found in an old house hard by the spot where they had been cast away, and I considered our sufferings already too lively to demand the supplementary punishment of a deadly stew-pan. However, the kettle was of iron, and the other things of stout block tin, and so I went back to my work, leaving her to go on with hers.

I remember I was sufficiently silly, as I cleared this cavernous retreat of such grimy furniture as we did not need, to continue in some small hope of meeting with something unexpected. Must I confess it? I was weak enough to suffer myself to be haunted by a little dream of treasure. I was but a young man, with much of the boy still clinging to me. After all, this was a sort of adventure to make even an older heart than mine feel virginal with romantic fancy. A cave into which the light of day may not have penetrated for above a century—as true a copy of a pirati-cal lair as the most ardent imagination could body forth—into which the dullest eye could not have peered without peopling it with a score of spectral things vital with the colours of imagination, and gathering a character of substantiality almost from the odd fantastic surroundings of dim silk and drapery, of a bedstead that carried one's thoughts to the great galleon with its bristling broadsides, and its mast-long pen-nons; of cutlass, matchlock, and hanger charged with suggestions of the Tortugas, Panama, the train of mules laden with silver, bracelets of gold on arms of ebony, and the citadel ramparting store-houses of ingots built roof-high—why, I say, it was impossible for me, with such young eyes as I then carried in my head, man though I was in years, to dismantle such a retreat as this without the sort of hope that must have set me laughing had it been told to me of another. But I explored to no purpose. Floor and wall were solid; no hint of a trapdoor, no sign of a secret hiding-place. Whether the discovery of a chest of bullion, or a sack full of ecclesiastical furniture in precious ore would have served to reconcile us to being marooned, I don't know; but on looking back I cannot but think that we deserved some such reward, and am still weak enough to imagine that had I hunted more diligently yet, I might have met with it.

I again examined the charts in the chest, with the hope of being able to make a guess at the name or situation of this island, but to no purpose. Mildew and dirt had done their work, and the tracings were as indistinguishable as the black background of an aged portrait. I let the chest lie as it stood. When I came to look at the chairs I found them very finely carved, and old enough to have formed part of the equipment of a manor in Henry VIII's time. The part of my work I least liked that afternoon was the handling of the mattress. It was a great bloated bed. I laid it upon the floor, and when I had knocked the bedstead to pieces, was about to lay hold of it to drag it up above, when I thought it stirred as though something were inside it. It was mere imagination, of course, yet I own that the fancy so frightened me that I stood staring at it for some moments like a fool. Then I gave it a pull to make sure that it was as light as I had before believed, and not yet being satisfied, I jumped upon it, trying to make out if I could feel anything inside with my feet. This I managed so cleverly that I fell plump over the odd inflation of the thing just as Miss Grant arrived for another pan to polish. I saw her start as I got up, and toss her hands with a brilliant stare of sudden fear, then she burst into a fit of laughter.

"Oh, Mr. Musgrave," she cried, laughing continuously whilst she spoke, and pointing to the mattress, "for a moment I actually believed it was a man that you were wrestling with."

I rose crimson with my fall and with the exertions I had been undergoing, and said, "I believed something was alive inside it."

"*Something alive inside it!*" she exclaimed, in a tragic voice, with her gravity coming back to her in a breath, and recoiling a step.

It was now my turn to laugh. "It's all right," said I, giving the thing a hearty kick; "it was mere fancy; but something seemed to move, and so I jumped upon it." I then seized hold of it to drag it up the steps, and I laughed again to see how she ran. She would have confronted a band of savages, I do believe, with a resolute face, but this mattress was too much for her. I did not let go until I had got it down to the sea, where it floated away handsomely and sank. It is odd how, in such a situation as we were placed in, little things will affect the imagination. I am sure that had that mattress remained in the cave, I should never have been able to occupy, or at all events to sleep in, the place. I believe I could not have consigned a dead body to the deep with graver satisfaction at being quit of it.

There was no chimney to the kitchen, but on making up a fire of wood, dry grass, and the sweepings, so to speak, of these rooms, in order to test the furnace, I found that the smoke passed out freely through the open skylight, whilst despite the apparent want of draught, the fire burnt briskly enough to roast us a leg of mutton, had we such a thing. I should have been glad to take up my abode that same night in these secret chambers, for I could see my way to as comfortable a bed of leaves and grass, with a rug for a sheet and another for a coverlet, as I needed to lie on, with promise besides of escape from the mosquitoes and the cold clip of the land-crab's jaws. But Miss Grant's soft shake of the head determined me to say no more about it. It was her humour to sleep another night in the hammock under the trees, and it was my duty to be near her. I thought to myself, should the bell toll to-night, her mind may come more willingly to the underground shelter to-morrow. For my part it seemed like mocking at luck to lie all night with nothing but blue atmosphere betwixt the trembling stars and one's body, when there was as good a roof for one as old mother earth could supply close at hand. But he must be a clever man who can even dimly guess at but a portion of what goes to a woman's timidity and reluctance.

I was mightily glad when sundown came. The fierce glare of the day striking down out of the swimming brassiness of the skies, and flowing back in intolerable sheen, like an *echoing* of light, if such a thing could be, off the dazzle of coral sand and silk-smooth water, made a veritable anguish of the eyesight when clear of the shadow of the trees. The evening fell upon us sweet as a blessing, with its dewy richness and coolness of air, and the hush of the discordant voices of the island, in a pause between the ceasing of the cries and screams of birds, and the small, fierce, sultry concert of the insects, and the first notes of the crickets, and the sullen croak of the frogs. We sat or strolled, as on the previous night, till the moon was high, talking of Rio, of what my cousin would be thinking, of the probable fate of the *Iron Crown*, of our prospect of escape, and a score of such matters. Once, on the sheer rim of the sheet of glory lying under the moon, we both thought we could make out a black speck, and I never could have imagined how wildly passionate was the desire for deliverance in us both—so smoothly would we talk of our rescue, so quiet was the face we had put upon our distress— until, as we stood gazing with our hearts in our eyes at the extremity of the silver wake with the purple gloom lifting like the banks of a river to it on either side, I felt her hand in mine trembling, and damp with the dew of an ungovernable emotion, whilst on my side my breath came and went as thick, dry, and difficult as though a poison worked in me. That it was a ship we neither of us could say. Sometimes we fancied we saw it, then it would go, then seemed to blacken out again into a tiny spot. So dead was the calm the lightest craft could scarce have floated the distance of a fathom in an hour. There was something almost of a physical burthen to the sensibility in the profound, stirless tranquillity that seemed to come weighing down with the fine clear dusk of the night. You almost blessed the crickets for the rising and falling of their bell-like chirping, and bent the ear to the delicate ripple of surf, for the relief you got out of the soft simmering noise of it. But let it have been a ship or fancy, 'twas all the same to us. The spangled indigo of the dome went down with its stars to the lustrous sea-line, smoothing it there to a flawless rim; and Miss Grant let fall my hand with a deep sigh, and a sudden look of grief at me in the moonlight, for which there was no answer but silence.

However, partly with the wish to distract her mind, and partly because of the necessity for such a thing, I thought I would see if there were any craw-fish to be obtained; so first of all I cut a bough from a tree which I had previously observed to be of a resinous nature, and on putting fire to it found that it made just such a torch as I needed. I then fashioned a shawl into a sort of bag, which I requested Miss Grant to hold, desiring her also to take her stand close by the wash of the water on the beach, ready to pick up and pop into the shawl such fish as I might have the luck to capture; then turning up my trousers to above my knees, I waded a little distance into the sea, not without some anxiety regarding my toes, for I knew there would be plenty of crabs hereabouts, big and powerful, with the jaws almost of a young shark in their gripping and cleaving qualities. The smoky flame of my torch threw a yellow illumination through the water to the bottom of it, and after waiting a little I was rewarded by the sight of several black objects crawling like lizards to my legs out of the darkness past the sphere of the sulphur-coloured radiance. I dipped briskly, and in a few minutes had chucked a good round score of craw-fish on to the beach, and as fast as they fell Miss Grant picked them up, till the improvised bag writhed to the movements of the creatures as though it were something living in her hand. She had recovered her spirits, and called out laughingly to me that some of these days she would endeavour to draw my portrait as I then stood, for she could not imagine a more romantic scene. Romantic it was, I doubt not, and she meant what she said, spite of the touch of banter her cordial girlish laughter gave to her speech. To see that it was so, one has but to think of my figure, black to the moonshine on the water, spite of the yellow tincturing of it by the flame of the torch; twin shadows of me flung by the firebrand and the moonbeam slightly swaying on the dusky ripple that floated shorewards into a mere wire-like breaker, my companion's fine figure pallid in the showering of the silver light, but clear-cut too against the snow-white softness of the sand which went shelving up behind; her dark eyes nevertheless stealing out even to a brief gaze at the glimmering phantasm of her lineaments; the island background of huddled blocks of vegetation; the stars jewelling the fibrine outlines of the trees; the sweep of the land to the hummocks looking mountainous and remote in the illusive atmosphere, and then the smooth plain of ocean glooming out into the vast distance with a sudden arrest of it against the sky, and a stern bending round of its confines that made the imagination desolate with the sense of irremediable imprisonment.

There was some labour in the occupation of dipping for the fish; but the water circled cool to my knees, the breath of it too floated refreshingly to the face, and flinging away the smouldering remains of my torch I waded ashore brisk as from a bath and lighted a cigar with immense relish of the fumes of the tobacco. I dropped the bundle of craw-fish down the hole that led to the underground rooms, and sat for a long while with Miss Grant; our camp-stools in the heart of the ivory whiteness of the tract on which I had slept last night, and on which I was again to sleep. Occasionally my companion would look a little nervously towards the forest. Now that the silent night had come, thoughts of the mysterious bell-ringing troubled her afresh. Since it was impossible for the bell to ring itself, she said, it must have been tolled by human agency of some sort. No bird or beast alighting upon or thrusting against it could have produced the varied ringing we had heard, and consequently she was certain there was a man hidden in the wood.

"Why should he hide?" said I, wanting to reassure her, for some hours of moonlight and gloom yet lay betwixt us and the daybreak.

"For fear of us, perhaps," she answered.

"If that be so," said I, "would not he be mad to make his presence known by ringing the bell?" She could not answer this. "Besides," continued I, "where would he hide himself? I searched the forest pretty narrowly. 'Tis true he might have a lodging in the hollow of a tree, but you can't reconcile any motive that a man would have in concealing himself, with his lusty ringing of a bell at midnight—raising about the most alarming clamour that human ingenuity could hit upon."

"Then, Mr. Musgrave, you wish me to believe that the bell rang of its own accord, or that it was struck by some spirit hand?"

This silenced me in my turn. For my own part, I could not make head nor tail of the matter, though, spite of the clear expression of human agency that I had found in the *changes* of the performance of the mysterious bell-ringer, I would have been willing to bet all I was worth that I was the only man on that island, as Miss Aurelia was the only woman. But it was not a thing to bother ourselves *too* much about. It was an odd ocean puzzle, which grew a bit wild with the deepening of the night, and the thickening out of the dusky shadows of the little forest to the westerly drawing down of the moon. But my mind was too greatly worried with other considerations to give it heed enough to render me restless on its account.

Whilst we sat conversing I spied the black shape of a turtle creeping out of the creek, with the moon sparkling in the wet of its shell. "I must have that lady," said I; "she looks but a tortoise, and a small one at that." I fetched the handspike I had manufactured that day to prize open the skylight casement in the sand, and then waiting till the creature had put a good distance between it and the water's edge, I made for it, and with more dexterity than I should have believed myself capable of, I slipped my pole fair between the flippers, and with a hearty spring turned the thing fair on to its back. I then opened my knife and cut its throat, feeling as remorseful through the horror of the needful operation as a conscience-stricken murderer, despite my perceiving how needlessly inhuman it would have been to let the poor creature lie all night in the torment of its capsized posture, only to decapitate it next morning after all. It was a small hawk's-billed turtle, I believe weighing less than one hundred pounds, or I should never have been able to deal with it single-handed. I returned with a guilty feeling of blood upon my head to Miss Grant, and told her what I had done.

"How shipwreck—to call our condition shipwreck," said I,—"forces one's hand! I should have thought myself no more capable of murdering yonder creature than of slaughtering an ox. How much of what is ignoble, of what is purely animal, comes out of one in stresses of this kind! A man, to remain only a little lower than the angels, should be luxuriously fed and housed, I think. His vileness grows with his needs. The nature of beasts remains the same in essentials, whether they be pursy with food or mere ribs with famine. But bring human nature down to such destitution as an open boat, for instance, expresses, without a crumb of bread or a thimbleful of fresh water, and how base, oh, how base it will show in its instincts!"

"And all this," she exclaimed, smiling, "because you have killed a turtle! Yet I dare say your appreciation of the god-like qualities of man in you would not suffer through your chasing a hare, in company with twenty horsemen, over miles of ground, or killing a long afternoon by shooting at harmless little pigeons." She rose. "It is too late to provoke you to an argument," she continued; "what is the time, Mr. Musgrave?"

I brought the face of my watch to the moonlight. "Twenty minutes past twelve," said I.

"Have you my pistol?"

I had it in my pocket. I loaded, primed, and handed it to her; she adjusted it in her belt as on the previous night, then removed her hat, and gave me her hand, as her manner always was ere retiring to rest. I pressed my lips to it in the old-fashioned salute, grieved to the heart to think of the hardships that had befallen this brave and beautiful girl, and deeply moved too by the pathos I found in her uncomplaining acceptance of our sorrowful and seemingly hopeless condition.

When she was fairly in her hammock, I rigged the mosquito-curtain over her, and turned away from the beauty of her face, complexioned to marble by the transparency under which she lay, with a feeling that made me almost wild at heart for a little with the sense of betrayal of the trust whose obligation, confound it! Grew more imperious in proportion as it taxed my weakness. I threw a rug upon the sand, rolled up a coat for a bolster, saw to my pistols, threw the mosquito-net over my head, and lay down. This was our second night on the island. I felt the solitude of the place and the dismalness and melancholy of our look-out far more keenly than I had on the previous day. There was something of novelty about our situation during the first few hours which worked with a little quality of buoyancy in the spirits; but that was gone, and there was nothing now between the heart and the crushing burden of imprisonment. The fire-flies swarmed in brilliant constellations, the tingling horn of the mosquito sounded shrill against my ear, odd midnight notes of dreaming fowl broke into the silence out of the inland dusk, down upon the ivory of the creek side lay my slaughtered turtle, with a look in it of a great stain of ink upon the moon-whitened sand that importunately and unpleasantly sent my thoughts straying away to the murder of Mr. Bothwell and the ugly blotch on the cabin floor. The brig, the mutineers, the loss of Gordon and the men, Broadwater's mysterious disappearance—why, these were things already growing dream-like, so heavy was the thrust this last experience of ours gave even to the freshest memories, sending the latest incidents reeling back into a sort of antiquity, till, on my oath, it seemed as long as twenty years ago since we had embarked on the *Iron Crown* in the Downs. How were we going to escape? If we lifted no hand to help ourselves, what was to become of us? Yet, great Heaven, I thought to myself, mechanically eying the soaring of a cloud of fire-flies till they looked to dance into the stars and make a green and silver whirlpool of the firmament just over my head, by the mingling of their phosphor with the diamond points past them, how is a man to deal with timber which he has neither saw nor chopper to level it with? What sort of ark is he going to contrive when he is as destitute of all appliances for building such a thing as he is of knowledge of what to do, though he had the conveniences of a shipwright's yard within hopping distance of him?

I was restless and hot, and was in the act of sitting up with the design of listing the mosquito-curtain high enough to bring a cigar to my lips, when the bell hidden away in the blackness behind us began to toll.

"There, Mr. Musgrave! There it is again!" cried Miss Grant almost hysterically, and in a breath she had sprung from her hammock and was alongside of me, with her hand on my shoulder, listening. The ringing was much the same as on the night before—first a slow and solemn tolling, making one think of some mortuary bell timing the melancholy pacing of a funeral winding along a cyprus-shadowed path to an ugly rent in the earth; then after a pause, as though the ringer had halted to refresh himself with a drink, a hasty clattering, a most alarming, clamorous vibration; then the dirge-like chiming again, followed on by all sorts of beatings, fast and slow.

"Will you say *now*," cried Miss Grant, holding my hand tightly, "that there is no man there?"

"Be it man or devil," I exclaimed, "ghost or goblin, it is a riddle we must solve for our peace' sake. Wait you here."

"What do you mean to do?" she cried, still clinging to me.

"Why, since it is impossible to see, let drive in the direction of the sound anyhow, and listen for some squeal to follow, that we may know the ringing is not an hallucination; for I protest to Heaven, the incredibility of such a thing is enough to make one think one's self mad for hearing it."

She dropped my hand, and I walked towards the trees with a pistol in either fist. She followed me however, holding her own little weapon, but the dense tangle, I knew, would stop her presently. I had no intention of penetrating the wood by the road I had taken when the morning shone brilliant. If it were dark *then*, it would be blacker than thunder now, which necessarily increased the astonishment I laboured under at hearing the bell; for unless the thing that rang it lived within a pace of it, its power of being able to find it amid that blackness was as astonishing as the sound itself. Yet all this while the chimes continued. Whatever the ringer might be, its mood seemed merrier on this than on the last night. It rang heartily, with a curious suggestion of enjoyment in the sound produced. The disturbed birds sent a hundred remonstrant cries, yells, and whistlings from the trees, which apparently merely increased the appetite of the ringer for his labour, for 'tis not in mortal pen to express the preternatural wildness, melancholy, and I may say horror of the sound of that secret ringing echoing through the island out of the central midnight fastness, and dying away in ghostly tones far out upon the silent sea. I was as angry as I was bewildered. The character of the sound staggered my doubts of there being a man there. It seemed impossible that anything but a human hand should produce such noise. Closely followed by my companion, I skirted the trees to that thin scattering of them whence I had emerged after my morning's hunt, and where I had tripped over the ring in the sand. Methought from this point I could better collect the bearings of the bell. Miss Grant soon came to a stand. Her clothing rendered the growth impenetrable by her.

"Oh, if I were only dressed as you are, Mr. Musgrave!" she exclaimed, in a voice so charged with bitter vexation that it was almost like hearing her sob. "Do not venture too far. Be cautious, for my sake. What shall I do if I am left alone here?"

"I will not go far," said I; "stand you in this black shadow. In the haze of the moon you will be able to see anything that may run this way. Let fly at it, will you, should it come. Only please take care not to shoot me."

With that I left her, and drove with drudging steps through the coarse wiry undergrowth, helped somewhat by recollection of the road I had taken in the morning, and aided also by the sound of the bell. From the whole area of the island the concert of the crickets rose in a volume of chirruping; the croaking of the frogs was distracting; everything seemed awake, and nothing could be imagined more confounding than this sweep of multitudinous noise, closing to one's very ear as it seemed with the notes of unseen things crying out of the grass upon which one trod, and from the near hidden trunks of trees, and the stoop of the dusky boughs overhead.

However, I had not advanced fifty paces when I found further progress impossible. There was no question however that the chimes came from the bell I had inspected in the morning, so I levelled a pistol at the blackness in the direction whence the sounds were coming, and fired. The trees all about me glanced out yellowly to the flame; the bell instantly ceased; but one had to *listen* to make sure, so deafening was the noise among the branches of the terrified creatures roosting up there. I levelled a second pistol, and fired again, with a renewal of the distracting outbreak overhead, rolling in a wave of discordant uproar, so wild with intermingling of tropic throats, with single near yells, groans, snores, gasps, and pipings, following as it were in the wake of the rushing clamour, that the effect upon the hearing defies language. I waited a little, eagerly hearkening. The ringing had ended. The forest noises died away, and in a few minutes you heard nothing but the familiar croakings and chirrupings, chiefly out in the open. There were too many trees in the road to render it likely I had hit the ringer; indeed I had not fired with that idea. But I thought that whatever it was that rang the bell might come sneakingly my way, and I strained my hearing for any sound resembling the rustling of the coarse growth pressed by the foot; but nothing of the sort was audible, so I returned to Miss Grant, and walked with her back to where the hammock was.

Well, it was a mystery not to be solved by wondering at it. I own I slept but little that night through thinking of it, whilst Miss Grant next morning confessed that she had not closed her eyes.

END OF VOLUME 2

Volume 3

Chapter I
I Shoot the Bell-ringer

INDEED, THIS MYSTERIOUS MIDNIGHT bell-ringing was a puzzle that presently threatened to render the island solitude desperately uncomfortable whilst the sun was up, and absolutely hideous when he had gone down. It was time it was dealt with some way or other. A few more such nights as the two we had passed might play havoc with Miss Grant's nerves; and our loneliness and helplessness were already so extreme that one felt it might presently go hard with one's brain if the paralysing conditions of being marooned were to be supplemented by an element of mystery nicely calculated to finish off in the intellect the work which grief, suffering, and despair had begun.

So when the morning came I slipped away for a plunge, feeling the need of a refreshment of that kind, after lying long in my clothes upon the powdery dust of my sandy couch; then returning, and asking Miss Grant to spread a little breakfast for us meanwhile, I clapped my pistols into my pocket, and plunged into the wood. I steered a pretty straight course for the bell, looking earnestly about me as I thrust my way along; and when I arrived at it, I stood surveying it for several minutes, wondering if the problem of the ringing was to be solved by an explanation that should be ridiculous for its simplicity when hit upon. But not the ghost of a solution offered. No; some hand—man's, beast's, or ghost's—must have rung the thing. I touched it, and it swung so heavily and stiffly that it was impossible any bird, even the biggest on the island, alighting, could have swayed it to the emission of a single chime. I peered curiously at the adjacent trees, but witnessed no sort of hollow in which anything of bulk could hide itself. I stared searchingly round for mark of human or any other tread, for hint of subterranean habitation, for any sign, in short, to resolve me this bewildering mystery; but the scene, to as far as I could see, was as bare of such suggestion as I sought as the bell itself. I considered for a minute whether I should return for a musket and beat down the green and mouldering frame, but on peering close at the bell I observed that it was suspended to an iron hook in the gallows-like beam. This gave me an idea, and putting my hands to the bell I lifted it off its hook and placed it upon the ground. 'Twas a tolerably heavy piece of metal, though not so weighty but that I could easily carry it. There has been so little change for centuries in the fashion of bells, that no man could have told how old this one was by the look of it. No doubt I was right in reckoning it to have been a ship's bell. Its sonorous notes may have been reverberated in its time by the long-ago-vanished timbers of a carrack, or some tall ship belonging to old Spain or England.

I was for letting it lie, but thought, no! for the thing that hammered it last night may have sense enough to sling it afresh and worry us as before; so I seized hold of it and succeeded in staggering with it painfully out of the wood, the thing occasionally tolling in a very melancholy way to the swaying of my figure as I lurched, through the knee-high tangle. I succeeded in lugging it to where our luggage was, and sat down hot as fire and pretty nearly spent.

"There," said I, "if the bell-ringer has a mind to enjoy himself to-night, he'll have to show himself, and if he does I'll *pot* him, if I never forgive myself for his murder afterwards."

"One wants to know the cause," she returned, peering at the bell much as she had at the mattress when I told her I believed it moved; "this is the effect only. The mystery will remain the same although the bell may not ring."

"May not! Should there be any further ringing to-night," said I, "I vow to steadfastly believe in ghosts for the rest of my life. As for the mystery, what we want is to be able to sleep when we lie down. It will be nothing to me what made the noise, providing we don't hear it. Of course the puzzle is a supreme one, but that need not signify. We shall be sailing away before long, please God, and it will be something for us to be able to boast about in such an age as this, that the villains of the *Iron Crown* marooned us on an enchanted island."

She looked pale and worn, her eyes were listless, but this might have been owing to want of sleep, and to the harassment of fretful semi-superstitious thoughts; yet the set of her beautiful mouth showed a spirit of resolution staunch in her still. The refreshment that was to be obtained by privacy I felt would help her, and I resolved to devote the morning to conveying her luggage to the inner chamber, to suspending her hammock, and to isolating the little room by draping the door that led to it. Speaking from experience, I know that the misery of such a situation as ours is to be lightened not a little by the comfort of a shift of garments, by a plunge in the blue water, and the like. Robinson Crusoe dwells at large upon the sweetness of the feel of a clean shirt. It looks but a light stroke, yet it is as deep a touch in its way as any of the best of the others in which Defoe's marvellous romance abounds.

After breakfast I climbed with her to the summit of the little hill. It was all bare sapphire sea, streaked here and there with long shining curves like a running of quicksilver on the surface. The sky was brilliantly blue and cloudless, the wind a faint, parched draught from the north-east; the bite of the sun upon the exposed flesh was as though his beam touched the skin through a burning-glass. It was insupportable, and we descended the hummock, my companion pale and silent, I sick at heart; for though I had not dared hope to see anything, yet the fulfilment of such an expectation as this brings a rage and grief with it, as of madness almost, with every recurrence, though you should look for a ship fifty times a day, and always be sure in your soul before lifting your eyes that you will see nothing.

"Can it be possible," exclaimed Miss Grant, "that no ship ever passes within sight of this island?"

"Don't let us think that," said I, "for a long time yet, at all events. We only came ashore here the day before yesterday. The speck that floated last night on the rim of the moonlight might have been a sail. This island lies very low, and there is plenty of ocean beyond the line of it all round us, so that a vessel might be within four or five leagues of us without seeing this Cay or we her."

"But there is land down in the west, Mr. Musgrave?"

"Yes, the film of it, so the men said, was visible from the *Iron Crown*'s cross-trees."

"Then," said she, "that stretch of water yonder must be a passage between this island and the land there; so that a sail ought to be visible now and again."

"The mischief lies," cried I, "in my not knowing where we are. Those days of thick weather, with a head wind and some sort of current of which I knew nothing, threw me all adrift; not to mention old Broadwater's chronometer, which in my opinion just ticked close enough to Greenwich time to tell him when the hour for another glass of grog had come round. Of course, this island is one of the Bahamas. There is sure to be shipping hereabouts, making for the West Indies, or the Panama or Mexican sea-boards, or steering eastwards for European ports. We must be content to go on waiting and hoping. We have the materials ready stocked for a great smoke, and who knows but that before even sundown to-day we may be safe on board some craft, bound to a port whence we may easily make our way to Rio?"

This was a fancy to put a little light into her face. "I suppose," she exclaimed suddenly, with a slanting glance at me as though she could not summon courage to look at me fully, "you would never again undertake to escort a girl to her sweetheart?"

"Why should I?" I answered, wondering at the meaning of the very faint smile that hovered airily as a shadow about the beauty of her lips. "It is thankless work, after all."

"Indeed, you may say that," she exclaimed.

"Oh, understand me. I don't mind the horrors of a mutineering experience, or of being marooned. No, there may be a companionship sweet enough to neutralize the direst conditions. I mean, 'tis going through a very great deal, you know, to oblige another."

"Poor dear Alexander," she cried, "he will *feel* obliged, I know; at least—" she paused suddenly with a reining in of her speech that made her cheeks flush somewhat to the effort. She struggled with an instant's confusion of mind, and then asked me calmly what I proposed to do that day, and what help she could be to me, but I saw in her eyes that she was still under the surprise of the thought whose utterance she had narrowly arrested. I could have sworn that she had only just saved herself from saying something which she would rather have bitten her tongue in halves than express. I looked at her again for a moment or two before answering; she was gazing seawards, as though the question she had this instant put was gone from her memory. Something in her manner—a subtlety as indeterminable as the aromas floating into the hot still air out of the hearts of the thousand secret and nameless flowers scattered throughout the island—quickened my breathing, till I broke with a start from a fancy that might have held me profoundly meditative for the rest of the day, and told her what I meant to do.

"But is there nothing for me?" she inquired, bringing her eyes to mine, though I seemed to miss the peculiar, familiar steadfastness that I had again and again found as fascinating as it was perplexing.

"Can you cook, Miss Grant?"

She clasped her hands, sunk her head with a little shake of it, and said, "Not nicely, I fear."

I said, "You will not mind trying your hand at a dish of turtle soup?"

"How is it made?"

"Why," said I, "by boiling the meat, I suppose. It will be something to do. Then there are those craw-fish. I'll make a start by lighting the kitchen fire."

I forthwith fell to work to collect a quantity of wood, which I carried to the furnace, where it was soon blazing merrily, with the thin blue smoke of it passing fairly out through the skylights, which I took care to open to their fullest extent; so that though at the start the smoke set me coughing a bit, the atmosphere all round the spiral volume was presently clear enough to enable me to breathe without inconvenience.

Indeed, I learnt from this subterranean kitchen how our forefathers had managed without chimneys, a matter that must have puzzled me all my life had I not observed how this smoke going straight and clean to the roof formed a cloud there that drained away through the skylight as cleverly as if its vehicle had been a smoke-stack. I then filled the vessels we had discovered in the cave with fresh water, and put on a big saucepanful to boil. 'Twas roasting work, what with the fire inside and the sun out, and I had to strip to my shirt and trousers, with a big straw hat for the protection of my head, though there were several times even then when I came very near to fainting. Meanwhile, to make sure of something to eat, I popped half-a-dozen of the craw-fish into the saucepan, and then knife in hand went down to the turtle; but was a very long while indeed coming at the inside of it. It was like jobbing at a man in armour; but the secret dawned upon me after many experiments, though I confess I never fell to any work that was more distasteful to me in my life. That the sun might not corrupt my turtle, I dragged it at the expense of many groans and much perspiration to the entrance of the underground rooms, down which I tumbled with it as though marooning had converted me into a sort of ant; and indeed I felt like one, I can assure you, as I painfully dragged my prey to the hole and staggered with it into subterranean gloom.

I see now with the eye of memory the stately and beautiful figure of Miss Grant stepping from the furnace, as I call it, after a peep at the humming saucepan, to the short length of passage for the cool of the shadow, though there was no breath of air to descend. I had left her at work when I went on one of my errands to the brook, or to the turtle, habited in her long dress, the clinging folds of which, with a yard-long measure of it trailing astern, I saw must bother her presently, and I looked forward to the pleasure of helping her pin her gown clear of her feet; but on my return I found that she had divested herself of the dress, and that her attire now was an under-skirt of brilliant hues. I imagined she had changed her gown, so ignorant was I of the mysteries of ladies' apparel, and thought that never could any sort of female garb more gracefully harmonize with any particular kind of beauty than did this short, richly-coloured *frock*, as I supposed it, with the fine form of Miss Grant. I've heard it said that the Spanish are the only ladies in the world who can *walk*, all others waddle, glide, amble, do anything in short but step with a proper sort of grace. I might believe this after recalling the gait of the ladies I have known, and contrasting them with Miss Aurelia's—another maternal legacy, no doubt, as I might suppose now that there was sufficient disclosure of her movements to enable me to appreciate the perfection of their freedom and their inimitable, easy, gentle dignity. She had removed her hat; the furnace flames tinctured her soft hair with their yellow hue; and in the subdued shadowing of the room her eyes looked to have recovered their earlier brilliance. Her arms were bare to the elbow—limbs of moulded ivory. I stood at gaze for some moments, as startled by this new revelation of her charms as I had been on the day when I had first met her. I know this dwelling upon a girl's perfections in the face of the acres of paper which have been covered again and again with like accounts is but poor work, and can but make tiresome reading; but one is not often marooned with such a woman as Aurelia Grant, and seeing even then how it was with me in my thoughts of her, I ought to be forgiven for this trick of pulling out her likeness, and asking you just to look at it once more.

By noon I had managed to transport the luggage to our underground home, lightening the burthen of the larger boxes by conveying parcels and bundles of their contents in my arms. I also took care to bring the bell along and place it in the kitchen, on the left of the entrance, where it was out of the road; and it will be strange, thought I, as I gave it a benedictory kick, if anything resembling this blessed thing torments us again to-night. My next business was to drape the entrance of the room that Miss Grant was to occupy. I had slung her hammock, spread rugs to serve as a carpet, and put a couple of high-backed chairs into the apartment; so that with the boxes convenient to her hand, and the sunshine streaming fair upon the skylight, and flooding the atmosphere with its radiance, whilst the tropic perfumes floating heavy and languid above came sifting down to sweeten the air, as though you should have wasted a nosegay of flowers there, the odd, earthy chamber looked positively habitable. The entrance was low, and a single shawl effectually served as a curtain.

"Yonder turtle-shell," said I, pointing to the creature I had killed, "when cleaned out and purified will make an excellent hand-basin. You have a looking-glass, and all other toilet requisites, as the hairdressers call the things. As matters are, Miss Grant, we might be worse off. Better surely this roof than the two trees 'twixt which your hammock swung. Confess now that you have no longer any reluctance in taking up your abode here?"

She smiled, casting her eyes over the room with a glance at the skylight; and I observed the tremble of just a little faltering of resolution, so to speak, in the delicate pout of her under-lip.

"I have one small misgiving," she answered.

"What is it?" I asked.

"Suppose there *should* be a man on this island?"

"Well?"

"You don't believe there is; but somebody must have rung the bell."

"And supposing there *should* be a man?" said I.

She shot another glance at the skylight, and answered, "He might shut us up down here."

"How?" I asked.

"Why, Mr. Musgrave, by closing the skylights, and covering them with sand, and then putting the cover on to the opening, and piling sand on that too."

"Well," said I, smiling, for my mind had long since got rid of the fancy that there might be a man somewhere hidden, though, as I admit, the midnight ringing was all the darker as a puzzle to me for that very notion, "there is but one way of checkmating the skulking rogue, assuming him to be of flesh and blood, and I'll attend to it immediately lest it should escape me," and mounting to the open, armed with one of the old muskets, I hammered at the hatch-cover until it lay before me in several pieces. These I carried one by one below, for the hatch was not to have been squeezed through the opening in its entirety, and stowed the fragments hard by the bell. "Now," said I, "your friend the ringer may indeed close the skylights, but it will put him to his trumps to cover that entrance. Think—there is nothing on the island that would serve him for such a purpose, unless he should cut down a tree, and whittle out a balk of it as a cork for that mouth. No, Miss Grant, little risk I think of our being buried alive."

My talk and the knocking to pieces of the hatch-cover reassured her, and as we might hope now that our turtle-broth had been boiling long enough, we prepared the little rustic table for dinner, and put on it a bottle of wine, a few biscuits, the remains of a tin of meat, the cooked craw-fish, along with a big bunch of plantains I had cut after bathing. But alas! we had but one knife between us, no forks, spoons, nor plates. How then were we to ladle up the soup! Hitherto we had eaten with our fingers and drunk from a meat tin; but the broth demanded an effort of ingenuity.

"I have it," I exclaimed, and stepping into the sunshine I made my way to the beach, where, collecting an armful of shells, big and little, I carried them to the brook, thoroughly cleansed them of the sand and salt, and returned with them to the kitchen. Better soup-plates than the large shells made we could not have desired, and the smaller shells made excellent spoons. How the soup relished it boots not to say. Wanting salt, herbs, and the like, it lacked perhaps the savouriness that a City alderman is accustomed to meet with in a potage of turtle, but the meat proved juicy, and the liquor grateful enough in its way, and though, to be sure, it was a sort of mess that I could not look at now, I swallowed it then with enjoyment and appetite, giving secret thanks to Heaven that there was plenty more of it.

It is quite likely that any Jack coming ashore to peer about, discovering these underground rooms, and looking down into them, might have taken Miss Grant and myself for a corsair and his leman. The rich dyes of her petticoat made her apparel romantic to the eye, and the poetic suggestiveness of her attire was heightened yet by the free graces of her roughened hair, and her fair and most shapely arms bare to the elbow. I, habited in shirt and trousers, needed but a red sash round about my loins to present a very fair copy of a pirate. It was entirely in keeping too that we should appear as though we were feasting, and the picture would have been faithful enough, I doubt not, to the liveliest imagination, of a piratical lair, coloured as it was with details of aged muskets and cutlasses, the venerable cooking utensils, the two century-old chairs, the queer, aged, straddling table at which we sat, if, instead of lifting shells to our lips, my lovely companion and I had been able to pledge each other in cool sparkling draughts from richly-chased goblets of precious metal. In truth, what the picture wanted to complete it was a hint of plunder. Miss Grant's sparkling rings were but a meagre intimation in that way. You would have looked for a golden candlestick or two, a silver crucifix, a sack in a corner bulged into a glittering *yawn* at the mouth by the pieces of eight which filled it.

"This is a sort of experience," said I, "which a man should need to be very young indeed to enjoy. One should be quite a little boy to think it fine. Yet I am realizing the dreams of millions of small lads. To think of being all alone with a beautiful lady upon an uninhabited island—to live in a cave that in bygone years resounded the revelry of the sea-robbers again and again—to have within arm's-reach several of the exact sort of muskets which Crusoe carried on his shoulder—to live upon turtle and plantains, with the delightful prospect of having some day to fell a tree and scoop out a canoe—oh! the bliss to countless small boys of such realization! What spasms of envy would thrill through the schools of Great Britain were the young friends of the old Whackums to learn that at this moment there was a young gentleman in company with a young lady living in a pirate's cave in an island hard by the Spanish Main."

"I am afraid school-boys would not envy you quite so much as you think," said she; "they do not greatly value ladies' society either in books or in life. To be cast away with a beautiful female—to be marooned even with a lovely princess, and live all alone with her in a cave—" She shook her head, laughing quietly. "No, Mr. Musgrave, if I know boys at all, they would not thank you for such an experience. Give them guns and canoes and pirates' caves, with plenty of oranges; but no girls, if you please."

"It is strange that little boys should ever make men," said I, going to my coat for a cheroot. "I am not very old myself, yet I find it difficult to believe that I could ever have been younger than sixteen. Would to Heaven that the light and colour and fancy of childhood attended us to the end! 'Tis miserable to have to sail out of a glowing horizon into the grey of the middle sea, and thence onwards yet to gloom. It is Byron, I think, who asks who would not be a boy again. Not I, for one, unless I could remain so. If a man has to turn out, it is better he should get up at once and have done with it. I love a sweet dream as fondly as any, but since the awakening is inevitable, don't delay it, say I; and then let the vision pass away for good. Who would live again through a mere phantasy, knowing it to be such? For those who incline that way we build lunatic asylums. No, I wouldn't be a boy again. The opening of one's eyes upon the reality don't make it worth while, as the tailor says when you offer him less for his coat than he can cut it for."

She listened to me with her cheek resting in her hand, her figure inclined, the swell of it methought gathering a particular beauty from the white of the arm on which her head reposed, her dark eyes fixed on mine with a hint of mingled merriment and puzzled inquiry in their serene scrutiny. But when I ceased she changed her posture, removed her eyes, and with a careless look around, said almost abruptly, as though the shift of mood in her was an effort rather than an unconscious transition, "How are we to get away from this island, Mr. Musgrave? You have been a sailor—is there no remedy for people in our situation? I wonder what Alexander would suggest if he were here."

I lighted my cheroot stolidly. There seemed to me something insincere, though I protest I don't know why I should have thought so, in her speaking of my cousin at that moment. I eyed her in silence a minute, and then said, "I believe if Alexander were here he would take my view of our condition. There are plenty of trees, but we have no tools. Had we a chopper we might fell a trunk, and in the course of months, perhaps of years, succeed in hacking and hewing the timber into the aspect of a canoe. But then how to launch it? The trunk of a tree, even when shaped into a canoe, is not to be whipped under the arm as though it were the model of a boat and carried to the water. I think if Alexander were here,

Miss Grant, he would agree with me, that our one chance lies in our making our presence known to a passing vessel; which reminds me," said I, rising and looking at my watch, "that it is about time I should take a peep seawards, for it will be some hours now since I visited the hummock." I was walking to the steps. "You do not ask me to join you," said she. I turned and noted a look in her, half wistful, half amused.

"Do pray join me," I cried; "I was afraid that the heat—"

"No," she interrupted; "I expect there will be nothing to see." I smiled at the coquettish feigning of gentle resentment in her manner of drawing aside the shawl that screened her room. She disappeared, closing the drapery afresh, and I climbed through the opening into the sunshine.

My hat was wide-brimmed like that of a southern planter. It sheltered me as effectually as an umbrella, and under the shadow of it I paced leisurely towards the hummock, but puffing perhaps with unnecessary energy at my cigar, to certain thoughts of Miss Grant which rose in me as I advanced. "Pooh!" thought I, "what a madman must I be, situated as we are, to think of *anything* under this wide blue sky but our deliverance, and how to effect it!"

It chanced just then that, my eyes happening to turn towards the scattering of trees which came thinning out of the mass of the forest round to that part of the sand where I had met with the iron ring of the hatch, I spied, or seemed to spy, a human face peering at me from the midst of a huddle of leaves big enough to serve for the foliage of a cotton-tree. I stopped dead like a man transfixed, the cigar I was about to raise to my lips arrested midway, as though my arm had suddenly been blasted. The light rained in a blue dazzle betwixt me and the heavily-leafed bough, and the glare of it obliged me to blink, that on looking again I might make sure. Yet when I stared afresh the face was gone. I hollowed my hands into the form of a binocular glass to shelter and strengthen my sight, and gazed again, but there was nothing to be seen saving the surface of green leaves which seemed to arch the solid bough they draped, as though each was of the weight of a giant banana. It seemed incredible that I should have been mistaken. The vision, if it were nothing more substantial, had been that of a swarthy face with white whiskers, and eyes that might have been of a reddish tinge, glittering under shaggy white brows. I listened, but nothing was audible save the humming, chirruping, and whistling, which swelled to the ear like the commingling of the notes of a bagpipe with the vibratory hum of a church organ. All was stirless in the tree, though I watched it attentively. I had left my pistols in the kitchen as I must call it, or I should certainly have let fly at the branch, and taken my chance of a murdered man falling out of the foliage of it. Still thinking it impossible that my sight could have been deceived, I walked briskly towards the tree, and looking upwards searched it as penetratingly as the greenery would permit; then seeing nothing saving a parakeet or two, I walked a little further towards the forest, still gazing upwards, but nothing answering in the least imaginable degree to the object, real or imaginary, that had confounded me, met my eye. I again strained my sight, sending glance after glance around, then returned to the open, and proceeded towards the hummock, satisfied that what I had beheld was a deceit of the imagination, though this notion did not help to soothe my secret perturbation. Unless the man actually lived inside the trunk of the tree out of whose leaves he had peered, 'twas impossible if he were human to have escaped the searching gaze I had directed at the intermingling of boughs. I said to myself it was some illusion of the sight, some fantastic creation wrought by the trembling flash of the sand and the wide blue brilliance of heaven and ocean upon the ball of the eye. And yet it was an apparition, too, to so fit the bewildering enigma of the bell-ringing, that, spite of my declaring to myself it was fancy, I was as uneasy as if I had been sure it was real.

However, on reaching the hummock my thoughts underwent a sudden and violent change, for on glancing leisurely along the sea-line, thinking of nothing but the man's face in the tree, I caught sight of a ship's canvas down in the south, like the point of a sea-fowl's pinion, projecting white as foam and lustrous as pearl above the horizon. I clapped my hands with the sudden transport the sight awakened in me, and without pausing to consider the distance at which the craft hung, I set fire to the pile of faggots. There was but the mildest breathing of air. The wood took some time to kindle, and then the smoke, darkening and fattening out in thickness to the green coating of grass and leaves with which I had covered the faggots, went nobly straight up to a great height—a grand signal indeed, as I thought, where it lazily arched over plume-like and floated softly into the east. I stood watching for upwards of three-quarters of an hour, with my eyes thirsting for a sign of the growth of the sail, staring with such tormenting intensity, that again and again the vast plain of sea brimming out to the brassy azure of the sky, steeping to it streaked with the silver lines of currents and turquoise-coloured swathes, winding and dilating and melting into the richer hue of the brine, would start as if to spin with gathering speed round and round, and I had to blind my sight with my hands to check the mighty waltz, the first reel of which was as sickening as a swoon to the brain. I was alone, and exerted but little judgment, or I might have guessed that on that stagnant surface the sail must hover for hours apparently motionless. Yet it was certain that she had hove in sight since the morning, that is to say, since I had last viewed the sea, and either a faint breeze of wind had brought her to where she was, or she was a small vessel stemming the water to the propulsion of her sweeps or long oars.

The fire was burnt out; the smoke drained dimly into the air off the smouldering embers, and was of no more use as a signal than the flourish of a handkerchief. Then, after waiting a little while, and watching as intently as the heat and glare of the giddy atmosphere, swimming to the sea from the dazzling brass of the heavens, would suffer, I could no longer doubt that the distant vessel was drawing down the slope into the south-west; whence, as there was no wind to propel her, it was certain that she was being urged by oars. In that case she would probably be some small drogher or coasting craft.

My disappointment was not so bitter as I should have expected to find in me at sight of a ship lingering long enough to wildly tantalize hope, and then tardily melting out of view. Maybe I found a large stroke of comfort in the very vision of her, for now I might suppose that the speck we had seen in the wake of moonshine last night, and taken to be a deception of the fancy, was a real ship after all; so that with yonder one we might say that two sail had hove, in near upon twelve hours, within reach of our eyes, even from the very low elevation we occupied. This was as good as understanding that the sea round about us was navigable water, that the ocean betwixt us and the film of land away down west might be a sort of highway, as Miss Grant had suggested, and that therefore a ship might at any hour pass close enough to our little principality of crickets and parrots to catch sight of our smoke and send a boat. So, not very greatly disheartened, I sent another look at the pearl-like fragment in the south, and making sure now by the airy blending of it with the azure that the craft was heading away and would be out of sight presently, I descended the little hill, purposing when the cool of the evening came to build up another fire ready to signal with.

As I approached our secret chambers, Miss Grant came out of the opening. It was the strangest sight in the world to see her rising, as it were, out of the earth; that was the impression you got from the flat of the sand. It put a fancy into me of the resurrection of the body, followed on by a daintier imagination of Venus shaping white out of the foam—though the girl's apparel was a little in the way of *that* idea. You saw nothing of the grave-like hollow, merely the figure of the beautiful girl that seemed to float up out of the blinding silver of the sand. Her apparition in this way was as sweet a surprise as could fascinate the eye. She had changed her attire, robed herself in a white gown, dressed her hair afresh, heaping it on her head, with a wide straw hat tilted on it like a picture of a beauty in George III's day.

"You have been a long while watching the sea, Mr. Musgrave," she exclaimed, smiling as if to the surprise and admiration with which I regarded her.

"I have been endeavouring to signal a ship," said I.

"A ship," she cried, approaching me close, and staring at me.

"Yes," I answered, "she will have faded out by this time like the smoke of my fire. But no matter. The sight of her is a warrant of more to follow. All I have to do is to keep a bright look-out. We shall be rescued yet, and *soon*, depend on it."

We strolled together to the shadow of the trees where our camp-stools were, and seated ourselves. For a long time she talked of nothing but the ship, and I could see, by the flush in her cheeks and the gathering light in her eyes, how useful to her spirits was the hope that my news of having sighted a vessel had brought with it.

"We ought to feel grateful to the crew of the *Iron Crown*," said she, "for having sent our luggage with us. Oh, Mr. Musgrave, how am I to express the refreshment of a complete change of apparel? It robs the island of half its terrors."

"Rather lucky," said I dryly, "that I kicked up that iron ring, though it cost me a sprawl. Is not the privacy of a bed-chamber in such a place as this almost as nice as a change of clothes?"

"Well, I didn't like the idea, I confess," she replied, with a pretty shake of the head. "I don't like it much yet, I admit. Those tomb-like rooms are very well in the day; but when the long dark night comes!" she added, with a light shiver.

At this I involuntarily turned my eyes towards the forest, with a glance up aloft and at the trees beyond, thinking of the demoniacal white-whiskered old face, with its Cairngorm eyes brilliant in the midst of its swarthy countenance, that had seemed to peer at me a while gone. But I would not even hint at the possibility of such an apparition. I was still inclined to reckon it a mere fancy; besides, I knew that even though I should vaguely refer to it as some optical delusion occasioned by a fantastic writhe of the leaves to the folds of the hot blue air between, sleep would be murdered for her that night. Nevertheless, I made up my mind whilst the sun was still high to put my pistols in my pockets and search the little forest afresh; for, to speak honestly, the memory of the swart malignant countenance coming into my mind again rendered me secretly very uneasy, and I felt, when the night drew down and I was at rest in the profound stillness of the underground kitchen, that I should regret not having made again a careful investigation of the wood.

I got up, saying, "I'll just take another walk through those trees, Miss Grant. I want to satisfy myself that there is not a second bell hidden somewhere in the green thickness. It would be insupportable, you know, to be awakened by a new kind of chiming tonight."

"Why should you imagine there is a second bell?" she asked, with her eyes seeming to enlarge to the very thought of it.

"I *don't* imagine there is," said I, "but no harm can follow another look round; besides," I added, smiling, "I might chance upon the fellow that has troubled us for the past two nights, so that even should we be unable to hang him before sundown, we might seize him to one of those trees as Broadwater seized the half-blood to the foremast, and go to our rest without apprehension of being corked up."

I laughed out to let her suppose that I talked for talk's sake only, and fetching my pistols made for the forest, taking the road into it past the tree in which I had seen the real or imagined face, waving my hand to her as I strode into the shadow. And a shadow it was when you penetrated into the thick of the trees, coming as you did from the sultry whiteness of sand, and the hot radiant stare of the unwrinkled deep up at the sky that opened and contracted its atmospheric folds of sapphire as it seemed—a shadow cool, dark, green, and as slumberous a spot as one could have pictured, with its sombre, pillar-like trunks of trees rising out of the stillness of the tall and prickly undergrowth into the cathedral hush of the gloomy density of boughs and leaves, but for the incessant splitting of the silence by the cries, whistlings, and croakings, as familiar now to my ear as the twitter of the London sparrow, or by the airy disturbance of the plumes and pinions of birds rustling on the wing with a sound as of the rending of satin as they sailed from one tree to another, brushing the foliage as they flew.

The direction I was unconsciously following brought me, with some painful thrusting of my legs—for in places the tangle was as hard and stubborn as a fence—to the spot where the gallows-looking frame from which I had unhooked the bell stood. It was scarce within view of me when I caught sight of a large hat placed exactly over the hook from which the bell had depended. I looked and looked, greatly amazed, and, let me frankly own, with a mind for some moments not a little disordered by consternation. I was of course as sure as that I lived that no hat was upon the frame when I had unhung the bell. I stared nervously around me, mechanically drawing a pistol from my pocket, and looking first into one twilight avenue and then into another, then gazing narrowly at the herbage round about, afterwards staring overhead, listening meanwhile intently. I approached the hat by a step, and inspected it. It was such a piece of headgear as might have been washed up by the sea. I raised my hand and pulled it down, but instantly dropped it, for it was horribly clammy and cold, and made you think, from the sensation you got from it, of groping in the dark and stroking down a dead man's face. It was apparently a felt hat that had once been black, but it was now green and bronzed with time and wet. It was very broad-brimmed, with a sort of sugar-loaf crown; much such a sort of hat indeed as the boys clap upon Guy Fawkes' head when they carry him off to the stake. I turned it over with my foot to see what the inside of it looked like, but it had long since been divorced from any lining that may have garnished it in its heyday. It was old enough indeed both in fashion and aspect to have belonged to one of the people who had dug out and used the underground chambers. But who or what since the morning had placed it upon that bell-frame? It gave me a kind of shrinking feeling, I can tell you, to think that there might be human eyes watching me out of some of those green dyes of shadow round about, and as I stood there I never knew from instant to instant but that the flame of a firearm would leap from behind a tree, or an arrow sling past my ear.

The sight of this hat convinced me that I had not been mistaken in supposing the wild, grotesque face I had caught a glimpse of to be that of a *man*. Miss Grant was right. There must be one or more human creatures in hiding here. The bell could not ring itself; the hat had been brought from a distance—I must certainly have seen it when I first explored this place, and stood looking from the scaffold to the grass far as my sight could follow it; I say, the old hat had been brought here and placed upon the frame, and if this did not signify human agency, then it was not to be accounted for but by supposing the devil himself to be at large upon the island. I was startled, astonished, alarmed, as I believe any man would have been; but I was resolved, nevertheless, not to quit the wood without a further good hunt, and so pushed on, pausing incessantly to listen and to look, to kick at some suspicious huddle of huge blades of aloe-like growth, to stare into the trees, or to fight my way to some trunk looming with a yawn in it in the twilight so as to make one suppose it hollow. But to no purpose. I believe there was no part of that forest I did not traverse, and in all I spent a full hour in making the rounds of it; but not the least hint of anything approaching humanity did I see.

The puzzle was so supreme as to depress my spirits by the heaviness of the perplexity it excited; but I made up my mind to say nothing about the hat to Miss Grant. I was now as convinced as she that there were more people than ourselves on this island, though but one more only, and I believed that it was *his* face I had seen amongst the leaves. All sorts of wild notions occurred to me as I staggeringly made my way out of that little forest. It had been the face of an old man. Was the bell-ringer some aged pirate, who had gone mad, and wandered about the place, living upon such fruit and herbs as he could grub up, grown expert in the art of climbing trees, and secreting himself by such years of practice as had enabled Selkirk to hunt the goat more fleetly than the goat itself could run, using the spreading branch for his bedroom, through not having intellect enough to hunt after and dig out the sand-covered portals of his subterranean home? Or, thought I, is it conceivable that there *are* such things as spirits?—that the old navigators' fables about demon-haunted islands are not the lies which our scientific age protests them to be? Upon my word, thought I, as I broke my way along with a nervous glance over my shoulder, how many weeks, nay, how many days of marooning go to the addling of the most healthy brains?

"What have you seen, Mr. Musgrave?" asked Miss Grant, as I approached her.

"Just a parrot or two," said I.

"You have been a long while watching them," said she, eyeing me so attentively that I feared she would find in my face some small signs of the astonishment and misgivings which filled my mind.

"Oh," I exclaimed carelessly, "the forest is dark, as you know, and a sheer maze in its way, with spots where the high guinea grass leans to you tough and piercing as a crop of bayonets. I was resolved to hunt the place through and through, a thing not to be done in ten minutes. Now, Miss Grant," I went on, with a glance at my watch, "suppose we go to tea, as I must call the meal—though for a real homely cup of tea just now, served up with buttered toast and a new-laid egg, with a plateful of watercress, I'd part with every inch of turtle betwixt the shells I opened this morning. Heaven bless us all, to what weak desires will marooning reduce a man!"

I had to build up the beacon fire again that evening, and when we had made a meal off some cold turtle and plantains, a sweet biscuit or two, and a shellful of sherry, and water fresh and cool from the brook— a sort of incipient sangaree—I fell to collecting as much wood as would go to the making of a great smoke, but the sun had been sunk some time before I had stacked and got ready the pile for firing. When I had made an end of this, I gathered a quantity of grass and leaves, and took the heap to the kitchen to serve me for a mattress by and by. Again and again I looked at the ocean, but it always stretched out blank, without a tip of cloud even to quicken the pulse for an instant with the fancy of a sail. As the evening darkened into night, with the moon rising slow and red directly in the face of us, where the eastern sea, black as ink, washed to the huge dull gold shield of the sulky-looking planet, as though the orb was some glorified head of land against whose very face the deep brimmed without a ripple of breaker, the disquietude raised in Miss Grant by the prospect of a night underground increased in her. I *felt* her uneasiness rather than gathered it from her speech; but it would have been unkind to us both to humour her—a mere provoking, in short, of some wretched tropic distemper—to sling her hammock between the trees again, and to make my bed among the land crabs. Indeed, though to be sure we had passed two nights safely in the open, the memory of the ugly glimmering face amongst the leaves, along with the odd and astonishing sign of the hat would have rendered the obligation of sleeping out here again very disagreeable to me, I can assure you. Why, it was only necessary to fancy that there *was* a man on the island to suspect that he might cut our throats if we gave him the chance. Underground, at all events, we should feel tolerably secure, by which I mean that the courage that would bring the wild creature, whoever he was, to the side of a girl motionless in a hammock, or to a man slumbering peacefully on the sand, with his figure clean cut on the face of the coral dust as though it were an inlaying of jet, and a very visible mark therefore for the assassin's knife—I say, the courage of the mysterious creature might fail him when it came to his having to seek us in a dark vault. He knew we were armed, and though he might have a knife, or spear, or something of the kind, it was a hundred to one if he had a musket or pistol, or ammunition for it at least. So, to my companion's disquiet, obvious in her fits of thoughtfulness and her uneasy glances towards the cave, showing where her thoughts lay, I seemed to pay no heed.

The night came on very glorious, with the soaring of the moon, the stars thick strewn, just stir enough of night air to send the sweet smells of the dew-washed island flowers lazily floating to us in folds of aromatic atmosphere, and a delicate seething of surf to blunt the edge of the shrillness of the inland concert. To kill the time, I proposed that we should go and hunt for turtles' eggs, and we went together to the creek, keeping a bright look-out for the impress of the tread of the turtle. But though we saw marks in the sand which fairly well resembled the tracks we sought, they led us to nothing.

"Perhaps," said I, "the turtle doesn't lay in this month. If I could have foreseen our adventure, I should have read a little in the natural history of this part of the world."

We continued our search for some time, probing at the sand, but if there were any eggs about, they were too cleverly hidden for us to come at, so we stepped down to the beach, facing the moon, where there was a clear, long, white walk, flat, and but a little less hard than a ship's deck, and paced to and fro for a long while; though there was no complete surrender of ourselves to each other this night as on former occasions, when she would reflect my mood, or I hers. The fact is, she could think of little but the underground bedroom, and I of the hobgoblin face and the old Guy Fawkes hat. Indeed my imagination was so wrought up, that twice when glancing towards the forest I could have sworn I saw the shape of a man flit a little way past the two trees where the hammock had swung; for the shadows there wore a greenish faintness of dusk with the pouring of the moon, and one's sight went a little way into the block of blackness. But the hour came round at last when it was time we should endeavour to take some rest. Miss Grant reluctantly walked by my side to the entrance, looking down a little into the hatch as though her heart failed her.

"Indeed there is nothing to fear," said I.

"Oh, but it is like being buried alive," she exclaimed, descending nevertheless, but with a quickened breath. I lighted one of the wax candles and carried it to the inner room, where, wanting the convenience of a candle-stick, I stuck it in the mouth of a bottle, earnestly looking round me to see that all was well. The skylight lay open. I asked if I should close it.

"No," she exclaimed, quickly.

"But supposing it should come on to rain in the night," said I, "an electric storm say, with a West Indian *shower* pouring off the edge of it? Besides, the mosquitoes will find their way in."

"I must take my chance," she exclaimed. "If that glass were shut, I should feel as if I were buried alive."

"Then good-night. May God bless you, and send you refreshing sleep and sweet dreams," said I, bringing her cold white hand to my lips. "My bed will be there," I added, pointing to the threshold of her door, "so that literally nothing could enter this room without treading on my body."

She glanced at the skylight, and looked at me wistfully, as though she would have me linger yet. I lifted my hat and quitted the strange chamber, carefully drawing the curtain after me.

The moon rode high over the island; her radiance lay upon the skylight, and on the hatchway, as I may call it, and light enough came sifting in to enable me to see without a candle. I gathered the dry stuff I had collected for a mattress close against the shawl that hung from the doorway of the inner room, and made me up a bed of rugs, with a rolled-up coat or two for a bolster. I then carefully looked to my pistols and placed them on the floor, one on either hand of me; which done, I threw off my boots, removed my light camlet jacket, and lay down. The skylight was open, but I needed air, for the atmosphere was close with the furnace-brickwork that still retained the warmth of the fires which had been kindled in it during the day, and since Miss Grant's skylight lay open too, it mattered little that mine should be so; for, should a downpour happen in the night—and I knew of old what a downpour in these parallels meant—the rooms would be flooded very nearly as swiftly with one as with both windows to let the wet in, specially with the entrance gaping like the mouth of a funnel to vehicle any deluge that might come. I lay down, I say, but not to sleep. I could hear Miss Grant moving with something of restlessness in her pacing, then all was still in her room; and I heartily hoped she would soon forget our situation and her fears in slumber. The stillness was deep. I had anticipated a pretty deep hush in these under-sand cells, but the reality was oppressive beyond any kind of breathless repose that I could have imagined. Not so much as the hum of a mosquito stirred upon the hearing; the metallic-like chirruping outside was a little storm of noise in its way, I knew; but not an echo of it penetrated underground, spite of the open skylight. I lay musing upon our extraordinary condition. It was difficult to credit that my beautiful companion and I were finding shelter and seeking rest in what was practically as much a grave as any hole in the earth that should in God's own time receive our bodies. Up above in the moonlight, with the spread of the sea widening out black from the shaft of silver in its heart, the trees overhead, the stars beyond, the innumerable voice of insect life in the air, our condition was real enough to the imagination—heart-breakingly real indeed; but down here it was like some wild fancy, one of those strange dreams which hover in the brain betwixt waking and sleeping. Besides, it was a time and an occasion too for whatever was superstitious in the soul to creep into self-assertion away from the clutch of reason. I don't know that I should have felt nervous but for the memory of the face I had seen; but

I confess that I was more uneasy than I should have been willing to admit to Miss Grant, as I lay in the dim, ashen-tinctured atmosphere of that underground apartment, running my eye from the grim memorials of sabre and musket on the wall, to the old table over against my head, on to the short corridor going black to the square of faintness that overhung the extremity, thence to the skylight, through which I could see a hundred soft and trembling stars.

However, after lying awake for a good long while, I fell into a vein of dozing, rambling thinking, the sure precursor of sleep, more like the shadows of dreams flitting before me than the presentments of waking thoughts; a sort of stupid confusion of pirates, mistily and so uselessly flitting about the chamber, with a few turtle mixed up amongst them, and God knows what besides; saving that, though reason was faltering, I was sensible enough to know I should presently be fast asleep.

I was in this condition of mind, my eyes fixed upon the skylight, though the lids were drooping fast and I was scarce conscious of what I viewed, when I saw a shadow as of the hat that I had met with in the forest, as it seemed to me, overhanging the open space. The posture of this shadow was that of a man peering down. 'Twas unmistakable; I could not be deceived. The dark outline was clear against the stars, and it was the head of a man wearing just such a steeple-crowned hat as I had encountered, bending over and gazing down.

I was instantly startled into broad wakefulness. Brave I should be sorry to call myself, though I think there is no man whose nose I should hesitate to pull who called me otherwise to my face; but at sight of that sugar-loafed hat and the motionless peering human shape revealed to a little past the shoulders, I must confess to having burst into a cold sweat. It was the being shocked perhaps out of the drowsiness into which I had sunk that made me think the thing a phantom for a minute or two. I lay stirless, softly sneaking my right hand to the pistol, by which time I had come to a sense of the reality of the vision; but before I could point the weapon, being resolved to fire cost what it would, the hat vanished. Now, thought I, the fellow has been able to obtain a tolerable view of this interior, and concludes I am sound asleep. His next step will be to come below!

I rose very lightly, being anxious not to disturb Miss Grant, and holding both pistols in my hands, I stepped in my stockings over to the corner made by the projection of the furnace, where I crouched in the deep shadow that lay upon this part of the room, with my head lifted over the edge of the brickwork to enable me to command the entrance. Hardly had two minutes elapsed when I spied the hat again overhanging the skylight, but it did not offer such a mark as I could hope to *pot* from the place I stood in; so I continued to wait and watch. I could hear no sound, not the faintest crunch of a footfall upon the grit of the sand outside; but the quick breathing of the fellow was as audible as the beating of my heart in my ear, and as full a warrant as I could have asked that the thing was no ghost. The peering and meditative posture of the hat was preserved whilst I might have counted twenty; the shadow then disappeared. Now, thought I, will he return to the forest, or will he descend? Is he alone, or was the second apparition that of a companion wearing such another hat as the first had on? Suddenly I saw the sort of film of light that came clouding a little way into the corridor out of the hatch die out, and in an instant, with the swiftness of a leap almost, the man was in the room. Softly as the footfall of a cat I got my pistol to bear upon him, but before I could pull the trigger he fell upon all fours, and a moment after I heard the clank of the bell grasped and overset. I sprang out of my hiding place, took full aim, and fired. The explosion made a thunder in the room. By the flash of the powder I saw the creature spring to the height of the ceiling whilst he uttered the most piercing scream that ever broke from mortal lips. The wild cry was echoed by a shriek in Miss Grant's room. I was half-crazy with rage and consternation, and flinging down the pistol I had fired, I levelled the other at the creature as he ran, dropping to the earth with one hand as he went in staggering leaps through the dark passage, and sent a second ball at him. The report was followed by another ear-piercing shriek horribly human. The curtain behind me was dashed aside, and Miss Grant stepped forth.

"What is it?" she cried.

The silver mounting of the pistol she held gleamed in her grasp as she raised her hand in addressing me.

"I have shot something," I exclaimed; "but whether man or beast I know not. Be it what it will, it has two bullets in its body. Let me have your pistol."

I took it from her, and walked right to the steps which led above. There was nothing in the passage. I sprang into the open and looked around. The moonlight lay bright as day, the shadows of the trees sloping eastwards black as indigo where they rested on the sand. Within a stone's throw of me was a dark object that looked like a small tortoise at the distance whence I viewed it. I approached and found it to be the hat that I had found in the forest. Miss Grant had followed me noiselessly, and I only knew that she was at my side by her breathing, the sound of which was not a little startling to me, bending down as I was to examine the hat.

"Look, Mr. Musgrave!" she exclaimed, in one of her tragic whispers, "*that* must be the man you shot." She pointed with her white arm to the stretch of sand some distance past the opening that led to our cells, where I instantly observed a figure prone and motionless. In a moment I was making towards it, but with increasing bewilderment as I advanced; for as the outline stole out clearer and clearer in the icy radiance to my steps I witnessed features which gradually but surely changed my alarm into a conflict of quite other emotions. The body lay on its back; its half-closed eyes looked straight up at the stars out of a brown and puckered face ringed with white whiskers; its arms were stretched out in the posture of a crucified person.

"It has three legs!" cried Miss Grant.

"By thunder, no!" I exclaimed, bursting into a wild laugh; "that is no leg, but a great tail! As I hope to go to heaven, 'tis a huge Madagascar ape!"

Chapter II
A Gale of Wind

THE MURDER WAS NOW out, the mystery made very plain indeed, and the solution, like most others which come to a man in this life, looked so simple that one seemed half a fool for not having hit upon it at once. How this great monkey happened to be in the island who is to say? Not very likely, I think, that he was born here, unless he happened to be an only son, and both parents dead. Most likely he had belonged to a ship, and been cast away with the crew many years before. I do not know how long monkeys live, but this fellow, as he lay in the moonlight with his teeth gleaming in the grin of death out of the wrinkled leather of his face, framed by a pair of long snow-white whiskers, seemed eighty years old. It was likely that he had belonged to a ship because of his bell-ringing trick, and then his wearing that Guy Fawkes hat looked as if he had been bred in his youth to a knowledge of clothes.

But be this as it may, the bell was rung no more. I pitched the hat into the sea and met with no other; no wild convulsed face looked at me out of the high greenery, and the skylight remained unshadowed by any outline of sugar-loaf headgear in peering and hearkening posture.

Miss Grant and I talked late into the night, for tame as the issue proved, it was, I can tell you, hotly exciting whilst it lasted. But we got some rest towards the small hours, sleeping well into the morning, and then my first business was to drag the monkey down to the creek where the sand was steep with a depth of three fathoms to the shelf of it; and with no further service than a few sea-blessings upon its head for the worry and alarm it had caused me, I rolled the body overboard, guessing that it would presently float seawards, where John Sharkee lay in readiness to provide it with a sure tomb.

And now for three weeks nothing that I need tease you with happened; no such incident, I mean, as that of my discovery of the underground rooms, or the midnight tolling, and the sight of the hat on the bell-frame afterwards; but it grew into a bitter distressful time for us as the hours swelled into days, and the days rolled into weeks, and found us still imprisoned upon this island, not utterly hopeless indeed of deliverance, though we presently scarce dared to expect it. God knows that never a shipwrecked eye kept a steadfaster look-out for vessels than I did; but though during those three weeks I reckoned that I had sighted ten sail in all, none of them ever grew to more than a glimmer of white upon the distant line; so showing and so fading—worthless to us as though they had been no more than the wreaths of steam or little curls of white vapour which they resembled. Only twice indeed did I fire my faggots and make a smoke. The distance the vessels showed at made my heart hopeless, and I could scarce step a pace from one shadow to another through the roasting dazzle of sand without asking myself how it must have fared with us had there been no fresh water on the island. For food, there were turtle and craw-fish in abundance, along with an occasional parakeet which I would knock over with Miss Grant's pistol, the precisest little weapon of the kind I had ever handled. We brought at the start no great relish to these birds, but they proved dainty eating for people in our situation, when carefully plucked, cleansed, and boiled. We found a plentiful growth of plantains, citrons, whose juice mingled with water furnished us with a refreshing drink, wild oranges, and a small delicious fruit resembling the Australian passion fruit, but its proper name I do not know. There were, as you have heard, a large stock of fish-hooks in the little black chest in Miss Grant's room. I had no means of pushing out seawards to any distance to fish, so between us Miss Grant and I manufactured lines of twisted linen, which we laid up to strengthen the least rotted portions of the small stuff I found in the chest; then attaching a sinker to the baited hook, I buoyed it to a little piece of timber, the sinker going about two fathoms below the surface, and let the apparatus drift out from the mouth of the creek to the end of the line which I held in my hand, and in this manner I caught a great number of fish, incredibly various in hues, shapes, and sizes; some of them coming out of the water like flashes of dark gold light, others green as emeralds, others with half-a-dozen of brilliant colours glowing upon them as though fantastically painted, yet with exquisite cunning, by an artist. It was merciful that we did not poison ourselves with some of these fish, for we ate all we took, if I except a great bloated, spotted thing with a green back, fins like a man's arm amputated at the elbow, and a white breast freckled with sulphur-coloured spots. Even this creature I think we should have devoured but for its ugliness, yet nothing that we ate hurt us. Indeed our health continued very good, which I attribute to our being lodged out of the touch of the night air, to our exposing ourselves as little as possible to the sun, and to the sweetness and purity of the water we drank.

As you may suppose, it was impossible for such an association as ours not to deepen in me the sentiment that had been excited so long before as the first week or two of our being aboard the *Iron Crown*. We were hour after hour together; it was indeed almost only during those intervals when I would walk to the hummock to take a view of the sea that we were separated. My couch of leaves and rugs was at the threshold of her doorway. All through the night there was nothing betwixt her and me but the curtain I had contrived. In the deep hush of that strange interior, made solemn to my mind by thoughts of the grave, and sanctified to my imagination by the presence of the beautiful woman it sheltered, I would lie listening to the regular respirations of her slumber, disturbed at long intervals by some low melodious flutterings of speech breaking from her dreaming lips, and sometimes I would catch my name clear in these unconscious utterings; and it was significant to me almost to an emotion of grief that I would notice myself hearkening for the name of her lover, and smiling when her babbling died out in a long sigh, followed on by peaceful regular breathing. It seemed a sort of mocking of fate, so to speak, to think of *love*, to be sensible of the stir of the emotion, in such a situation as ours was; but then, unhappily, it was no more to be helped than the thirst that would come upon me, or the yearning after our deliverance. That I concealed from her what was in my mind I cannot say. I strove most strenuously to do so, not only from love of my own honour, and because it would have wrung me to the heart to have been the occasion of a pang in her, but because I instinctively feared—indeed let me say I clearly foresaw— that should she guess at my thoughts of her, a sort of alienation must follow, a condition of inexpressible embarrassment to us both, banded as we were in intimate partnership by our imprisonment. I could foretell pity, shyness, reproach in her; an estrangement which would be as a perpetual wound to my pride; a cessation of our free communion, to end maybe in a mere bleak civility of intercourse; the inspiration of our requirements rather than of her desire. You will think me unduly sensitive; yet when I look back I cannot but think that I rightly governed myself in the matter. If ever this fair and charming woman was under my protection she was so now, with infinitely deeper claims on me than she could have had in our darkest hours aboard ship. Her very defencelessness, me-thought, was God's own protest in her against the lightest exhibition of passion that would give her uneasiness. If I was in love with her, it was for my honour as a gentleman to wait until our escape should strengthen her womanhood by the surroundings of a civilized life to tell her so, or enable her to conjecture my mind. Thus I reasoned with myself, and so reasoning I acted; but I must admit the weakness of a deep wish in me at times to interpret her by looking into her eyes. She was heavily subdued, as you will conceive, by the conditions of our life, otherwise I witnessed no change in her manner. There was nothing to be divined from what she said, by what she did, or what she looked, and no gaze was ever more eloquent, more darkly beautiful with spirit, thought, and intelligence.

But to proceed, for this threatens to become mere parish chatter.

For days and days the weather had been lovely and quiet, the sun regularly going down behind the island rayless in the whirl of his crimson haze, the evening opening to his descent soft, dark, and fragrant as the heart of a violet; nights of marvellous stillness, saving always the island voices, with the firmament that seemed to hover like a sheet of silver dim in places, so lustrous was the star-shine, so thick the dust of the constellations when the moon was gone and left the heavens uneclipsed from sea-line to sea-line; with calm blue dawns dazzling fast into tropical glory, and then the long, brassy, fiery day, and the silent sea sparkling with the tingling glitter of new tin under the soaring luminary. At intervals a cloud would show no bigger than a man's hand, like a burst of steam from a boiler on the horizon, and then melt out into the blue air as though the heat within the cincture of which our island was the centre were so fierce as to absorb the substance of it ere it could float to its shoulders.

But one afternoon, three weeks after the date on which we had been set ashore, there came a change. That a shift of weather was at hand one might have gathered by the general uneasiness expressed by the life on the island. The birds' whistling had a subdued note, the parrots' scream was softened somewhat, the ear detected a hint of agitation in the peculiar snoring noise made by the tree-toad; there was a constant hurried flight of feathered things amongst the trees, the continued restless glint of coloured plumage darting like prismatic rays amongst the leaves. The insects bit fiercely, and the universal humming rose with a sharp note of anger and fear in the shrilling that was new to me. Miss Grant told me that these queer symptoms of disquiet might be prophetic of an earthquake, and certainly the intolerable heat of that day should have led one to expect such a thing. Indeed the sultry air seemed to press down upon one with a sensible weight, and with the stifling breath of the atmosphere of a hot oven.

When I saw the blue thickening into a kind of dinginess of no colour that I could give a name to, with a rounding of the sea at the edge of it like a lifting up of its flood, though it would be no more than the shadowing it got from the sky, with a sort of airy whitish gleam the whole horizon around, I thought to myself, if a tropical outburst is to happen, it is as well that I should turn to at once and provide that all things under hatches shall be as snug as possible. So I fell to work to bring up the hatch-cover I had knocked to pieces, and shipped the fragments into a compact form over the opening, regretting that ever I had been fool enough to break it up. I then took a view of the skylights and mused a while over them; for, thought I, when they are shut, the sweep of wind and wet will speedily load them with sand, and then, with the entrance covered by the hatch, how is fresh air to enter these cells so that we shall be able to breathe? But it was imperative any way that the skylight should be closed, if, supposing the rain to fall heavily, the rooms were not to he swamped out of hand. I tried to consider how the buccaneering folks who had dug out the place dealt with an extremity of this kind, but was quite at a loss. Some trick they must have had, but it was above my art. I conferred with Miss Grant, and she was for facing the approaching tempest above. I told her that she must know more about tropical weather than I did, but that it seemed to me, is a West Indian tempest was threatened by the gathering gloom, we were bound to perish if we did not shelter ourselves from it; and what shelter was there on the island save the vaults in which we lived.

"Yes," she exclaimed, "but should they be flooded we must be drowned; for how shall we escape when the water is pouring in?"

Well, I understood this danger clearly, and was fairly nonplussed; and indeed how we should have managed, had the weather fulfilled its threat of tropic storm, I don't know. But very fortunately for us, a little before sundown the sulky dimness above shaped out into bodies of clouds heading south, with a sea-board full of well-defined shaggy heads, showing rusty to the sun, lifting fast in the north. Then it came on to blow, in small moans at first, a sullen swell leagues in length rolling along the course taken by the clouds and swinging silent to the island, where it burst in thunder with a roaring, foamless slide of it past the eastward-facing beach. But the moans quickly grew into the hooting and whistling of a brisk wind increasing yet, even as one listened to it, to tempestuous bellowing high aloft, with a wild flying of the dry white sand, a fierce stooping and shearing of the trees, through which the wind seethed with a sound as of red-hot hissing, and a magnificent smoky scarlet that put a lining of blood whilst it lasted to the shadows flying athwart the angry beams. I saw, or hoped perhaps, that there was to be no rain, and that was comforting; but the weight of wind, and the blinding flashing into the eyes of the flying coral grit soon forced us below; though not before we had seen enough of the suddenly enraged ocean to stamp a memory fit to last for life. You almost feared for the island, so thunderous was the blow of the surge, so scaring the sight of the pallid bodies of foam sweeping in shrouds of faintness—like the colour of the brow of the snow-cloud discharging its white burthen to the tempest—through the evening gloom that rapidly followed the sun's going. The wind struck the cheek, salty and heavy with spray, which swept through the lashed and writhing trees with the crackling, rending, and tearing noise of storm after storm of bullets volleying into them.

In this way the sand became in a very short time too wet to fly, nor was the briny showering so heavy as to excite in us the least apprehension of being flooded by it. With the skylights closed and the hatch-cover on we were snug enough in our underground chambers. As for fresh air, more than we needed came blowing down through the cracks of the cover I had broken up, and whose fragments I had put together over the orifice. But though we were sheltered, and safer maybe than we should have been in a house, having regard to the wind only, there was to be no rest for us that night. The mere fear that the tempest might play us the familiar tropic trick of ceasing all at once with a driving up of the hindmost clouds into a compact blackness of vapour, breaking on a sudden into a mighty roar of rain heavy enough to swamp a city to the very roof of its cathedral, was enough to keep us wide awake; for should such a downpour happen, there would be nothing for it but to instantly rush into the open, before the rooms filled, and perish—if perish we must—in sight of the sky, instead of drowning like rats in a hole!

'Twas as wild a night as ever I remember; the glass frames above were soon coated with wet sand, but the occasional flash of lightning darting out of some rushing cloud glanced with a violet glare in the passage through the chinks in the cover; but if ever thunder followed it was out-bellowed by the hurricane, or swept by the headlong rush of the blast clean out of hearing. Our cells hummed to the elemental torment for all the world as though there was an endless procession of locomotives dragging heavy trains of cars over the island. We had husbanded our slender resources so carefully that we had a few wax candles left, and most grateful were we this night for the light one of them gave us. Without it we must have sat in total blackness throughout those long and raging hours.

"It is the proper sort of storm," said I on one occasion to Miss Grant, "to blow vessels ashore here. It should be an ill wind indeed if it blows us no good. What an imprisonment is ours! Enough to make one so wicked as to pray for a shipwreck, on chance of the sight of a survivor, or of a boat washing ashore, or material to help us to get away."

"It should frighten a poor shipwrecked sailor horribly, I think," she said, "to cleanse that glass up there and look through, and see an illuminated room with a man and woman sitting in it."

She gave a little hysteric laugh, bringing her hands to her eyes.

It was a very nightmare of an experience then to my mind, and her beauty was powerless to soothe or soften it. There were three weeks of this life working in us, and had I been alone, though I should have kept my senses sound as a bell to this moment, I believe I must have fallen mad as a thirst-crazed sailor before the dawn broke. Expectation rose into positive agony with waiting for the thunderous subterranean humming to cease, for *then* the rain might come, and the necessity of carrying my companion into the open to face the black deluge, and whatever else might happen there, was only less frightful to my overstrained nerves than the fancy of such a quick flooding of these chambers as would give us no time to escape from them. A man should wield a pen above my power to put such a picture of us and of this room before you as might make you witness it even dimly. I see at this moment the candle stuck in a bottle, with the remains of our poor supper of such odds and ends as we had been able to collect still upon the table—as mocking a regale as ever eye rested upon!—shadows like the reflection of human forms moping and mowing on walls and ceiling to the slant of the flame stirred by small hurryings of draught coming out of the black corridor; the black shapes of the old muskets and hangers, the doorway yawning past the half-drawn curtain, courting the glance to the dungeon gloom within—the whole gathering a preternatural element to my imagination, stirred to its depths as it was by the trembling of the earth to the shocks of the sea upon its northern board, from the look of wild beauty my companion's eyes got from the candle-flame, as they showed dark to it out of her face, whitened to the very complexion of a spirit by our vigil and the thoughts that worked in her.

All through that night, down to an hour past dawn, it blew a fierce and heavy gale of wind, never rising, however, to the hurricane force that is to be expected in weather of this kind hereabouts. We knew by the cessation of the humming noise in our rooms that there was tranquillity overhead, but the skylights were so thickly coated with sand that no ray of light broke through, and the change in the weather was only to be gathered by listening. It took me some while to break my way out through the entrance in consequence of the heavy plastering of the hatch-cover by the wet soil hove by the wind upon it; and seeing that our dwelling-place must have been air-tight for some time, it was strange that we found no inconvenience from breathing the atmosphere. But then, to be sure, the chambers were tolerably big, and there were but two of us to breathe in them, with but a single candle-flame besides. I battered the hatch with one of the muskets, and so forced it open, and on emerging found a sullen, wild, though silent morning, dense masses of white cloud hanging, brooding fashion, over the sea, with their violet shadows lifting up to them, as it were, great lagoons of blue sky between, the sun in one of them shining with a fiery and piercing light.

Indeed the wind was all gone; but there was a great swell still running which made the sea a noble and majestic sight. The polished flowing of the vast folds caught the sunlight as they rolled, till under the luminary the ocean seemed to be formed of sweeping hills of molten silver. The gale had played havoc with the island; many trees lay fallen, and the weather side of the little forest showed as though the branches there had been trimmed by the shears of countless gardeners during the night. But the insects and flies had come off with their lives. Their concert was prodigiously shrill, with a note of thanksgiving in it, Miss Grant thought; but it sounded to me more like an impertinent hymn of triumph, the clamour of multitudinous insignificance, as one might say, over the defeat of the mighty forces of nature. We stood eagerly looking towards the sea and along the sands far as our sight could trace them, not knowing what might have happened during the long, dark, howling hours; but there was nothing to be seen saving the mighty, brilliant blue welter sending its brows washing to the edge of the distant sky. We then made for the hummock, and took another view thence; but the prospect was barren of wreck; not a glimpse of the wet flash of a fragment of black timber wallowing—no hint of any sort of disaster at sea.

I will not say I was disappointed, for I had scarce felt expectation; but my sickness at heart was deep—never had it been deeper in those three weeks that we had spent upon this island—when I sent my gaze around the winding and waving horizon, and found no vaguest symptom of life in it outside its own ponderous turbulence. Down on the northern strand the surf was vast and glorious, with the bursting of the swell arching into giant breakers upon the beach. The giddy dazzle, the creaming splendour detained us. The prismatic, snow-white boiling, along with the cold thunder of the headlong and recoiling masses of water, were grateful beyond expression to every sense in us, coming now to loathe, as we did after many days of it, the stifling stagnation of the great plain. However, the swell of the sea soon flattens when there is no wind, and by noon the heave of the deep was languid enough, the clouds gone, saving a small, pearl-coloured heap in the south, and here and there out at sea faint tricklings of air delicately smearing the glassy blue, like the tarnishing of moistened fingers upon a looking-glass.

The sight of the fallen trees raised an idle hope in me of manufacturing some sort of fabric out of them by which we might escape; for we were now arrived at such a condition of hopelessness that, sooner than go on lingering in this island, which we dared no longer believe any vessel ever approached close enough to witness a signal of distress in the smoke of our fire, we thought it would be better to take our chance on the roughest contrivance we could put together, and launch. We had material to stitch into a sail, which, under Providence, might blow us within eyeshot of a ship. But it was not necessary to look long at the fallen timber to understand that, without help and without tools, it was as useless to us as the coral sand under our feet. What were we to do? Was it the will of Heaven that we should end our days on this beautiful but most melancholy island?

As we sat conversing, Miss Grant on a sudden gave way. Never once during our imprisonment had she let fall a tear; but now she broke down. She covered her face with her hands, wept most piteously, sobbing as if her heart were broken. If ever I had wondered whether I was in love with her, my doubts would have ended as I watched her in her grief, waiting for the first passion of her sorrow to spend itself before I addressed her. The natural timidity of a woman she had indeed exhibited on several occasions; but taking our wild, miserable, most distressful experiences throughout, her spirit had shown clear, noble, heroic, and it was this fine character in her that made her sudden outbreak miserable to witness. One would have given little heed to such a display of emotion as this in a woman who had been fretful and mopish during our trials, with tears always at hand, and a weak heart aggravating with repinings. But here was a girl whose courage had proved superior to every demand made upon it; in those darker and sterner experiences, I mean, which might well have caused the spirit of the stoutest-hearted man to shrink within him. The sweetness of her nature had never failed her. Again and again had our gloomy underground haunt resounded with the gentle melody of her laughter, often uttered, as every instinct in me knew, for no other purpose than to cheer me; and to see her giving way now——

I waited a little, and then I could no longer bear it. I took her hand and put it to my lips and fondled it, and said—but I know not what I said, only that I was sensible my secret had slipped from me. Whether she gathered the import of my words, whether indeed she even knew what I spoke, I cannot tell. The cloud passed presently, and she was again meeting my gaze with steadfast, shining eyes, the more brilliant they looked for the very tears she had wept. Well, thought I, everything that happens is for the best, we must believe; yet for the rest of the day the memory that I had been hurried into saying more, much more, than I felt I ought to have addressed to her, haunted and bothered me; but though I would eye her keenly, if furtively, and listen to her with an attention so strained that it could not have missed a single note in her utterance interpretable by my sensitiveness, I could no more have told, when the night came and we had parted to take our rest, that she had heard or heeded what I had said to her, than I could have predicted what was to happen to us next day.

It was the morning of the twenty-first day of our captivity. I was awakened from a dream of my old home in England—a cheerful vision of an English landscape, with the soft May sky shining over budding hedgerows and the delicate green of spring vegetation—by the loud singing of a bird perched on a ledge of the open skylight, which I need hardly say I had long before purified of the sand that the storm had accumulated upon it. This singing had something of the note of a linnet in it, only very strong and piercing, and doubtlessly it was the melodious piping that set me dreaming of English meadows and woods, and the house in which I was brought up till I went to sea. I had passed a good night, felt strengthened and refreshed by the long rest, and at once kicked off my rug with the design of taking my usual morning plunge off the sand away round past the creek. All was quiet in Miss Grant's room I climbed the steps, and found it a brilliantly clear morning, roastingly hot after the pattern of the days here, the sea very calm, with a light swaying like a long sigh running through it, and a soft air floating languidly down out of the north, with just weight enough to put a trembling into the needle-like rays spiking off the edge of the sun's light in the water, as though the seams of his wake were ravelled. I cast a careless look around the ocean, thinking more of my bath, maybe, than what might be in view; for this looking for ships had grown into a habit, and habit becomes mechanical. I then undressed and waded to the height of my hips, a depth I durst not exceed for fear of sharks, and after revelling for nigh half an hour in the cold blue swing of the little breakers, whose caressing foam sang to the ears like the seething of the froth of a sparkling wine, I stalked again on to the beach, dried, and fell to dressing myself.

Whilst I was thus occupied I suddenly spied something black out upon the water, but how far off I could not tell. I took it to be the back of a shark at first, or the black spine of a porpoise that would round away out of sight in a minute; then I thought it must be a piece of wreck; but as it seemed to me to be very slowly growing, I walked to a clump of trees to shelter me from the heat of the sun, and sat down to watch the thing. It was little more than a speck when I first sighted it, but after waiting some time, and observing that it increased in size, I could not question that it was approaching the island, and that it was either a boat or canoe impelled by human agency, for there was no sail to bring her along, though the faint breeze favoured her; nor, though the tide might be helping her a bit, was the set of it swift enough to account for the thing's growth. I was gazing intently when I heard Miss Grant calling. I hallooed back, telling her to come to me. She arrived presently, exclaiming, as she approached, that she was growing alarmed by my long absence. I pointed to the object on the water.

"It must be a boat, I think," I cried. "I am watching it—waiting to see what it means."

She looked, instantly saw it, and cried, "Oh!" starting violently, with a quick clasping of her hands, and then, with her manner full of excitement, came and sat close beside me. "Oh, Mr. Musgrave, if it should prove a boat!"

"It *is* a boat; it is being rowed too. Look attentively, and you will see the glint, on the right hand side of it, of the wet blade of an oar lifting to the light."

"I see it!" she cried.

My mind was agitated beyond my capacity of expressing the commotion raised within me by the sight of the boat. I seized Miss Grant's hand with both mine, pressing it whilst I cried out in my transport that a chance had come, that we might now regard our deliverance as certain, that my frequent bitter, imploring prayers were heard at last, and we were now to be supplied with the means of escaping. The distress of the sea makes a very child of a man. I felt the tears which my eyes refused to distil scalding at my heart. One may bear up stoutly for days, for weeks, for months amid the misery of solitude; hope dying out in one to a mere spark amid the embers of dreams and expectations—I say one may endure the heaviest afflictions the sea can heap upon the soul with a lion's spirit; yet it will be strange if, when succour comes at last, one do not give way as a little child might.

Within three-quarters of an hour of my first catching sight of the minute speck, it had enlarged upon the calm white heave of the sea to the proportions of what was apparently a ship's quarter-boat, with a spot of red in her that puzzled me, a mast like a hair rising out of the black rounding of the gunwales, and an occasional gleam of oars wielded most languidly and intermittently, as though handled by a dying man. Indeed, I cannot convey how suggestive of distress was this slow and irregular motion of the oars, gatherable from the sparkle of them whenever the blades rose languidly from the blue surface. Presently I saw that what I had taken to be a spot of red in the boat was a soldier's jacket, and waiting yet a little while longer, I observed that the fellow was a negro. There was no other occupant of the boat to be seen. I ran down to the beach, followed by Miss Grant, to motion the man to head for the beach at the head of the creek; for small as the breakers were, it would have been madness to imperil so precious an object as the little fabric by grounding her amongst them. He evidently understood me, for he pulled a little with his left hand to point his boat according to my gestures, and then let go both oars to stand up, with his hands clasped above his head, and his face lifted as in a posture of entreaty to God, whilst his body reeled in such a way that I expected to see him go overboard. He next made certain signs, pointing to his mouth and then down into the boat, and then clasped his hands again, but I could not understand him. I shouted, to encourage him, continuing to point towards the creek, which would be visible to him, and presently he sat down and fell to his oars afresh, but rowing so weakly that it was miserable to watch him. He made shift, however, to bring the boat within a fathom or two of the head of the spit of sand that formed one side of the entrance to the creek; then looking round, he got his port oar inboard out of the thole-pins, and had his hand on the loom of the other, when he fell back and disappeared.

My terror lest the boat should drift away rendered me as reckless as if I had fallen crazy. Without giving a thought to the sharks that might be about, I waded into the water till it was out of my depth, then swam with the utmost fury, and after a few strokes caught hold of the gunwale, and with a hard spring rolled head over heels into the little fabric, and seizing the oar that lay jammed in the tholepins, I headed the boat into the creek, and sculled her right fair to the gleaming round of the little inlet without so much as glancing at what lay inside the craft, till her forefoot was aground and I had leaped ashore.

Chapter III
A Startling Apparition

THERE WAS A SECOND man in the boat, a negro also. He lay dead in the bottom, a dreadful sight, naked to the waist, and clothed with a pair of sailor's old drill trousers, the right leg discoloured by many blood-stains. He was twisted, as though his spine was broken, with his breast partly turned towards the stern of the boat, whilst his knees, which were drawn up, pointed forwards, and his face stared straight up, the eyes open like dull glass, and the skin of that indescribable sort of greenish ashen hue which death contrives as a complexion for the dead black man. The other fellow was on his back, as he had fallen, with his head in the bottom of the boat, and his legs over the thwart. He still breathed, but I noticed the foam gathering upon his lips even as I looked on for a moment or two at this terrible picture. He was dressed in a soldier's or marine's coat, a cloth round about his loins, and his attenuated cucumber shanks naked; an old ragged Scotch cap clung to his woolly head.

It would be impossible for me to tell you how this little ocean tragedy was heightened by the element of the grotesque in it. There was no sail in the boat, no breaker that might have held water, no hint of the miserable blacks having sailed or been blown away with so much as a bite of biscuit. The oars were scarcely more than paddles, and evidently had not belonged to the little fabric. She was black outside, painted white within; clearly, as I had thought at the beginning, a ship's quarter-boat. The words *Prince William* were painted in small black letters on her stern, inside of her. Miss Grant overhung the craft in a posture of pity and horror.

"This poor fellow in the bows is still alive," she cried.

"I see that he is," said I; "we will help him in an instant; but the value of this boat signifies the worth of our lives, and we must make her a bit securer yet. Please pull at this rope as I pull."

I handed a bight of the line in the bows to her, and then put my hand on the gunwale at the head, and together we ran her another few feet out of the water, the wet keel and bottom of her slipping readily enough up the ivory-like grit of the sand. All this was done as swiftly as I can write it. I then jumped into the boat, and with some trouble, for he was an exceedingly heavy man, I raised the negro on to the thwart, and set his back against the mast. His head lolled upon his shoulder like that of a person hanging. He looked at me with a gleam of intelligence in the lift of his bloodshot eyes, and his lips moved, but the merest rattle of noise trembled through the foam that filled his mouth. He raised his hand and pointed to his throat.

"Why, of course!" cried I; "I must have been mad not to perceive it. The poor fellow is dying of thirst. Will you get some water, whilst I keep him propped up here?"

She was off in a bound like a stag, and in the briefest imaginable time returned with a preserved meat-tin full of water, which I put to the negro's lips; but the moment he tasted the cold of it against his mouth a frenzy seized him. He grasped the tin, throwing me from him with a jerk of his elbow that was like to have broken my back for me against the gunwale, and uttering a strange throaty cry that made one think of the yell of a hunted negro to the first leap of a bloodhound upon him, he drank the whole of the water at one draught—a full quart, as I should reckon, for the tin was a big one—let drop the vessel, flinging both his hands against his breast in the manner of a man furiously striking himself, stood bolt upright with a most mad and murderous look in his eyes as they met mine, ere they rolled right up till you saw nothing but the crimsoned whites of them, and then without a groan fell backwards across the other body and lay motionless.

I looked round at Miss Grant. "The draught has killed him, I fear," said I.

She turned away her head with her hands over her eyes. I kneeled down and grasped the poor wretch's wrist that showed like a bit of ebony forking out of the ragged sleeve of the red coat, but could feel no pulse. I then felt the arm of the man beneath him, designing to gather if *he* lived, but instantly twitched my fingers away from the clammy chill of the unmistakably dead flesh. I next soaked a handkerchief in salt water, plucked the Scotch cap off the head of the man who had fallen, and bathed his brows, but nothing followed. Once a movement as of muscular contraction went in a twitch through him, but the drop of the jaw told me all I needed to learn.

It was proper, however, that I should let him lie for a while to make sure that he was dead, and so I stepped ashore, and to still further secure this precious gift that had come to us, I carried the end of the painter, which was a good long length of coir rope, with the strands at the extremity showing that it had parted, to a tree which stood near the head of the creek, and secured it, then withdrew with Miss Grant to the shelter of some tufted heads of the cocoa to sit down and rest and think a little, and wait to observe if the man had actually expired.

My companion was greatly overcome. The appearance of the negro, the white foam blanching his purple lips, and the short, stubborn hair under his nose and chin, the deeper horror that was put into his anguish by the absurdity of his apparel, the suddenness of his rising, the frightfulness of his collapse after he had drained the tin, with a swing of his hands to his heart, and the terrifying glare of his eyes, had proved so overwhelming a picture, with the unexpectedness on top of it besides of the body in the bottom of the boat, that she could scarcely raise her head; shudders went through her, and I feared she would faint. Dreadful indeed it was, but the pitifulness of it, I am almost ashamed to say, was largely qualified to my mind by the transport of joy with which I viewed the boat, and understood that the time of our deliverance—a chance not to have been dreamt of two or three hours before—had come to us. It needed but a very brief spell of thinking to arrive at how this thing had happened. As one who had used the ocean, I could not fail to see it all clearly and quickly. In fact the parted strands of the coir line told me the tale. It was no painter, but such a rope as a boat would ride astern of a ship by. It had broken, maybe, in the gale that had stormed over us two nights before, and the boat had gone adrift with these negroes in her, without a sail, with a rudder that was without a tiller, without water, and without food.

I waited for some time, and went to the boat to have another look at the man, and then his appearance persuaded me that he was dead. I was heartily grieved that this should have been so, for now that he lay at rest he showed, methought, a very bland and honest countenance, besides being of a most muscular and robust make; and I felt that had he lived he might have proved of the utmost use to us, not as a pilot only, and as one perhaps who would know the situation of this island and its name, but as an assistant to help me to rig the fabric and navigate her. However, the truth lay before me; and I suppose these hard island-experiences of ours having rendered me extremely prosaic and matter-of-fact in directions which at another time would have stirred all the sentiment in me to its depths, I determined to deal with the bodies without ado. So looking around me, I picked up two good big stones, one of which I secured to the body of the man who had just died by the cloth round about his middle, whilst I attached the other to the second body in a manner I need not describe; then without saying a word to Miss Grant, who sat watching me, clearly understanding my intentions, I unhitched the line from the tree, shoved the boat afloat, and sculled her clear of the creek where the water was deep, and tumbled the bodies overboard. It was as odious a bit of necessary work as ever mortal man could put his hand to. Hot as the sun was, the job made me feel as cold as if the chill of an English November night were upon me; but I breathed more freely when I came to scull myself back to the shore, and when I stepped out with the end of the line in my hand, the earlier emotion of joy that the possession of the little craft had raised was again so active in my heart that I could scarce hold myself from singing like a boy at the top of my voice.

The morning was already advanced, and we had not yet broken our fast. I disliked the idea of turning my back upon the boat, lest on my return I should find her gone. However, her forefoot being hard and fast ashore, and the line in the bows secured to the trees, it was impossible that the flow of the tide in the creek could play me any ugly tricks with her; so we walked to our underground chambers to get some breakfast. I remember that our repast consisted of cold turtle-steak, plantains, sweet oranges, and a draught of cold water from the brook. The stock of provisions that had been set ashore with us was now exhausted; we had a small quantity of spirits left, but the biscuit, tongues, preserved meat, and the like, were gone. Such a breakfast as ours was hardly fare to grow fat on, but it was wholesome and cool, and perhaps the sort of food that nature intended for the use of such human beings as should live in this island. It seems to me that the properest food for the people who inhabit a country is that which grows good for eating in it. Think of Broadwater's bill of fare, for instance, under such a dog-star as raged over the spot of earth we had been marooned upon!—roast pork, massive sausages, turbid pea-soup, and the atmosphere all the while so hot that you heard the spikes and leaves and tendons of the breathless vegetation quivering with tingling noises like the faint crackling in burnt paper, or in a sheet of tin curling to the roasting glare of a furnace! I was mighty sick of turtle, and so was Miss Grant, but then it was a sort of meat in its way, and combined to make out a meal of the fruit, which was too delicious to weary us. One helped the other, and rendered the whole diet nutritious; and maybe it was the simplicity of the fare that kept us well. We had been a long three weeks upon the island, yet Miss Grant had never once uttered a complaint of indisposition, whilst for my part I was almost unreasonably hearty in face of the heavy anxieties that weighed down my spirits.

"Thank God," said I, with a look round the room, as I seated myself with my companion to our lenten meal, "we shall soon be taking a long farewell of this most melancholy haunt. It would have been strange indeed if that ill wind the other night blew us no good. A boat is the next best thing to a ship."

"How strange it is," she exclaimed, "to watch the working of the hand of fate! Ashore, it is an influence, a hidden government; but at sea it is as apparent as a billow, or the rising of a cloud. One saw *that* in the boat as she approached. Fate was at her helm, and if I were an artist, and desired to materialize the conception of fate, and make it a visible thing, I should figure two people standing as we did, hopeless and imprisoned on this island, watching the boat coming out of the tiny blot it made in the far blue distance, gliding towards us without a swerve, with a final complete surrendering of itself to us, as it were, through the death of the two poor creatures in it." Her fine eyes shone to the high religious mood that was in her. "Little wonder," she continued, "that we should always be saying God's hand is most plain on the deep. The Ancient Mariner was not mad when he spied the little bark with Death on board gambling with a woman for human souls. The sea is to me so much more wonderful than the land, that I believe I could credit any amazing thing that should be related of it. Where else does one come closer to one's Maker? Oh, Mr. Musgrave, it seemed to me like seeing the Divine finger itself when I watched that boat growing upon the calm sea, urged, as we know now, by dying hands."

She shuddered, and pressed her fingers to her temples. She had been overtaxed, nor was the horror wrought in her by the incident of the morning to be soothed by the deep excitement that the opportunity for escaping from this island brought with it. Hysteria, I thought, was bound to dog the heels of such moralizing as she had started on; so there was nothing for it but to be blunt and prosaic, though, but for the fear I had that the humouring of the mood she was in would be bad for her, I could have listened all day. It was not so much what she said as the thoughts which lay behind her words, which spoke in her face, making her beauty eloquent with the rich fancies flushing to her delicate cheeks, and flashing a brighter light yet into her eyes.

"We shall have to go to work briskly," said I; "if all were prepared I would start at once."

She came back to herself with an effort, and brought her hands from her white brows with a faint smile, as if she understood what was in my mind concerning her.

"What is to be done, Mr. Musgrave, that I may know my share?" she asked.

"Well, first of all we must victual the boat," said I; "we have bottles enough for the storing of fresh water, and you can do a useful hour's work by hunting for the corks which we have drawn and thrown away, and fitting them to the bottles afresh. For food we must be content with the handsomest stock of craw-fish, fruit, and turtle that we can contrive. The boat wants a tiller. *That* is easily managed. She also wants a sail, which we shall have to manufacture out of your shawls. I must likewise make a yard for the sail, which may be got from a bough off one of the fallen trees. This done, our business will be to embark and head away west."

"It is a little boat for so great a sea," she said, in a low voice.

"Ay," said I, "but then the film of land that was visible from the cross-trees of the *Iron Crown* is not too far distant for her to fetch, and it will be mighty odd indeed if that streak of blue haze which the men talked about be not an inhabited island, with houses to lodge in, and the means of proceeding to Jamaica, which can't be far distant; whence our next departure will be for Rio, and for Alexander."

She looked down suddenly, with the pearl of her teeth showing over the under-lip she slightly bit, then her eyes sought mine again with a soft gaze so full of inquiry that my heart seemed to stop for a breath, as though to catch the words that must follow her look; but she did not speak. I jumped up.

"I must go to work now," cried I; "in fact it frightens me to think of the boat, lying half dry as she is, being unwatched."

She rose too, with the air of one starting from deep thought. "My business then," said she smiling, "is to look for corks, and fit them to the bottles?"

"If you please," said I.

For the rest of the day I worked very hard, stripped to my trousers and shirt, with my wide straw hat to shelter me, scarce intermitting my labour but to eat and drink, and obtaining quite fortitude enough out of the prospect of getting away from this island with Miss Grant, to enables me to defy the intense heat. I found amongst the fallen trees the very bough to serve my turn, and without much difficulty I severed it with my little saw, trimmed it of its leaves, and proportioned it to the size of the required yard. I also cut a tiller for the boat. This work I was able to accomplish under the shelter of the trees. Miss Grant possessed several shawls of different textures and colours, and when she had collected the bottles, and gathered what corks there were to find, I set her tacking some of these shawls together into the shape of a sail, which she managed by perforating them with a bodkin, and then connecting them with tape, of which she had a little parcel. She made no trouble over mutilating her shawls, though I cannot but think that the first thrust of her bodkin into them must have caused her a pang. I cut off a short length of the coir-rope, and got yarns enough out of it to convert into as many robands as were necessary to connect the head of our queer sail to the yard. There was still plenty of line left for a tack and sheet and halliards, which I rove through a sheave in the head of the mast. My impatience gave me very great energy indeed. We had a good supply of fresh turtle, which needed boiling, and this, with other matters which it would only weary you to specify, gave my fair companion plenty to do. I was resolved not to quit the island without being well stocked with food, for should it come on to blow from the westwards, I foresaw that our sail would not help us, that we should not be able to lay up to the wind more than six or seven points, so that we should stand to be blown away into the Atlantic eastwards, where we might spend days without view of a ship. My hope was too high perhaps to suffer me to contemplate such a probability as this with the least notion of its coming to pass, but my seafaring instincts governed me without my perhaps being very sensible of their influence, and I schemed, in a mechanical sort of way almost, so to provision the boat that you might have thought we intended to sail to England.

When the cool of the evening came, I plucked some hundreds of plantains and oranges, which I carefully stowed away in the little lockers aft that served as seats in the boat's stern, and I then fired a torch and waded into the sea for craw-fish in the manner I have before described, meeting with a more plentiful harvest than had at any other time happened to me, insomuch that I had to give up stooping and throwing them to Miss Grant through sheer aching of my back, though the sandy bottom was still black with the dusky, lizard-like shapes of the creatures crawling into the sheen, when I extinguished my torch to step ashore. I also provided the boat with a stock of coconuts, but I never could discover a single turtle's egg, spite of my earnest exploring of the sand for several nights running during those three weeks.

We were wearied rather than sleepy when the darkness was deepening into midnight. There was a young moon in the sky, with a wire-like waving of silver under her in the glooming sea, that spread very darkly to the stars. I had still several bundles of cheroots left, and lighting one of them, I brought our camp-stools close down to the wash of the ocean, where the sand stretched like ivory glimmering to the dusk, for the cool of the atmosphere upon the water, and to get away from the trees, in whose shadows the suffocating air of the day seemed to linger as though imprisoned. This was to be our last night on the island, and neither of us could think yet a while of shutting ourselves up underground. The phosphorescence of the water was shown by the light-green flashings which broke from each little purring breaker, as it melted into yeast and seethed soft as snow up the coral strand. But the ocean lay too silent and still for the fires to show themselves out upon its breast, if it were not that here and there at intervals you spied a greenish, smoke-like burst, as though some huge jelly-fish were shining under the surface, in the black brow of the silent swell that ran without sound and without break. The outline of our boat stood clear like a sketch in ink against the sand on the other side of the creek.

"We shall have much to tell," said I, "when we are released from this place; more than many will think credible, I dare say. 'Tis almost like some old Arab's yarn, this marooning of a young man and a lady, the old piratical lair underground yonder, the incident of the monkey, and strangest of all, at least to my mind, the arrival of that boat there this morning with its tragic burden of dead and dying blacks. What will Alexander think?"

"If our meeting is much longer delayed,' she answered, "he will think us lost."

"What grief for him, poor fellow!" said I; "but then, you know, the meeting will be the sweeter for its unexpectedness."

She made no answer; nor indeed was I much surprised by her silence. In truth, I had grown somewhat accustomed to a reserved attitude in her whenever I spoke of her sweetheart. However, I was in the humour, I cannot say why, I am sure to twang this chord just a little longer.

"Now," said I, "as to-morrow will see us under way—and the night, please God, safely on board ship, or within view of the lights of a little town in some island hidden behind the sea-line—I feel equal to talking a bit freely, Miss Grant. I have not set eyes on Alexander for years. He was a fine, handsome young fellow when at sea with me; always bold enough to excite my admiration; but since then his courage seems to have increased. Do I admire it in its excess? I will not say so. The emotion it excites is one, I fear, of supreme wonderment only."

The moonlight was thin, but I could see her looking at me by it, with a little contraction of her white, brows as evidence of the intensity of her gaze. "Some satirical fancy about Alexander has occurred to you?" she exclaimed.

"No, Miss Grant, nothing of the sort, on my honour."

"What is this courage of his that you wonder at?"

"The astonishing pluck he showed in confiding you to my care." She did not or would not understand. "Here am I," I continued, "a young man, for days and days in the society of a lady of whose charms he has proved himself very sensible indeed." She uttered a soft laugh scarcely above her breath. "Now, would not my cousin, as a young man himself, conclude that it could be scarcely possible for me to be so incessantly with you without—without—well now, what I mean to say is, without my falling in love?"

"He would not think of such a thing, Mr. Musgrave."

"Oh, I fancy he would. A thought of the kind is bound to occur, and it is this triumphing of hope in him over what must lie at his heart with the strength of a conviction, that—"

I was arrested by her suddenly clutching at my hand; her swift *fierce* grasp, as I thought it for the instant, almost took my breath away. "Heaven forgive me!" I mentally ejaculated, "I have aroused the Spanish blood in this woman. I—I—"

"Look, Mr. Musgrave!" she exclaimed, in a tone that thrilled to my ear with the fear in it, what is *that?*"

Her face was turned towards the creek, and following the direction of her glance, I observed the figure of a man standing a little on this side of the spot where our luggage had been deposited by the boat's crew. He was clear of the shadows of the trees, and it was bright sand where he stood, and in the light of it lifting into the atmosphere he resembled a statue cut in ebony. He was motionless save for the occasional raising of his hand to his mouth from time to time, as of a man taking a bite at something in his fist.

"Gracious mercy!" I exclaimed, a little above my breath, "not another monkey, I hope. The deuce is in this island. But he is too big surely even for a baboon."

"It is a man!" whispered Miss Grant, "and a black man too."

"There must be another boat come ashore," said I.

I stood staring a little, waiting to see whether he would advance, and what he meant to do. My heart beat fast. It would be impossible to express to you how startling was the apparition of that black figure. The suddenness and unexpectedness of the apparition was rendered the more alarming by the faintness of the moonlight. Standing where he was, the brilliance of the full orb would have interpreted him; but though he stood jet-like upon the sand, he yet seemed to mingle with the dusk in a visionary sort of way, and this blending of the blackness of him with the gloom caused him to appear as phantasmal as though he were the veritable shade of some negro anciently murdered for the sentinelling by his spirit of hidden treasure in the place.

"Are there others about, I wonder?" said I. I sent a swift look towards the forest and past it, but all was motionless. I bent my ear with the fancy of catching the notes of voices beyond where the man stood, suspecting that his boat had arrived off the western sand; but no sound of the kind penetrated the distracting shrilling of the crickets.

"He is watching us!" exclaimed Miss Grant.

It was time to end this. In fact the more one stared at the dusky shape, with its rising and falling arm, the more one stood to grow afraid of it.

"Hallo there!" I sang out, walking a little way towards the figure, "who are you, and where have you come from?"

No answer was returned, but the figure moved uneasily, as if uncertain how to act. I hailed again, still advancing towards him, Miss Grant keeping close by my side; and then he approached us, but very slowly, whether through physical weakness or fear I could not say. He was sufficiently close now to enable me to make out that he was a negro, and I was sensible at sight of him of a sickening chill coming into me, though at that moment certainly I could not have accounted for the sensation. A wild fancy entered my head, working almost like a touch of insanity there, that I had seen the man before. Was it the build of him? Was it his gait? I could not say. He was still too far distant to enable me to see what clothes he wore, if indeed he were dressed; but I remember coming to a stand with a coldness about my forehead as though some icy air were fanning me, whilst I let fly my breath with a sound that came very near to a cry. On a sudden Miss Grant screamed out, stepping in a terrified way backwards, then coming to me again and clutching my arm.

"It is a ghost!" she cried; "it is one of the men you buried to-day. Look at the soldier's coat on him—at the white cloth under it!"

He was now near enough to render these features unmistakable. The red of his ragged jacket stole out ashen to the wan light; round his loins was the cloth to which I had secured the stone I had sunk him by. Nothing was wanting to him but his Scotch cap, and that I knew he would not possess, as I had removed it to bathe his head, whilst on noticing it that afternoon lying in the bottom of the boat, I had chucked it overboard into the creek. I stood stock still, as though some blast of lightning had struck me dead. Very distinctly indeed do I recollect the sensation of the stirring of the hair upon my head, an effect I had once looked upon as a mere poetic imagination, beyond the reach of the extremest form of terror in real life. The dew started from my brows, and my hands turned as wet as though I had lifted them dripping from a basin of oil. Had I endeavoured to run away my legs must have failed me. I felt Miss Grant trembling from head to toe, in the vibratory, nervous grasp she had of my arm. Why, here was a man who had at least twelve hours before fallen dead in our presence, and whom I had soon afterwards buried in the sea, securing him against the possibility of rising by a sinker weighty enough to keep two such fellows down; here was this same man, I say, now standing before me, stalking out of the forest, it would seem, instead of out of the ocean, dressed as I had buried him—a dusky outline with a black face combining with the gloom, and his eyes touched with the faint sparkles of the moonlight that he confronted.

"Oh, speak to him! What *is* it?" exclaimed Miss Grant.

Thrice I endeavoured to articulate, but my tongue clove to the roof of my mouth, dry and parched as the sand upon which we stood; but at the fourth effort I managed to find my voice, and nothing huskier ever rattled in human throat.

"In God's name," I said, "who *are* you?"

He answered, but in a language I did not know.

"It is Spanish," whispered Miss Grant, "negro Spanish. He is not a ghost then; but oh, what can he be? He was dead, Mr. Musgrave, when you buried him."

"Do you speak Spanish, Miss Grant?" said I.

She answered, yes.

"For Heaven's sake then, address him, and resolve this horrible mystery," I cried.

But she was too terrified to speak to him yet. She continued to cling to me with shivers chasing her. Why, the heart of a Boadicea might have swooned to such an apparition. And then the time of its coming too!—this dimly tinctured gloom—the streak of westering moon—the dark sea floating into the distant silence, with *our* supreme conviction that the corpse of the black object we were looking at lay with a stone attached to it fathoms beneath the surface!

He addressed us again in the same tongue, in the thick, throaty guttural of the African, this time delivering a pretty long sentence, whilst he stood before us with his arms hanging up and down, and a supplicatory inclination of the head towards us, and an occasional totter of his black shanks.

"What does he say?" I cried.

"It is hard to catch his meaning," she said; "he speaks a very strange kind of Spanish. I think what he wants to say is, that he is alone and ill, and asks us not to hurt him."

It was about time now that I should see something miraculous had happened in the shape of the preservation of this negro's life. I was still prodigiously amazed and confounded astonished almost to the height of imagining that my mind was all abroad, and out and away more scared than a natural danger could have rendered me. But common

sense was beginning to break through, and after a little I had sufficiently mastered myself to think intelligently.

"This is no ghost, Miss Grant," said I; "the poor devil has in some
astonishing fashion come off with his life, and we must learn how.
There's a sup of spirits below; a dram along with something to eat will
help his tongue."

I stepped up to him, Miss Grant meanwhile keeping a tight hold of
my arm, and with a motion of my hand invited him to accompany us.
He at once complied, and the three of us walked to our underground
chambers. We had made a very thrifty use of our candles, and had still
a few wax ends left. I asked Miss Grant to request him to remain outside till I called him. She did so, and then said, "Do you mean to ask
him to come down here?"

"He won't hurt us," said I; "he is no ghost. Kindness will make him
grateful."

"But suppose he believes you meant to drown him?" she exclaimed.

"Oh, we'll clear his mind of that notion," said I, for I was now rallying fast, with a hope rising in me that something helpful to ourselves
might come out of this business, and consumedly curious besides, as
you may suppose, to learn how the fellow had come to life again.

"I will go first," exclaimed Miss Grant.

Indeed the negro was still little more than a ghost to her mind, and if
she led the way, then of course I was between her and him. It was pitch
dark, but we were most sorrowfully well acquainted with the road by
this time, and easily making our way to the kitchen struck a light, and
then called to the black man to come down. He arrived, staring about
him with an air of stupid bewilderment, apparently thunderstruck at
the sight of our hidden lodging. I lighted a couple of wax ends to have
a good view of him, and found him sure enough the same Quashee
whom I had supposed dead, and whom I had buried, and whose very
existence, I may say, so full of business had the hours been between, I
had almost forgotten. His soldier's coat sat dry upon his shoulders, his
loin-cloth was also perfectly dry; so it was clear his resurrection had
not been recent. His grotesque garb and ebony figure formed a detail
to fit this subterranean place to perfection. Indeed, somehow it was
impossible to glance at him and around the chamber without finding
a new kind of significance in everything the eye rested upon stealing
into it out of his presence; the muskets and cutlasses looked as grim
again, the walls and ceilings more wildly and piratically rugged than
ever they had shown, to the turning of the black, wondering face upon
them, as the fellow stared here and there. We had still a drop of the

ship's rum left; I mixed a dram for him in a soup and boulli tin, noticing that he threw the remains of a plantain which he had been eating into the furnace, to receive the draught. Indeed, as he afterwards told us, he had found a tolerable meal among the fruit past the forest, and he was eating plantains when he first hove in sight, as I had gathered from the motion of his arm. However, he could find a corner for a large piece of turtle which I handed to him, devouring it with great relish and avidity.

Miss Grant posted herself on the other side of the table, away from him. She stared incessantly, as if she could not realize his existence, and indeed, though one saw him eating and drinking, sitting solid and substantial, with the whites of his eyes rolling most realistically over the room, whilst he chewed upon the turtle with the true negro smacking of the lips over every bite, yet when I reflected how stone dead he had been, and how completely I had buried him, I would start to the fancy that if it were not all some odd and ugly dream, why then the black creature *might* be a spectre after all, a solemn intimation to my incredulous mind that such things were. But I must say that these notions grew feebler with their recurrence.

"Let us get his story, Miss Grant," said I.

She addressed him nervously; he stood up on being spoken to, but sat again on my motioning to him to resume his chair. I shall not in this life forget the peculiar magic that Miss Grant's beauty took on this silent night in our underground haunt, from the emotions which were in her; the struggling of her brave spirit with the superstitious fears excited by the negro, and *his* black face at hand to contrast her whiteness with. She sat beside but behind me, having regard to the black man's position; and full as my mind was of the fellow's startling apparition and miraculous recovery—if recovery it were, and not some baleful bit of fetish necromancy—I'd find my thoughts scattering away with confusion when I'd look from the bland ebony countenance on my left, with the whites of the eyes glowing out into orange to the candle light, to the loveliness of the face on my right, charged with the revelation of new beauty to every glance I gave it. I had never heard her speak Spanish before. Nervous and agitated as she was, the rich syllables of the noble tongue rolled in honey from her lips, and as was her face by the negro's, so was the melody of her Castilian utterance inexpressibly sweetened and heightened by the hoarse, thick speech of the red-coated fiend. It was like the warbling of a flute alternating with the gong-like roll of a tom-tom.

"What does he say?" said I, after he had been spinning a twister lasting over five minutes.

"Why," she answered, "that he woke as if from a long sleep this evening, some time after sundown, and found himself lying on the beach on his back, on the west side of the island, as I suppose, from his speaking of the situation of the hummock. He does not know how he came there. He recollects arriving here this morning in a boat, and fainting away after drinking the water you gave him. He says, after lying a little he rose and walked towards some trees, where he presently heard a sound of running waters. It was the brook that he means. He drank, and then sought for fruit, but appears to have lost himself in the forest; though a little before he made his appearance he came across the plantains. That is his story."

"Then," said I, looking at him, "it is no great mystery after all, though a mighty wonder all the same. He was not dead, *of course*, when he dropped after the drink. Well now, the big stone that I jammed into his waist-cloth must have rolled out of it when I hove him over the side. It was a sickening business, and the instant I had cleared the boat I sculled up the creek without looking astern. Then what could have followed? The poor fellow floated up on to his back, for he must have drowned with his face down, and was carried away by the tide to that part of the island where he stranded. Had we looked we might have seen him floating, but we were too busy with the boat; and when he had weathered the spit of sand he would be out of sight to us at the head of the creek. Ask him if he knows what this island is?

She addressed him again, speaking now with growing confidence, though her first superstitious fear hung a little lightly upon her. He shook his head whilst he answered. She spoke to him afresh, and then told me that he was not only ignorant of the name of this island, but had not the least idea of the situation of others in these seas; so there was an end of my expectations of him as a pilot. She questioned him further, and his story was to this effect:—First of all, he and his companion had been runaway slaves. They stole a boat, and blew out to sea from somewhere near Point Maysi, thinking to land at Tortuga, but were sighted and picked up by an English craft, and were entered as seamen aboard her; but the usage they met with was so barbarous, mainly owing to their inability to understand the orders addressed to them, that they resolved to run from the ship at the first opportunity that offered. A chance was provided by the master of the vessel bringing up under the lee of an island, probably not very remote from our own, to seek shelter, as was to be supposed, from the storm that had swept these waters the other night. There was a boat riding astern to a long line, and when the night came down dark, and the hands were below, saving the anchor watch, look-out, the blacks dropped over the side, their dusky skins making their movements very secret in the gloom, and swam stealthily to the boat. But it was already blowing with a bit of a popple on in the bay where the ship rode, with the flight of the wind scurrying down the mountain side, and they had scarce rolled in-board over the gunwale when the line parted, and they drifted out to sea. So this was the fellow's story, a bit of which I had anticipated hours before at the sight of the shredded strands of the rope. Trusting he might have a few words of English sufficient to understand my questions, so as to save Miss Grant the trouble of inquiring and then interpreting, I sang out to him—

"You speakee English?"

"No, no; no speakee," he cried, shaking his head vehemently.

"You no sabbe how to pilot boat?" I roared.

"No speakee, no speakee," he bawled, wringing his hands; and then looking at Miss Grant with eyes full of piteous entreaty, oddly accentuated by a broad supplicatory grin that bared his great ivory teeth to the junction of his jaws almost, he poured out a whole torrent of words in Spanish to her, clasping his hands whilst he rattled on, and then dropped plump on both knees before us when he had finished.

"What is it all about?" said I.

"He swears by the Holy Virgin and all the saints that he does not speak English," said Miss Grant, "and implores you to believe him. The poor fellow has been horribly cowed by ill treatment. He thinks because you are English you will punish him for not being able to speak our language."

I motioned to him to rise, and to top the encouragement of my face I mixed him another dram, which he drank on his knees, making some mysterious motion of amity, or perhaps affection, by holding one arm stiff upright after the manner of certain South African tribes; then rose and seated himself.

"It is getting very late," said I, looking at my watch; "there will be a long day before us in that open boat to-morrow, though pray Heaven it may not prove longer than a day. I would urge you to take some rest."

"I am not at all sleepy," she replied. "I am too excited to lie down; what with this apparition and the prospect of our sailing tomorrow, I shall not be able to sleep indeed."

"That poor fellow will want to turn in," said I. "Rolled up in a rug, he'll lie snug enough near the furnace. You will not object to his occupying this room?"

She looked askant at him, and said a little doubtfully, "No, I should have no fear of him at all but for the really terrifying wonder of his restoration to life."

Here the negro yawned prodigiously, uttering a bawling sound as he gaped.

"There is indeed nothing to be afraid of," said I. "Harmlessness in natures nearly allied to the animal as his is, is almost always expressed in the face, and I'd stake my right arm upon his being honest to the core—abjectly so indeed. For my part, humanity aside, I consider it my duty to cherish him. A hand to help in the boat will be invaluable. Imagine, for instance, a dead calm, with the gleam of a ship's canvas just visible on the horizon from the low level of the gunwale. Two of us might manage to row the boat to her; whereas my single pair of arms would give up exhausted long before I was able to rise the ship's hull. He is a powerful fellow; observe the breadth of his chest. Besides, he is a child of the sun, and the fittest help in the world for such an excursion as we are meditating under these heights, as the Ancient Mariner would call them."

So speaking I took a rug and handed it to the black, motioning him to make a bed of it against the furnace, to which I pointed. He understood me promptly, grinned gratefully, and wrapping the rug around him as he stood, with a proud glance at the embellishment, he lay down with the docility of a trained dog, using his arm for a pillow, and in a couple of minutes was snoring like thunder, sound asleep. Miss Grant withdrew to the inner room, whilst I stole up the steps to take a peep at the boat and see that all was right with her. Her outline showed black against the sand. The ebb of water had almost left her dry, and I had no fear of her. 'Twas a breathless night, with its odd accompaniment of whistling lizards, snoring toads, and chirruping crickets. It wanted but three hours to dawn, and at the first peep of the sun it was my intention to be up and away. The slip of moon glowed rustily over the western rim of the forest, where the heads of the trees spread like funeral plumes motionless against the sky. I lingered a little, earnestly contemplating the heavens in search of any hints of weather, then went back to the kitchen and lay down, but not to sleep. Indeed if the agitation of my spirits at the prospect of getting away had not kept me restless, I must have been held so by the negro's snoring. He now lay flat upon his back with his mouth wide open, and I can only compare the sounds he produced to the noise made by the keel of a boat dragged over shingle.

Presently Miss Grant called softly to know if I was awake.

"Very much awake indeed," said I.

"All is well whilst he snores like that," she exclaimed.

"Yes," I answered. "But it is happy for us that he should be our guest for one night only. Imagine three weeks of this!"

Chapter IV
We Leave the Island

I HAVE HEARD SWEETER MUSIC in my time than that negro's snore; but though it might have disturbed the repose of the dead, nothing was ever more comforting and soothing to me, as you will believe, when I say that I could not listen to the poor fellow's gasps without reflecting how very near indeed I had come to murdering him. My restlessness was a sort of fever, and six or eight times before the daylight came, I crept softly up into the open to take a peep at the boat, and make sure that she lay safe. Indeed, we had met with so many surprises on this island, that I was in a manner prepared for the strangest thing that could happen; and I believe had I looked forth out of the hatch and found the boat gone, whatever might be the emotions which would have helped to the madness such a loss must have raised in me, wonder would not have been of them.

I had made up my mind to steer west, knowing that the American seaboard lay that way, to say no more; but it was very vexing that the negro should be ignorant of the situation of this island, and unable to pilot me to the nearest inhabited land. The joy caused by possession of the boat had overwhelmed all other considerations; but now that I lay sleepless upon my bed of grass and rug, waiting for the skylight to glimmer out to the dawn, I found myself a bit disheartened by the prospect of the new voyage. That there was land down in the west within view from the ship's masthead, I did not doubt; but then it might prove such another little spot as this, verdant and uninhabited; in which case we should have to push on; and how far off might the nearest land to it be? It was a great ocean, as Miss Grant had said, for so little a boat. Strange, too, that one of my minor, seafaring nightmares should be fulfilled long after I had abandoned the profession, for I recollect that when I was at sea I would think with horror of exposure in an open boat, which to my young imagination threatened an experience scarce less fearful than the raft. Indeed, of the two, perhaps, the raft was the less horrible, for a man was not likely to linger long on such a contrivance, whereas in an open boat he might go on languishing for days until he died, and then be found a skeleton in the bottom of her, with the little craft afloat and buoyant after months of different kinds of weather. Nay, had not that morning indeed illustrated the significance of the open boat at sea: the dead man in her, that creature yonder pointing with ebony forefinger to his mouth filled with froth, the empty locker, the thirsty, oily smell of the paint, inside and out, exhaling to the roasting glare of the sun! Well, well, thought I, the sort of spirit I require is not to be got out of thoughts of this kind; and my eye then catching the dim, greenish lustre of the dawn, lying like waning moonshine upon the skylight, I started up, thanking God for daylight, and feeling that, let the future hold what it might, the bars of our prison here were broken, and we could now free ourselves from an unendurable confinement, which but yesterday morning was as hopeless to the heart as the bald sweep of the sea was to the eye.

"Is that you moving, Mr. Musgrave?" exclaimed Miss Grant, from behind her curtain.

"Yes," said I; "the dawn has broken. You have not slept, I fear?"

"No," she answered, "I have not closed my eyes."

"Pray endeavour to get a little sleep," I exclaimed. "Mumbo-Jumbo here can help me in the few preparations that remain, and I don't doubt of making myself understood. Even an hour's sleep will be helpful. Don't doubt that I shall call you when we are ready to get under way," I added, laughing.

She answered me by whipping back the shawl along the rod, and stepping forth.

How can you talk of sleeping *now?*" she exclaimed; "the instant you are ready, Mr. Musgrave, let us start."

I was glad to hear her say this. There was no fear of her hesitating to sail in the little boat into the vast sea that stretched around; but I had suspected she would express in her manner that her mind hung in the wind a trifle, and that she would show herself a little scared by a prospect that was far more formidable than it appeared, as *she* would know, as well as I.

The negro was snoring as briskly as ever. Heaven knows, this miserable old kitchen was only too familiar to us; yet it seemed to be made fresh, as though in faith we had stumbled upon another underground room, by the novelty to our eyes of that black man, resembling some immense performing monkey in his red coat, lying flat on his back, his mouth wide open, his arms extended, and the palms of his hands showing like dirty yellow paper inlaid in his skin to the jetty points of his thumbs and fingers. I stirred him with my foot, but I probed him in this way for some time before he opened his eyes. He then sat up with a glare of astonishment, whilst he grasped his wool, and whipped out in a thick, half-awake voice with a string of Spanish, sounding like the gurgling of water in a sucked hubble-bubble. However, he speedily grew conscious enough to understand Miss Grant when she informed him that it was time to get up, and that we wanted him to help us complete our arrangements for promptly leaving the island. He rose slowly on to his cucumber shanks, scratching his head with a dull stare of mystification, as I thought, in his dusky eyes as he rolled them from me to my companion, and then addressed her. She answered; he spoke again with growing energy; she nodded, on which, to my astonishment, he clasped his hands and dropped upon his knees, and fell to pouring out a whole jumble of words, the imploring character of which was gatherable from the tone of his voice.

"Why, what *is* the matter with the poor wretch?" said I; "have his wits left him during the night?"

"He is entreating me to beg you not to take him away from the island," said Miss Grant, viewing him with surprise and pity.

"But does he know," I cried, "that if we leave him here he will be all alone; not another black even to keep him company?"

She spoke to him again, motioning to him at the same time to rise from his knees. Her question produced a very long answer. His looks and inflections of speech pronounced him desperately in earnest. I could not follow a syllable; time was pressing, moreover, for I desired, when afloat, all the daylight I could get, and I was growing a little impatient, when Miss Grant turning to me said, "He desires to stop here. Indeed, I believe, could you even carry him to the boat by main force, he would jump overboard and swim back to the island on your letting go of him. He says it would be like being a king in his own country to live in these fine rooms, and have the island all to himself."

"Humanity forbids it," said I, amazed.

"But what is to be done?" she exclaimed; and I instantly echoed the question mentally, when I glanced at his robust figure, with some stupid thought of compulsion in my mind, and then reflected that he might detain us here for hours whilst we endeavoured to persuade him, without perhaps altering his resolution, after a most wearisome course of exhortations and representations, all of which would have to be translated if he was to understand them. I noticed him ogling the old muskets and cutlasses upon the wall, with a negro's affection for such toys kindling in his eye. No good could come of bothering ourselves over the matter, so I formed my resolution.

"If he won't come, why then of course he must stop."

"He will not come," she exclaimed; "he is a runaway slave, remember, fresh too from being cruelly treated even when dealt with as a freeman. He means to stop here, indeed."

"Then please tell him, Miss Grant, he may do as he pleases; but I should have been glad to have the use of those brawny arms. He can't starve, I believe and maybe when he wishes to leave he'll know how to go to work. We have no powder, but he is welcome to those muskets yonder," nodding towards them—I caught him watching me eagerly as I did so—"and he may as well take possession of all the traps we must leave behind; so there'll be clothes enough for him," said I, with a look at his shanks, "not to mention some pretty dresses when he has worn my coats out."

On this being interpreted to the poor fellow, he burst into a hundred passionate exclamations of joy, was so convulsed with delight, indeed, that I expected to see him plump down upon his nose and roll upon the floor in his ecstasy. He clapped his hands, made as if to embrace me, recoiled a step with a frantic skip, leapt with such agility that he struck his head against the ceiling with force enough to have stretched him motionless had his cranium been a white man's.

"Pretty good all this," I exclaimed, laughing in spite of myself, "for a man who was last night a ghost, and yesterday morning a corpse."

I had nearly completed all necessary preparations on the preceding day. The halliards formed of a length of coir rope, the strands unlaid, halved, and laid up again into a smaller line, were rove; the sail of coloured shawls was bent to the yard. There remained but little more to do than fill a few outstanding bottles with water, stow away the craw-fish, and the like. The boat was a roomy little craft; yet though there were but two of us, we found there would be space for no more than a small bundle of necessary articles chosen from the luggage we must perforce leave behind us. I asked Miss Grant to make a collection of such things as she might deem needful, taking care that at the utmost the parcel should be but a small one; and then putting the negro to the job of filling the remaining bottles with water from the brook, I slipped round past the creek for my morning plunge, from which I returned as much refreshed as though I had slept soundly all night. My next act was to climb the hummock, and take a last view of the sea from a spot whence I had surveyed it again and again, with many contending emotions of misery, hope, and despair. There was nothing in sight, a light air was fanning out of the north and west, with weight enough in it to put a blinding twinkling into the water where it was sun-touched; the heavens spread in a soft light blue, without the phantasm of a cloud anywhere visible. Sheltered by my wide, sombrero-like hat from the bite of the sun that, low as he yet hung over the sea, stung the naked flesh like nettles, I lingered a little, after bringing my eyes away from the silken brimming of the blue ocean to the azure distance where it blended with the heavens, to rest them for a few minutes upon the island.

The harsh *squawk* of the macaw, or some such fowl, came like the edge of a saw out of the heavy greenery of the forest; to every pause in the fitful blowing of the morning breeze a hundred sounds of bird and reptile life on the island—whistlings, croakings, rook-like cawings, the jabber of green and golden shapes, with short notes as of bells accompanying, chimes-fashion, the clear, melodious pipings of the very few birds who really could sing on that island—came stealing in a growing volume upon the ear, then softening again to some hot, soft gush of the wind that floated the strains of the concert backwards to the trees. The tall guinea-grass stirred to the creeping of invisible things; the draught of air breezing upon the weather-side of the forest set the branches dancing, and the verdure seemed to flash again to the lift of the foliage, as the silver under-lining of innumerable leaves shone out with the stirring of the air. Maybe I did not loiter above a couple of minutes, but thought has lightening rapidity, and I lived again throughout the three weeks we had spent on this beautiful island in the few seconds during which I stood contemplating the sunny scene. The setting of us ashore by the cold-blooded rascals of the *Iron Crown*, the crushing weight of hopelessness upon us as we sat together yonder, where the white sand wound in ivory to the creek, with our luggage heaped about us, no shelter for our heads, no prospect of deliverance; then the hollow and startling notes of the midnight bell, my strange discovery of the sand-covered hatch, our life in the darksome chambers underground there, the fright occasioned by the monkey, and now that boat snug in the creek yonder!—memory affected me like a succession of wild dreams. The mighty surface of the sea stared blindly at the sky, and for the life of me I could not repress a shudder as I glanced at the boat, and thought of the tiny speck it would presently be making upon that huge, broiling, merciless expanse.

I broke from my thoughts, and quitted the hummock with an odd and most bothersome fancy in me—so perversely does the imagination steer the mind—of what my cousin Alexander would say and think, supposing we should live to tell him the story, of the intimate association forced upon Miss Grant and myself by the perils of the ocean, of our living as though we were a couple of Indians underground, of our being thrown together for another spell of yet deeper intimacy in an open boat—pshaw! thought I, 'tis high time we got away.

But first it was our business to make as good a meal as we had appetite for. The negro ate like a cormorant, and since his resolution was formed, I hoped for his sake that there would happen no dearth of turtle whilst he chose to remain all alone by himself here. It made one think of Juan Fernandez and the solitary Mosquito Indian, to look at him. I asked Miss Grant to again endeavour to persuade him to accompany us, thinking that the fellow might now have changed his mind. But the moment he gathered her meaning his face filled with alarm; he stared at me so appealingly that it was impossible to watch him unmoved, and I think he would have gone down on his knees again but for something which Miss Grant said that reassured him.

"It cannot be helped," said I; "he is not a little boy; I cannot carry him to the boat. He may be even more lucky than we—I mean that a vessel may heave-to off here even before he is tired of the place. Have you collected what you want, Miss Grant?"

"Yes," she exclaimed, rising, and going to the inner room she brought out a little bundle. "I have shown great self-denial, don't you think?" she exclaimed, laughing, as she held it up.

I did not ask what it contained, though I afterwards came to learn that it consisted mainly of a few parcels of letters and bits of jewellery, and the like, prized entirely for the givers' sake. "It seems hard," she added, with a wistful look at her trunks that showed through the opening, "to leave all my pretty purchases behind. How patient you were, Mr. Musgrave, when you accompanied me on my shopping trips! What a number of things I could have done without if this experience had been foreseen!"

"Better," said I, "that this honest negro should possess them than that they should have foundered with the *Iron Crown*; for the bottom of the sea was bound to be their destination had they remained aboard. Now, if you take my advice, you will put on your broadest-brimmed hat, and our stock of umbrellas must go with us, lest a breeze of wind should carry one or more overboard."

I beckoned to the negro, and Miss Grant made him understand that he was to carry certain articles to the boat, and then entering her room I took down her hammock, which was a thing that stowed very compactly, and might be of use to her were we driven ashore upon such another island as this. I also gave the negro a good warm cloak to carry, a well-lined garment, that would serve as an excellent wrap for Miss Grant at night; but though we took these things, there was little more we conveyed to the boat—my monkey jacket, I remember, her and my pistols with powder and ball, a few remaining bundles of cigars, all the umbrellas we possessed, some rugs, and a few other items which I need not tax my memory to recall.

All being ready we slowly left the underground rooms which had sheltered us for three weeks, both of us sending lingering glances around as we quitted the dreary, dream-like haunt, and accompanied by the negro walked to the boat.

She was lying, half the length of her dry, upon the sand. The negro placed the parcels he carried in the bottom of her, then came to me, and letting go the line which held her, we put our shoulders to the bows, and drove the craft afloat. I jumped in as she slided into the brilliantly clear, calm surface, and throwing one of the paddles over, got her head round, then sheered her alongside the bank of the creek, extending my arm to Miss Grant, who sprang aboard. My next business was to coil the line away in the bow, then to thoroughly overhaul our little ship to see that her freight—more precious to us, mere craw-fish, turtle, bottles of fresh water as it was, than the richest treasure that ever put to sea in the hold of a register ship—was properly trimmed, and that nothing the island could supply us with was wanting. Miss Grant sat in the stern-sheets, sheltered by an umbrella. The radiance of the early sunshine came streaming down from the far eastern sea-line hot as moulten silver into the creek, and the glare of it, rising off the surface to the face, which it stung as though the lustre was formed of flaming needles, furnished a mighty uncomfortable hint of the sort of roasting that awaited us outside, when the luminary should rise to the middle of the sky. I threw the paddles over, and rowed slowly down the creek. There was no draught of air to be felt here, though the water outside was wrinkling to the fiery breathing that came softly out of the north-west. The negro walked along the bank to the edge of the spit, where, drawing his figure erect, he held his right arm high, and so stood watching us motionless, like a black statue whose nobly-proportioned trunk and arms some fool had smeared with red paint. I noticed my companion gaze wistfully landwards as we drew out. You saw in the expression of her eyes how busy her memory was, with a change in their soft, brilliant depths into a look of mingled wonder and uncertainty rather than of dismay, as they went seawards from the bright vegetation, the arid hummocks, and the tracks of white sand, whitening out from the dense undergrowth to the long space of dazzling coral platform on which the blue breaker was melting.

There was scarce an experience of mine on yonder island that did not recur to me as a passage in a dream might, so vague did the memory of it offer to my imagination through the sheer strangeness of the whole adventure. But nothing approached the dreaminess which the reality of this our departure took. It was not only the feeling that we were leaving the place for good—a prison from which we had again and again feared we should never have power to deliver ourselves;—no! the realization of escape, when the hope of escape has long lain dead, will always affect the mind at the first start as something visionary, something that one durst not believe. But it was not *that* only. It was the manner also of our going. It might have seemed to a strange eye, ignorant of the truth, as though this young girl and I were some young bride and bridegroom, with a little summer ocean home hidden away among the cool trees up there, and that we were starting upon a pleasure cruise, intending maybe a survey of our tiny principality, to which we should be returning anon. This was my fancy as we glided down the creek, and it was this that made the thing as unreal as a dream to me. It was sitter for a summer Thames scene than an illustration of human distress at sea. Who would have imagined, watching me in shirt and trousers and shoes, bare-armed, slowly plying the flashing paddles—who would have conceived, observing the quiet figure of the girl seated aft draped in white, carefully sheltering her face, the shadow of her wide hat enriching her warm beauty with the softness of the tint it made, though there was sparkle enough in the water alongside to touch her hair with a delicate light of gold—that we were quitting the island in search of succour, that we had launched ourselves on a boat voyage which might prove darker with peril to us than the blackest hour we had yet passed since we boarded the *Iron Crown* in the Downs, that instead of a sultry morning jaunt alongshore we were going to lose ourselves in the heart of the mighty ocean yonder, with no further hope in the result than we could get from confidence in the Divine guidance?

Once clear of the creek I hoisted our sail of shawls, flattening in the sheet and putting the helm down to test the little craft's capacity of looking up to it. The colours of the shawls were red, white, and blue, and at a distance the boat sliding out of the creek might have passed for a huge aquatic parrot, outward bound on some predatory excursion. The negro, with his figure standing boldly out at the extremity of the tongue of sand, now held up both arms, slowly moving his hands at the wrists. It looked as if he were blessing us, but I suppose it was his country's way of saying goodbye. Miss Grant waved her hand to him, and I bade him farewell with a flourish of my hat, whereupon he turned on a sudden and ran with incredible swiftness to the underground rooms, down whose hatchway he shot with the rapidity of a skip-jack plunging from its leap out of water, and so vanished.

"He has gone to clothe himself," said Miss Grant.

"Wonderful how he could have held out so long," said I; "the desire to squeeze himself into my patent leather boots and frock-coat, not to mention my green satin stock and several coloured shirts which he will come across, must have risen into madness whilst he stood holding up his arms. One guesses that by the rush he made when nature gave in. And now, Miss Grant, how is this little craft going to serve us?"

There was, as I have said, a draught of air fiery hot as the waftings of the atmosphere of a furnace blowing out of the north-west, with just weight enough to keep the water twinkling, and to thread it here and there with long, silken, dark blue shadows with the heavier scoring of its sparkling pressure. I hauled the sheet of the sail as flat as it would come, but could not get the boat's head round to within six points of this air; and even at that, when she had got way enough upon her to set the water slobbering and tinkling a bit along her clinker-built sides, I noticed a leewardly trend that sent her fathom or two of wake, oil-smooth with a few holes of eddies in it, veering away upon the weather quarter. I had no compass, and when we lost sight of land there would be nothing but the sun or stars to steer by; meanwhile however I made up my mind to head away north, keeping the boat as close as she would lie, and then supposing the breeze to hold, when we had put the island a mile or two astern, to go about on the starboard tack, and blow away as best we could, south and west, partly with the hope of rising the land in the west before sundown, and partly with the expectation of thrusting into the fairway south; for it was nearly always in the south quarter that the sails we had sighted from the hummock hove into view, with one or two in those three weeks gliding blue and ghostly in the far east, but none that ever we saw north or west.

"Our sail should make a brilliant signal," exclaimed Miss Grant, "if a ship should come within view of it."

"Yes," said I, "that was the thought in me when I hoisted it. Red, white, and blue, the proper sort of colour for English hearts to beat under. Ouashee's soul will have yearned for them. The red shawl would have made him a fine turban; indeed it would be finer as a turban than as a sail," I added with a glance at the yawns where the shawls had been taped together.

Yet the fabric was giving the boat some sort of way, and the island was slowly dwindling. It looked a radiant, gem-like spot now upon the ocean, that brimmed with a line of silver to the white sand. I sat watching it, the boat steering herself, for which I was mightily thankful, for the little tiller I had shipped grew into a heated bar of iron to the touch, and my bare knuckles felt as if they were flayed after keeping my hand spread to the sun a few minutes. I could not but hope that I was acting rationally in quitting the island in this little boat, for the solid land there at least supplied a certainty of refuge, which induced a wild emotion of misgiving when I glanced away at the huge sea, and thought of the gale that had swept it the other night. Yet we had both of us pined and prayed for such an opportunity of escape as had now come, and there seemed something like the profanity of ingratitude in hesitation, natural and reasonable as misgiving was at such a time.

I was startled from the reverie into which I had plunged by a sudden exclamation from Miss Grant, who sat near me bending over the side. She pointed down into the water, shrinking a little as she did so, with an expression of consternation glittering in her glance and dilating her eyes as she looked round at me. I peered over and saw immediately below, scarce six feet deep in the clear, blue, glass-like profound, the long dark form of a great shovel-nosed shark, with the upper barb of its tail rounding out like a scythe, the whole outline absolutely motionless, without a tremor in its fins that I could witness, though we were sliding along at some two or the miles in the hour, and the thing held its position as though it were our shadow. For the life of me I could not help a sudden recoil. It was as big and ugly a monster of the kind as ever I had seen, and by simulating, as it were, the reflection of our boat, furnished an appalling mockery in that way to the imagination—to *mine*, at least, which instantly went to work to construe the grim and foul adumbration into a foreshadowing of our fate.

But I pulled myself together quickly, and said, "One cannot sail these waters without sights of this kind happening. Stop! he may be routed out of this."

I took an oar and plunged it harpoon-wise at the brute, and struck him fair on the back. Ugh! the touch, the feel of it threw me into a cold sweat. It would have been otherwise with me had I barbed the beast, but the soft slippery contact was like the blow of a baby's fist upon the snout of a tigress. Yet it startled the creature nevertheless. With a sweep of its tail it drove ahead, sending a shoal of bubbles to the surface, with a line of sparkles in the blue beneath, and when we came to look for it again it was not to be seen on either side the boat. I met Miss Grant's eye thoughtfully fixed upon mine. The whole weight of my responsibility came upon me *then*, somehow. I knew that her trust was in me— that wherever I led she would follow in full faith in my judgment. Her life had grown so precious to me, that the mere fancy of imperilling it by any resolution I might form, hoping always for the best, was unendurable. I sent a glance into the hot azure distance, then at the island, then met her eyes afresh.

"If you are in the least degree timid—it is not too late. We can be ashore again in an hour," I exclaimed.

"I am not timid," she replied; "the sight of that great fish frightened me. Why should we return? Here is our chance for escaping; why should we neglect it?"

"True; but often bitter perils and privations attend attempts of this kind," I rejoined. "Your life is dear to me, Miss Grant;" her lips stirred, but I did not catch what she said. "Is it right," I continued, "that I should subject you to the risks and exposure of such a venture as this? I may have acted in too great a hurry, scarcely shown prudence in my hot desire to break from that jail there. This proposal now occurs to me. Let us return to the island. The negro will help me in my new plan. Here is a boat in which he or I may every day row or sail away into the southward, which is apparently the navigated tract of these waters, and it will be strange indeed if we do not meet with some vessel before long to which we can make our condition known."

"You would take me with you on such excursions?"

"No need. I should leave you on the island until we could obtain help."

She shook her head. "No," she exclaimed slowly, with great emphasis; and then she added, "Imagine the evening to come on one day and no sign of your boat. The night passes, and next day, and then weeks pass, and I am still alone. Oh, Mr. Musgrave, how can you *suggest* such a thing? When we were set ashore you said it made you happy to think that we were together. That was my happiness too," she continued, dropping her eyes for an instant, and then lifting them again to mine, "and now you will risk a separation—that—that—" She shook her head again almost bitterly, but smiled a moment after. "Besides," she went on, as though she had no patience to hear me, nor indeed meant to give me a chance to speak, "you would not get the negro to accompany you. No threats, no entreaties would prevail upon him, I am sure. He would dread to be recaptured. He has that island all to himself now, and a hole to live in, and is as free as a monkey in any forest in Brazil, and should you attempt to persuade or force him, what might happen? Another mutiny, Mr. Musgrave, more dreadful than the one on board the *Iron Crown*, with a chance of his taking your life, and of my being left alone with him!"

"Be it so," I said; "we are together, and together we will remain—at least for the present," I added, cooling down my voice suddenly to check the gathering ardency of it.

She made no answer.

Chapter V
A Day of Peril

B Y FOUR O'CLOCK IN the afternoon I reckoned the island to be about two leagues distant, scarce visible, so low it lay, save when the slide of the boat to the brow of the swell showed it "dipping," as they say at sea—just a blot of indigo blue upon the gleam running to it, and against the whitish azure behind. At about this hour the small, scorching breeze, that had held fairly steady from the north-west since the early morning, died away as though devoured out of the atmosphere by the blazing eye overhead, and the deep turned into liquid glass, with the heave of it due east. It was not an undulation to notice from a ship's side, or from the low elevation of the island; but to us in that boat it seemed as heavy as a strong sea, with the rise of it putting the horizon out of sight one moment, and the next making the bright line look to spread twice as far as it went in reality. One may talk of getting a sense of the mightiness of the deep when aboard a great ship that is hove by the surge with her thousand tons of freight, and the massive fabric of her spars and rigging roaring into the gloom of the tempest as a boy tosses a ball; but it is surely in the little open boat that one feels the power of the giantess most. You lie close to her heart, you feel the beating of it, your eyes are within arm's-length of the mysteries under her shining breast, the spirit within you takes measure of the volume and altitude of her respirations, and you are oppressed by an indeterminable emotion of awe, of a kind different from any the mind is sensible of in viewing the sea from an elevation, whether it be the edge of a range of coast or the rail of a tall vessel.

I had put the boat's head round for the south-ward a little time before the stark calm fell, but without her measuring a quarter of a mile of water in the time, I should say, so faint grew the breeze whilst slowly slackening into breathlessness. I said to Miss Grant that I could not imagine it hotter in the most scorching circle of Dante's Inferno. Why, I had but to stand up and let my arms hang up and down, and the sweat drained from my fingers' end, as though I had just been fished out of the sea. It was not the blaze coming down that one felt so much as the dazzle that rose off the edge of the water, lifting into the face as though from polished copper, and making one writhe and twist about in search of the shelter that neither umbrella nor hat could provide. At one or thereabouts we had made a little meal of plantains and craw-fish, along with a small draught from one of the bottles; and then—

though there was wind enough blowing to keep the feeling of fever out of the blood—even then I remember contemplating our stock of provisions with a melancholy eye as I ruminated upon the perishable qualities of them. But when this "furious calm," as the Spaniards call it, came, the fear I had for our food deepened. Though everything was cooked barring the fruit, it seemed cock-sure to me that our miserable store of boiled turtle and the like must putrefy right away off, and leave us nothing but our oranges and bananas to eat. We were without bread, biscuit, flour. People putting away from a ship in our condition will, for the most part, unless they are very unfortunate indeed, carry with them food that defies climate—meat in tins, bags of bread, with other matters designed for seafaring use. But two-thirds of our stock might not keep sweet through the night, and the very plantains me-thought must rot speedily to such a blasting and withering eye as the sun looked down upon us with. But though now and again I would send a wistful glance at the blue smudge in the distance whenever it showed, I said nothing. The die was cast, we had to abide by the throw. It would have been wanton in me to suggest a return to the island after what Miss Grant had said; and as to the provisions, I comforted myself with reflecting that the coconuts, at all events, would hold their virtue, whilst I also considered that I had done my best—that what the island yielded we had taken—and that no man, though he thought with the spirit of a prophet in him, could do more.

Miss Grant made no complaint. It was seldom that I met her eye but that she had a smile. It seemed to me that now she was confronted with something tangible, a condition she could realize, a situation of which the issue, whether life or death, was within the grasp of her mind, her spirit rose to it. It would make me shrink at times to cast a look around the sea, for when the island disappeared the vast solitude in which we floated became sheer ocean to every sense, full of the desolation which the distressed heart would give to it, and which there was nothing in the glory of the day to mitigate. But her eyes sought the distance fear-lessly; twenty moods alternated in her, as I saw in her varying expression; but no hint of timidity was ever visible in one of them. Indeed it was the heroic tranquillity of her look that kept me still. The heat tried me fearfully, the dead calm was like a sensible weight upon my spirits; I had worked hard on the previous day, and had not closed my eyes for twenty-four hours; and such was my temper, as I sat in that small scorched boat dodging the swing of our preposterous sail for the idle comfort of the shadow of it, that I needed but a face opposite me to reflect mine to have exhausted myself with grumblings and lamentations, and maybe to have resolved, the instant the cool of the evening came, to hark back again for the island as nimbly as our paddles would sweep us there.

However, I got the better of all this unmanly weakness after the sun went down; though whilst he was going I could have stood up and shaken my fist, as Tom Cringle did, at the vast red, rayless body that looked, as his lower limb hovered a moment or two on the sea-line, to be sipping the blood streaming from his own fiery substance into the water beneath him. There was no air, not the fluttering of a breath, to touch with the shadowing of a feather the immeasurable liquid surface breathing in oil with the sluggish panting of some sentient thing half dead with the day-long pouring of the luminary upon it. Whilst the last beam of daylight sent its red flash across the sea, with a running of the crimson stream of wake to the orb as though 'twere a length of cloth of purple gold that he dragged off the sea with him as he slipped down the side, I stood up on the thwart with my arm around the mast, and carefully scrutinized the horizon. There was nothing to see, no longer even the island's dim shadow, which was already absorbed by the airy gloom creeping with tropic stealthiness and celerity also into the atmosphere now that the hour of sundown was passed. I lowered the sail to save the chafe of it, and carrying a bunch of plantains into the stern-sheets, made with Miss Grant a little supper of them, helped with a bit of cold turtle.

"Do you remember," she said, "when we walked together at Deal on that moonlight night, the day before we sailed, that I said the beauty of the sea frightened me with its immensity, that the magnitude of its sublimity was an oppression which forbade delight? I remember some fancy of the kind occurring to me," she said, musingly, her face stealing out pale in the shadow, with a corresponding deepening of the luminous dusk of her eyes. "But how should such beauty as this," glancing round, and then up at the sky that in the east was already velvet-like, with the young moon in the midst of it, whilst the stars seemed literally to shower out upon the gaze if you did but watch any space in the heavens for a little, "affect people situated as we? How *tremendous* it all is, Mr. Musgrave! There was never this sort of repose on the island. Listen!"

I strained my ear, whilst she looked at me with a faint smile.

"Not a sound," she exclaimed, after a few moments; "not a breath, not a whisper of air. Ashore there was always the simmering of the surf, some stirring of breeze or pinions amidst the foliage, and the song of the crickets, and the rest of the midnight concert. But here; oh, listen!"

She paused again, with her hand lifted.

"Holy Mother of God!" she cried, with a passionate toss of her arms. "Only think of being *alone* in this boat!"

"I don't think my loneliness would last anyhow," said I; "I guess, as Jonathan says, I would give myself about two such nights as this to have a whole ship's company of spectres along with me. There are plenty of green navies under our keel for marine phantoms to rise up out of. Yes," said I, pulling a cheroot from my pocket for the blessed solace of the mere smell of the weed, "it would not take me two such nights as this to introduce a very attractive society betwixt these gunwales. With my mind's eye I already see it clearly: here, where you are sitting, some mariner that fell overboard when Columbus was sailing this way, his eyes full of Spanish fire, moustachios curled upon his cheeks, and the body sheathed in old metal, for they wore armour in those times, though I won't swear that the forecastle Jacks went so clad; yonder in the bows a grim old buccaneer, some tough, sun-blackened rogue of the days of James I, wearing a spiked beard, and grizzled locks flowing upon his back, a great fusee across his knee, and a murderous hanger against his hip; it is not hard to see him sitting yonder in the bows, his arms folded, his head drooped, and a falcon-look fixed upon me under the sleepy lid—— Why, Miss Grant, these imaginations won't do, you know," I added, chipping at a little flint for a light; "but this silence is wonderful though, and Lord, how the dew falls!"

It was the dark roll of the swell perhaps that rendered the hush more oppressive to one's thinking of it; for the silence with which the folds swung along put an inexpressible quality of ghostliness into the reality of the dusky run of the water. Expectation seemed to crave for sound with the sight of such voluminous movement, and it made me feel deaf sometimes to look at it and hear nothing.

You would suppose that a couple placed as we were would find nothing to talk about but our situation, of ships heaving in sight, of the time our stock of provisions and water would last, and so forth. Instead, we conversed on any other subject. Not that we desired to shun such topics; we would recur to them at intervals; but in the main our chat was on matters in which it seemed almost like a sort of impiety to take interest at such a time as this. I very well recollect that, one thing leading to another, she gave me a description of society at Rio, of the balls, the dresses, the dances; how the English held aloof; the brutal treatment of negroes by blacks who, having been themselves slaves, had ended by becoming the possessors of slaves. There were long spells at a time when we forgot where we were in listening to one another. I had been struck by her exclamation when she spoke of how she should feel were she alone in this boat, and asked her if she was a Roman Catholic.

"No," she exclaimed; "how strange, now, that we should have been together for so long a while, and that you should not know what my faith is!"

"Not so strange if you will but think of it," said I. "There are no churches at sea, and old Broadwater's discipline was not of a sort to furnish one with a chance of discovering a fellow-passenger's religion."

"My mother died a Catholic. She wished me to be of her faith, and of the faith of her forefathers. My father belonged to the Kirk, Mr. Musgrave, and my mother was a very sweet, yielding, docile woman, and I am glad it is with me as it is, though I feel that to be good is to be all. To be able to say that if God can read your heart you need not be afraid, is to be happy within yourself—"

Hark! what was that? We both started. A strange sound came sweeping along the polished brows of the undulating water, as though some steamer at the distance of a mile or two were letting off steam at regularly respiratory intervals. It was a long, seething, blowing noise, followed by the sharp showering sound of water foaming into water from the height of a cataract. It was right astern of us. I turned and peered into the dimness there, but could see nothing.

"What is it, do you think, Mr. Musgrave?"

The girl's question was answered by the sudden upheaval of a long black line floating up like the keel of an inverted ship, with a brilliant sparkling of phosphorescent light all along the ebon side of it, off which rose a faint gleam to the reflection of the horn of moon and to the shine of the planets and bright stars in the wet blackness, instantly followed by the same steamlike hissing we had before heard, only that it was now so close the blast of it came tingling to the ear through the dead hush; and with this sound there rose into the dusk a great feather-shaped, cloudy spout of water, green as emerald, and radiant as though it were vapour illuminated by the glare of a signal-light with the sea-fire that swarmed in it.

"A big whale, by Jove!" said I, "and unpleasantly near to us too."

Indeed the black mass had risen within pistol-shot; but the very element of fear its proximity induced deepened the impressiveness of the dark grandeur, the majestic, mysterious beauty of the show. Oh, never to be forgotten was the sight of that leviathan shadow oozing out of the indigo gleamless stagnation, looking half a mile long with the loom of it upon the clear obscure, the sea rippling in fire against its sides, and its liquid spout shooting up into a column like a dull green flame, arching over at its summit as though curled by a breeze of wind, and falling in a burning shower into the water that flashed to the discharge, till the curved substance of the big fish loomed as big and black again as it was against this mystic radiance of its own making. Presently the huge shape melted out, but some time afterwards it spouted afresh down in the south-west, the bulk of it rising fair in the slender feathering of silver under the moon, whilst a second monster blew about a mile away down in the north, the sounds following one another through the silence for all the world like some mighty giant rumbling into a few snores in his sleep; and then we saw no more of the creatures, though the notion that there might be others about kept us both exceedingly uneasy with the fancy of a sudden shattering hoist-up starwards with the rising of one of these monsters under our keel, its blow-hole right amidships of us.

Not a breath of air yet. You saw the exquisite polish on the water in the untarnished flake of some large star's reflection as it rode the black brow of the swell, widening as it went. During such dead hours as these I knew there would be no earthly chance for us; for, as I have long ago said, steam was not as it is now. There was but sail to think of, and nothing could be stirring on such a night. The atmosphere was heavy with dew that made it cool. The thwarts and the line of the boat's gunwale sparkled with the moisture as though crystallized. I shipped my pea-coat to keep my shirt dry, and wrapped a shawl round Miss Grant. As bad a part as any of it all was the want of space; the cramped feeling that came into the body with the very look of our narrow quarters, let alone the reality of them. She was a fat boat happily, of a lubberly, motherly roundness, like the half of an apple, staunch and comparatively new, an honest ship's quarter-boat, in a word, worth dollars enough I dare say to have brought some evil mutterings into the throat of the skipper of the ship she had belonged to, when he peered over the stern and found her gone. Her beam and the heaviness of her build, that gave her a firm seat on the water, enabled us to move without fear of capsizing her, and from time to time I would give Miss Grant my hand, and get her to step from thwart to thwart for the ease and comfort of the motion after the long spells of cramped sitting.

At last it came to an hour when I told her she must lie down and sleep.

"I shall be able to doze as I sit here, I am sure," she answered.

"Be guided by me, my dear Miss Grant. Every bone in you will ache like the gout if you slumber seated on this hard board with your back against the side. See, now, the sort of bed I have had in my mind for you all along."

I placed a strapped rug in the bottom of the boat, close against the stern-sheets, to serve as a pillow, then spread other rugs along with shawls, as a mattress, reserving yet a rug, for we were well supplied in this way, to cover her with.

"Now," said I, "if you will remove your hat, and pull the hood of your cloak over your head and lie down, you will rest as comfortably as ever you did in your underground room."

"Why will you not take some rest first, Mr. Musgrave? I can keep watch, if indeed any sort of watchfulness is necessary on such a death-like night as this. Sleep whilst you can. There may come a change of weather which will prevent you from obtaining repose. You can trust me to awaken you if the need for doing so should happen."

But I said no; she had not closed her eyes last night. I would call her by and by, and then she could relieve me, as the sea-saying is. She would have remonstrated, but I took her hand, pressed it to my lips, with a gentle courting of her, by retaining her hand, to leave her seat, so without saying more she removed her hat, turned that I might adjust the hood to her head, and lay down. I covered her carefully, snugging her little feet which extended under the thwart, and then fitted a small umbrella over her head to shelter it from the dew. I asked her if she was comfortable, peering as I spoke under the umbrella at the deli-cate glimmer of the beauty of her brow and cheek in the shadow there. She answered gently, yes; and disengaging her hand from the shawl, extended it to me.

"How good you are, how kind you are!" she exclaimed. "Oh, Mr. Musgrave, how would it have been with me but for you? And how do I repay you?—by bringing you into these cruel experiences and wretched adventures."

I again pressed my lips to her fingers, that being the only answer I dared make just then, and sat down to chip in an agitated way at my tinder-box for a light to consume the cheroot that was but half smoked out. When I hear people talk of romantic situations, picturesque sur-roundings, and the like, I sometimes look back and recall that night, and put it before me. Romance!—let the reader, if he be a man, take my place in fancy—as my place then was—and shut his eyes and think. Why surely, if poetry is ever to be found in conditions of human dis-tress, I fancy you will find the sanctification of it in our situation this night in an open boat—alone—amidst the scarce visible undulations of the dark ocean, stretching with a measureless shadow into the liquid gloom that looked as far off as the celestial lights which shone in it; alone!—but the more alone for the sight of the stars trembling their multitudinous, unsympathetic gaze at us—eyes as they seemed to me of countless phantoms heedful of us only out of curiosity—with the vast silence between, that you *felt* as a breathless pause up there, as if some expected end were at hand which the Spirit of Night, inclining towards us with respiration checked, was awaiting. And that was not all either; indeed it was the least part of it to my mood then. Add the lovely form of the woman, for whom my passion was already deep if secret, reposing at my feet. The eyes of a lover's imagination, like those of a cat or an owl, see best in the dark; and the wan gleam of her face— for a *gleam* the whiteness of it looked—was wrought by my fancy into the damask beauty and rich impassioned glances of the sunlit reality; till, though she lay there vague as the dusk could make her, she yet slumbered before me in her perfections, so that through a long spell of that watch 'twas a sort of doting with me, from which I was not to be broken away by an occasional thought of Alexander clipping in between.

Indeed, I was beginning to think that I had earned this woman; that our association was now, as it had been all along, of a kind to render possession an obligation; nor was my honour any longer startled by such fancies. In love, I suspect a man's conscience towards others is sensitive as his passion is weak. His fine talk of duty is proportioned to the slenderness of his stake of emotion. As his heart sinks into a woman's, moral obligations are left behind, floating atop like bladders whose support he no longer requires. Whilst I sat swaying with the heave of the boat, sucking at my cheroot, my mind went to Alexander, and I thought to myself, as I glanced at the sleeping girl, and then swept my sight over the great desolation of the star-touched sea. Does not my cousin *deserve this*? Has he not brought it about? He knew that I was a single man, accentuated it, indeed, that he might correct any hesitation in me. He was also aware that I was young. Was it just in him to urge upon me a long shipboard intimacy with a beautiful woman, and expect me to emerge unscarred from such commerce, whole-hearted, capable of resigning her with a smile and a handshake, as if she were some parcel of precious stones of which he was the consignee? When the hour to surrender her arrives, I thought, looking down—but, Lord, will it ever arrive? And I remember shuddering wildly and on a sudden, with an involuntary hugging of my pea-jacket to me, as though a chill had come into my marrow, to the presence of this high and sparkling night, and to the black sweep of the sea-line, and to the solitude made awful by the silence and enormous by the low-lying stars.

I dropped my extinguished fragment of cigar over the side. The water was so full of fire that the fall of this mere morsel of leaf chipped a flash out of it like a spark from a horse's hoof against a flint; and as though the lambent flame had ignited some fantastic firework shape beneath it, there sparkled out, green and bright, the huge outline of a shark, the beast of the afternoon maybe. The creature looked as if it were the sketch of such a thing, painted by a brush dipped in flame in the dark water. It was moving stealthily; the tremor of its fins made just a little showering of spangles at those extremities, with a thin, green, fiery vein of wake streaming out from its tail like a rubbing of phosphorus on the wall of a darkened room. The shining configuration drove ahead a short way past the bows, and then the lines of light blackened out, whereby I knew that the beast had come to a stand. But the shape shone again presently, heading towards the moon's reflection, and vanished. However, it was horribly uncomfortable to feel that such a creature was lurking near, and it checked my romancing in a most magical manner. I could think no more of Alexander. My yearning now was for a breeze. But the star-flakes rode as unblurred as droppings of quicksilver upon the swing of the swell, and there was not the sound of a sigh of air to be caught stealing through the silence of the night.

It would be about three o'clock in the morning—some three-quarters of an hour before dawn at all events—that Miss Grant suddenly sat up with a little exclamation of astonishment, to which cramp might have added a note of its own.

"Oh!" she cried, "I have been dreaming. I did not know where I was. Pray help me up, Mr. Musgrave."

"The dawn will be here shortly," said I; "why not sleep the night out?"

"The dawn! Then you have let me take more than my share of rest. Pray help me up. I have slept soundly."

On this I cleared away the umbrella, removed the shawl that wrapped her about, and assisted her on to her feet.

"Still the same dead calm," she exclaimed, looking round her. "Now, Mr. Musgrave, you will please lie down."

"No, I can get the forty winks I want here quite comfortably."

"But you will go on talking, if you sit instead of lying down, and thus a second night will pass without your having closed your eyes."

"But I don't need to plank it to sleep," said I. "I won't talk, I promise you. Observe now how in earnest I am," and so saying, I turned up the collar of my coat, folded my arms, and let drop my chin in a proper sleeping posture; and sure enough, in less than three minutes I was in a sound slumber, for I never could have imagined how worn out I was until I shut my eyes and fairly got under way for a doze.

It seemed to me that I had not been sleeping five minutes when I was awakened by Miss Grant moving; I started, and found myself leaning my full weight against her, my head very coolly resting upon her shoulder.

"I am so grieved to disturb you," she said; "but a little breeze has sprung up, with some clouds darkening down in the west there, and I knew you would wish me to arouse you."

The dawn lay green to starboard, a queer, most melancholy smudge of muddy light, looking to ooze rather than to flow up into the dusk, as though it was some dull, thick, luminous atmosphere lifting with difficulty against the palpable obscure. The raven-hued sea-line ran straight as a rule against it. A twinkling of running waters was in the air, with delicate seething noises of ripples coursing nimbly into foam. Indeed, it was blowing a pleasant breeze of wind, with a hint of briskness presently in the hum of it sweeping out of the western gloom; with the stars all eclipsed down *there* by range upon range of dusky shadows, which gave a significance to this wind that woke me to my full senses promptly enough, I can tell you, as soon as ever my sleepy eye turned to the larboard seaboard.

"Due west, as I live!" said I, "since that faintness yonder must be in the east. Heaven deliver us! Why couldn't this blessed air have come away with the sun?"

"It may give us the sight of a ship though," she exclaimed, "let it blow whence it will."

"Ay," said I, "and thanks for that grain of comfort. But it is abominably mortifying nevertheless. Needs must, however, where Old Nick drives, and so, Miss Grant, for a ratch to the southward, if our shawls will suffer this little hooker to look that way."

I rose, and added, "How good of you to pillow my head! We are supposed to be irresponsible in our sleep; but I think I showed myself pretty rational—I might have swayed towards the gunwale instead—but you should have shaken me off."

"Indeed," she answered quietly, "you *did* sway towards the gunwale, and that you might rest, with some little comfort, I coaxed your head to my shoulder."

"And it went willingly enough, I don't doubt," said I, somehow wishing she had made more of this by her voice, for it was too dark yet to see the expression of her face. But then it was impossible not to forget at moments that she and I were alone.

I laid hold of the halliards and mastheaded the yard, and bringing the sheet aft, got it flat with a good lee helm, and in a moment or two the breezy ripples were washing along the boat's bends; but though I dragged the sheet as flat as I durst, dreading to rend the shawls by too hearty a pull, I found I could not bring the dawn, that was brightening fast, on our lee-beam. In fact, the sun rose broad upon our bow, and there were we heading away southeast, with a westerly breeze in chase of us, and no chance of the boat making a better course, trim as I might. But this, like everything else that had happened, could not be helped. So soon as the sunlight flashed fair over the sea, I stood up and took a long look around, then seated myself again with a momentary sickening of heart to the bitter familiar sterility of the broad spread of ocean. There was no sign of our island either, though it was impossible it could be many miles below the horizon. The clouds that at dawn had looked swollen and dark as thunder, showed white and swelling as snow-covered mountains now that the sunlight was upon them; but though they rose slowly, I was sure they meant wind, the more so from the colour of the sky floating out of them, a dimmish blue, moist and filmy, to where it brightened into the dazzle of the sun. But spite of its being a bad wind for us, the sound of it in the air, the sparkling movement of the waters, the life that the blowing put into the whole scene, came grateful as a relief after the clock calm of yesterday and the night. Some hope was to be got out of it, at all events; not a flicker of foam but that might at any moment change into the star-like shining of canvas; whereas the roasting tranquillity of the hours we had passed through, topped by the deadness of the night, forbade so much as a wistful fancy in that way.

I glanced at my companion to observe how she was weathering this bad time. There was a little languor perhaps in her eyes, a suggestion of weariness in the set of her lips, and her face was pale; but I witnessed nothing beyond; no symptom of the haggardness which follows long exposure, and the sort of anxiety that is bred by the constant confrontment of danger. She met my gaze with a smile full of spirit, and patience, and serenity.

"You are bearing all this far better than I should have dared hope," said I, "but some sort of end must be at hand surely. Why, it would imperil the reputation of a writer of romance as an artist to add in his book even but one more adventure to the catalogue we have left astern."

"We have been so mercifully watched over so far," she answered, "that I am sure we need not fear what remains to come. And then when it is all over how small it will seem!" I shook my head doubtingly. "Oh yes," she cried, "it is the same with all sorts of trouble. People when they are ill think they can never forget their sufferings; but they do, or at least they make very little of them when they get well. It is like the weather that is hot or cold, or wet or dry, outside the memory of the oldest inhabitant. But it passes from the mind, and at the end of the year it is all one, Mr. Musgrave."

"Well," said I, "yours is very good philosophy to help one to triumph over ills which have passed, but whilst those ills are with us, the victory, I fear, must remain with them."

Slowly the breeze freshened, but scarce with weight sufficient in it yet to raise sea enough to render me uneasy. The clouds in the west gradually soared, and some scatterings of them in feathers and crescents of vapour, blown from the brows of the main body, sailed like so many new moons into the blue mistiness. The sun glared strong over the bow, with so much throbbing brilliance in the ocean all that way, that the eye wept if you but rested it there for a moment. But the wind took something of the sting out of the heat, and the plash of the foam over the side was so refreshing to the ear that the sound of it seemed to melt with a sensation of coolness through and through the system. We broke our fast with some craw-fish and oranges, and a drink of water; meanwhile incessantly directing glances round the sea in search of a ship, for it seemed impossible that such a wind as this could hang steady, with our own southerly trend besides, without heaving something to help us in sight.

As the morning advanced the breeze freshened. The clouds were now broken up into vast puffs of vapour, white as steam, which came rolling stately out of the west, darkening wide spaces of the running, frothing blue with violet shadows. The sea was beginning to hollow a bit, too; the ridges growing wider and deeper, along with the sound of snarling in the seething slide of their heads. The yawns in the sail where the shawls had been united widened; the yard I had manufactured from a bough of a fallen tree fell to buckling uncomfortably to the growing leaps and plunges of the boat. Indeed, I presently found that if the shawls were to stand the sheet must be slackened out yet, so that before it was ten o'clock that morning we were running eastward with the wind almost astern of us, blowing away as fate would have it in the quite wrong direction; a windy sky behind, a hollow sea all about us, and nothing in sight save a dull, slate-coloured smudge just visible

when a sea threw us up, far away down upon the starboard quarter—
our island no doubt, for its bearings, according to my calculation, were
thereabouts. Could we only have hoisted cloths on our masts fit to sail
such a boat as this by, I believe I should have tried for that island again,
if only to freshen ourselves up by a rest ashore, and to lay in a further
stock of fruit. It was some years since I had handled a boat, but it would
all have come back to me quickly, I dare say, had we had shipshape
and seaworthy materials to deal with; but there was nothing to be done
with the shawls. They would have parted to any approach to tension of
the sheet, and so there was no luff at all to be got out of them. However,
by noon I had begun to think that were we under as honest a lug-sail
as was ever mastheaded, I should have had to up helm and run for it,
for it was now blowing fresh; indeed such a wind as a ship on a bowline would offer a main-topgallant-sail to, and nothing above it. Under
our queer sail that looked like a Dutch flag, the colours up and down
instead of horizontal, we stormed along, driving God knows where,
saving that we knew the great Atlantic Ocean stretched past the throbbing boundary over our bows. The little boat sheered through it like an
arrow, making one long floating slide after another, with a short pause
in the drop of her stern to the yawn of water, and then a lightning-like
rush forwards as the running sapphire knoll in chase washed brimming to her, giving us a hoist that caused the ocean to look as wide and
wild again; with the flash of the wind too into our gaudy spread of sail
that made me regularly expect to find it in rags next minute. The little
craft needed nice steering. The foam would come boiling to your fingers as they clasped the gunwale, and the least swerve at such a moment
must have swamped and drowned us out of hand. It was a rushing
scene indeed, and there was something of madness to our distracted
brains in the eager flashing life of it all. The rolling of the clouds along
the sky; the headlong passage of their shadows over us; the leap of the
sun from the edge of one wide mass of vapour to the next; the swift
hurl of the seas—the swifter to the eye for their impatient, impetuous
heave of the snow from their brows to ahead of them—the sparking out
of flying-fish from either side our running boat; the shriek of the wind
past our ears when it swept fair and full at us to the rise of the little fabric to the height of the surge; the blue finger-like dartings of the breeze
upon the smooth sides of the liquid slopes ahead, combined with the
sensation of our helpless velocity, offered such a picture of movement to
the imagination, that the mind might be defied to witness the like of it
even amidst the commotion of a tempest from the deck of a large ship.

Miss Grant sat by my side, apparently unmoved. I'd see her some-times glance astern in the moment of some unusually high billow run-ning us up with a roar and dazzle of foam to the level of the quarters, but without a hint in her face of quailing to the sight, without a tremor in the decision you saw in the marble-like set of her lips. This was one of the realities indeed her spirit could confront. She had shrunk from entering the underground rooms, she had been exceedingly perturbed by the midnight tolling of the bell in the forest, and now amidst a peril that might most honestly have blanched the cheek of a tough old salt, she was as calm as though she slumbered. Sometimes, but at long inter-vals, she addressed me. It was almost impossible to converse, however. The mere sight of the flying sea kept one's thoughts in a wild popple, like the water, disjointing the links of coherence almost. The noises too were horribly confusing—the ceaseless hiss of billows breaking into foam, the distant thunderous sound of warring waters swelling into volume, with the scream of the wind cleaving *it*. Besides, what wits I had I required to devote to the steering. Our salvation indeed might lie in the holding out of our sail, and in the drag of it that was rushing out keel clear of the smother of the avalanches chasing us; but then it was just the sort of navigation to be tyrannic in its demands upon the nerve and eye; the swiftness of the boat made her responses to the movement of the helm so instantaneously sensitive that the controlling of her to the course of a dart engrossed every thought I had mind enough to summon. One heedless movement of the tiller, and the next minute would have seen the boat bottom up.

And still the sea went frothing to its confines tenantless, our little craft the only object visible upon its breast for leagues and leagues. Were our adventures to end then in our being drowned after all? Had we quitted the island where at least our lives were safe if our existence was miserable, to court, as my fears had sometimes foreboded, a miser-able fate? My unemployed hand instinctively sought that of the girl by my side. She held it as if she would comfort me by so doing, smiling to my swift glance at her, for I durst then have no eyes but for the boat.

"You are steering the little ship admirably," she exclaimed; "the wind does not increase, I think, and if this be so, then since we have been safe so far, we have a right to hope that all will continue well with us. Don't be dispirited. Your old instincts as a sailor are equal to worse difficul-ties than this."

"Blessings on my head for having brought you here!" said I. "You speak of my old instincts as a sailor; they should not have driven me into acting the fool. We ought to have remained on the island. I was mad to subject you to the experiences of an open boat."

"I would sooner be here," she answered. "There is hope for us in this little flying shape; there was none on that dismal rock, with its gloomy cave and the silence of the night there."

This was as much as we could say at a time.

The strong breeze held all day, freshening at moments with noisy guns and spiteful blasts, but happily these stormy intervals were of short duration, otherwise such a sea must have been set running us would have yielded me but a poor chance indeed of keeping the boat afloat. I thought the day would never come to an end, though I dreaded its ending too, when my mind went to the prospect of the dark night that was to come, with the added weight of wind, which in all probability would follow the sun's departure. From time to time a sea dissolving in foam under us would lap inboard on either hand, with a pouring of seething white water that hissed to our ankles as the little craft swung her nose up; and on these occasions, not daring to let go the helm, I was forced to put Miss Grant to the job of baling, which she managed with wonderful spirit and swiftness, flinging the water out over the side with the soup and boulli tin that we used for a drinking vessel as fast almost as the second-hand of a watch travels, till the boat sprang forward again freed from this cold, sobbing, and sinister freight.

A little before sunset I spied a sail right ahead. The angry crimson in the west seemed to roll like the clouds into the far east, where it hung in a smoking red haze that looked cyclonic with the huddled loom of the vapour behind it, driven in a heap down there by the wind, and in the heart of this stormy radiance I saw the sail. But whatever the craft might be she was hull down, and the red canvas of her, more like a live cinder than the fabric of a vessel, was to be caught only from the head of a sea when it lifted us. I pointed it out to Miss Grant, rather for the hope the sight might yield her than for any imaginable good it could be to us; and she rose, passing her arm round my neck to steady herself, and there was so much of an unconscious caress in this action, as though her heart dictated a gesture unnoted by her reason, that it was through Heaven's mercy alone the thrill of delight the contact of her white hand against my neck sent through me, did not cause me to head the boat off and founder her.

She had barely resumed her seat, and was seemingly about to address me, when the wind breezed up with a shriek, the puff taking us precisely as we swung to the ridge of a billow, and away went the shawls, all three of them vanishing ahead like a fragment of rainbow, leaving the yard in halves, hanging to the halliards like the legs of a pair of compasses slightly open. I half rose with the intention of converting the shawl that had been wrapped about Miss Grant during the night into a jib-headed affair, which might provide surface enough to scud under, with some promise of the pull of it keeping us ahead of the seas, but I changed my mind on second thoughts. "Where are we going to?" I asked myself. "Here I am, suffering this boat to be blown out into the Atlantic Ocean, when our hopes of salvation lie over the stern."

I said to Miss Grant, "Please catch hold of this tiller—so. Hold it steady as you have it, straight fore and aft, that you may keep the boat dead before the wind."

She did as I bade her. I sprang forward, unstepped the mast, and taking the two paddles bound the three together securely by the halliards. This done, I secured the bundle to the end of the coir rope that lay coiled down in the bows. I then called to the girl to put the helm over, motioning to her that she might know which way to thrust the tiller, and the instant the little craft came broadside to the sea, I flung the bundle of mast and paddles overboard, then floundered aft, moving as low as I could in the boat, scarce knowing whether the next minute would not find us drowning. It was a necessary but a most dangerous manoeuvre in that sea. She rounded quickly head on to the pull of that rope; but ere the drag of her could tauten the line she hung a breathless moment or two in the trough, with the sea like a dark wall to windward rearing its head to the height of my own stature, flickering duskily against the crimson in the west, and I could not fetch a sigh, so sure was I that the sweeping volume would tumble sheer over us. But the broad-beamed little structure went floating up it broadside on, with her keel at right angles, whilst I gripped the gunwale with one hand, my right arm encircling Miss Grant to save her from sliding into the water to leeward—and this without shipping more water than a small thunder-shower of spray blowing over us off the brow of the surge as we mounted it. Then as the boat swept into the hollow behind, she tautened the rope and whipped her nose round to the sea, and so lay rising and falling, heavily indeed but comparatively safely, behind the breakwater of the mast and oars to which she rode.

"It was the only thing I could think of to do," I cried. "Thank God it is done, and well done. You have a magnificent nerve, Miss Grant. For my part I thought it was all over with us, and was too frightened to bawl out."

"We are safer like this than with the sail set?" she said.

"Yes," I exclaimed; "we shall be able to make something like good weather of it now, even should the breeze freshen. I ought to have thought of this old-world nautical stratagem long before it grew perilous to practise it."

It seemed to be blowing as hard again now that we faced it. Our running before the wind had taken half the spite out of it, and it was almost like the change from a pleasant breeze to a sharp gale to feel the hurl of the damp wind rushing down upon us, spray-laden, from every liquid acclivity we rose to. I dropped on my knees and baled till I cleared the boat. The sun was gone, but the scarlet of his setting flooded the sky to the zenith, and went down rusty red to the opposite sea-line from which the sail I had spied had disappeared. The clouds rising out of the western horizon were darkening to the fading illumination, and the seaboard that way looked as though it reflected the lustre of some mighty conflagration, with smoke in volumes pouring from it. The ocean turned green as the North Sea in winter, with a hardening of the shape and outline of every running ridge, and the rise and fall of the long tracts of snow-like froth upon it rendered its aspect so indescribably bleak, chill, desolate, that the sparkling stagnation of yesterday seemed as a dream, and it defied the imagination to realize that this melancholy picture of froth and warring waters was looked down upon by the heaven of the Antilles. But the boat rode well and buoyantly, and how the breakwater helped her you saw by the savage leap of the froth against it; though it was smothered again and again, yet it made a sort of "smooth," as sailors say, for our keel, and the prospect of the night was no longer unendurable to me. Before the darkness fell I got some fruit and turtle out of the locker. Miss Grant shook her head, but I insisted, and then she ate a few mouthfuls, but merely to please me, as I could see. Happily we had a drop of rum with us, and I persuaded her to take a small draught, and afterwards I carefully wrapped the rug round her, and made her as snug as the horrible plight we were in would permit.

Chapter VI
Rescued

T HE WIND FORTUNATELY DID not increase when the darkness
fell, but the gloom of the night gave so stormy an aspect to the
ocean that you would have thought it blew as hard again as it did. I
cannot express how dismal was the appearance of the weltering liquid
blackness in whose heart our tiny ark laboured, one moment flung to
the sight of the stars, the next plunged into the momentary stagnation
and midnight of the Atlantic trough, with long dashes of pale foam
heaving like great winding-sheets all about us, and the slender moon
leaping with a troubled silver face from the rims of the flying clouds,
to render the picture ghastly with the cold, death-like complexion of
her light. There was to be no couch for Miss Grant at the bottom of the
boat. The fabric rode well, and took but very little water over the bows,
but the wet came in fast through the showering of the spray off the seas
curling into foam ahead of us, and obliged me again and again to bale,
though it occupied but a very little while to free us.

My companion sat beside me in the stern-sheets, to which place
indeed I had transported most of our little cargo of fruit, water, and
the like, that the combined weight aft might give the boat's nose a good
cock-up for the run of the surge. Happily, though it all looked chill as
a wintry Channel scene, the wind blew warm, wet as it was, and the
water was warm too with the first touch of it, though, to be sure, if
you let it lie long trickling upon your face the breeze made it frosty.
There was a great deal of fire in the sea; a constant sparkling of pallid
flames flashing like summer sheet-lightning as they rose incandescent
against the sweep of blackness over the horizon where the night lay
deepest. Conversation was out of the question. The roaring of the near
seas drowned our voices. To render ourselves audible we had to put our
lips to each other's ear, sheltering our mouths even then with the hand
against the blast, that would otherwise have clipped our words away as
you'd snick the twig from a bough with a pair of shears. I saw that the
night was to be a fearfully trying one for us both. My own attention
was kept so much on the strain by observing the plunges of the boat,
and watching the seas rolling at and past us, that I protest my very soul
ached as if it were some physical faculty in me. Our misery, too, was
increased by the obligation to keep seated. In calm water, as you have
seen, we moved about and eased our cramped limbs by passing to the
end of the little craft, or standing; but now we durst not stir, not only

for fear of throwing the boat out of trim, but lest we should be flung overboard by one of her many extravagantly wild leaps.

Thus passed the time. I occupied my mind by considering what we should do on the morrow, if the dawn found us alive and the weather moderated. The one ship we had seen at sundown made me hope that others might show next day, but I could not forget that we made but a minute speck on this mighty surface, invisible at very short distance away, and that our chance of being picked up must lie in a vessel passing close to us.

Whilst I thus sat pondering, with my heart so heavy in me that I could not have felt more melancholy had I been sure that the sun was never again to rise for us, I felt the pressure of Miss Grant's form against mine, and bringing my eyes close to her face I saw that she was asleep. I passed my arm round her that she might have the support of it, and yielded so as to bring her head to my shoulder, as she had mine on the previous night; and thus she lay worn out in a deep sleep, breathing regularly. The moon sliding into some indigo opening at times would shed its light upon us, by which I could see Miss Grant's face as it lay pillowed close to mine in the hood with which she had replaced her hat. It was a radiance to spiritualize her beauty. How passionately my heart had gone to hers, how deep was my love, I never could have guessed so truly as now, when her beauty was close to my lips, and she lay at peace against my breast amidst this thunder of warring surge, this long howling of the ocean night wind, this convulsive tossing of our little boat. Murder! what a passion is this same love that it should triumph over such a time as *that*; dominating every consideration of the horrors of our situation, and forcing my spirit to secretly whisper to itself, that in this delight of slumberous embrace—for an embrace it was in its way, with her head upon my shoulder, her form against mine, and my arm clasping her to me—there was solace enough for as many days of this sort of thing as might go to a month of Sundays! I'd often fancy that the poets mightily exaggerated when handling the subject of love, as though the world's main occupation lay in thinking of that, and nothing else; but I now know better. Indeed, I have only to think of that night to know better. Alongside this passion, the passion of life itself is a feeble sentiment. Death seemed to have no terrors for me whilst I held that girl to my heart. The grim feature grinned in every black trough to the glare of the graveyard lights scintillating in each ebon steep, but I was without fear; I was tranquil, at peace, even happy. But I must own not for very long.

For an hour, perhaps, my enjoyment lasted, whilst I sat snatching at every opportunity which the glance of the moon would give me to look at her as she slept, sorely tempted indeed at moments to touch her lips, whose nearness made the black, damp gale aromatic to me, only that my alarmed honour would spring to the succour of my manhood, and transform my desire into a vein of self-reproachful musing for which I thanked my good angel; for I vow to Heaven that I never afterwards could have forgiven myself the lightest act of disloyalty to the noble faith this woman had in me. For an hour, I say; at the expiration of which time my eye was suddenly taken by a pale shadow a trifle on the starboard bow of the boat. It came and went with our tossing. I sent a careless glance at it at first, for it had the look of a small cloud, or some white boiling of water, like to the many scattered all around, that seemed to glare out in ivory heaps to the touch of the moonbeams; but it hung steadily and grew rapidly, enlarging out of the western dark- ness with a steadfast spectral sheen that presently assured me it must be the canvas of a ship. The involuntary start I gave awoke Miss Grant. She sat up, unconscious of the posture her sleep had taken, and I with- drew my arm from her waist.

I pointed whilst I put my mouth to her ear, and cried out, "A ship!"

The mere sound of the word instantly brought her to her full senses. She exclaimed, "She will not be able to see us! Can we not signal? Can we not show a light?"

Alas! I had no means of making a flare. Swiftly I over-hauled the contents of the boat mentally, but there was nothing in her that would burn. The shawls, the rugs which, wetted with the drop of spirits we possessed, might yesterday have been kindled into a flame, were now saturated with the flying spray. More over, the vessel was approaching us too rapidly to have enabled me to act, even had an opportunity for doing so offered. It was very soon after I had sighted her that she had shaped out to the proportions of a large vessel of eight hundred tons at least, running under a press, all three royals set indeed; for what was half a gale of wind to us down here, lying in the eye of it and receiving its full pressure, would be but a pleasant breeze to yonder tall craft, who, by giving it her stern, took most of the spite out of it. But my agony of annoyance at being unable to signal her vanished on a sud- den to the horror which her approach excited, for as her hull stole out black against the dusk beyond, blacker yet under the pile of glimmer- ing cloths, with a faltering streak of a white line broken by ports run- ning along it, it looked to me as though she were heading dead for us, and that in a few minutes the thunder-cloud of her shadow would be upon the boat.

I sprang to my feet, in my anguish sending a wild yell against the gale to her, but was immediately flung down again by the jump of the boat. I again staggered up, but only to fall afresh, this time fetching myself a thump that had like to have broken my back. All the misery of our adventures boiled down into one instant of time could not have approached the torment of feeling with which I watched, breathless, helpless, mute as a corpse, the drawing down upon us of that great fabric, storming under cloths that, from the low point at which we surveyed them, seemed to sweep the very clouds that rolled onwards with her speeding trucks. The wind so drove her that she heaped the foam to near the height of her spritsail-yard, and the raging sound of the parted water there, along with the hissing of the acre of white smothering spume which she sent in thunder ahead of her with every stately stoop of her bows, swept a noise along that rose high above the crying of the wind and the clash of colliding surges, even when she was many times her own length distant from us. It was impossible to suppose that the mere black dot we made upon the tumbling waves was visible to her people, but it did so happen that when she was not above two or three hundred fathoms away from us her head drew a point out, and a minute or two afterwards she was rushing past us close, with ourselves becalmed for an instant in the hang of her shadow as it were betwixt us and the wind, till we rose high to the shriek of the gale again on the breaker-like curl of sea that swelled in a long coil from her cutwater, flashing into a snow-storm when abreast of the gangway.

Terror had constricted my throat; I could not find my voice. The mere effort to shout wrenched me as though some hand were upon my heart striving to tear it from my breast. I could see no light along her until she gave us her stern, when there shone out some squares of illuminated windows with a gleam of gilt-work writhing round about them, and the wake rising hump-backed from the blackness under the counter to the stare of the lights above, as though it found its milkiness in their lustre. She had the look of a frigate, and may have been one for all I could tell, though more likely she was some fine West Indiaman, well to the westwards for the usual course of such craft bound home. As she had risen as a cloud, so did she vanish like one; her squares of canvas paling to the moon, then darkening to the brief eclipse, then brightening out afresh into visionary fragility, till the stars were trembling once more where her stately, rolling spread of cloths had hidden them, and the sea went frothing to the mere smudge she made in the desolate, windy, distant dusk.

Miss Grant took my hand and held it, crying to me, "God watches over us, Mr. Musgrave. To-morrow will bring us help, I'm sure."

But the agony of expectation I had endured, the reaction following the horrible suspense caused by that ship's approach, the bitter grief, the wild feelings excited by her blind, thunderous rush past us, had done their work with me, and I could not have answered the girl to have saved my life.

It was shortly before two in the morning, as I might guess by the passage of the stars, that the wind slackened, shifted into the south-west, and hung there a soft and pleasant breeze, with a thinning away of the clouds, a brighter glory of starlight, a more diamond-like edge to the curl of the moon now sailing low, and a spreading out of the sea into a large, round swell, the sleepy cradling of which was like a bene-diction to the senses after the sharp, snarling curses of the surges which had been racking our bones and bewildering our brains for hours. We sat talking awhile, but my companion's voice was broken by weariness, and presently she made no answer to some question I put, and on look-ing at her I saw that she had fallen asleep. I supported her as before, but it was not long ere I was nodding too. Her soft and regular respiration was an invitation to slumber; the rhythmic swing of the boat too was poppy-like in its influence. My eyelids turned into lead, my chin sunk upon my breast.

I was startled by a voice hailing me. It aroused me from a nightmare, and I woke in a fright. It was daylight, so I must have slept for an hour and a half.

"Boat ahoy!"

I started to the cry that came ringing harsh and loud close aboard, and Miss Grant opened her eyes and sat erect, with an exclamation of astonishment, and a lifting up of the hands as though to fend off some phantasmal object. The sun was just rising, and his first beam like a liv-ing lance of light came hurling along the swelling surface of the waters, which brightened out to the stretching of that magic wand of glory into dainty turquoise even as you looked.

"Boat ahoy, I say!"

I turned, and then sprang to my feet with a shout of joy. Close astern of us, within toss of a biscuit, lay a little fore-and-aft schooner, with her canvas shaking to the light south-westerly wind, into the very eye of which her jib-boom pointed. She was a craft of some twenty-five tons, painted black, sitting low on the water, a beautiful model to the eye, schooner-rigged as I have said, her canvas old and grimy, and liberally patched, her masts badly stayed, the standing rigging grey for want of tar. A fellow in a red shirt and a blue cap, like a French smacks-man's, leaned with his bare arms upon the rail, staring at us with a face of a dark yellow. Over the forecastle bulwarks were the heads of four negroes attired in bright colours, and another negro stood at the long slender tiller that swayed in his hand, whilst he gazed at us with his mouth open behind the yellow-faced man. All these details were swept upon my mind with photographic swiftness and fidelity.

I cried out, "For God's sake, take us on board. You shall be hand-somely repaid for any trouble we give you. We have out-lived a terrible night, and are in the greatest distress, and must perish if you do not receive us."

"Can yah manage to scull dah boat 'long-side, d'yah tink?"

"Oh yes!" I cried, "oh yes!"

I whipped out my knife, sprang forward deliriously, dragged at the sea-anchor, hauled it streaming into the boat, severed the ligatures, and seizing a paddle floundered aft with it, and fell to sculling the boat towards the schooner. Once a horrible swooning feeling seized me, and I was forced to pause to rally my senses, on which the yellow man bawled out, "Look out for dis yeerie line," and hove a coil of rope into the boat, which Miss Grant caught, and we were dragged alongside. I thrust my companion's parcel of letters and jewellery into my pocket, and helped her up the side. But the moment we gained the deck the brave and beautiful girl broke down. She hid her face and sobbed bit-terly. Her emotion was tonical as an obligation upon me to bear up, otherwise I believe I should have given way as weakly as any woman, so true it is that sudden joys, like griefs, confound at first. I drew her gently to the side, longing to soothe her with a lover's caress, though I started to the mere fancy of such a thing, and half turned from her, for now that we stood upon a vessel's deck again she seemed to slip magi-cally back to the old bearings she had aboard the *Iron Crown*. It was the mere sensitiveness in my humour then, no doubt, but I felt it as a sud-den chill at my heart, that my lovely associate on the island, my patient, tender, heroic companion of the boat, had changed into Miss Aurelia Grant *merely*, the young lady whom I was escorting to Rio to oblige my cousin, who would marry her on her arrival.

She looked at me through her tears, smiling.

"What would yah like done wid dis yeerie boat, sah?" exclaimed the yellow-faced man.

"Get her aboard, if you please," said I, "or take her in tow, or cast her adrift. She's of no use to us now, thank God."

"Them rugs is yourn, I reckon?" said the man.

"Yes," I answered; "I shall be glad to have them. We may need them here."

He took a look at the boat, and then ran his eye along the little schooner's deck in a sort of calculating way, and exclaimed, " 'Tain't good enough to send de likes of her adrift. Dere's room yeerie, I guess. Hi! Toby, Hebenezer, Jupiter, lay aft, you tree dam niggers, and git dis boat inboards. Daddy, jump for dah lufftackle; jump, mah Hafrican, and stop scratching your head. Quick an' lively's dah word all roun' now."

He clapped his hands, and fell to cutting several queer capers, as though striving to work himself up into a state of excitement, perhaps with a notion of putting life into his niggers. Indeed, he was the oddest figure that could be imagined. His nose was that of the negro, and his mouth so twisted, whether by disease or disaster, that the left-hand corner of it was on a line with his right nostril, whilst the rest of it went up into his cheek in the shape of the paring of a finger-nail. One eye was larger than the other, the dusk of them indicating African blood. His beauty was further improved by a strange growth of short black hair upon his chin, every fibre as wide apart as the teeth of a comb, and as coarse as the bristles of a hog. There was the negro twang in his voice, and he seemed incapable of speaking without ballooing. He wore, in addition to the cap and shirt I have already named, a pair of dirty duck trousers which ran flowing to his naked yellow feet; but grotesquely ugly as he was—and the more so for the contrast of his twisted, guinea-coloured face betwixt his old blue cap and faded red shirt—he could not have been more beautiful in my sight then had he been one of those dewy, ambrosial, lovely spirits who, in *Paradise Lost*, with flaming lances keep the devil at a respectful distance from Adam and his wife asleep.

All was now bustle; the negroes walloped about, tumbling into the boat, bawling out like school-boys at play, making the craft we had vacated splash to their tumbleflection as though they would capsize her. Suddenly the yellow-faced man, who was looking at them over the rail, roared out, "Hallo! What you do, hey, you black teeves? What! you steal my goods, hein! Tunder and flames! I gib you someting proper to eat, my dickey-birds. Stop now!" with which he plumped right into the boat, jumping as though he meant to go clean through her. I looked to see what was the matter, and observed all three negroes with their mouths full; one with a lump of turtle in his hand, another with a craw-fish, a third with a bunch of bananas. Their greedy gobbling was like to choke them. Apparently they meant to stow a good cargo away before they could be stopped. The instant, however, the yellow-faced man was in the boat he let drive with his head at the stomach of the negro near-est him, who fell with a crash as if shot; but the other two showed fight, poising their heads in a butting posture and awaiting the onset in that attitude, though they continued to cram their mouths nevertheless.

"Drop what yah're eating, you black teeves ob de world!" shouted the yellow man, who wisely came to a pause on observing their hostile demeanour. "Yah both hang for blasted pirate when we gets to Nassoo! you see now! Yes, yah both swings for dis, high as de highest tree dere is. Yah'll see now. Drop it, I say."

But by this time the fellows had nothing left to drop saving some claws of a craw-fish, which promptly fell from the black paws that held them, whilst the men looked up at me grinning from ear to ear. Amidst the utmost confusion, the yellow-faced man remaining till the last in the boat to guard our poor remaining stock of provisions, the little craft's nose was got to the gangway, the block of the luff-tackle hooked on to the ringbolt in the stem, and then all hands came aboard to hoist her in. The fellow at the helm left it to help, and though my emotions just then leaned very little to the side of merriment, I laughed till I was breathless at the contortions of the blacks as they pulled in company with the yellow man, every dusky throat delivering a yell with each drag on its own account; till all at once, just as the bows of the boat were showing over the side, crack! The fall of the tackle parted, down tumbled the negroes in a heap, with the yellow man on top of them, where they spurred and kicked at one another like a lump of spiders in the bottom of a glass, filling the air with execrations and shouts, whilst they rolled over and over in an inextricable muddle of black fac-es, cucumber shanks, red, yellow, and white headgear, and shirts that threatened to become rags in a very little while if the sport went on.

I looked for the boat and sound her under water, floating with just the line of her gunwales above the surface, and the rugs, shawls, umbrellas, and the like quietly sinking past her in the blue heave of the swell. The yellow man scrambled out of the twisting group with his cap gone; and now he proved himself uglier than had been at all conjectur-able whilst his head was covered, for he was as bald as a turnip down to the semi-circle where his wiry hair bushed out thick as the frill of a Persian cat, and as coarse as coconut fibre. In fact his bald head showed now like the top of an ostrich's egg stuck in the hair of a mattress. He ran to look at the boat, and when he saw she was under water he yelled out, "Yah dingy villains! Look at yah work, yah black piggies!" and in a paroxysm of rage stooped his head and went butt in afresh for the first negro at hand; but Ebenezer, as the black was called, was too sharp for him; he sprang aside, and the yellow man drove head foremost against the single old pump that stood before the mainmast. The blow that he fetched himself would have lasted a white man for a lifetime, but it appeared to cause the fellow no further inconvenience than was to be remedied by a brief spell of rubbing. I was getting tired of all this.

"Better get the block unhooked and let the boat go," said I. "What I want has floated out of her, and there's nothing left in the locker that's worth the saving. Besides, I want to have a talk with you. You'll lose nothing by shoving ahead."

"Right yah are," he answered. "Jump now, some black debbil, and free de block. Way 'loft, way 'loft, Toby, and bring dot tackle down."

He looked about him for his cap, found it, put it on his head, and came aft to where Miss Grant and I had seated ourselves on some small raised contrivance just abaft the rudder-head.

"What's the name of this schooner?" said I.

"Dah *Orphan*, sah," he answered.

"Where are you bound to, may I ask?"

"We're out a wrecking," he answered. Then seeing I did not understand, he added, "Dah *Orphan*'s a wrecking craft dat wisits dah islands 'way from Providence down to Inaguey and dah Mona passage, to see what's to be got 'longshore."

I understood him now, for I had heard of such vessels.

"You hail from Nassau, I suppose?"

"Yaas," he said, "dat's my country," inspecting first Miss Grant and then myself with growing curiosity.

"I may take it you're captain here?"

"Dat's so, sah."

"Your name, pray?" said I.

"Capt'n Emilius Jeremiah Ducrow," he answered, drawing himself up and speaking slowly and emphatically.

"Well, Captain Ducrow," said I, preserving my gravity with an effort that was the harder for the demureness I noticed in Miss Grant's face, "before I tell you our story, let me thank you from the very bottom of my heart—and, of course, I speak for this lady as for myself—for your handsome and timely rescue of us. God knows how it must have been with us both had succour been delayed. I can afford to pay you for any services you may render us, and I simply tell you this, that you may know you and your little ship's company will not be losers by your complying with any request I may make you."

He kicked out with his heel as he scraped a bow at me and said, "I see yah a gent. I witness it troo dah accent of yah language. Dere's nebber no mistakin' a gent. I mix in fust-class company ashore myself, and could tell perlite breedin' blindfold by de mere smell of him. Now den," he roared, suddenly turning and looking forward, "get dat gangway shipped. Tunder and slugs! 'tain't dinner-time yet, yah blooming shark-fishes, and so I tells yah. Lay aft to dis helium, Moses. Beg a tousand pardons, sah," he continued, rounding upon me with another scrape and a kick up behind, "but niggers is de most excrooshatin' people to manage. Dey works 'pon your temper more nor aching tees," saying which he extended his arms, drooping his yellow hands, whilst he turned his head from the direction in which he seemed to point, with his face puckered up into an expression of loathing which the twist of his mouth rendered monstrously ugly and comical.

"Well, now," said I, "I want to tell you our story, but before I begin, I should be glad to know if there's anything to eat aboard this little hooker."

"Oh yes, sah; dere's eating to be had—middling coarse, jest sailor's eating, sah; not fit for dis lubberly lady," bowing low to Miss Grant, "but dah best Capt'n Ducrow can perwide."

"We have not had bite nor sup since last night," said I. "What can you give us?"

"Will yah hab it yeerie or in dah cabin?" he inquired.

"Here," said I, making a shrewd guess at the temperature below.

He called to one of the negroes and told him to put a pot of chocolate upon the fire, then to lay aft with a bit of cold salt beef, ship's biscuits, plates, and the like; "And bear a hand, mah humming-bird," he said, "for 'tain't dinner-time yet, yah know. Now, sah," he continued, addressing me, assuming a fine air of dignity in his manner, "whilst dah wittles is making ready I shall be glad ob yah story."

I at once went to work and related our adventures, and on coming to an end I asked him if he could give me news of the *Iron Crown*.

He answered no, he had not heard of the vessel, but that he had learnt about a fortnight ago, though he could not recollect the source whence he had received the intelligence, that a vessel bound to Porto Rico had been spoken, and reported that she had on board four men, whom she had found adrift in an open boat, and that the fellows said they had gone in search of a man and lost their ship in thick weather. "And I believe, sah," said Captain Ducrow, "dat dah name of dah wessel dey gave was dah *Iron Crown*; but I won't swear to it, for I ain't got no memory worf speaking of, 'cept for poetry."

Here he sent a languishing look at Miss Grant.

"For poetry!" I rapped out. "Do you know," I exclaimed, turning to my companion, "that this looks uncommonly like as though poor old Gordon and his men had been picked up."

"I hope so," she answered; "and it seems so indeed. It will diminish by so much the horror of our memories of the ship. And four men too, Mr. Musgrave! *That* must mean that the poor cabin-boy was recovered."

"Pray, captain," said I, "which is the nearest port hereabouts; some civilized place of houses and ships, I mean, where we may be able to put ourselves in the way of getting to Rio?"

He looked steadfastly around the horizon as though seeking for information on the gleaming sea-line, and then gazing at me with one eye shut full of thought, he exclaimed, "Dere'll be nuffen nearer than Nassoo."

"And how far off will that be?" said I,—"in the shape of time, I mean."

"Well, maybe a week, maybe a month. Dere's no predicating ob de winds. Perhaps yah know dem bootiful lines, Miss—

"Sometimes dah gale blow high,
 Ho! an' sometimes dah breeze blow small;
 Sometimes it breeves in a sigh,
 An' sometimes it blows in a squall.
 But ho, my lub, and my lub! Most often when I pants to get at yah,
 down yeerie it don't blow at all!

"You didn't happen to know dem werses p'r'aps, Miss?"

Miss Grant answered no, smiling.

"Waal, I ask 'cause dey're mine. When sung to dah accompaniment—"

"Beg your pardon, Captain Ducrow," said I, breaking in here, "but I want to settle some plan with you, for we're in a great hurry to get to Rio, and if you'll help us to arrive there you shall do so on your own terms. What do you advise now?"

This reference to his judgment flattered him. He drew himself up, folded his arms, and cocked his eye thoughtfully at the sky, with the air of a man who recognizes his opportunity, and means to make the most of it.

"Tell yah what," he suddenly exclaimed, "take mah advice, and let me bowl yah to Havana. Dere's breezes to be trusted off de Bahama Bank."

"All right," said I. "Havana will suit very well. And now to square the matter off whilst we're upon it—what about the passage money?"

Again he struck an attitude with another squint aloft, then fell to counting upon his fingers, as it were, whilst his lips moved. He uttered a few disconnected syllables. "De grub—lost time yeerie—nuffen p'r'aps 'long-shore arter all;" then bringing his eyes to me and staring a little without speaking, he exclaimed, "Say fifty dollar apiece?"

"You shall have it," said I, pulling out my pocket-book, and giving him a sight of some Bank of England notes in it.

The negro now came along, bearing the meal that had been ordered. A small carpenter's bench was brought from forward, a piece of sail-cloth spread over it, and Miss Grant and I fell to. The beef proved a piece of corned buffalo hump, and speaking for myself it ate with extraordinary relish after our three weeks of turtle and craw-fish. Even out of the flinty biscuit I could get enjoyment, whilst the chocolate was as well made and as handsomely frothed as any I ever tasted ashore. The light sparkling breeze, but with the fire of this torrid zone in its breath, hung steadily, crisping the large rounds of the darkly blue swell, and sending the little schooner cleaving through it in an airy, undulating sliding that was like flying, so buoyantly did the keen clipper keel mount the swelling hills, with a soft lean on their summits from the hot blue gushing that woke a note as of a fountain at the bow, and raised a sound alongside as of the dim melody of musical glasses chiming afar. Captain Ducrow stood by us whilst we breakfasted. I asked him to join us; but he said his own breakfast of tea, biscuit and molasses would be coming along shortly, and he'd rather wait. I then asked him if he could tell me the name and situation of the island we had been marooned upon.

"Waal," says he, "I've been tinking hard 'pon dat berry question whilst yah've been feeding, but what island it can be passes my apprehenshun, sah. 'Tain't Watling, dat's sartin; 'tain't Rum nor Samana. Your resemblance ain't nuffin like him. 'Tain't Guihaney, nor Planas, nor Cockus" (Caicos, I presume). He added, with an air of desperation, "De debbil only knows what island it is."

I was nearly telling him that we had left the most of our traps behind us, but on reflection I thought it was best to say nothing about that. Wherever the island might be, it now certainly lay out of our course. Time must be spent in seeking and making it, and time grew doubly precious when I cast my eye at the little companion-hatch, and reflected upon the sort of accommodation that awaited us below, and how for *that*, if for no other reason, we could not be in too great a hurry to end this trip. Our baggage would of course have been serviceable to us, but its recovery was not worth the delay of a deviation. And then, again, I believe the mere notion of going to that island afresh, lying off it, having it in view along with all its melancholy, wretched associations of hopelessness and privations, would have grievously depressed Miss Grant, as it must certainly have affected me, even into a superstitious dread that the mere loom of it above the sea-line would prove prophetic of further disasters to us.

When we had finished breakfast I asked Captain Ducrow what sort of accommodation he could furnish the lady with below.

"I can't praise him, I can't praise him," he answered, with a solemn shake of his head, to which the swinging of the tassel of his cap imparted additional emphasis; "but yah shall see him for yourself, sah," with which he led the way to the companion, and down the three of us went. The small skylight lay open, but it was a stifling little cabin for all that, about the size of a North Sea smack's, with a tiny room bulkheaded out of it, to which Captain Ducrow pointed, exclaiming, "Dat's where I lies, sah; but it is dah duty of ebery gent to make room for dah ladies,"—here he scraped another convulsive bow at Miss Grant,—"and if you will hab dah grace, ma'm, to hoccupy him till we gets to Havana, he'll be all de sweeter for me to use again. Dat's it, I reckon, and so, mam'selle, he is werry moosh at your sarvice."

"Ah, captain," said I, "I see now what a fine poet you are. Upon my word, Miss Grant, there's no finished courtier could have turned a neater speech."

The fellow grinned so exceedingly with his twisted mouth that you would have thought the emotion of delight must have ended in the wringing of one side of his face clean off the other.

"It all comes ob mixing in fust-class company," he said, in a voice whose natural negro huskiness was thickened yet by excess of gratification. " 'Tain't all nature in this yeerie yearth. Nebber knew a rale genteel man as didn't git his polishing from dah elbows of dah fust-class crowd he shoves in 'mongst. Yah may take it for dah Lord's truss, sah—"

I interrupted him. "Any cockroaches here, Captain Ducrow?"

"Waal, yaas; more'n one family, I'se afeered."

"Nothing *worse*, I hope?"

"Nebber's nuffin worse where dere's cockroaches," he said; "dah cockroach eats up what's worse."

"It's a pity," said I to Miss Grant, "that your hammock went overboard. We could have made shift to swing it in this bit of a room.

However, you'll want a place to sleep in, and we can't do better than accept Captain Ducrow's kind offer."

So it was arranged that the skipper should clear out his traps, leaving the bunk bare for the reception of a square of sailcloth, which, with a roll of the same stuff for a pillow, would provide my companion with a clean couch at all events. As for myself, I told Ducrow that one of his lockers in the cabin would supply me with as good a bed as I needed. On my asking him where he meant to sleep, he pointed to a hole in the cabin bulkhead forward, which I found to be a sort of bunk-place like to the orifices in which the hardy smacksmen aboard a certain type of vessels stretch their weary, sea-booted limbs when they turn in. This being settled, we returned on deck, glad to escape from the stifling little cabin.

The hours slipped by, the blue swell came running out of the south-west, with the fresh but burning breeze flashing off the heads of the brimming brine into our patched and grimy spread of cloths, under whose pressure the schooner swept along with the subtlety of the shark, and with such a whipping of her ill-stayed spars to every jump as made one look at times to see them go overboard. They rigged up a sort of awning for us, and under it Miss Grant and I sat throughout the greater part of the day, talking much of the perils we had come through, of our happy deliverance, of the honest prospect that had now fairly opened upon us of our arriving safely at Rio, at no very distant date either; with frequent interruptions from Captain Ducrow, who would entertain us with twenty odd remarks, with accounts of his wrecking experiences, with inquiries into our story, with several poetical quotations all of his own manufacture, as he protested, sometimes quitting his lofty air to let fly at one of his negro seamen, or even to chase him.

But in this time I was sensible of a change both in myself and in Miss Grant. There was a delicate suggestion of diffidence in her which I could see her struggling against in every smile she gave me, but which nevertheless remained as sensible to me as the aroma of her breath, or the spirit that shone brilliant in her eyes. Sometimes I'd think it the reflection of my own bearing; a sort of reserve came upon me which I could not control, though when I sought to interpret its impulse, I found I could but understand it in part. There would be sensitiveness too to increase suspicion. I fancied that now we were comparatively safe, thoughts of my cousin, sharpened by happy conviction that she would soon be with him, caused her to recur to our intimacy—perhaps to certain passages in our intimacy—with the resolution to once again clearly define herself to my mind as Alexander's sweetheart, but as insensibly as her sweetness and gratitude could contrive it, so that nothing of pain might be caused me by this new posture in her, or rather this return to an earlier manner. It was so reasonable, that I could not but think I was right in thus thinking. Most honourably cautious as I flatter myself I had been, glances, nay words, had escaped me in the hurry of my feelings which she would now recall. I remember once that afternoon, when her face was turned away from me, whilst she shadowed her fair brow with her hand as she gazed out to sea—I remember, I say, looking at her earnestly, my mind full of her, wondering what thoughts were in her heart, striving with a kind of passion in me to interpret her beauty into even the feeblest revelation that might correspond with my imagination of her. She was slow in looking round, and when she did so I grew immediately conscious by her manner that she knew I had been watching her. She let her eyes dwell on mine a moment with a softness that was like an appeal; then as her glance fell, her lips were parted by a smile I would have given all I was worth to know how to translate. I waited almost breathlessly for her to speak, and still watching, I saw a tear drop from her cheek to her hand. She rose suddenly and went to the rail, and stood there a little with her back upon me, and when she returned it was with some commonplace remark about the sultry glimmer of the air at the junction of the sea and sky.

Chapter VII
Aboard the Orphan

OUR LITTLE SCHOONER WAS named the *Orphan*. She had indeed a forlorn and melancholy look, strongly suggestive of friendlessness, with a dampness besides, owing to her being repeatedly pumped out, that gave her a tearful appearance. Her beautiful lines would have made me imagine that she had been a yacht in her day but for the homeliness of her fittings. She leaked considerably, and the negro who acted as mate aboard her told me her timber was so rotten forward that you could dig cubes of dry rot out of the knees and carlings as easily as you cut a cheese. Her aspect of decayed gentility was quite moving in its way. You witnessed the good blood in her, which perhaps rendered her uncared-for condition the more affecting. But she was an orphan that did not keep her woes to herself. There was not a tree-nail in her but complained, not a fastening nor bulkhead but mingled its groans with the lamentations which broke out from all parts of the little fabric. The very creak of the rudder on its pintles had the note of the sniff of a sobbing man; and then, as one or another of the blacks was repeatedly addressing himself to the gaunt old brake pump in front of the mainmast, there was constantly a choking sound of water in the air, with garglings of the bright stream as it sluiced into the sea through the little holes in the scuppers, which was perhaps the one and final condition needful to render the lachrymose air of this ill-clothed, sun-blistered, neglected, sieve-like *Orphan* completely effective. Whether such craft are still afloat at the work to which this vessel was put, I do not know. Perhaps the West Indian wrecking business is already an old world story, but in my time a whole fleet of small craft, sloops, cutters, schooners, and the like, were employed in the trade; that is to say, in hunting the many islands in these waters for wrecks of vessels, and for such commodities as might have been washed ashore out of them.

Havana, according to Captain Ducrow, was within eight or nine days' sail of us. The outlook of the run, if a run it was to prove, was not a thing to trouble either Miss Grant or myself at the first blush, coming as we did fresh to this little schooner from the horrors and perils of an open boat at sea, and from three weeks of hopelessness in an island prison. But it does not take long for the novelty of rescue to wear out. Before darkness closed upon that first day of our deliverance we had ceased to marvel at our happy escape. We had grown used to thinking of it, and though gratitude was always in our thoughts, there was no longer the first passionate delight and astonishment rising at moments to incredulity.

Hence when the evening settled down hot as iron that has blackened out of its white heat, along with a fining down of the breeze to a mere sighing of air that threatened a dead calm anon, Miss Grant's and my conversation naturally went to the prospect before us, of the passage in this stifling, leaky, ill-provisioned little schooner to Havana, that yet lay some hundreds of miles distant. The small awning had been removed; the dark velvet of the heavens showed from sea-line to sea-line fiery with stars. And the moon's reflection this night lay brightly upon the sea. The heavy swell of the morning had flattened; but there was a light movement yet to which the schooner kept time with her whip-like spars, every sail swinging in and out regularly, with draughts of dewy air scurrying cool to one's heated brows from these fannings. A negro stood at the helm, and when the stern of the schooner drooped to a hollow, the ebony figure melted out of sight into the blackness of the water beyond, though with the rise of this end of the craft he would stand out again in a sharp limning against the silver ground of the luminaries. Captain Ducrow had gone below to lie down, and we could hear him snoring in the cabin, a sound as persuasive as the heat as an influence to detain us on deck. The negro mate paced the gangway with naked feet, soundless as the footfalls of a cat, with an occasional halt to squirt a stream of tobacco-juice over the side. At intervals a black figure would come oozing out, as it were, from the deep shadow forward to the pump, the clank, clank of which was now a familiar sound in our ears, though I recognized it as a threat to our repose when we should come to stretch ourselves for a little rest; and you saw the fiery water creeping, dilating, fading upon the deck like sheets of wriggling glow-worms, with sometimes a faint flash of the sea-glow upon the swell of the jib, rounding to the roll of the little craft when some sudden brimming of the swell broke into light against the bows.

"I'm afraid," said I, "that this part of our experiences will be pretty nearly as tedious as our island life."

"But we are safe," she answered.

"I hope so," said I, "though I could wish there was less need for pumping. But I fear you will be horribly uncomfortable."

"Oh, but after last night, Mr. Musgrave!" she exclaimed, in a way as though she would tenderly rebuke me for the little show of irritation and despondency in my manner just now, quite perceptible to myself, though I would or could not cope with it. "You must not think of me at all—of my comfort, I mean," she added, and then stopped suddenly, as though she wondered at her own expression, immediately saying, however, "The hardship now is very trifling compared to what we have endured."

"That's so indeed," I exclaimed, "but I shall be glad to exchange this existence though, all the same. Buffalo beef and flinty biscuit are not a fare upon which you can long thrive; and then what a bedroom that is down stairs! I dread the moment of your going to it. Yet it is absolutely necessary you should sleep under deck; for observe how dark these planks are already with dew."

"You will take more cheerful views tomorrow," she exclaimed; "you have suffered much in mind and body, and for your sake, not for mine, indeed, I could wish the cabin a pleasant, airy one, that you might be sure of a good long night's rest. Sleep is what you need."

"I am thinking," said I, waiving this point, and continuing to speak with a little irritation in me, due, as I should have known by giving the thing a thought, to my fancy of her changed attitude towards me, along with the peevish, secret, jealous dislike of the obligation of conveying her to my cousin, of losing her *then*, of quitting her, consumed by a passion which I was young enough to imagine neither time nor distance could possibly cool,—"I am thinking," said I, "that if we were to come across a good, comfortable, roomy craft, it would be as well for us to trans-ship ourselves without regard to her destination."

"I will do whatever you wish," she said simply.

"Only," said I, "suppose she should be bound to a European port?"

She seemed to be sunk in reflection.

"It would be rather a blow perhaps," I continued, feeling a bit cynical as I progressed in this talk, "to be borne off to England or to France or to Spain even, or say North America—"

She interrupted me: "The ship might be going the other way; she might be sailing to the East Indies perhaps, or to Australia."

"Oh," cried I, with a short laugh, "in that case then of course we should stop where we are. But suppose the vessel bound to Europe, would you be willing to go on board her?"

"If it were your wish—yes."

"But, Miss Grant, so grave a matter must not lie altogether upon my shoulders. Remember your sailing to Europe again would greatly prolong the term of your divorce from your sweetheart."

I could see her smiling softly in the moonlight, though she hung her head. "We may not sight a ship," said she, presently.

"But if we do," said I, "shall we leave this crazy old hooker for her?"

"Yes," she exclaimed.

"Without regard," I said, striving to steady my voice, though my heart just gave a flop that was like to choke me, "to the port she is bound to?"

"Oh yes," she responded, with a note of archness in her voice; "the captain would not alter his course to oblige us, you know."

"It would only signify a little further delay," said I, "with the comforts of civilization between, and that's what we both want now. Of course on our arrival, be the place the Tagus or the Thames, be it Boston or Marseilles, I should *immediately* go to work to equip ourselves afresh for a second, and I hope a successful, voyage to Rio."

"You are very kind," she answered, a little above her breath, whilst I could see her biting her lip to another smile.

Late as it was, and wearied as I was when I saw her to her miserable little hole of a berth, I yet paced the deck for above an hour afterwards in as odd, unreasonable a temper as ever possessed me, full of the agitation of fifty wild thoughts all rolling one to another in as lively a play as ever the sea showed off a harbour, with the water shoaling in spouts to the sweep of the wind one way, and a current seething into it the other. The fact was, a resolution to keep Miss Grant by my side, no matter what the name of the stars might be which looked down upon us, had been growing and hardening in me, till I whipped out with it in the suggestion that it would be good for us both to transship ourselves at the first opportunity that offered, no matter where the vessel we entered might be bound. I should have guessed from her manner all day that such a proposal must have instantly won an eager anxious *No!* from her—instead of which she had promptly assented, saying without hesitation that she would do as I wished; and she had made nothing at all, as you have seen, of my remark touching the destination of the ship we might exchange the schooner for. This was a sort of acquiescence, let me tell you, to excite me not a little, when I came to turn it over during my solitary march to and fro the lightly swaying deck, specially when I coupled it with what I seemed to find in the memory of her down cast eyes, her quiet smiles, and a something more significant than either in her *way*, to use the old phrase, though I could not give it a name.

This, to hark back to the image I have just employed, was the intellectual gale that set my thoughts running in surges one way; and all would have been an easy rhythmic motion with me, but for the strong adverse tide of fancy which came washing into the run of feeling with consideration of my cousin's claims upon me, my honour as a gentleman, my duty as a man. Heaven save me!—in my temper I could have struck my foot clean through the deck. I wanted her, I felt that I must possess her, that I had a higher right to her than ever my cousin could advance; and yet the thought of the poor fellow stuck in my throat, and I grew so mad with the bother of the whole thing, that I'd gladly have given the darky who stood at the helm half a sovereign for liberty to kick him fore-and-aft until I was tired. After all, thought I, it is for Miss Grant to decide—*she* must settle it. If she persists in making for Rio—if, in short, she'll have none of me, though mightily obliged, and all that sort of thing—and here my mood grew so outrageous that it was an exquisite relief to me to see Ducrow's face sallow even to the starlight, fork up through the companion with a "Hallo, sah. Keepin' mighty late hours, ain't yah?"

"Oh, go to the deuce!" I cried. "Look here, man, hark to *that* now, bad luck to you!" and as I spoke, the clank of the old brake pump recommenced for the fiftieth time, it seemed to me, that night. "What's the good of going to sea in an old basket?" I shouted. "Why, damme, Ducrow, don't you know that a dollar's worth of oakum is all that's needed to keep your abominable old pump from disturbing the sleep of the green seamen who lie in shoals here under your keel as you jog along in this weeping bucket?"

He stood staring at me from the companion, as though he thought I had gone mad, and small blame to him for that; then approaching me cautiously, he exclaimed.

"Berry good job, sah, I'm a man of perlite feelings, odderwise I might tomble into a passion, and say someting to wound yah sensashuns."

"What d'ye mean?" I cried, hoping he *would* fall into a passion, as I felt the need of the relief of a row.

"Sah," he exclaimed, drawing himself erect, "a man what keeps de select company I comingles wid ashore am slow in shocking dah feelings ob folks. But what I should like to say am—mind I don't say it—I merely intends dat what I should like to say am, if yah ain't satisfied wid dis little hooker, I'm werry mosh sorry indeed yah ebber came aboard her. Pump!" continued the poor fellow in a broken voice as though he must presently weep, "whar's dah wessel what don't pump? Whar's dah man-ob-war sloop dat don't pump? Whar's dah Indieman as glorious as sunlight wid gilt and windows wot don't pump? Whar," he continued, raising his voice, "is de noblest frigate ob dah King of Yengland wot don't pump? Whar—" and this he delivered in a shriek—"is dah magnificentest line-ob-battle ship wot was yebber launched wot don't pump?"

He plucked his cap from his head and flung it on deck, grasped the bush of hair over either ear with his hands as though he intended to tear out by the roots what nature had left him in that way, and then, swaying to and fro in the moonlight like a drunken man, he exclaimed in a blubbering voice, "An' you specks dah poor little *Orphan* to keep dah seas widout pumping?"

Tush! thought I, I'm acting like a fool; and moved by the way in which the poor creature had received my insulting language, I strode over to him and clapped him on the back. "It's all right," said I; "I don't feel very well to-night. Pump away as briskly as you please, my lad, I'll not complain again. I have come through some infernal adventures, Captain Ducrow, and though I sneer at your little craft in my ill-temper, I am grateful to Heaven for the privilege of feeling her under my feet."

He unclinched his dingy fingers out of his hair and let his arms droop slowly, whilst he looked at me with his head on one side, with a slow twisting up of his eye that was in inimitable correspondence with the absurd cast of his mouth.

"I see how it am, sah," he exclaimed; "yah feels a bit low."

"Worn out without being sleepy," said I.

"Sorter hankering to be soothed, preehaps?"

"Yes," I answered, "but your cockroaches won't help me there."

"Tell yah what will though," said he.

"What?" I asked.

"A little poetry," he answered. "If yah'll sit down I'll gib yah as pretty a half-hour ob sentiment as ebber yah could buy for hard money in dis yeerie airth."

"Much obliged," I answered. "Since I've been talking to you I've grown a bit sleepy. After all, that pump may be more soothing as you call it than I had supposed. Can you find me anything to serve as a pillow?"

He picked up his cap reflectively and presently said, "I hab it," and stepping to a raised contrivance abaft the rudder-head, he produced an ensign rolled up. "Dere," said he, "dere's dah British colours to lie on. I'll warrant it agin all dreaming, onless it be a wision ob de Income Tax."

I took the roll of bunting, and wishing him good-night went below, and stretched myself upon a locker. A slush lamp swung from a blackened beam. It looked like a coffee-pot with the spout vomiting forth a lump of wick burning in a dim flame that blackened into a line of smoke, which went writhing and quivering to the upper deck, whence, spreading, it loaded the atmosphere of this interior with the flavour of hot fat. The beams were lined with cockroaches, wriggling and heaving in dusky lengths, with a frequent skirr of one of the abominable creatures swinging past my ear or dropping upon my face. It was roastingly hot, and I feared to find Miss Grant suffocated in the morning, if indeed the sun should find me still alive, after such a course of air as I was now booked to breathe. But miserable as it was below I durst not lie on deck. The dew was like rain, and the light breeze was wet with it. Further exposure, moreover, following on top of what we had already suffered in the boat, would have been sheer madness, seeing that we had managed to come off with our health, which might receive lasting injury from another night spent unsheltered in the warm, moist, fever-breeding atmosphere of these parallels.

I had thought the *Iron Crown* as noisy a ship as was ever built, but compared with the creaking of this schooner, as she rose buoyant to the dark heave of the swell, floating down into the hollow for another slide upwards, the straining sounds inside of the brig were as the soft singing of a woman to the clatter of a watchman's rattle. But I was dog-tired, as they say at sea, and my cheek could not have pressed the ensign ten minutes before I was sound asleep.

It was a night's rest to refresh me, and though, when I woke up and rolled off the locker, my back ached from the hardness of my couch, I felt a new man, hearty, hungry, and even cheerful. But it was sickening though to go on deck and find a dead calm, the sea molten glass, scarce stirred by a delicate undulation, the sun an intolerable flame of fire four hours high, with the heavens half full of his white dazzle, and the rest of it hot, silver azure, down to the opalescent edge of the water. In the far east was a dot of light—a sail; and some four points past it to starboard a streak of greenish colour swimming a finger's-width above the horizon, and winding like a small sea-snake in the hot air. It was some Cay, the name of which I have forgotten. There was nothing besides it and the sail in sight, not a pinion of cloud to give us hope of so much as a catspaw.

Miss Grant was on deck when I arrived there. She had slept—not very well she told me; but she had managed to obtain rest enough to refresh her spite of the oven-like sultriness in which she lay. She was awake when the day broke, and rose soon after the light had filled the cabin.

"You were sleeping heavily as I passed," she said, "and in spite of being covered with cockroaches."

"Would you think me querulous and ill-tempered now," said I, looking at her, "after such a night as we have passed, for advising our transshipment at the earliest possible opportunity?"

"Did I not say, Mr. Musgrave," she answered, with a demureness that was full of archness, "that I am willing to do exactly as you please?"

I sent a glance deep into her eyes, but the riddle went the whole length of my sight and beyond it. Does she guess that I love her? I thought; and can I suppose that she is even a little bit fond of me—in the right sort of way, I mean? But here Ducrow stumped up to ask us where we would breakfast.

Our first day in the open boat had been a dead calm, as you know, but this was deader yet as it seemed to me, perhaps because of my impatience, that would grow to a torment when hour after hour passed, and the spot of light that signified the sail still hung stirless in the same quarter, with the streak of green past it flickering like a blowing pennon on top of the white gleam that trembled betwixt the blue of the sea and the blue of the sky, and never a shadow of air from sunrise to sundown to dye a fathom's space of the fiery, breathless surface. There was no comfort to be got out of the schooner at all, saving the news that there was plenty of fresh water aboard. The pump clanked steadily at regular periods throughout the long hours. Now and again would come a brief bit of diversion in the shape of a quarrel between two negroes, and in Captain Ducrow's airs and talk there was much to laugh at; but the calm was in all things and over all things, flattening down the spirits to its own monotonous level, with the heat so great besides that it prohibited one the ease of venting one's self by eager exercise; though again and again I'd half start from my seat with a longing of my temper to exhale itself in a spell of swift, passionate pacing from the taffrail to as far forward as I could have got. On the other hand, Miss Grant was reserved, quiet, thoughtful; always gentle and kind; welcoming my lightest speech with a smile; humouring my little fits of petulance, and making the best of our situation by recurrence to the misery from which we had been delivered. But her gaze no longer met mine with the old brilliant, intrepid steadfastness. There was, methought, a suggestion of coyness about it that showed somewhat oddly when I contrasted it with the dignified sweetness and fearless candour of her earlier bearing. It chilled her manner, to my fancy, as something foreign to her nature, and complicated the conundrum for me yet, for there were times when a look from her, a gesture, a smile, would convey notions that set my heart off at a rapid trot, and then the surface would thinly ice again, and leave me as bewildered as a man who struggles to hunt out another's meaning in a book, the pages of which have been wrongly stitched.

Chapter VIII
We Quit the Orphan

WELL, WE HAD THREE days of this sort of thing—three days and three nights of it; and then on the morning of the fourth a breeze of wind darkened and roughened the western ocean, and presently the little schooner was again under way, off her course by some three and a half points, but sweeping through it gaily nevertheless, showing herself as rejoiced at her release as if a human heart beat in her, with sharp clips of her sheering stem at the frothing surges melting to her bow, and a saucy whisking of crystals to the wind, and much coquettish prancing and whipping of her ill-conditioned spars, all as though the little crazy beauty should say, "I have started on a dance; the fiddles have struck up; hark to their strains in the rigging!—no white foam-finger along my path shall detain me; every offered kiss of the blue billow will be repulsed." Ducrow slapped his thighs and urged her on, bursting into thick laughter at times in his glee, and pointing with a yell of applause to the sparking out of the flying-fish, as though, like an overgrown child, he tasted a kind of victory in the flight of the beautiful little creatures from the winged and buoyant and floating rushes of his leaking, trembling, pump-sodden, worn-out old *Orphan*.

This day, shortly after noon, a small brig passed us. When I first sighted the squares of her canvas I took her to be a big ship, for she showed a sky-sail on the main, which threw her up tall and spire-like as she came blowing up, radiant as cotton could make her, over the blue edge. I had not said a word to Ducrow about our intention of leaving his schooner if a chance came, but I thought I would do so now, specially as yonder craft promised the opportunity I had fallen half crazy in yearning for during our time of stagnation. But first I spoke to Miss Grant. We were sitting under the little awning aft, whence we had a good view of the distant sail as it slowly enlarged.

"If that ship there will receive us," said I, "shall we exchange this schooner for her?"

"You must think me very capricious, Mr. Musgrave," she answered; "have I not again and again answered yes to such another question as that? When my mind is made up, I do not quickly change it indeed without excellent reason."

"But I want you to reflect. I wish you to think for yourself, and of yourself wholly. Be that fellow's destination what it will, he is bound to sail as straight for it as the wind will let him. He is heading about east. Now that is a direction exactly contrary to your wishes."

"My wishes!"

"I mean that his bowsprit points to any other quarter of the world than where Rio lies."

She looked at me an instant with an expression in her eyes which showed her mind to be full, though I was too blind to make out a shadow of what was there—too sensitive perhaps I should say, for to be over sensitive is to be worse than blind sometimes; and then after a little pause, she said quietly, "Once more, Mr. Musgrave, I'm quite willing to leave the schooner."

"Captain Ducrow!" I sung out.

"Hillo, sah!" he answered from the rail, where he was standing with his arm round a backstay, watching with a grin the flash of his little ship through the small ridges which whitened into cream along the dirty green of the vessel's sheathing.

"Step this way, will you?" said I.

He sprang to the deck and approached.

"We want you to speak that vessel," said I, pointing. "In a word, we wish you to stop her so that we can go aboard of her, as we find your accommodation scarcely all that we require, at least under these burning heights; otherwise, we're both of us quite in love with your charming little vessel, whilst we highly value you for your good breeding, and thank you excessively for the attention you have paid us."

This bit of troweling I deemed necessary that the rest might be easy, but his surprise mastered his gratification, and with a sort of grin in his twisted mouth, whilst his eyes on the other hand stared their amazement, he cried, "Yah want to leave dah *Orphan*, hein? 'commodation not good? But I know dah reason. De calm's disgusted yah. Yah was werry mosh satisfied afore de wind fell."

"Come, captain," said I, "it shall be all the same to you. See here?" I pulled out my pocket-book and produced a bank-note for twenty pounds. "There," said I, slapping it, "place us aboard yonder craft, and this is yours. Of course, if she's bound to some outlandish place we sha'n't quit you; but put us within hailing distance, will you?—signal to speak her; and if she will receive us, and her destination be some port convenient to ourselves, you shall have this money the same as though you had landed us at Havana."

He eyed the note greedily as I folded it up and returned it to the pocketbook, following *that* too till it was hidden, and then said, "All right, sah. Yah'll miss de *Orphan*—dere's nuffen afloat—but den ob course if dah lady hain't comfortable—" He suddenly roared out "Hi, Moses! you black tees, lay aft, mah bird ob Paradise, an' hoist dat ensign half-mast high. Dat'll make 'em reckon we've got someting on our minds."

The negro came shambling along with the ensign that I had slept on, and a very tattered symbol of Britannia's mercantile sovereignty floated slowly aloft, and then blew out when within a dozen feet of the topmast-head. The stranger, however, appeared to take no notice of this. There was no telescope aboard us, but she was near enough now to enable me to distinguish her with the naked eye. She showed no colour, nor indeed exhibited any disposition to shift her helm to bear down to us. Ducrow luffed till our canvas was shaking fore and aft, so that nothing could have been more expressive of our desire to speak than the posture of the schooner, almost at a stand, plunging to the short sea that she had now brought almost right ahead, with every dingy balsamed cloth on her trembling, and the half-masted ensign streaming like a flame aloft, and giving deep emphasis to every hint discoverable in the schooner's attitude. As the stranger drew out she showed herself a brig, a smaller vessel than the *Iron Crown*, though large enough to have stowed the *Orphan* between her rails. She was under all plain sail, with the weather-clue of the mainsail up, and she slided past with graceful courtesyings upon the swell, a streak of gold gleaming at her forefoot to the light of her bows, with a yeasty, trembling hurrying along it like a ball of white wool there, which unwound itself as she thrust it forwards. But though she did not alter her course by so much as a quarter of a point, our own wind-jamming brought her close enough aboard to enable us to see her people clearly. A couple of figures were pacing the poop under the snow-white awning. There was a group of heads forwards, and a sailor in the foretopmast-rigging swinging out with his face towards the schooner watching us. What her nationality was I do not know. I fancied I could trace something of a Yankee paternity in the colour of her cloths and the hoist of her topsails; but be this as it may, had we been some green old water-logged hulk, hoary with barnacles, we could scarce have won less not ce. Nothing imaginable could be more provoking than the sight of those two figures on the poop, coolly stumping to and fro with our halt-mast ensign fair in their view, and our little ship all in the wind, piteous to the eye with the trembling solicitude her shivering canvas gave to her mute appeal.

"Dem's no sailors," cried Ducrow, "dey's what's call scow-bankers. Moses, mah honey, yah may haul down dah ensign. Ebenezer, my lub, up helium an' fill on de little beauty agin. Dere'll be more ships passing presently," he added, addressing me. Then clapping his hands together, he yelled at the top of his pipes, "Tail on to dah troat halliards, mah sweet and pleasant livelies; gib dah *Orphan* a chance, boys. Look at dah set ob dat sail. Whar's de gal whose gwine to dance wid de heel ob her boot wore down?" saying which he flung himself excitedly upon the tackle in question, roaring out in thick negro accents—

"Wah're dah dandy ship an' dah dandy crew.
(*Chorus of black throats pulling behind him*)
Hi, sah ! ho, sah! slap 'im up cheearly!
We am dahboys who's dah lady's only joys,
(*Chorus of black throats pulling*)
An' dah gals dey lub us dearhly.
(*Full Chorus.*)

"An' it's yo hi ho! dah breezehim do blow,
An' dah tack will come taut wid dah jigger!
An' dah ship she roll along
To as lubberly a song
As was ebber sweetly sung by a nigger."

The job of sail-setting being ended, Ducrow looked at me to see what I thought of his song—manifestly a composition of his own, sung to an air that had an odd touch of African wildness in it, at least to my fancy, as it floated ventrally through the enormous mouths and blubber lips of the chorusing niggers. But I was too keenly disappointed and mortified by the cool behaviour of the brig to heed him.

Our chance however was presently to come, though we had to wait for it a little while longer. It was the sixth day of our being on board the schooner *Orphan*. Long spells of dead calms, of light head-winds, and small baffling breezes had resulted, spite of the subtle quality of sneaking through it possessed by the little craft, in our discovering that Havana still lay a fair week's sail away from us, even supposing a prosperous wind every day, and an average run of a hundred miles in the twenty-four hours. At wide intervals a sail would show remote and faint upon the horizon, often vanishing magically, like a wreath of mist devoured by the sun. Life even on board a large West Indiaman in these waters, the most roasting liquid tract on the face of the world, is unendurable enough even with a wide spread of snow-white awnings to cool the deck, with shadow from the forecastle to the taffrail; great cabin-windows wide open, the heels of windsails penetrating every aperture, with a constant sluicing of the planks to keep them cool.

But think of a small red-hot schooner, that in moments of a breathless calm, when the sun stood almost overhead, tingled with sounds as though she were actually frying! the cockroaches multiplying day by day, the cabin atmosphere growing more and more difficult to breathe every time one entered it, no shelter save a strip of awning aft, nothing better to eat than salt meat and ship's biscuit, nor to drink than cold water, of which, though the stock was plentiful, the quality was by no means good, and which was certainly not to be rendered more palatable by the one jar of fiery rum that Ducrow kept secret in his lazarette, never producing it without taking a dark and suspicious view of the little skylight, or going on tiptoe to the companion to make sure that no man of his crew was peering down.

But there was bound to come an end some day or other to these faint gaspings of catspaws; to the intolerable brassy dazzle of the noontide heavens, to the putrefying calms of the night, with dim configurations of phosphorus and graveyard glowings of ghostly fires, making one think with the poet that the very deep was rotting.

It was the morning of the sixth day of our rescue from the perils of the open boat. All night long the weather had been breathless, but with the rising of the sun there had come a small breeze of wind, a little to the eastward of south, which as the morning advanced freshened, and the schooner was sliding through it once again, heading saucily along her course, with Ducrow strutting the deck in high spirits, a couple of negroes repairing a sail forward, another at the tiller, a fourth perspiring at the old pump.

Suddenly Ducrow bawled out, "Sail ho!" pointing ahead.

I looked languidly in the direction he indicated, not rising even, so sick was I of this cry of "Sail ho!" heretofore as barren to my purpose as a parrot's meaningless croak of the words. I was conversing with Miss Grant at the time, and turned to her afresh, proceeding in what I was saying without giving the vessel ahead another thought. Time passed; presently Ducrow said, "Dat fellow's a big 'un what's coming 'long dah. We mustn't hab de go-by given us this time, if it's to be helped, sah. Must make more fuss, odderwise dere's no chance ob getting compassionated." So saying, he went to the little locker, took out the ensign, and bent it, Jack down, to the halliards, and ran it half-mast high, belaying it slackly that it might blow out with a good visible curve. This done, he bawled to his men to shorten sail.

"Down jib, mah blackbirds! down wid both tawpsails! jump, mah blacks, jump! Hurrah now fo' de ship. Up maintack, let go mainpeak-halliards. Now den, Hebenezer, you black teef, down hellum, and trow us right up into de wind—up into de wind—up into de wind, I says," walloping about in a most extraordinary manner as he bawled these orders, and springing from the deck on his naked feet as though the planks were too hot—and well they might be!—to suffer him to stand upon them. Thus all in a moment, so to say, the little schooner was brought to a halt; her mainsail "scandalized" her masts half denuded of canvas, her bowsprit pointing to the wind, the few cloths she showed shivering to the breeze with such a symbol of human distress flying aloft as richly coloured and most admirably rounded off the picture of misery which the posture of the vessel now submitted.

The stranger was heading dead for us, as though she must run us down indeed, so immediately were we lying athwart her hawse. She came steadily along, with her yards braced forward, a vessel apparently of six hundred tons, painted black, standing high out of water, a fore-topmast-stunsail set, her royal yards close to the trucks, with a glimpse to be had of large black tops under the curve of her topsails. I went with Miss Grant to the side to watch the stranger. My heart beat fast with expectation, yet I struggled hard with my impulse of hope, dreading in the mood I then was the effect of a second disappointment. Suddenly the vessel took in her foretopmast-stunsail, then a spot of colour floated aloft past the shining round of her courses to the gaff end. It blew out, and I muttered just above my breath, "Thank God!" as I recognized the English flag.

"He means to speak us, at all events," I cried. "Pray Heaven he will show mercy, and take us off this schooner. Why, if he were bound on a search for the Nor'-West passage I'd go with him."

"I dare say," Miss Grant exclaimed, in a musing sort of way, "that the captain of that ship will wonder at our wish to leave the schooner when we are within a week's sail of Havana."

"Yes," said I, looking at her, whilst she kept her face averted by continuing to gaze at the approaching vessel; "but *we* are not bound to Havana, you know. Rio is the place we started for; and besides, are we within a week's sail of Havana? Perhaps to-morrow may introduce a succession of calms that shall last a month, during all which time we are to lie here in this bescorched schooner, with our lovely countenances slowly roasting into a rich brown under yonder heavenly furnace! Eh, Miss Grant? Never mind about that skipper there *wondering*. Better Van Diemen's Land in a ship like *yon*, as they'd say in the north, than Havana with Rio close on its heels in this little frying-pan."

She turned just to glance at me, with a gleam like a smile in the look she shot through the dark fringes that drooped again as she resumed

her attitude of watching the coming ship. 'Twas not often that I got
a view of her mind; but by her manner then, it seemed to me it was
her intention to let me know she had obtained a very accurate sight
of mine. Be it so, thought I; but if that craft there will receive us, we'll
board her all the same.

She was a handsome picture as she drew close, becalming the blue
under her lee into a tremorless mirror, in which the reflection of her
swelling canvas sank in cream, but lustrous as silver too. She had so
keen a stem that she clove the rippling surface with scarce the disturbance of a flash of froth in the wrinkles which broke from her brows,
and which went away astern of her in lines of light when her shadow
was off them, and when they streamed fair to the sun. She was heading as if to run us down, but on a sudden her main-topsail was braced
aback, with a falling off of her head that gave us a view of her decks,
with two white quarter-boats swinging at the weather davits; a couple
of men standing at the poop-rail clothed in white, with broad straw
hats; beyond them the flutter of woman's apparel, as I thought; several
sailors on the top-gallant-forecastle, their whole shapes plain through
the low open rail that protected this part of the craft. As she came
floating alongside within easy talking distance, she seemed to tower
above us like a line-of-battle ship. One of the two men dressed in white
approached the mizzen-rigging to hail us. I now saw a woman standing near the skylight, and at that moment another woman came up
through the little companion-hatch and joined her.

Ducrow sprang upon the bulwarks, and pulling off his cap he wildly
flourished it, whilst he vociferated, "Ho, dah ship ahoy!"

"Hallo!" responded the man standing at the mizzen-rigging.

"What ship am dat?" bawled Ducrow, but with a fine air of importance in his manner, as though this were a ceremony to yield him dignity, and therefore to be made as much of as possible. I secretly bestowed
a sea-blessing or two upon his bald head in my impatience; but it would
not do to interrupt him.

"The *Bristol Trader*," came back the answer, "of and for Bristol from
Havana, five days out. And what schooner's that?"

"Dah *Orphan* ob Nassoo, bound to Havana, but percastinated by
calms and head-winds. We hab somet'ing pertikler to communicate,
and will send a boat."

"Ay," cried the other; "but can't you tell us what's the matter with
you without sending a boat? You have your ensign Jack down; what is
wrong? Bear a hand, for time's precious."

On hearing this, and fearing that Ducrow would muddle this opportunity away for us with his negro dandyfications and fine airs and words, I sprang on to the rail beside him, and with a thrust of my elbow tumbled him inboard.

"Ship ahoy!" I shouted.

"Hallo!"

"The case is this. This lady," pointing to Miss Grant, "and myself sailed as passengers from the Downs in June last aboard the brig *Iron Crown.* There was a mutiny. The mate was killed, the captain disappeared, and the brig was headed for Cuba. One of the Bahama Cays was made, and this lady and I were marooned on it. A boat came ashore, we left the island in her, and were picked up by this schooner, and we desire to exchange her for your ship, if you will receive us as passengers."

The man in white flourished his hand. "Come aboard," he exclaimed; "I dare say we can arrange."

"Over wid dah boat, over wid dah boat, mah darkies," screamed Ducrow. "Hurrah now, bullies, no stopping now to shave, if yah please; 'taint dinner-time yet, so no loafing."

The schooner carried a boat on chocks amid ships; as leaky, sun-blistered, paint-denuded a fabric as the mother whose child she was. The gangway was unshipped, the three negroes and Ducrow yelling and bawling all together, and stamping with their naked feet till the thrashing of the decks sounded like twenty or thirty people clapping their hands, ran the boat to the gangway, and launched her smack-fashion. The excitement of one negro however carried him overboard with her. He fell plump, but his black head instantly shot up alongside like a sweep's brush out of a chimney-pot, and in a trice he was in the boat, combing the wet out of his breeches and grinning into Ducrow's face, who shook his fist at him as "dah clumsiest son ob a hog wid a sow for a grandmudder as was ebber to be met 'pon dah high seas."

A second negro then jumped into the boat, into which the water was beginning to drain in twenty places, so that I saw if we did not bear a hand we should be awash before we had half measured the distance between the schooner and the ship. The negroes threw the oars over, and splashed me alongside the *Bristol Trader* as though rowing for a wager, with a dollar for the man who should catch the most "crabs." I sprang into the main-chains, and in a minute stood upon the ship's poop.

The captain, as the man who had hailed us proved to be, was an intelligent-looking, weather-darkened, iron-haired fellow of some forty-five years, thin, smooth-faced, with a grey, seawardly eye, kind in its expression. I raised my hat, he did the same. I repeated my story, now relating it circumstantially. The two women drew near as I talked, and he inter rupted me once to introduce me to one of them as his wife, to the other as a friend of hers, who was going home in his ship as a passenger. My romantic story seemed quite to the taste of these ladies, who frequently broke out into exclamations of astonishment, whilst they sent glances full of curiosity at Miss Grant, who had withdrawn to the shelter of the awning on the schooner's quarter-deck, and sat there watching us, too far off for her beauty to be evident, though one might have guessed her charms even at that distance by the delicate light of her face under her broad hat.

"But you were bound to Rio," said the captain.

"Yes," I answered.

"You may easily get to Rio from Havana," he continued. "That schooner should carry you to Havana in a week. It seems a pity to travel all the way home again, when your port is comparatively at hand. We could provision you too with a few articles to render the run more tolerable."

"No," said I warmly, "there is nothing in food and drink to render that schooner tolerable. Her cabin creeps with cockroaches, the atmosphere can scarce be respired for the heat and smell of it. The lady and I have talked the matter over, and we are earnest in our wish to return to England. Why, see here, sir; you'll be able to land us at Bristol before we could hope to reach Rio, even suppose yonder schooner should convey us to Havana in a week's time, which I gravely question when I recall the spells of weather which have nearly murdered us. Of course," I went on, seeing him look a bit reflective, "we should ask you to receive us as passengers, that is to say, as people who will be glad to defray all charges for accommodating us."

"Oh," he said, in a tone of indifference, "that matter can be hereafter settled. As a mere question of humanity it would be my duty to receive you. You have no luggage, you say?"

"None."

"Well, sir, the lady can come along at once." He looked over the side. "Hi, you Jumbos! shove off now, and bring the lady aboard."

I hailed the schooner: "Miss Grant, the negroes will fetch you. Ducrow, come you along with the lady that you may receive your money."

Ten minutes later I had assisted Miss Grant over the side, and escorted her on to the poop. She bowed with stately grace to the two women, who courtesied to her as though she were a princess. The captain, whose name by the way was Foljambe, held a trifle aloof at sight of her, eyeing her with a mixture of astonishment and admiration. Perhaps now, with a couple of her own sex at hand to contrast her by, helped by such definition as her fine figure would obtain from the white and roomy deck, the clean brass-work, the sparkling skylights, the snowy awning, with the wheel in the sunshine past it, at which stood the smartly-dressed figure of an English sailor carelessly leaning upon the spokes, watching us under the spread of a great Cuban hat—perhaps now, in the swift glance I threw at her, I could see in a manner scarce to be managed before, how little her beauty had suffered from the trials we had come through, from exposure to the high sun, from the many bitter anxieties which had clouded her mind. The glow of the tropics was in her cheek, and seemed to clarify the brightness and to enrich the loveliness of her full, dark, speaking eyes; the very neglect of apparel enforced by privation appeared as a grace in her, as the dishevelment of her soft brown lustrous hair gave a character of romance to the dignified sweetness of her countenance. I could not wonder that Mrs. Foljambe and her friend stared, nor that the captain should have fallen back a step to her approach, as though veritably startled by her beauty, as I had been indeed when I first met her.

Captain Ducrow came up to me, cap in hand. His strut was incomparable. I heard the half-smothered laughter of men forward as he bowed first to the captain's wife, then to her friend, then to the captain, bringing his cap to his heart, and slowly bending his body, till I thought he had a mind to double himself up after the manner of stage contortionists.

"Berry sorry to lose yah, Massa Musgrave," he said to me, "and berry much sorrier still to say good-bye to dis most bootiful lady, which," he added, with an emotional grunt in his voice, "I may nebber, nebber see agin in dis yeerie earth—" He was proceeding, but I could see that Captain Foljambe was impatient. So I cut him short by handing him the bank note, and then shook him warmly by the hand, thanking him with the sort of sincerity that a man who had gone through what I had could hardly miss of, for his rescue of us and his subsequent kindness. Miss Grant also gave him her hand, addressing a few words of gratitude; but my gravity vanished when the poor fellow suddenly plumped down on one knee and lifted her fingers to the side of his face where his mouth was.

"Now then, skipper," cried Captain Foljambe, "away with ye, my lad. This is the breeze to make the most of, so please don't keep me waiting."

"Gor bless yah! Gorramighty in hebben bless yah both, an' make yah happy," cried the poor fellow, backing to the gangway as though from the presence of royalty, and speaking with so much emotion that I looked to see him blubber. "May dah good Lord look down pon dis ship, and send yah ten-knot breezes all dah way;" and arrived at the gangway, he dropped over the side, and was pulled to his little schooner.

"Get your topsail-yard swung, Mr. Murphy," exclaimed the captain, addressing the mate who was the other of the two men I had noticed clothed in white, and who had been standing quietly on the lee-side of the poop, waiting for this business to end.

The sailors sprang to the braces; the great yards came slowly round, the sails, silk-white to the sunshine, swelled out to the blue breeze, and the *Bristol Trader* was heading along on her course again. Meanwhile the two negroes had splashed Ducrow aboard his little schooner in hot haste, to save themselves the job of baling the boat, as I suspected; but I gathered what the hurry was about, when the poor yellow-faced fellow, who had drawn his cap down over his ears in his excitement, floundered as though pursued by a bull to the signal-halliards, hauled down the ensign with frantic gesticulations, bent it on afresh with the Jack right-side up, and then sent it aloft again, yelling to one of his negroes to lay aft in a voice that was distinctly audible, though the distance between the vessels was being magically widened, considering the lightness of the breeze. The negro seized one length of the halliards, Ducrow the other, and between them they dipped the flag, that is to say, they lowered it as a token of farewell—hoisting it anew, and then lowering it—not once, not five times, but over and over and over again; the whole dusky crowd of them howling a good-bye at us every time the flag rose to the masthead, until the schooner had slipped so far astern that their voices could no longer be caught, whilst the flag itself had dwindled into a mere red spot.

It was the last I saw of the little craft ere I turned to accept Captain Foljambe's invitation to step below. I behold her now again with my mind's eye, heaving to the long ocean swell, with a tremor of light in her black side, as she lifts it wet from the brine, slowly paying off with her jib rounding, her main-peak hoisting, a dingy white topsail slowly creeping to the masthead, the Liliputianized figures of her crew making a very toy of the little fabric indeed as she heads slowly into the mighty loneliness of the ocean past her bows, with the glare of the sun in the sky over her going down like a wall of dazzling brass to the sifting into it of the whitish blue of the heavens trembling upon the remote western confines. Ah, there are no memories so dream-like as those one carries away from the ocean.

Chapter IX
Home

THE *BRISTOL TRADER* WAS one of the most comfortable ships of her class that ever I was aboard of. Her cabins were tall and roomy, her decks spacious, her port-holes large, her hatchways big enough to serve for an emigrant ship. After our experiences on the island, in the open boat, and on the schooner, it was like arriving at some cheerful, hospitable inn, with the welcome of a blazing fire, a hot supper, and a warm bed, after hours of blind groping over miles of snow-clad moors, to find one's self in such a ship as this. One needs to be marooned to appreciate comforts made cheap by homeliness and familiarity. We had been absolutely destitute aboard the schooner, without the commonest and meanest conveniences—no hairbrush, no towels, soap, sheets, and what not; nay, there had not been even a looking-glass, and neither Miss Grant nor I had the least idea of the sort of faces we submitted until we had been conducted to our cabins by Captain Foljambe and his wife. I borrowed a razor from the captain, and shaved myself for the first time since I had left the island, and I protest the sensation was as though nature had clothed me in a new skin. It is the common-places of life which make themselves heard of in maritime disasters. The captain was good enough to lend me a clean shirt and collar, with other articles of underclothing, all which sat very comfortably upon me, as we were pretty nearly of the same build. He told me that his wife was taking care of Miss Grant, that she (namely Mrs. Foljambe), together with her friend Mrs. Tweed, had between them a plentiful stock of clothing, so that my companion could be at once made comfortable, and kept so until our arrival at Bristol.

He was a man that improved on acquaintance, shrewd, respectful, sailorly in a sort of careless manner that was a grace in its way, well spoken, with something of the manners of a well-bred gentleman, roughened without being coarsened by the usage of the ocean.

He sat in my bunk whilst I dressed, and asked me many questions about the *Iron Crown*, and our life on the island. He could give me no news of the brig, did not seem to know of her name even, but he told me that whilst at Havana he had heard of a vessel which had fallen in with a boat containing four men, that had gone adrift during thick weather from the craft that owned it; and this coming on top of Ducrow's narration, confirmed my belief that Gordon and the others had been saved; for which I was heartily thankful indeed.

It was long past the dinner-hour, but neither Miss Grant nor I had broken out fast since the morning.

On my telling Captain Foljambe this he immediately gave orders to his steward to prepare a meal for us in the cabin, and by the time I had finished civilizing myself with the razor, hairbrush, and the skipper's linen, the meal awaited us: cold roast chicken, fine white biscuits, ham, several plates of fruit with the sweetness of the tropic soil still in their flavour and freshness, a decanter of brandy, a *monkey* of cold water—why, Heaven bless us! after poor Ducrow's brine-toughened buffalo meat and his caulkers of water warm from the scuttlebutts, this was such a princely regale that the recollection of it bids fair to outlast the memory of many a sumptuous banquet that I had before and have since sat down to. The afternoon sunshine flashed azure off the water through the open ports, and filled the interior with a soft golden haze that floated cool to every sense in me after our days and nights of the *Orphan's* cabin, upon the atmosphere freshened by the gushings of air from the white canvas tubes of the windsails, whilst the eye was soothed by the violet shadow cast by the awning down upon the open skylights, in whose gaping casements the hot breeze hummed as though it echoed the burden of the island insect chorus.

I was conversing with the captain's wife and Mrs. Tweed, two very homely, unaffected ladies, brimful of kindness and sympathy, when Miss Grant arrived. I had never seen her beauty look so rich. The peculiar complexion of the atmosphere in the cabin just then may have helped her, but methought there was the glory of the newly-blown flower in her as she stood a moment after coming out of her cabin, instantly smiling as our gaze met. I brought her to the table, and we seated ourselves. There was a West Indian plant, bearing a starshaped flower lovely as the lily, but inodorous, trained against the handsomely-framed trunk of the mizzenmast, sloping abaft the table from the deck to the cabin. The captain cut one of these flowers and presented it with a sailorly bow to Miss Grant, who thanked him, and put it in her bosom.

"This sort of thing," said I, almost jealous to think that the hand of a stranger should have touched a stem that was to find so sacred a resting-place, "makes one feel alive again. I fancy I must have been dead for a month, perhaps a little longer. Everything strikes me with an astonishment that is preposterously unnatural. This damask table-cloth, how white it is! this crystal tumbler—I never before knew glass to sparkle so! and yonder roast chicken!—upon my word, I thought there had been an end of hens."

The captain laughed. "I have been ship-wrecked, sir," he exclaimed. "I've known the time when the hairy face of a seaman, all knobs and warts, has set me weeping as though I was taking my last view of the only man left in the world besides myself."

"How very odd!" exclaimed Mrs. Foljambe. "I've never heard you say that before, William."

"My dear," said he, "had it been the last *woman* perhaps I shouldn't have cried."

"Because I dare say you'd have taken care it shouldn't have been your last view of her," observed Mrs. Tweed dryly. This lady was a widow.

"Now, Miss Grant," said I, working away at the roast fowl and ham, and immensely enjoying Captain Foljambe's excellent old brandy "shall we ask our kind friend here to shift his helm and give chase to the schooner, that we may overhaul and board her afresh, and make our way to Havana in her?"

"If you will return to her, I will," she answered.

"That means no," said Captain Foljambe. "No for all hands. Bad look-out to shift the helm now, Miss Grant. It blows a pretty six-knot breeze."

"Hurrah!" cried I. "Why, with this clipper keel under us we shall be heaving Bristol into sight whilst the little *Orphan* is still dodging the ghost of a catspaw in waters not yet hull down. No, no, it was a voyage not to be pursued. A twenty-five-ton boat, Mrs. Foljambe! her one pump going day and night! all the plagues of Egypt rolled into one, in the shape of cockroaches! Think of *that*, Mrs. Tweed."

"Shocking, sir," she cried, "the horrid creatures! But there are none here, thank goodness."

"Here and there one," said the captain.

And so we went on, chatting and eating, then mounted on deck, I with a big Havana cigar in my mouth, so joyous in spirits that it might have needed but a band of music to have started me off dancing for the rest of the day. What words have I to describe the delight that filled me, as I looked at the sparkling blue sea, sloping between the awning-stanchions to the heavens, which were reddening all round to the westering of the luminary, and at the swelling folds of the courses, which, past the edge of our canvas shelter, rose in stately cloud upon cloud, every cloth silently doing its work, rounding marble-like to leeward, the shadows of the rigging lying in delicate curves in each still, snow-like heart, and the tinkle of water swiftly shorn at the stem faintly sweeping a bell-like note through the steady breezing of the wind! The ocean looked boundless from the height of the poop-deck, and the way before us was yet a long road. But my heart beat the more gladly for the very thought of it when I turned to look at Aurelia Grant, and reflected that she was still by my side; that for many a week we should be together; that, in short, I had by this manoeuvre indefinitely postponed the hour of our separation. Was I dishonourable? Was I disloyal? Was I unfaithful to my trust? Maybe, maybe. How *you* would have acted in my case I cannot tell. Fallibility must fail somewhere, says the old moralist. And I was in love.

But you have made one eventful voyage with me, and I am as little desirous possibly as you that you should undertake a second uneventful one—uneventful, I mean, in respect of incident, for we were a smart ship, and the crew hearty and honest, the captain a wise disciplinarian, and his two mates plain, sturdy, steady-going seamen. Yet though uneventful in the sense of gales of wind, collisions, lee-shores, leaks, mutinies, and the rest of the list of maritime perils, for *me* it was marked by a passage that rendered it more stirring than all the experiences we had gone through boiled down into one could have proved. I have spoken of a quality of reserve in Miss Grant's manner when aboard the schooner, of my own sensitiveness to it, and how between us there had come something that seemed to hold us a bit apart; but this had made way before we left the little vessel for the old frankness, the warmth, the sweet and fearless cordiality of her bearing towards me when on the island. Yet we had not been twenty-four hours in the *Bristol Trader* when I noticed that her behaviour was once more charged with a chilly and uncomfortable element of reserve. Then she even grew timorous at times, shunning my gaze, though sometimes I'd catch her unawares watching me with an expression of wistfulness that lay sad in her eyes, like a shadow of melancholy there. I very well knew she had guessed that my proposal to sail home was merely that I might possess her society for some weeks or perhaps months longer, and I would fancy that in thinking over this she had come to resent it, as though she was now clearly seeing that my duty lay in proceeding with her in the schooner to Havana, whence, as Captain Foljambe was constantly saying—and I certainly did not like him the better for this confounded trick of iteration—we would have met a ship to transport us to Rio without delay.

All this secret worrying in me over what *might* be in her thoughts resulted in cooling my manner too, though my love for her increased as my demeanour became inexpressive; and sometimes it would happen that we were together only at meal-times, by which I mean that I would go and sulkily post myself in some corner with a book, which I would read upside down, whilst she paced the deck with the captain's wife or

Mrs. Tweed, or remained below in the cabin. I was for ever seeking to interpret her, but never could find the hints I sought. When with her I would constantly talk of Alexander and of the plans I had formed: for instance, we should arrive at Bristol; we should then proceed to London, where she would take up her abode at the hotel she occupied before she left England, whilst I made all necessary preparations for a second attempt to carry her to her sweetheart. But I took notice whilst I thus talked that she had very little to say to it all. She'd thank me and tell me I was too good, and protest that it was not likely she would put me to the trouble of escorting her again; that most probably on her arrival in London she would write the story of our adventures to Rio, and wait for my cousin to fetch her—*most probably*; indeed, she would add with a sigh, she had not made up her mind. There was plenty of time to think the matter over, and meanwhile I was not to dream that she would again subject me to the risk of under-going perhaps worse adventures than those which we had happily come safe through. This and the like she would say, but always with a sort of air of in difference, as though she talked to a person whose programme she did not regard as a very sincere one, and as though in consequence she could take no interest in it.

There came a day however when feeling grew too strong for me. Conscience had wrestled hard with inclination, but to no purpose. Often, whilst tossing in my bunk at night, whilst seated alone on the deck by day, I would ask myself if I had not acted dishonourably in falling in love with this woman, and whether I should not be rendering my sin heinous beyond forgiveness by proposing to her. But it was like putting some insoluble riddle to my heart. I gave it up. Had Alexander been my brother instead of my cousin it would have been all the same. I was head over ears in love with Aurelia Grant, and I made up my mind to marry her if she would have me. And there came a time, as I have said, when patience gave way, when passion grew too powerful for restraint, and when I determined to put the matter boldly to her and see what she had to say to it.

The ship was then on the equatorial verge of the Bay of Biscay, so you will gather that I did not make up my mind in a hurry. Our clipper had made a noble run through the trades, with fine weather and pleasant breezes to follow, and now on this day at noon we found ourselves under all plain sail on the port tack, bowlines triced out, a light breeze off the bow, and the vessel sliding quietly through it over the long undulations of the Atlantic swell, flowing with pulse-like regularity from the westward. When the dusk settled down, the half moon shone in the sky. Her light lay soft and white upon our high-reaching canvas, and filled the shadow between the rails with a silver tint, through which the forms of the seamen moved in dark outlines. The awning was furled, and the poop-deck lay almond-white to the stars, with many quicksilver-like ripplings of radiance in the polished brass-work, and the man at the helm rising with the lift of the stern against a faintness like the after-glow on the sea-line there, his shape sharply wrought upon it, and the circle and spokes of the wheel keen as though he and it were an etching in India ink.

I came on deck after an hour spent alone in my cabin, and stood a little at the head of the ladder that led to the poop, trying to persuade myself that I lingered to admire this fair ocean night-picture; but I found my eyes quickly going from it in search of Miss Grant. I saw her in a moment standing in the dark shade flung on the deck by the reflection of the mizzen-mast. She was talking to Mrs. Foljambe and Mr. Murphy, the chief mate. I put on the lightest air I could summon, and approached the group in an easy saunter.

"Pleasant weather this for the close of October, Mrs. Foljambe," said I; "it won't be quite so nice a little higher up."

"There's no climate after all, Mr. Musgrave, that beats the English," said Mrs. Foljambe.

"Well, madam," said I, "I might agree with you if I were a slug or a water-rat."

"You must go to the west of Ireland for a fine climate," quoth Mr. Murphy.

"Too much steam," said Mrs. Foljambe. "I once stayed a week at Ballyvaghan, and it was like looking at natural scenery through the smoke from a bowl of hot punch."

"You should have thried Ballaghaderreen, ma'm," said Mr. Murphy.

"Say Ballydehob at once, now," answered Mrs. Foljambe; "and I am sure a hob the poor creatures who live there must find it—a hob with a steaming kettle on it."

"Well," said I, "this evening is a fine one, but it is a bit chilly for all that. What say you to a stroll, Miss Grant?"

She assented, and we left Mrs. Foljambe and Mr. Murphy arguing on the climate of Ireland.

"Will you take my arm?" said I. "This long heave is gentle, but it doesn't help to steady one."

She did as I asked. I thought I felt a little tremor in her fingers; she was silent and pensive, looking away from me towards the ocean; but this had been her demeanour of late, and was therefore not new in her.

"This is the Bay of Biscay," said I; "not many more days now before us."

"I shall be glad when the voyage is ended," she answered; "the Foljambes are very kind, everything is nice here, but I am weary—weary—*weary* of the sea, Mr. Musgrave."

"You had need be; it has used you very ill, and something of this weariness of the ocean you are extending."

"Extending! I don't understand you."

"Well now, to be plain, Miss Grant, you have had enough of my company."

"You don't *think* so," she answered quietly; "why do you *say* so then?"

"I say so because I think so, and I think so because the fancy has been forced upon me by your manner. Since we have been in this ship you have ceased to be what you were."

"What was I?"

"Warm, cordial, frank, making our association to me so sweet an intimacy, that though I was clamorous to leave the island, I now vow to Heaven I would be glad to go on suffering a lifelong imprisonment in it to preserve what I have lost in you."

"You have lost nothing," she exclaimed, speaking in a subdued voice, that did not however conceal her agitation; "if you have noticed any change in me, it is but the reflection of your own manner."

"My manner! It should be warm, not cold; it should be bright, not gloomy, if love be the hot and radiant emotion the poets tell us it is, Aurelia—"

She fixed her dark eyes upon me as I pronounced her name, and halted, looking at me intently, but for a few seconds only, then her gaze fell, and she resumed her walk, still holding my arm.

"Aurelia," I said gently, "you heard what I have said—you know now that I love you."

"I have known it a long while," she answered, still looking down, but speaking with composure, though I have little doubt I should have felt her heart in her finger-tips had I brought them to my lips.

"You say I have no sympathy; but I am quicker to see than you—quicker to recognize."

Her meaning was as clear as the sound of a bell. We were to leeward, forward as far as the deck extended; the sheet of the great main course curved like a dusky wing betwixt us and the moonlight on the water, and we stood in this dusk, concealed from the others, obscured from all eyes in the fore-end, though clearly visible to each other. It was my turn now to halt. I let fall her hand from my arm, then clasped it and the other as well. She stood passive. I drew her to me till her face was close to mine, and kissed her sorehead. She released her hands with a manner of tender agitation, and went to the rail and looked over, and I heard her draw her breath in a sob.

I stepped to her side and said, "If I have grieved you, forgive me. The time had come when I could not help speaking. I have loved you from the hour I first saw you. It has been a hard fight. I have endeavoured to do my duty, will still attempt it if you command me, but your beauty and sweetness have conquered my resolution of silence."

She wept silently.

"See now how I have vexed you," said I.

She shook her head. "No, I am happy," she answered, in a voice so low that I had to bend my ear to catch the words. "I am indeed happy in knowing that you love me. It is as it should be. It is—it is—as *he* would—as he *might* desire it. Poor boy. But—but—"

She raised her head, and the next instant her face was hidden on my shoulder, my arms around her, and her heart beating against mine.

And thus it was that we managed to round off in true poetical style our most eventful experiences as a marooned couple. That this was a right and proper ending I will not affirm, but that we could help it I do most vehemently deny. And, after all, if you will but gravely consider the matter, you will see it was scarce possible but that two people thrown together as Aurelia and I were should fall in love, to the exclusion of all promptings of loyalty and conscience on the one hand, and of all impulses of an earlier passion on the other. Nor was this all. The character of our intimacy demanded our union. Indeed, Aurelia did not scruple to tell me afterwards—I mean when she was my wife— that even had her love been made to falter by thoughts of my cousin's claims upon her, and by the memory of their vows and betrothal, the recollection of the island must have sufficed to rally her into accepting me as destined by fate or old ocean, which is the same thing, to be her husband. But why enlarge upon this? It would have been easy to shift the helm of this yarn towards the close of it, and submit myself as having cut a highly virtuous figure. But then is it highly virtuous to heave one's emotional obligations overboard?—to confront a pure and ennobling passion with a countenance acidulated by some bolus of conscience that is, strictly speaking, neither here nor there, though it works very uncomfortably in the moral system, without leaving one much the better for it?

We arrived at Bristol on the 6th of November, after above four months of much livelier experiences than I should again care to undergo on any account whatever, and proceeded to London, where before the month was out we were married. The wedding, as will be supposed, was a very quiet one, so quiet indeed that there was nobody but ourselves present; I mean nobody in any way concerned in it. Privacy of this kind is a happiness that attends the nuptials of those only who are without relations; that is to say, when the marriage is an honest one, done in the light of day, and not what one may call a window-and-ladder match. Aurelia was as good as alone in the world, and for the matter of that so was I; so we drove one morning to church and returned man and wife, and I remember saying to my blushing beauty as we stepped arm-in-arm from the sacred building, that if all marooning experiments had ended as ours did, the punishment must long before have become so fashionable that there would be no uninhabited islands left; the most sterile rock would be occupied by some languishing couple, and it might come to skippers being handsomely rewarded for reporting so much even as the creation of a volcanic spot of earth.

But before I was married I wrote a letter to my cousin, Alexander Fraser. It was a very long letter indeed. I gave him the full relation of our adventures, and do not know that I spared him the most trifling detail, so anxious was I to submit the whole picture to him, that there might be wanting no incident which, omitted, I might have regretted as helpful to the general apology of the missive. I told him that of course I expected he would resent my conduct at first, that he would consider I had taken a mean advantage of the trust he confided in me, but that when he came to think the matter carefully over, he would understand that nothing else than what had happened was possible. I touched very delicately upon Aurelia's and my enforced intimacy of association on the island; delicately, I say, but I indicated it too, for therein, methought, lay the very handsomest excuse any man could seek or expect for what I had done. Whatever occurred to me to say in self-extenuation, I said; but though I took great pains, wrote in a subdued strain, with plentiful appeals to his sailorly instincts as a man to judge me kindly, to believe that I had embarked most honestly, that for weeks and weeks I had never thought of the girl but as his sweetheart, that even after we had quitted the island I was still for conveying Aurelia to Rio, though I was loving her passionately then, and abhorred the thought of parting with her—I say, that though I did my best in this letter, I felt at every word which dropped from my pen that it was like rubbing a cat the wrong way, as uncomfortable to the stroking hand as to the creature thus dealt with. Perhaps I said too much; then it would occur to me that I had not said enough; and sometimes I thought it would have been best to say nothing at all, and leave him to conclude that the *Iron Crown* had foundered, and we with her.

Well, a few months after I had dispatched this epistle—this great bundle of manuscript I should call it, for it ran into many sheets—during all which time not a syllable reached me from Rio, I received a letter from Captain Foljambe, in which he gave me two items of news, both of great interest to me.

The first concerned the *Iron Crown*. It seems that this vessel had been found derelict at sea, about a hundred leagues westward of the island of Cuba. She was fallen in with by a French barque, whose people on boarding her discovered a couple of auger-holes in her bows, one of which had been plugged, whilst the leakage of the other had been, strangely enough, stopped by a fish that lay jammed in the orifice, just leaving room enough for a small draining of brine, scarce as much as would have raised a foot of water in her hold in a fortnight. On entering the cabin they found the ceiling, stanchions, and a portion of the forward bulkheads scorched, with other signs of a fire having been kindled, manifestly for the purpose of destroying her. There were traces of blood upon her quarter-deck and waist, whether human or not could not be told. A loft she was a complete wreck; most of her sails in rags, her main-topmast gone, her fore-topgallant-mast hanging by its gear, and about ten feet of her starboard bulwarks smashed level to the covering board. Her name was plain upon the stern, and she was unquestionably the brig in which we had sailed. She had apparently encountered a violent storm, but whether before or after her abandonment was not to be guessed. There was nothing to be done with her, and as she would prove a formidable obstruction to drive into in the dark, the Frenchmen knocked the plug out, cleared away the fish, and left her to drown. Nothing was known of her crew, and I may as well say here, that though I continued long afterwards to make inquiries, I never got to hear of them, and therefore remain to this hour ignorant of the manner in which Broadwater had met his end—whether he was murdered, or perished by his own act.

Foljambe's second item of news was to this effect. During his outward run to Havana, when somewhat to the southward of the Great Bahama Bank, he sighted a little schooner which, on his nearing her, proved to be the *Orphan*. Ducrow, standing at the rail, recognized the *Bristol Trader*, and yelled in his demonstrative fashion to be permitted to step on board, that he might make inquiries after myself and the lady. There was very little wind at the time, and Foljambe told him he was at liberty to come, but that he was not going to back his topsail-yard to oblige him. On this the schooner's boat was thrown over the side,

Ducrow and two blacks jumped into her, and in hot haste and shouting loudly swept the little leaking fabric to the main-chains of the ship, over which Ducrow floundered, smirking, flourishing his tasselled cap, and bowing as of old with many contortions. The main purport of his visit was, that I might be told through Captain Foljambe that he had found out the island on which we had been marooned, and had carried off not only our luggage, but the Spanish negro whom we had left there. The fellow, he said, was now aboard the schooner, and he pointed to a black who stood surveying the ship from the schooner's forecastle. He told Captain Foljambe that he did not know there was a man on the island—and indeed I had said nothing about the poor runaway, as I supposed that he desired to lie in hiding for the rest of his life in that ocean retreat. Ducrow and one of his darkies—Moses—went ashore, and after a short search found the open hatch in the sand. They peered in—the evening was then gathering—and Ducrow, being afraid to go first, told the negro to lead the way, giving him a kick to help him to a proper posture of resolution. Moses plumped down, and Ducrow was in the act of following him, when he heard the negro yelling, "De debbil, de debbil!—here's de debbil himshef,—here's de debbil himshef!—oh, Lord!" followed by sounds of wrestling and hard breathing, whereupon Ducrow instantly took to his heels, but before he could reach his boat he was tripped up by some one who pursued him, the man in chase falling over him heavily. This fellow proved to be the Spanish negro. Ducrow, jumping up, concluded that his end was arrived, and whipped out with a long knife, intending, as he told Captain Foljambe, to sell his life at the highest price he could get for it. Then followed a parley. The negro could only speak Spanish. Luckily for Ducrow, he knew a few words in that tongue, enough with gesticulations to let the negro understand that he meant him no harm. Ebenezer, the mate of the schooner, was in the boat. This black had been a Cuban slave, and was able to converse with the other, who was speedily tranquillized by his pacific assurances. When he was told that he would be a free man under the British flag, and that whilst that bunting continued to fly over his head he need not fear of being recaptured, he told Ducrow that he would be willing to enter as a sailor with him. In short, he had had enough of the island, though I believe he had not lived alone upon it above a fortnight. He said it was haunted. One evening he saw the ghost of a black man come out of the sea and pass into the forest and vanish, and he declared it was the spectre of the dead negro who had been with him in the boat when they drifted to the island. It ended, Ducrow told Captain Foljambe, in their clearing the underground rooms, not only of our luggage, but of everything else in it—the chairs, table, pots, and pans, muskets, and so forth. This was good booty to Ducrow, who made a division of it amongst the men, the Spanish negro being very well satisfied with his share. Ducrow sent many flattering messages to Aurelia and myself, and particularly begged the captain to compliment me in his name on my taste in shirts, and to inform me that he had never worn anything choicer in the way of linen. I confess we both begrudged the rogues the apparel they had come by. I know that Aurelia's and my outfit had cost me a round sum of money, and that she had left enough dresses and other clothing behind her to have furnished her with a trousseau.

It was eighteen months before I heard from Rio, by which time I had arrived at the conclusion that either my cousin Alexander was dead, or that he hated me too violently to put pen to paper. Aurelia believed that death was the reason of his silence. He had died, she believed, of grief, and I was heartily glad, for my own sake as much as for my wife's, when one morning I received a letter from him; for I may as well say her notion that he had died of a broken heart was the cause of many fits of melancholy in her, which rendered me a little peevish with jealousy; so that had Alexander not written, there might by and by have come some little unhappiness into my married life.

He began by saying that he had made up his mind not to write to me at all. He had hated me consumedly for months after reading my letter, and would have been pleased to kill me, only that the voyage home was too tedious and expensive an undertaking for so twopenny an issue. News of the *Iron Crown* having been found abandoned and in a wrecked condition had reached him before he got my letter, and he concluded that Aurelia and I were at the bottom of the sea. He had written home to the owners of the brig for information, but his inquiries remained unanswered. His getting my letter, he said, was like receiving a missive from the other world, and he swore that before he was one-third through it he heartily wished that it *had* come from the other world, and from the deepest and most fiery part of it too, for to that place did his temper consign me at every full-stop he came to. Of Aurelia he desired to say nothing. Women were sent into the world to make fools of men, and not even old age hindered the most of them from struggling on in fulfilment of this mission. But a woman could sometimes make as great a fool of a man by marrying him as by jilting him. For many months he had been wondering which of us two—meaning himself and me—was the more deserving of compassion, but now he was no longer in doubt, and he could only hope I was happy, he was sure. Aurelia was a beautiful woman, and he had been very much in love with her; but after all beauty is but skin deep. And then, again, people's feelings change wonderfully. Time converts the loveliest face into a mask, and often into a very ugly one; and how swift is the flight of time! We clasp a beautiful creature to our heart, and when she lifts her face from our bosom, lo! we find the angel of Time has been with her, and 'tis all pucker and rheum, crows'-feet, sausage-curls, and the deuce knows what besides! As to the *durability* of sentiment—Stop! he'd give me a yarn. He was at a funeral last year. A young wife had died, and the husband was inconsolable. His grief at the grave-side was terrible to witness. His friends had to grasp him by the arms and coat-tails to hinder him from precipitating himself into the yawning chasm when the coffin was lowered into it. He wept, he howled, he tore his hair, he shook his fists at the sky, and asked with streaming eyes what he had done to deserve this dreadful affliction. This emotion was sincere down to the very heels of it. "Four months later," added my cousin, "I received an invitation to his wedding!"

"And now," continued the letter, "since I, have made up my mind to write, I may as well give you and Mrs. Musgrave *all* the news. Will you ask your wife if she remembers Isabella Radcliffe? No doubt she does. Mr. Radcliffe and Mr. Grant were, I believe, friends, but a coolness sprang up between them some time before the latter left Rio. Though Isabella has not the *good fortune* to have Spanish blood in her, being indeed purely English, and eminently gifted with her country woman's noblest quality—the grand characteristic of the *entirely* British lass—I mean loyalty, Dick, she is exceedingly beautiful, nevertheless. Her eyes are violet, richly fringed, her hair auburn, rarest of tints; there is nothing *majestic* and *stately* about her; she is merely *lovable*, plump, fragrant, sweet to see and to hearken to, with so exquisite a contralto voice that everybody calls it a fortune to her. Her papa is dead, and his will appoints that the sum of eight thousand pounds is to be settled upon her when she marries, providing that she does so with her mother's consent, presuming of course the mother to be living. The mother *is* living, and *I* have her consent, and perhaps some of these days I may have the pleasure of introducing the prettiest woman that was ever seen in South America to Mr. and Mrs. Musgrave. Happily she resides at Rio, so I shall not be obliged to ask any relative to bring her to me. Be good enough, when you next write, to let me know what I owe you for Mrs. Musgrave's outfit, and for the hire of the cabins of the ship you embarked in. Convey my kind regards to your wife, and believe me, my dear Dick

"Yours very truly,
"Alex. Fraser."

Poor Alec!

Yet this letter magically cleared our home atmosphere. There were no more melancholy references to my cousin's broken heart. I have drunk many a bottle with Alec since, and he is godfather to my second boy, and Aurelia is godmother to his third girl.

So passes the procession of life across the stage of the world. I had advanced but a few steps, so to speak, on the boards when this experience I have written about befell me. My wife and I were young, our hearts had a strong beat, the sun was yet in the eastern heavens, his light very glorious, and the land fair and gay with flowers; and now I am hobbling off within a few paces of the dark wing whose shadow, when the actor has entered it, shrouds him for ever from the gaze of the company that sit watching the show. But the western radiance still lingers, the dusk has not yet fallen, and my wife and I, though our clasped hands tremble with the infirmities of age, still walk in sunshine, finding cheerfulness in the lingering lustre, though we know it to be waning fast.

THE END